MONUMENTS

MONUMENTS

CLAY REYNOLDS

TEXAS TECH UNIVERSITY PRESS

Monuments, a Sandhill Chronicle

© Copyright 2000 Texas Tech University Press

This book was set in Revival 565. The paper used in this book meets the minimum requirements of ANSI/NISO Z39.48-1992 (R1997).∞

Design by Tamara Kruciak

Printed in the United States of America

Library of Congress Cataloging-in-Publication Data

Reynolds, Clay, 1949-
    Monuments / Clay Reynolds.
       p. cm.
    ISBN 0-89672-433-6 (alk. paper)
    1. Teenage boys—Texas—Fiction. 2. Texas—Fiction. I. Title.

    PS3568.E8874 M66 2000
    813'.54—dc21
                                          99-089489

00 01 02 03 04 05 06 07 08 / 9 8 7 6 5 4 3 2 1

Texas Tech University Press
Box 41037
Lubbock, Texas 79409-1037 USA

800-832-4042

ttup@ttu.edu

Http://www.ttup.ttu.edu

This book is dedicated to my friends, for their faith, their loyalty, their love . . . but mostly, it's for Wes, and for all those same, enduring reasons.

Also in the Sandhill Chronicles

Time does not relinquish its right, either over men or over monuments.—GOETHE

PART I: THE BOY

CHAPTER ONE

No one was sure where the movement to save the Hendershot Grocery Warehouse started. Everyone had heard the rumors that the old building was going to be razed, everyone was concerned. But it wasn't until the bulldozers and wrecking balls showed up in the weedy field around the building that the citizens of Agatite took a serious interest in the project.

Hendershot's Grocery Warehouse was the tallest building in over two hundred miles. It sat on a large, overgrown vacant lot a hundred yards north and slightly east of the parking lot where once had stood the Fort Worth and Denver depot. Built around turn of the century, it also had the distinction of being the only six-story structure of that vintage in the state, maybe the only one in the Southwest. Now just over eight decades old, Hendershot's was a practical building that boasted no frills, no aesthetics, only grim utilitarian solidity. It was constructed of poured concrete, had yellow adobe brick and fieldstone facings, and was lined on three sides by a huge wooden loading dock that stood six feet off the ground. Some said the joists inside were petrified and that the structure would stand forever. But no authorized person had been inside the building in over twenty years, and even those who spoke the loudest in the attempt to save it had to admit that it had long been an eyesore the whole town would be better off without.

Hugh Rudd first heard about the planned demolition of the building while he was sipping a lime Coke in Central Drugs on a delicious June morning and trying to forget the afternoon before. Then, he had played in what was the final Civic League baseball game of the year. But for him, the season might have continued for a while, and that was not a pleasant thought. He came up to bat with the local championship game on the line, his team down by two runs, one out and the bases loaded. And he had let himself be fisted by an inside curve. The ball bounced once, right to the shortstop for a season-ending double play. He dragged himself home and went to bed early, burdened by the weight of disappointment. Even Coach Kruickshank hadn't had much to say to him afterward. Nor had Hugh's father. They had always assumed Hugh would make the high school team, would easily segue from the Civic League at least to the junior varsity even in his freshman year. Now, for the first time, he had his doubts.

The new day, though, turned his mind in new directions, toward new ambitions. Hugh had lined up twenty regular lawn mowing jobs, which should carry him through the remainder of the three months' vacation and send him to school in the fall on a new Yosemite Mountain Bike. He had spotted it in a catalog and lusted for it since Christmas. He knew he could make more money working for Mr. Hadnought out near Blind Man's Creek, plowing and mending fence, tending to the old rancher's stock, but he also knew Mr. Hadnought had a reputation for working his boys from sunup to sundown every day it didn't rain, even Sundays. At fourteen, Hugh wanted to enjoy his last summer before high school as much as he could, and he figured he could mow four or five lawns a day and make enough to buy the bike and still have some left over for an occasional movie and pocket change. A job in town would permit him to get out to the high school and take some batting practice several times a week, as well. If he was lucky, some of the older boys would be hitting fungo, and he could get in some work that way, also.

"Going to have to blow her up," Hugh heard one man say from down the counter. "That sucker's built solid as a brick shithouse, and there ain't no way in hell they can take her down with a bunch of piddling little old bulldozers. I was in the Seabees, and when it comes to dozer work, I know what I'm talking about."

Other men sipped their coffee and agreed with nods and murmurs. Hugh squirmed around on the counter stool and tried to hear better. He knew better than to ask a direct question of the men in the drugstore. In the fall, they gathered to discuss the football scores from the Friday night game, and in wintertime, the high school basketball team's failure to get past district dominated their conversation totally. But in summer, when no one but distant pro baseball players were doing anything worth mentioning, the men found little to argue about. Most of them couldn't have cared less about baseball, Hugh knew, unless they had a kid or grandkid playing on one of the local teams. Although none was a farmer, they sometimes bewailed the drop in grain or beef prices, something they invariably blamed on the Republicans. Other times, they gave the Democrats trouble for one "goddamn socialist" policy or other they identified. But mostly in the summer they confined themselves to whatever juicy gossip might be handy. Hugh was too canny to listen too obviously, for he knew they didn't like to think anyone overheard what they said, especially a junior high kid.

"What I don't see," George Ferguson, the town's single independent insurance agent, spoke up, "is why they want to spend money to tear it down in the first place."

"Goddamn railroad," Phelps Crane, who ran the Downtown Chevron Gas and Tire Service, swore. "Burlington Goddamn Northern. Ever since they took over the old FW&D, they've torn up every goddamn thing they ain't put out of business. Not a man in this town ain't been hurt by the Burlington Goddamn Northern."

Phelps, Hugh recalled his father, Harry Rudd, saying, had worked as a conductor for the Fort Worth and Denver until Burlington Northern exercised its corporate might, bowed to the inevitable in the nation's love for the automobile and airplane, and ended passenger service. His refusal to accept relocation to all-freight work running out of Tulsa had ended his career, and he had managed the gas and tire station ever since. The truth, Hugh also had heard his father say, was that Burlington had owned the Fort Worth and Denver since the line was organized, and they had kept the passenger line running long after it ceased to show any profit whatsoever, mostly for the sake of the railmen who relied on the train for their livelihood. Such charity was lost on Phelps Crane, though, who told everyone he met how he had been "shucked and ground up" by the railroad, then offered a pension no one could live on.

Another truth about Phelps, Hugh knew, was that he was close to retirement age when the railroad pulled out, and that probably he wouldn't have worked but two or three more years anyway. Phelps's local claim to fame was that in 1942 he lied about his age and enlisted in the U.S. Army when he was only fourteen, no older than Hugh, actually. He collected three Purple Hearts and had been decorated for bravery more than any man from that part of Texas. Any time the words "war hero" were mentioned, Hugh and everyone else in town instantly thought of Phelps Crane, although the heavyset, gray-faced, balding man who seemed to wear a perpetual scowl and to hate everyone he didn't agree with was hard to reconcile with the image of the heroic GI he must have been at one time.

Phelps also was known to Hugh—through his father's occasional remark to his mother—as a man familiar with heavy drink. This morning, Hugh noticed as he had many mornings, a small flask appeared over Phelps's coffee cup, flashed quickly, and then was stored deeply in the faded bib overalls he always wore. Hugh shook his head. To him and most of his friends, Phelps Crane was something of a joke.

"Say they want to build a new wye," Harvey Turnbull, the former Seabee and one of the three barbers in town, put in while he fetched the coffee pot from the Serve Yourself table and splashed refills all 'round.

"Don't need a new goddamn wye," Phelps shouted at Harvey as if it were Harvey who had thought of it. "Never turned nothing around here, anyway. If they wanted to turn around here, why'd they tear down the goddamn roundhouse? Answer me that one."

"That old roundhouse was falling down," George said softly. "It was dangerous with kids playing in it all the time."

"Well, the goddamn depot wasn't falling down," Phelps whined. "They come in here and bulldozed it in the dead of night."

"It wasn't 'the dead of night,'" Harvey corrected. "It was broad daylight. Fellow in a hardhat come right in here of a morning and asked if we could direct him to the depot. Next thing we know, it's gone. You know that, Phelps. Hell, you're the one told him where it was."

"Well, if I'd of known what he was going to do," Phelps grumbled, "I'd of kicked his ass around the block for drill. Wasn't nothing but that goddamn Ronald Reagan done that. Prissy little dipshit son of a bitch. 'Trickle down economics,' my sweet ass. Only thing got 'trickled' on 'round here was our shoes."

The men murmured their agreement with that assessment. Like everyone else in town, Hugh knew that every town up and down West Texas's Highway 287 had suffered from the loss of the railroads. The decline had started in the late sixties and continued steadily for the next twenty years. There were a dozen such small cities between Fort Worth and Amarillo, county seats mostly. Mr. Diamond, Hugh's history teacher, said they had been deliberately spaced almost precisely thirty miles apart, the approximate maximum a steam locomotive could travel without needing more water. Some of these towns were actually built by the railroad companies, and in the first half of the century, they flourished.

But diesel locomotives didn't require water, and nobody took a train where they could fly or drive themselves, anymore. Freight now moved through without stopping. Only the local mill kept the local switching crews working, Hugh had heard his father say, and every day more and more of their plaster and wallboard product was moved out by eighteen-wheeler. By and large, the local yards were being used only as a transfer and switching point. In time, some said, even that wouldn't be required. In time, his father said, freight-by-rail would become a thing of the past.

Hugh knew that the days of the railroad as a local industry were over. It was a reality he had practically grown up with. A generation before, boys his age couldn't wait until they turned eighteen so they could go to work for the Burlington Northern. Now, it wasn't even an option. The depot was torn down the year he was born, and he was aware of its existence only because of the broad blacktopped area off Main Street at the north end of the business district that everyone identified as the "depot parking lot." The railroad had never mattered to him one way or another. Hugh had no ambition to work for the railroad. He was planning to play professional ball. Or go to college.

He drained his lime Coke and got up to leave.

"Tell you one goddamn thing," Phelps was saying as Hugh departed the cool air-conditioned atmosphere of the drugstore, "I don't think we ought to let a bunch of goddamn Chicago lawyers tell us what we can have in our own goddamn town."

By the time Hugh had mown his fourth lawn of the day and had serious second thoughts about signing on with Mr. Hadnought, he had forgotten all about the drugstore conversation. His main worry was how much it was going to cost him to buy a new mower to replace the old family rattletrap that kept stalling and stopping every time he made a turn. The last thing on his mind was the Hendershot Grocery Warehouse.

Hugh used his next two weeks' earnings to put up a down payment on a new self-propelled Grassmaster, and he calculated it would take him the rest of June and some good portion of July to acquit the debt, even if he took on four or five more lawns a week. He had no time at all for lime Cokes and casual eavesdropping in the drugstore, but one night at supper, his parents took up the topic of the Hendershot Grocery Warehouse.

"They tried to organize a committee to save it," Harry Rudd explained to Hugh's mother, Edith, as she served fried chicken and mashed potatoes. "But there's nothing they can do. The building sits right on Burlington Northern property. They can't stop them from doing what they want."

"What about getting it declared a historical monument?" Edith asked as she poured the iced tea. "I mean, they did that with the hotel."

"I think somebody's already tried that. Not time, now." Harry bit into a leg. "Even if there was, doubt they could do it. There's nothing really historical about the building itself. Could I have some gravy? It might have some architectural significance, but to most people, it looks exactly like half the old buildings in half the towns up and down the highway around here. I don't think it ever had any historical importance. I mean, it was just a business, a warehouse. Nothing ever happened there except that Old Man Hendershot made a fortune before he left his wife and ran off with that waitress from Chillicothe."

"Harry," Edith warned with a nod toward Hugh. His father coughed, wiped his mouth with a napkin, and went on in an indifferent tone. "Where're the biscuits? Main thing is that they can't really do anything to stop it. Word is a bunch of folks went to Judge Parker, but he couldn't find any grounds to grant an injunction. So I guess they'll just tear it down. Are we having any vegetables?"

Edith bustled efficiently around the kitchen, and he stopped shoveling food into his mouth long enough to watch her. She seemed almost to glide from stove to countertop to refrigerator to table, her arms laden with steaming bowls and platters. Her face always wore a determined smile, and her total concentration seemed to dwell on the multiple tasks at hand. Somehow, though, she kept up a running conversation with her husband and even reached down to straighten Hugh's napkin on his knee as she swept by.

"It's an eyesore anyway." Edith was finally seated and was trying to stir her potatoes sufficiently to generate enough heat to melt the pat of margarine she had placed on top. Now she rose, went to the stove, and brought over a bowl of green beans. They were stone cold, but Harry didn't seem to notice as he spooned them onto his plate.

Sometimes, Hugh thought, it was almost comical the way his mother behaved. She often reminded him of the television-perfect mothers he saw on the rerun cable TV channels. But Donna Reed and June Cleaver were different. It wasn't that they always were dressed up in heels and pearls and had perfect hair. It was something about the way they did things, as if household chores were second nature to them, not a delicate balancing act between perfection and utter failure.

Edith Rudd's house wasn't perfect, but it wasn't exactly a disaster area, either. She took a lot of pride in how clean she kept everything, and Hugh was seldom in greater trouble than when he left a wet towel on the bathroom floor or forgot to rinse out a milk glass. But then, Hugh was almost never in any trouble anyway. That, too, was something that Edith Rudd bragged about.

Still, his mother's suppertime routine bothered Hugh. But if his father noticed, he never mentioned it. He just ate his supper and talked to her as if she were sitting across from him, relaxed and comfortably eating her meal right along with him, something she almost never got to do.

Hugh was aware that his father's one true passion was good food. Harry asked for very little from life, he always said. But one thing he insisted on was a "good supper." That meant a full meal every night, "and none of that low-fat bran crap and raw fish, either," Harry good-naturedly chided Edith. "A working man needs *real* food, and if it's bad for me, so much the better." She did what she could for his arteries and heart by substituting margarine for butter and frozen yogurt for ice cream and by using low-cal salad dressings. But Harry refused whole wheat bread, and he wouldn't touch lite mayonnaise.

"And it's probably a firetrap," Edith went on, reseating herself. "It's all grown up with weeds and probably has snakes all around it." She stirred her cold food around a bit, then pushed her plate away slightly. "We're better off with it gone."

"Dangerous place, all right." Harry cleaned his plate with a masterful stroke of his fork that removed the last of the green beans and potatoes at once. "Is there any pie?"

"Kids play in there, I hear." Edith rose and moved to the sideboard where a fresh peach pie awaited her knife. "You never play in there, do you, Hugh?" she asked.

"No'm," Hugh muttered around a mouthful of chicken. He resented her notion that he still "played" at all.

"Well, see that you don't," she said automatically without hearing him. "It's still a shame to see it go. It's kind of a landmark, I guess. A reminder to a lot of folks of the way the town used to be." She cut the pie, and steam rose out of it.

"I'll get the ice cream," Harry said.

"When do they start?" she asked.

"Tomorrow." He placed a carton of frozen yogurt in front of her. "It ought to be quite a show."

"You stay away from there," she said as she spooned the white confection onto the pie. "It's likely to be dangerous."

"Yes'm," Hugh responded. He had already decided that the Smiths, Hendersons, and Tallwaters could wait one day to have their grass cut. He was planning to be downtown at first light.

─┤

The demolition crew contracted by the railroad had arrived the evening before, and they spent the first two hours of daylight off-loading their yellow Caterpillar bulldozers and arranging a huge crane with a wrecking ball on the back of a flatbed semi-trailer. Within a few hours, the high Johnson grass and scraggly mesquite trees that filled the vacant lot around the warehouse were beaten down under the wheels of the vehicles. A travel trailer sat off to one side.

A small, angry crowd gathered on the site of the old Fort Worth and Denver Depot and glared at the workers about a hundred yards below them. The vanished depot's parking lot and the double set of railroad tracks that still ran parallel to it marked the unofficial northern boundary of the small town's business district. On the other side of the tracks, an overgrown vacant lot flattened out and spread about a hundred yards down a steep slope, terminating along the southern wall of the old Hendershot building and its loading docks.

Because of the difference in elevation between the downtown area and the Hendershot building, the workers had to look up to see the crowd, who gathered behind a line of old wooden pylons that ran parallel to the near tracks and was joined by a single strand of cable running from pylon to pylon. The barrier terminated at the eastern easement to Main Street, directly across from another abandoned building, a red-bricked Railway Express Office.

For years, long before the razing of the depot, the parking lot had been an unofficial turn-around for vehicles circling and seeking an opening in the slant parking spaces of the three blocks of the downtown area. When downtown was crowded, the drill was to circle the depot parking lot in a broad U-turn, then scout the west side of Main as far as the courthouse square. Then, if no spaces were open, to go around the square and try the east side as far as the depot parking lot, where the process would begin again.

Today, though, too many people were gathered in the old parking lot to permit even a kid on a bicycle to make a U-turn. More folks wandered down as the sun warmed the early morning air. The work crew knew nothing of the town's hostility toward the project and only waved and offered large, friendly smiles.

Hugh arrived at seven in the company of Tommy Quisenberry, a smallish boy his own age who had been fired by Mr. Hadnought the day before. They had met on their bicycles near the old water tower just west of his house and pedaled slowly off while Tommy explained the circumstances of his sudden unemployment.

"Said I had to take too many shits," Tommy confessed to Hugh as their bikes raced parallel toward the downtown blocks. "Said I was spending more time squatting off by the fence line than I was plowing." He grinned sheepishly. "I guess I was, too."

"Why?" Hugh asked. "You sick?"

"It's my mom," Tommy said, casting his eyes downward. "She won't cook any meat anymore."

"Why not?"

"Oh, she says we have to 'eat right.' She says my dad's cholesterol is too high, and we have to become vegetarians."

"Vegetarians?" Hugh was dumbfounded. He thought all vegetarians were some kind of religious nuts.

"Yeah," Tommy said. "No meat. I mean, not even chicken. No meat at all. Just vegetables. It's driving us all nuts, especially Dad. But Mom's stubborn. She won't budge. She won't let us eat 'anything that has a face,' she says. It's horrible."

Hugh tried to imagine his father's reaction to such a thing. It wasn't possible. Harry lived for a good cut of meat, especially steak, cooked bloody and rare.

"Anyhow, it's giving all of us the runs. Mom says that'll go away after a while, but I don't know. Seems I'm farting as much as I'm shitting, and half the time I can't tell the difference before it happens." Tommy shook his head. "Old Man Hadnought's probably right. My ass was so sore all the time, I couldn't walk. But it doesn't matter. I'm glad to be through with the son of a bitch, even if it means I'm broke. Didn't have time to spend any money anyway."

Hugh breathed a silent prayer of thanks that his mother never got such crazy ideas. "Well," he said, "maybe we can set up a practice schedule. Get some BP in."

Tommy's face adopted a serious expression for a moment, and he nodded. He and Hugh had been teammates since tee ball. Tommy was a quick second baseman and a fast runner, but he had never been much of a hitter. "Yeah. Maybe we can talk Coach Kruickshank into throwing us some. If he's ever sober," he added and laughed.

Their bikes swung into the downtown blocks, and they saw the growing crowd down by the tracks.

"Jesus," Tommy breathed aloud, "I haven't seen so many people since the fire."

A fire had broken out in Gilbert's Auto Parts Store two years before. Half a block of buildings had burned before the six fire departments from neighboring towns that came in to assist the local unit could bring it under control. Hugh chiefly remembered it as the first time in his life he had stayed out all night.

Just as Hugh and Tommy parked their bikes and moved in closer, Phelps Crane climbed up onto a small three-step ladder and started yelling at the two dozen men who made a knot around him. His face was red, and Hugh could see veins roping across his forehead.

"Can't you people see what they're doing?" Phelps cried. He pointed toward the distant roar of the bulldozers, which were gearing up and grinding through the head-high weeds down around the building. "They're tearing down the whole town! Bit by bit! Pretty soon, they'll be coming right into your homes! Taking your jobs! They took mine, and I ain't the only one. It's a plot! I'm telling you, it's a goddamn plot! We got to stop 'em. Somehow, some way, we've got to."

"Hey, Phelps," somebody in the crowd yelled. "You serve drinks after the sermon or just before?" Everyone laughed, and Phelps waited one angry beat, then climbed down, folded his ladder under his arm, and stalked angrily off toward his station.

Mostly the crowd was quiet after that, but in dribs and drabs more townspeople drifted up and joined the small gathering. The bulldozers and trucks moved into position, and soon they had knocked down the big wooden loading docks on the front and near side of the building. After workers secured the huge, rotting planks with chain, the tractors pulled them away toward a front loader, which picked them up and dumped them into the back of a truck to be hauled off.

"They're goddamn neat about it," George Ferguson remarked as men came in after the front loader to pick up loose boards and scraps that had fallen loose from larger pieces.

"Hell, yes," Harvey Turnbull agreed. "Pretty soon we won't even know it was there."

"Just like the depot," a woman piped up.

"Just like the depot," Harvey and George agreed together. They had a Thermos of coffee and some cups with them, and they replenished their drinks and lit cigarettes and looked around vaguely for something to sit on before resting again on their heels and continuing to watch the demolition. People were shading their eyes against the new sun, and dust from the bulldozers and trucks began to waft up through the rapidly heating air toward the crowd.

"It ain't like the depot at all," a calm voice suddenly spoke up from right behind Hugh. He jumped, startled. It had been a while since anyone had spoken, and for a moment Hugh had the feeling that there was a ghost standing right on his shoulder.

Harvey and George turned and looked curiously at the speaker, but then their eyes recorded the face, and they exchanged a grimace, turned around, and resumed drinking their coffee and smoking.

"It ain't," the voice said again, and Hugh stepped away and looked around.

An old man stood blinking into the dusty sunlight. He had on patched dungarees and ancient, cracked workboots. A plaid shirt draped down from a pinched neck and bloused over his waistband, and a pair of faded red suspenders hitched them up and seemed to prevent the shirt from taking off with the breeze. He had a battered fedora on his head. There were moth holes in it, and the band was stained from salty sweat.

"It's a whole 'nother thing," he said. "That depot was new-fangled. Made of Mescan bricks, it was. Wouldn't of stood by itself 'nother ten years without some major work. But old Hendershot's. That's a whole different tune. Them fellers'll learn that, by and by."

More people casually glanced back toward the old man, but as soon as they identified him, they turned away with disgust on their faces. No one but Hugh was paying any attention to him. Even Tommy had wandered off toward the edge of the crowd and was trying to talk to Mavis Patterson, a girl from their class.

The old man squinted down at Hugh, his only visible audience. "I'm telling you, boy," he said, "you can stand here and watch them dozers till pigs get wings, but you ain't going to see 'em bring down ol' Hendershot's with some piddling little ol' tractor. Going to take dynamite, and that might not do her. That's a good building. Take more'n that bunch of peckerwoods brought to take her down."

Hugh caught himself staring at the man, then, embarrassed, glanced off and started to turn away.

"What's your name, boy?" the man asked.

"Hugh. Hugh Rudd."

"Jonas Wilson." The man stuck out a gnarled hand and smiled.

Hugh was stunned by the sight of the paw thrust out toward him. It was scarred and battered, as if it had been broken in a vise. Scabbed-over sores ran across the back where the skin was papery, and large blue veins stuck out and seemed to pulse right before his eyes. No finger was straight or properly aligned. In fact, the third and fourth fingers were minus their ends. Yellow tusks of fingernail grew right out of the stumps, reminding Hugh of granite boulders he had seen embedded in the orange soil of the Wichita Mountains.

The second stunning thought that froze the boy was the man's name, for it immediately identified him as the town loony, the town drunk, the town pervert, the town "stay away from him or he'll get you" boogeyman about whom he had been warned every since he was old enough to leave the house without the company of one of his parents.

Jonas Wilson. The name caused giggles in groups of kids and occasioned nightmares when one awoke by an open window late at night. Jonas Wilson murdered children. He carried them out to the boxcar he lived in five miles from the city limits. They disappeared forever. He buried them in his garden—the size and success of which were grudgingly admired throughout the county—cut them up and fed them to the gray mongrel dog that accompanied him wherever he went. He always carried a tow sack over his shoulder, a butcher knife in his pocket, and when the sack bulged full, it was a safe bet it had the remains of some lost child in it.

Those were the stories, some of them, anyway. Hugh's eyes got large in spite of his efforts to control them. He had seen Wilson only at a distance. Because his boxcar was on the side of the road on the way to the mill where

Harry Rudd worked, Hugh passed by it when he rode out with his father to check on something that required an off-duty foreman's attention. Sometimes, they passed the old man himself, trudging along with his head down, usually pulling a child's little red wagon or carrying his infamous tow sack over his hulking shoulders. Hugh often wondered how many of the stories about the old man were true. Wilson never lifted his head, waved, or tried to flag a ride, no matter how laden the wagon or sack or how bad the weather. He just lowered his battered hat against the draft of the car when it passed, gestured to the large gray dog, and moved on. The boxcar itself was nothing more than a shack with a stove pipe sticking out of the top. Aside from the oversized garden, it was surrounded with old car parts, mattress springs, and other junk, and the whole abode was encircled by a rickety barbed wire fence.

Passing the man or his place always made Hugh shudder, and it almost always caused his father to remind him never to go anywhere around "the crazy old coot."

"Just stay away from him," Harry Rudd automatically warned. "He's no damn good, and we'd all be better off if he'd just go away."

Now, however, Hugh stood staring at Jonas Wilson's hand, which was thrust out right toward the center of his chest. He no longer believed the childish stories about kids being carried off and fed to the old man's dog, but all the warnings and taboos concerning Jonas Wilson froze his arms to his side, caused him to look at the ground in a mixture of fear and embarrassment.

"That's okay, son," Jonas Wilson said and dropped his hand. "When you get to feeling like it, we can shake and howdy. We've traded names. That's more'n most folks in this town'll do."

Hugh looked up at the old man to apologize. Somehow, he decided that his training in gentlemanly behavior took priority over his father's cautions. Anyway, both parents had always warned him against being rude, even to a colored man or a Mexican. And Jonas Wilson seemed polite enough. He was about to speak and offer to shake hands, but Wilson was no longer paying any attention to him. The old man's eyes were directed beyond him and down the grade toward the ongoing demolition project.

Hugh moved away through the crowd. The bulldozers had completed their work with the loading docks, and now they were shutting down. Crews were battering away at the huge, wooden double doors on the front of the building, preparing to enter and begin removing any other impediments to efficient destruction.

The work went on steadily, and Hugh went over to one of the wooden pylons that marked the barrier between the parking lot and the railroad track and perched there. Tommy soon came up and joined him.

"They're saying they'll be done before dark," Tommy leaned on the rusty cable. A green stench rose to Hugh's nostrils, and he turned away in disgust.

"Jesus!" he said. "Smells like something crawled up inside you and died."

"Beans," Tommy smiled grimly. "That and turnip greens. We had a mess of those last night, too. Makes a stink, doesn't it? Works on me all day long. Really, I think it was that more than anything that got me fired. Old Man Hadnought said he couldn't come near me without wanting to puke. Other kids, too." Tommy studied his sneakers and rubbed his eyes. "It's embarrassing, Hugh. It really is. But I can't help it. It won't stop if I don't get some meat to eat from somewhere. My mom won't even let us have tuna fish."

Tommy passed more gas and offered his friend a sick smile. Hugh stepped back, breathing through his mouth and fanning the air between them.

"Jesus, it makes my eyes water!"

"I can't help it, Hugh. Say," Tommy smiled, "what're you having for supper, tonight?"

"I don't know," Hugh muttered. The thought of Tommy sitting around their table and farting through supper made his breakfast cereal revolt in his stomach.

"Well, if there's going to be meat, count me in. Maybe I can come over once a week or so. That'll help. We're going to the Grand Canyon later this summer. I'll bring you a T-shirt or something if you can help me out."

The sun rose higher in the morning sky, and the temperature went up accordingly. Sweat began to break out on faces, and as handkerchiefs dampened, so did enthusiasm for watching the slow process of destruction of Hendershot's Grocery Warehouse. Tommy finally gave in and joined those departing with a caution to call him if the Rudd household was planning to enjoy some kind of meat that night. He looked so hopeless that Hugh decided to check with his mother and see if he could. Edith Rudd was a great cook, and there were always leftovers.

Eventually, the crowd thinned down to only a handful of men who stood leaning against the pylons or their cars, smoking and watching the crews move in and out of the big, yellow building. Now and then a worker would lean out of a window while he tried to pry off a board or chip away at a piece of brick. Hugh noticed that the pieces being thrown out of windows or carried out the big front doors became smaller and smaller. Eventually work seemed to stop all together.

"Broke for dinner." Jonas Wilson's voice came up behind Hugh and made him jump all over again.

"Jesus!" he spun around and swore at the old man. "Stop doing that! Just because I'm shorter than you, you don't have to sneak up on me."

Wilson leaned back on his heels and studied the young man. Hugh's blond hair stuck out of a New York Yankees baseball hat, and his white Red Sox T-shirt was damp with sweat. Freckles covered his nose, and his ears were slightly too large for his head, but he was already the picture of the handsome young man he would become. He had a slim but muscular athlete's build, strong arms, and clear blue eyes.

"You ought'n't to swear at an ol' man, like that," Wilson said calmly. "You might give me a heart attack. Wouldn't it be a shame for the last thing a mortal's ears should hear to be a blasphemy?"

Hugh's eyes fell to his shoes again. An adult's admonishment, even that of an adult such as Jonas Wilson, must be acknowledged. "Sorry," he muttered. "You just scared me, that's all."

"Seems like I do that pretty good," Wilson declared with a chuckle, and Hugh looked up.

The old man's face was splotched with brown spots and skin cancers. His gray eyes were rheumy as they peered out from under bushy, white eyebrows, and lines creased both cheeks from the crow's feet on his temples all the way down to the wattles of his neck. He needed a shave, but beneath the white whiskers, Hugh could see a strong chin beneath a mouth lined with clean, white teeth. He was thin, Hugh observed as he studied the loose skin around his neck, but his shoulders were broad, and he stood squarely in broken-down workboots, his feet solidly planted on the blacktop of the parking lot.

"Didn't get very far this morning," Wilson observed generally. "They'll find out what a job they took on this afternoon." He lifted his ragged fedora, revealing a full shock of white, sweat-washed hair, and studied the sun. "They'll be off for a hour or more. What say we have us a bite?"

Hugh looked around. Almost everyone had drifted off by now. He wanted to escape, but he didn't know how. He thought of just walking off, but somehow, he couldn't do it.

"I'm not very hungry," he said.

"Not hungry? Big boy like you?" Wilson scoffed. "Shoot, boy. When I was your age, I'd eat half a cow, hide and all, for supper and have the bark off a cedar post for dessert. C'mon, they's a spot of shade over by the hotel. We'll be back in time for the matinee."

Hugh was confused, and he stood where he was. Images of being grabbed and hauled off in the tow sack that bulged over the old man's back swam before his eyes. Jonas Wilson moved off toward the street and then turned.

"C'mon, boy," he waved and spoke gruffly. "I ain't made that many offers like this, and I don't take kindly to being turned down." Hugh felt as if his sneakers were melted into the blacktop of the parking lot. He couldn't move. "I said, 'C'mon,'" Wilson barked suddenly. "Ain't much going to happen to you in the shade of a chinaberry tree."

Hugh found himself moving, trailing after Jonas Wilson across the bricks of Main Street, down the old roadbed of the Fort Worth and Denver switching track that ran between the northernmost building of downtown and the abandoned Railway Express Office. Beyond that, a block and a half away, was the town's old hotel. He thought of the Pied Piper of Hamlin, of Fagan in *Oliver Twist*. He didn't want to go, but he couldn't help himself. Jonas Wilson called, and he followed.

─<

"You like 'mater sandwiches, or you prefer crookneck?" Jonas Wilson asked as they approached the overgrown chinaberry tree that grew haphazardly out of the weedy grass in the vacant lot next to the hotel. Two decades before, when the owners went bankrupt, the city obtained the property for back taxes. Ten years later, during the national Bicentennial celebration, the county historical society was given charge of it, and they found federal funds to restore the building to its former splendor in an attempt to make it a tourist attraction.

The plan was to convert the ground floor into a series of shops and stores and then rent out the rooms upstairs for high prices to rich tourists heading back and forth from the Metroplex to ski country in Colorado.

But money for remodeling proved inadequate, then somehow ran out completely. Now, except for a skimpy gift shop and tourist information center, there was no commerce going on in the three-story, whitewashed stucco building. The rooms upstairs remained untouched, as they'd been at the moment the establishment's role as a bona fide hotel ended years before.

The caretaker, Milton Kruickshank, coached Hugh's Civic League baseball team, and at the end of every season—which always ended in mid-June, as he never seemed to have a team that could win a championship—he stayed so beer drunk that he couldn't work up the energy to mow the grass more than once a month. He also ran the gift shop and handed out maps and brochures to the five or six tourists a week who wandered lost or waited for car repairs at one of the downtown garages. In exchange, he was furnished with a small salary and a room on the hotel's ground floor.

"I don't know," Hugh muttered as they stepped over the curb and worked through the weeds and sunflowers to a matted-down spot directly under the tree.

"Well, it's a simple enough question," Wilson stopped and sat down, folding his legs under him. Hugh heard the old man's knees crack when he bent them, but his wrinkled face betrayed no discomfort. "You like homegrown 'maters?"

"Tomatoes?" Hugh said. "Yeah, I guess," he nodded.

"You like crookneck squash?"

"I don't know." Hugh looked confused. "I don't know what it is."

"Yeller squash," Wilson explained. "Some folks call it 'summer squash.' Though I'd have to allow it's Yankees that do that, mostly."

"We eat summer squash," Hugh confessed, remembering that he didn't much care for it.

"Your folks Yankees?" Wilson asked, digging into his tow sack.

Hugh kept a nervous eye on the old man's movements. "My mom's from St. Louis," he said. "Or she was born there. She was in the military. Or Granddad was. The navy. They moved around a lot. All over the world. You know—"

Hugh's voice stopped and evaporated into raw breath. The first item Wilson removed from the sack was a long, black-bladed butcher knife. The carbon-steel edge was outlined by silver-honed sharpness. He could almost feel it slicing through his throat.

"Never was at sea," Wilson said casually. "Fact is, I only saw the ocean once, and that was just the Gulf of Mexico. Down to Galveston. Went down for a longshoreman's walkout. Had a heck of a storm. Hurricane of some kind. Durndest thing I ever seen. Biggest, too. Makes a twister look like a spring shower. That was back in '35. Or '36. I forget."

He put the knife down on his leg and reached into the sack and brought forth a small stack of wax-paper-wrapped sandwiches.

"Now they all got mustard on 'em," he apologized while he arranged the sandwiches on the grass before him. "Even the 'maters. I don't like it near as good as mayonnaise, but mayonnaise sours in the heat. Gives you the bellyache. Might even kill you. Heck of a note, ain't it? In cool weather you can use mayonnaise—which is the best thing with 'maters, crookneck, and the like—but them things ain't growed up in the wintertime." He pushed the sandwiches around with the blade of his knife. "You go right on ahead and take your pick. You're company."

Hugh reached out for one of the squash sandwiches. The knife flashed, and he jerked back his hand in a panic. When he looked, however, he saw that Wilson had brought it toward his own hand with the dull side down.

"Now, durn it," he frowned. "Don't you go taking crookneck 'less that's what you want."

"That's fine," Hugh said, realizing with regret that he was whispering. "I like it okay."

"Well, 'okay' just ain't good enough." Wilson said. "Take a 'mater, or a pepper, onion, and beet pickle. Them's the best with mustard anyhow."

"I don't think I'd like an onion sandwich," Hugh said.

"Well, you ain't tasted one of mine." Wilson frowned. Then he brightened. "Tell you what. I was going to cut 'em in two anyhow. Let's have half of one, half of the other. What'd you say?"

Hugh nodded, and Wilson smiled and sliced the sandwiches in two.

They were good, Hugh had to admit when he bit into the squash sandwich. The small, yellow gourd was crisp under his teeth, and the mustard enhanced the flavor perfectly. The bread was homemade. Thick and crusty, it seemed to melt in his mouth while he chewed.

Finally, as he bit into the tomato sandwich, he decided that this was the best noon meal he had ever had. At home, his mother would be sitting down to a can of Campbell's or a tuna sandwich. He wondered what she would think about his eating sandwiches of squash and tomato. She probably had never heard of such a thing.

"This is really good," Hugh said after wiping his mouth on his T-shirt's tail. "I mean it. I never ate a sandwich like these before."

"Secret's in the vegetables," Wilson said while he chewed. "Got to be fresh. Right out of the garden. These was growing last night. Picked 'em just after the moon set. That's best, Indians always said. They done that with wild onions, berries, herbs, and such, and that's what they said."

"The bread's the best part."

"Bread's easy, if you got the starter. That there's sourdough. I've had that starter for years. Got it from a ol' boy who used to chuck for the Matador Ranch."

"You worked on a ranch?" Hugh's mind suddenly filled with movie images.

"Worked on a ranch, railroad, farm, and factory. Drilled for oil, water, and gas. Went prospecting once down to Mexico. All that 'fore I was growed up, or durn near it. Done a little of everything, I guess." He smiled and folded the wax paper into neat squares, which he thrust into the sack. "Played piano in a fancy house once." He held up his abused hands. "Can't do that no more." He laughed. "What I like best is carpentering. Halfway good at that."

Wilson wiped the knife blade on the grass and then on his stained dungarees and thrust it into the sack, exchanging it for a small brown paper sack. "You take a smoke?" he asked, reaching into his pocket.

"Sure." Hugh's voice quaked with uncertainty. His father smoked in between bouts of trying to quit. Even his mother took a cigarette from time to time, especially when they were all at home alone watching TV or after something had upset her "too much to think," as she put it. But he had been threatened with the most unimaginable punishments if he even looked at a cigarette seriously.

Wilson's eyes focused vaguely on the boy. "You don't smoke, do you." It was a statement, not a question.

"No," Hugh admitted. "I never have."

"Well, if you want, you can try."

"I'd like to try."

"If you don't like it, don't do it no more. I've always believed a man needs to try things, see if they work for him. Smoke's always been a friend of mine. Stayed with me when shorter strings run out. Stayed with me longer'n any man or woman I ever knew or had dealings with. It's there when I need it, don't bother me when I don't."

"I'd like to try," Hugh repeated softly.

Wilson nodded and pulled a sack of Bull Durham from his shirt pocket. Hugh was taken aback. He expected to see a pack of Camels such as his father smoked. He was unprepared for home rolled.

"Watch me, and do as I do," Wilson said, handing him a thin paper and dabbing a measure of loose tobacco on top of it.

Hugh's fingers inexpertly followed Wilson's movements, but when the old man had a perfectly rolled tube sitting on his chapped lips, the boy's efforts lay uselessly in his hand.

"Try it again, and this time don't try to force it. Secret to a good smoke is not to force it."

Hugh worked through the process once more, and this time he proudly lifted a completed product for display, only to drop it onto the grass in astonishment. Jonas Wilson had removed a pint bottle of bourbon from the small brown sack and was tilting it back and allowing his large Adam's apple to pump it into him.

After two swallows, the old man looked at Hugh.

"Ain't going to offer you a drink of whiskey," he said, corking the bottle, thrusting it back into the sack. "Lot of folks 'round here'd like to see me hang just for giving you a sandwich and a smoke."

Hugh scooped up the cigarette and accepted a light from a kitchen match scooped in Wilson's hand.

"Don't nigger-lip it," he said as Hugh sucked in the smoke and coughed violently. "It ain't your mama's titty."

"Mr. Wilson," Hugh coughed again when he tried to speak. The smoke seared his throat and lungs and burned like dry fire.

"Don't call me 'Mr. Wilson.' Last man called me 'mister' died 'fore your daddy was out of diapers."

"What should I call you?" Hugh took another drag. It went down easier than the first.

"Call me 'Jonas,'" he said with a nod. "'Mister' is a title of respect. I got a notion you don't respect me. Not yet, anyhow. What you want to ask me?"

"I thought you always had a dog with you."

"Dog? Oh, you mean Goodlett."

"Goodlett?" It was the name of a near-ghost town fifteen miles to the west.

"That's where I found her. Just a pup. Some son of a buck put her out by the road to die, and I come along and just took her up. Been with me near ten years."

"Where is she?" Hugh sucked in another drag. His head swam with a light, not altogether unpleasant sensation.

Wilson's dark eyes sparked momentarily. "She's 'round here. Put out that smoke. Never take it all the way down to the nub. That'll give you the cancer."

Hugh ground the butt under his sneakers. He made up his mind to find a way to buy more makings and practice as soon as he could. He wondered what Tommy and the other guys would think. He *knew* what his mother would think—if she caught him.

"I'll call her, but you got to do as I say. She's a mean little bitch when she wants to be. Bitch dog's the best dog there is, but you got to handle 'em right. Now get up and stand real still."

Wilson got up on his knees. Hugh stood and looked across the street to the Goodrich Auto Store and the backs of buildings on Main Street. He saw no dog anywhere. A shrill whistle came from Wilson's lips between his chopped-off fingers.

As if she were a hallucination, the dog rose from beside the concrete curb directly across from the chinaberry tree. Hugh's eyes blinked several times as what he thought was merely a ripple in the gray curb rose and moved across the street and entered the grass. Her dirty gray color gave her a perfect camouflage against the concrete curb.

"Don't move, no matter what," Wilson warned him. She slipped through the grass and weeds to the tiny area where they had eaten.

Goodlett came silently through the grass and froze when she realized that Wilson was not alone. A throaty growl began deep in her throat as she stalked close to the quaking boy.

"Goodlett," Wilson ordered in a deep voice. "Okay." He pointed to Hugh and then to himself and repeated the command. "Okay."

The dog moved close to Hugh and sniffed his sneakers and legs. Her nose moved up to his crotch, and then as Hugh gasped, almost yelled in alarm, she rose on her back feet and placed her paws on his chest. He looked deep into her eyes, which he saw were dark yellow, felt her hot breath on his throat. Her growl continued to rumble deep inside her.

"Okay, Goodlett," Wilson ordered again. "Get down."

After a long moment, she dropped back on her paws, and with one more quick sniff, she went over, squatted, and watered the base of the china-berry tree.

"It's okay, now," Wilson said. "You can move. She's real partial to me, and she's jealous as any redheaded woman you ever seen. Like to killed this ol' boy who come up to the house when his car broke down."

Hugh didn't feel like sitting down. Sweat covered him, and his hands felt waxy.

"That's some dog," he said. Goodlett lifted her head and inspected his voice, then lay down next to Wilson's feet.

"She'll do," Wilson said. "More trouble'n she's worth is the truth. Won't let me keep chickens. Kills 'em every time."

From the direction of the tracks, they heard the engines of the bulldozers starting up.

"Well." Wilson cinched up his tow sack. "They're starting up again." A smile appeared beneath the whiskery wrinkles. It was as if he knew something no one else was aware of. "Reckon we'd best mosey back over and catch the afternoon show."

"Thanks for the sandwich, Mr., uh . . . Jonas." Hugh looked down again. "And the smoke."

Wilson smiled broadly. "My pleasure . . ." he started, but suddenly Hugh, without knowing why he was making the motion, thrust out his right hand. Goodlett looked up at it, decided no harm was meant, and put her head down on her paws once more. Wilson stared at the boy's outthrust fingers. "We'll do it again, tomorrow." He left his hands at his side.

"But they'll be done by tomorrow," Hugh protested. His hand was still thrust out, and he flushed, dropped it. Wilson taught him what that sort of rejection felt like. It wasn't good.

"Oh, no, boy." Wilson grinned and hefted his sack. "They're a long ways from being done with Hendershot's Grocery Warehouse."

CHAPTER TWO

When Hugh and Jonas Wilson returned to the parking lot, a few people had already formed up for the afternoon session. Some brought umbrellas and lawn chairs and set them in the backs of pickups, but as the afternoon grew hotter and the workers did little more than drive around in their bulldozers, raising dust and collecting debris from inside the building, they eventually grew bored and left.

Hugh noticed that Goodlett didn't like the crowd and shied away. She picked a spot by the curb near the Railway Express Office and lay down, almost completely disappearing against the concrete's gray background.

Phelps Crane showed up two or three times during the afternoon and tried to talk people into coming to a meeting that night at his station, but no one would commit. The flask in his overalls pocket had been replaced by a sack-wrapped pint bottle, exactly like Jonas Wilson's, and the old conductor often moved off by himself and sneaked nips from it. Each time he appeared he would march around talking earnestly to people. His face grew ruddier than ever, and small veins burst on his nose, giving it a red, almost clownlike appearance. The more he talked, the madder and hotter he became. Soon his shirt was stained dark blue with sweat, and people refused even to look at him. Eventually, he just stood around and mopped his balding head with a red bandana, swore softly in between sips from his bottle, and kicked at debris on the parking lot.

He refused to speak to Hugh or Jonas Wilson—to one because he was just a kid, and to the other because he was Jonas Wilson—but he glared at the two of them as they leaned against their wooden pylons and chatted idly about the workers' progress. Finally, he stalked over to a pay phone on the corner and started pumping coins into it.

Tommy showed up about midafternoon, but he didn't hang around very long, either. Hugh wanted to borrow makings from Wilson and show his newfound talent to his friend, but he was too fearful of smoking in public to do so, and he contented himself with ignoring Tommy until he got angry and left. It wasn't until after Tommy pedaled off that Hugh recalled Tommy's bid for a supper invitation and realized that Tommy was probably madder about that than anything.

About four-thirty the sun was behind some of the taller buildings on Main Street, and people began to gather once more in the shade. One or two brought ice cream freezers and sat down behind them on campstools and began churning away. Lydia Fitzpatrick, a tall, too-skinny woman with bright red hair and too-short shorts, showed up and started grilling steaks for her family on a portable propane grill mounted on a shiny new and pine-floored lowboy trailer that her husband, Carl, towed behind his dual-axle Ford 350 crewcab pickup.

"They going to work through the night?" Carl Fitzpatrick demanded of the gathering crowd when he walked up. When no one knew, he seemed disappointed. Carl was a handsome man about the same age as Hugh's father, but deeply tanned and careful in his appearance. His black hair was razor cut and silvery at the temples, and more than one of the men in Central Drugs had confided through chuckles that Carl—and Lydia—had availed themselves of cosmetic surgery. Hugh glanced into the cooler Carl opened and spotted several cans of beer in the ice. The Fitzpatricks were hoping for a party, he thought.

Carl winked at Hugh, the only person paying any attention to him, then he pulled a can of beer from the cooler, wiped it with a towel, and inserted it into a plastic Coca-Cola can wrapper to disguise it. Hugh moved off to watch the workers.

Just before five o'clock, a white Dodge sedan with the Burlington Northern logo on it drove down Main Street. The driver, wearing a suit, slowed when he passed the parking lot and studied the milling crowd, then gunned the car's engine and sped down to the worksite. He ground up next to the demolition crew's small trailer, jumped out, and talked to one of the hard-hatted men. Then he put on a white plastic hard hat, and they went inside the building.

"Told you they was in trouble," Jonas Wilson jeered, but aside from frowns caused by the source of the comment, no one paid him any attention. Hugh smiled.

26

Eventually, the men came out and talked a while longer. They looked at the crowd up by the tracks, and then the suited man got into his car and drove up to where everyone was gathered.

He parked the car, got out, and looked around, his hands on his hips, his head shaking in a kind of disapproving gesture. Settling on Carl Fitzpatrick, the only other individual present in a coat and tie, he took a visible deep breath and approached. Although he had fixed his mouth into a smile, he was not in a very good mood.

"My name's Grissom. I'm with Burlington Northern, Fort Worth Bureau," he announced to Carl, who refused to take his hand when he shoved it out. The smile evaporated. "I got a call this morning that a bunch of people were interfering with this project, so I thought I'd come see what the matter was."

"There's nothing the matter," Carl said. "We're just a bunch of folks getting together to watch a little bit. For the fun of it. I can't see that we're 'interfering' with anything. We're just having an old-fashioned picnic."

"Here?" the railroad man opened his arms and gestured to the parking lot between the tracks. Smoke from Lydia's grill rose from the lowboy. Card tables and portable picnic tables had appeared and were being arranged around the Fitzpatrick vehicle.

"Looks like," Carl said.

The young man walked away and over to the cable-connected pylons. He noted the lawn chairs, backed-in pickups, and general semicircle of people, all gathered around the perimeter of the lot facing the workers below. Then he turned and approached Carl again. His smile returned, but his brow wrinkled in a sympathetic expression.

"This is all just silly," he said in a pleasant but firm voice. "What is it you people find so fascinating down there? It's just a bunch of men doing their jobs."

"We're watching," Carl said and smiled. Carl was a lawyer, but he was also running for city attorney. "I don't think we're breaking any laws. It's a public parking lot."

"It's not," the man said. "This is railroad property. Everything between the tracks is railroad easement. Technically, you people are trespassing."

"People been using this parking lot for U-turns since before you was born!" Phelps Crane stepped through the crowd and strode up to the railroad man. "And long's anybody remembers, it's been city crews patched up the road between these two tracks. Ain't that right?" The crowd moved in closer to hear better. Some of those on the near side nodded wisely and murmured assent.

George Ferguson stepped forward and backed up Phelps. "I don't see as we're doing anybody any harm," he said.

"Don't you people have homes to go to?" The railroad man was not happy at the growing crowd around him. "I mean, Christ, it's hot out here." The crowd began talking among themselves, and the young man surveyed them with a wary eye. Suddenly the walking shorts, bright summer blouses, khakis, and workshirts began to form themselves into something resembling a wall. He turned in a complete circle as he spoke, opening his arms in a helpless gesture. "I mean, is this all there is for entertainment in this town? Don't you have a movie or something? What the hell are you people really up to?"

"What makes you think we're up to anything?" Carl asked, his smile plastic. "And I'll thank you to watch your language."

The railroad man pulled out a handkerchief and mopped his brow. Then he lowered his tone. "Look," he said, "I'm sorry. I had a long drive up here, and it's hot. Now, I know there are some people in this town who aren't happy about all this, but these men are down there to do a job. That's all. We don't want any trouble, and—"

"We wasn't having no trouble till you come up here and started it," Phelps yelled. "Why'd you come up here anyway if you didn't want to start trouble?" Phelps's hammy fists were clenched tightly. Sweat poured off his scowl. He looked like he wanted to hit somebody, Hugh thought.

"I just want to know what it is that's so fascinating about a bunch of construction workers," Grissom said softly.

"Well," the voice once again came from behind Hugh, once again from Jonas Wilson, but this time the boy didn't jump. "I can tell you that there ain't *much* interesting about *con*struction workers. But *de*struction workers. That's something else again."

People in the crowd glanced at each other for assurance, then smiled uncomfortably in agreement, but Carl Fitzpatrick took a breath and stepped forward to seize the moment for himself.

"That's right! We've been looking at that building all our lives. It's part of this town."

"Just like the goddamn depot was," Phelps put in hotly.

"And we're not sure we want it decon—uh . . . demolished," Carl finished, hooking his thumbs in his waistband. He looked about him as if he were searching for a platform. Finding none, he rocked back on his heels and waited for the railroad man to answer.

Grissom loosened his tie after glancing at his watch and frowning. "I think we've already been over that," he said. "Your own judge Parker—"

"*Our* judge?" Carl shot with a lawyer's grasp of a hole in a witness's testimony. "Who said he was 'our judge'? I mean, he *lives* here—lived here all his life—but I think if you'll check, you'll find he's a superior court judge. He's our neighbor, our friend, maybe, but he's not 'our judge.' That's sort of a dangerous thing to say, Mr. . . . Mr.?"

"Grissom."

"Mr. Grissom," Carl finished and flashed a toothy smile. "You seem to have a problem with your language, today."

"Anyway." Grissom recovered himself. "Judge Parker has already ruled that the building is to be razed, and there's nothing you people can do to stop it."

"Go on and raze it, then," George put in. "Who the hell's stopping you?"

"The building's going to stop 'em," Jonas Wilson said, but this time, no one paid him any mind. "It's like a monument," he finished. "You don't just tear down monuments."

The railroad man heard that and gave Wilson a quick look of dismissal. "You're crazy!" he shouted. Then he calmed himself. "That's just an old building. A derelict. Nobody wants it. We tried to sell it for years, and nobody even made an offer on it."

"How long you been with the company, boy?" Phelps accused angrily. "You don't know nothing about what's been done 'for years.' Hell, you weren't even out of short britches when I was busting my hump for the FW&D. And what did that get me? A pension a Mescan couldn't live on, hemorrhoids, fallen arches, and hives, busted bones and deaf in one ear from a hotbox that went up at Estelline. Hell, I worked so many nights, I can't sleep between sundown and sunup. Who the hell cares about that?"

Grissom stood aghast at the old conductor's tirade. "What the hell does that have to do with anything?" he demanded. "Jesus Christ! I'm not responsible—"

"I told you, damnit," Carl put in, "keep a civil tongue in your head, or I'll call the sheriff."

"And I told *you*," Grissom shouted to the crowd, "You people are on company property. I think you ought to move off before *I* call the sheriff."

"You go on ahead and call him," Phelps challenged. "His name's Anderson, and he's not worth a tin shit. This here's a public U-turn lot, and I don't give a good goddamn in hell what you got wrote down somewhere on a piece of paper. Folks in this town been using this lot for longer than you been born. Since before there was cars."

"How is that possible?" the railroad man turned around for support, but everywhere he looked he found hostility or, at the least, detached curiosity as to what he might say next. "You can't have a U-turn without cars."

"Yeah, you can," Jonas Wilson spoke up once more. This time heads turned around to look at him. A beam of sunlight snaked out from behind a building and fell across the crowd. Many hands went up to foreheads to shield against it. Hugh thought they all looked like they were saluting him.

"Folks was parking wagons and mules and horses here long 'fore the first automobile come into this country. Long 'fore there was a depot here."

"And just how the hell would you know?" the railroad man sniffed.

"'Cause I helped build the depot," he said calmly. He pulled the makings out of his pocket and began rolling a smoke. "And I seen the first automobile in this county. Cadillac, I think it was. Belonged to Jacob Hadnought, daddy to the boy who farms up on Blind Man's Creek. He was a big-time capitalist. Banker. Married money. Went bust in the Depression. Served him right. He skinned a lot of folks. His boy's all right, though. Works with his hands."

There was a moment of silence as Jonas completed rolling his cigarette and lit it with a kitchen match. People were looking at the old man with a kind of bewildered curiosity in their eyes. Hugh wondered if any of them had ever heard so many words from him before.

"Carl?" Lydia Fitzpatrick called from behind the cordon of people who surrounded Grissom. "Your steak's ready. Come get it before it dries up. You know how tough it can get when it dries up." Carl stood his ground, but he shifted his weight uncomfortably. "Look," Harvey Turnbull spoke up. "We're not happy about what you're doing down there. But I don't see how we're stopping you by watching."

Grissom gave Harvey a narrow look. "You're making the men nervous."

"What're they afraid of?" Phelps sneered. "That old Lydia might not have 'em up for ice cream after while?"

"The point is that we're not stopping you. We *can't* stop you," George Ferguson spoke up. "If we could, we would. But we ain't hurting anything by watching. Are we?"

"No," Grissom sighed. Hugh looked down and noticed that the workers were piling into pickups, quitting for the day.

"I guess you people aren't hurting anything standing around here in the heat," Grissom said at last. "But if you do anything to interfere with those men and their work, I *will* call the sheriff—" He shot a look at Phelps. "Or the Highway Patrol, if I have to. We're within our legal rights, you know. We're a federally protected corporation. If I have to, I'll call the FBI."

"The FBI!" Phelps roared with laughter. "Goddamn, Lydia! What kind of ice cream are you making?"

Grissom flushed and turned away, pushing through the wall of people and making his way back to his car. "The show's over for today, folks," he announced. "I don't know why we don't sell tickets." Then he stopped when he opened the door and addressed the crowd behind him. "That building's coming down," he stated. "Like it or not. It's just a building, and this time tomorrow, it'll be down."

"We'll see 'bout that," Hugh heard Jonas Wilson mutter from behind him. But when he turned around to speak to the old man, all he saw was his shuffling form retreating toward the hotel. Goodlett rose from her curbside position and padded along in his wake.

—‹—

"What I want to know," Edith Rudd demanded as soon as Hugh sat down to supper and winced with ironic reaction at the big tureen of pinto beans and plate of cornbread that dominated the center of the table, "is just where you think you've been all day?"

"The boy doesn't *think* he's been anywhere," Harry munched down on a fresh spring onion. "Bring some butter over here, please. He *knows* where he's been." He looked at Hugh and winked. "So, Sport, where *have* you been all day?"

Hugh dug his spoon into the beans and filled his mouth. "Downtown, watching—"

"Don't speak with your mouth full," Edith ordered. Then she sat down.

"I asked for some butter," Harry said. Hugh noticed for the first time in his life that his father looked old—not as old as Jonas Wilson, but certainly older than Carl Fitzpatrick.

"In a minute," Edith said. She waited until Hugh chewed and swallowed, and then she put out a hand to stay his second bite. "Now, where were you all day?"

"I was downtown," he mumbled. "For a while. I wanted to watch them tear down that old building."

"For a while," she repeated, her blue eyes fixed on him, searching his face.

"Well." He flanked her hand and picked up a piece of cornbread. "I was downtown most of the day."

"That's what I thought." She rose and fetched the margarine from the refrigerator. "And who were you with?"

"Tommy," Hugh said brightly.

"Don't lie to me!" Edith slammed down the margarine dish and splattered glass and the artificial butter all over Harry, who scooched his chair back quickly from the table and upset his iced tea.

"I will not tolerate being lied to!"

"What the hell is going on here?" Harry demanded. "Edith, what's wrong with you?"

"The boy has the gall to come in here and sit down at my table and *lie* in answer to a direct question," she shouted at Harry. "He's your son! Do something about it!"

"I was with Tommy," Hugh protested. "He met me at the water tower, and we rode our bikes down together. You can ask—"

"I *did* ask him," Edith said. "Harry, are you just going to sit there, or are you going to do something about this?"

"About what?" Harry Rudd's face was a mask of confusion rapidly changing to anger. His shirt and trousers were wet with spilled tea. "I don't know what the hell's going on!"

"He was downtown, all right," Edith bit her words off carefully. "And he spent the whole day down there. And do you know who with?"

Harry looked at his wife with a puzzled expression. "Am I *supposed* to know? Jesus, Edith, I was at the mill all day. How the hell am I supposed to know what's happening downtown?"

"Well, he's *your* son!"

"That's true enough." Harry stood up and wiped his wet clothes down with a paper napkin. Then he turned to Hugh, who had not moved through the whole ordeal.

"Who were you with today?" He put up his hand. "Don't answer 'Tommy.' We've had that answer, and it won't work. Now who?"

"Jonas Wilson!" Edith said. Her voice cracked as she spoke, and her eyes roamed the kitchen as if she expected to find some stranger lurking in a corner. "That old man! That's who! Your son spent the whole day with that awful old man!" She collapsed into a chair, put her hands over her face. Harry put out his hand, but she ignored it, rose, and raced out of the kitchen. "Talk to him, Harry. For God's sake, talk to him," she cried from the other room.

"You'd best go out onto the porch," Harry said. Hugh obeyed. Inside the house, he heard his parents arguing. They hadn't argued much in his life. His mother, he knew, was what his father called "fragile," and she had been for a long time. Hugh's brother—his baby brother—Larry died mysteriously in his crib shortly after he was born, and his mother never completely recovered from the ordeal. Ever since, both his parents had treated Hugh with a special kind of love, and Hugh's father had treated his mother with a special kind of delicacy, rarely raising his voice to her or to Hugh, being especially solicitous when she seemed overwrought for any reason.

Growing up, Hugh had been given more lenience than many of his friends. He was aware of the special status he owned, and he often was aware that he could abuse it if he wasn't careful. Somehow, he sensed, any misstep whatsoever could hurt his mother beyond repair. For that reason, he always tried to be especially good, especially trustworthy. It wasn't something he thought about, just something he did in response to his parents' attitude toward him as their sole surviving child. He was, as his mother so often called him when she bragged on him, "a good boy, a model child." Even before he understood what the words meant, he instinctively understood that his responsibility in the family was greater than that many of his friends had to bear. He had to be good, for his mother, fragile as she was, depended on it. If he failed, she would be the one who was hurt.

But this wasn't his fault, he argued with the twilight surrounding the porch. He hadn't *wanted* to spend the day with Jonas Wilson. It just happened. He couldn't see that it hurt him any or hurt his mother at all. In fact, he was already looking forward to seeing the old man the next morning. Except for the cigarette, he couldn't think of a thing Wilson had done or said that he couldn't tell both his parents.

Well, he remembered, the cigarette *and* the whiskey. But he hadn't touched the bottle. Wilson wouldn't let him, and Hugh knew that his parents kept a fifth of bourbon under the kitchen sink behind the drain trap, and he knew that from time to time, on special occasions such as holidays and celebrations, it was taken out and opened.

Wilson had only two swallows, Hugh continued in his silent debate, and he'd bet that his parents—or at least his mother—didn't stop always there. No, Hugh insisted to the buzzing June bugs smashing against the door's screen, Wilson didn't have any really bad habits at all. Hell, Hugh thought with a shake of his head, Wilson didn't even cuss.

He saw his father move back into the kitchen and scoop up a spoon full of beans and shovel them into his mouth. Heavy as he was, Harry always seemed to be hungry, Hugh thought. He came home, ate two helpings of everything, then had a smoke and fell asleep in the easy chair. Then he would wake up and have a dish of ice cream or a leftover piece of pie or cake before going to bed. He had a big belly and a double chin under his five-o'clock shadow. He wasn't strong or well built. But he loved his son, and he had a good heart. That much Hugh was certain of.

As Hugh peeked through the kitchen curtains and saw Harry Rudd fill his mouth once more before washing it down with the remainder of Hugh's tea, Hugh was already outlining the speech on personal trust and responsibility he knew he was about to receive. Tonight, he knew, it would be heavily laced with reminders of how delicate his mother's disposition was, how important it was for him not to upset her when he didn't have to, and how much she depended on his being trustworthy.

He had heard it before. All last summer, in fact, his father had provided him with a weekly recital of how much he loved him, how he wanted to be able to trust him. And when Hugh decided to undertake to mow all those lawns this summer, he had received a double dose every week, especially since his father agreed to co-sign for the new mower. Hugh knew the speech by heart. He prepared himself for it. But his father surprised him.

Harry came out and sat down heavily in the glider. He had the end of a cornbread muffin in his hand, and he polished it off, then lit a Camel before he spoke.

"I seem to recall something about co-signing a charge account at the hardware store for a lawn mower," he said quietly. Hugh nodded, and Harry took the cue and went on. "I seem to recall some promises being made about paying it off by the end of July at the latest." Hugh nodded again. "How many lawns did you mow today?"

"None," Hugh mumbled.

"How do you propose to keep up payments on that machine if you don't do work with it?"

"I just took off one day, Dad."

"Well, Sport," Harry sighed and flicked his butt out into the yard, "that's true enough. But you can't let it be a habit. One day off leads to another, and pretty soon, you're too far behind to catch up."

"I just wanted to watch them tear down that building."

"I understand that, Sport. I even understand all the excitement around town about it. It's like your mother said. It's kind of a landmark around here."

"It's a monument," Hugh said, hearing Wilson's voice echoing in his mind.

"A monument, huh?" Harry thought for a moment. "I don't know if it's a 'monument' or not, but it's been there a long time. I guess you could see it that way, though. These days, there aren't many things that last that long."

"Mr. Crane is having a meeting tonight at his station to try to stop them," Hugh said. So far the talk was going well. He hadn't spoken to his father this way before, and it relieved him and made him anxious at the same time. Further, he thought darkly, it kept the topic away from why he was out there in the first place.

"Heard about that."

"At the mill?"

"Phelps called up some guys who used to work for the railroad. He wants to get up a petition or something."

"Would you sign it?"

"I don't think so."

"Why not?"

Harry looked out into the gathering night. Hugh wondered if Jonas and Goodlett were sleeping beneath the chinaberry tree. Sheet lightning flashed in the distance. No storm was coming—not tonight—it was only heat flashes out on the prairie.

"I just don't think so," Harry said at last, firing up another Camel.

"Why not? Don't you think it's worth saving? Even if it's not a monument, it ought to be worth something."

"I don't know," Harry said. He used the cigarette end to burn a mosquito that had landed on his forearm. "Skeeters are bad out here tonight." He rose and moved out and sat next to Hugh. "I don't think they ought to tear it down, but I can't think of any reason to stop them. They own it. They need the land it's sitting on, I understand. For a wye."

"Just what *is* a wye?"

Harry forked his fingers and explained. "It's a place they turn the freight around. They back the train in from one direction onto a straight sidetrack, throw the switch, and take it out the other way. Saves a lot of time for the switch engines. Otherwise, on short runs, they have to back them all the way down from the mill here to Fort Worth. The trains make the mill's business work better. A wye will let them run shorter trains more often without losing money."

"So you're all for it," Hugh asked.

Harry sighed. "Don't know. Don't much care, to be honest. But since I'm sort of in management, now, it's better if I don't rock the boat."

"Would they say anything to you if you signed a petition to stop it? Fire you, maybe?"

Harry's form stiffened. "No, they wouldn't fire me. They wouldn't say anything. I don't think they would, anyway. But the next time promotions came around or a big raise, time off, anything like that, I might not get it."

"That's not fair!" Hugh declared. "In social studies, Mr. Diamond says that in America—"

"In America," Harry interrupted, "you have to learn pretty quick that you do what The Boss wants. He's The Man. He pays the freight." Harry sighed deeply. "You have to learn that you can do pretty much what you want. Say what you want. But if it goes against the flow, you pay for it. In the end you always pay for it, one way or another."

"I don't think they ought to tear it down," Hugh said softly. "I think they ought to just leave it like it is."

"Well, Sport, I agree with you," Harry smiled across at him. "But there's not much you or I or Phelps Crane or any petition can do about it. Is there?"

Hugh thought for a moment. "No, I guess not." They sat in silence for a long moment, and Hugh wanted to go back inside. Mosquitoes were buzzing his ear. He pulled one sneaker up beneath him to push himself up, but his father's voice stopped him.

"Tell me about Jonas Wilson."

"There's not much to tell," Hugh said quietly and resettled himself uncomfortably. He should have known he wouldn't escape so easily.

"What did you do with him today?"

"I wasn't *with* him," Hugh protested again. "I was just standing around, and he asked me to eat with him."

"Eat with him? What did you eat?"

"Sandwiches."

"God, that old man must live on road kills. What kind of sandwiches?"

"Well, one was just tomato and mustard, and one was squash and mustard."

"My God, Hugh, that sounds awful." Harry gagged slightly.

"No," Hugh turned to his father and looked across the backyard. "It was good! I didn't think it would be, but the vegetables were fresh, crunchy. He grew them himself. And it was good. He said they would be better with mayonnaise, but it goes sour in hot—"

"Did you have anything to drink?" The question hung in the darkness like a moth fluttering about in search of a flame.

"No," Hugh said sincerely. "I didn't."

"Did he?"

Hugh took two beats of a pause. "He had two sips, but he—"

"He wouldn't let you have any," Harry finished for him.

Hugh brightened. "That's right. He said I was too young."

Harry said nothing, but then he rose to his feet. "Wait here," he ordered, and he went inside.

In a moment he was back, and he sat down where he had been before and produced the bottle from under the sink. "Do you know what this is?"

"Whiskey," Hugh identified the half-full bottle.

Harry unscrewed the cap, tilted the bottle. He didn't pump it down his throat the way Jonas had done, but he sipped two quick swallows, then held the bottle out to Hugh.

"Go on," he nudged Hugh's arm with the bottle's neck. "It's okay. I said it was. It's not a trick."

"No." Hugh shook his head. He felt cold all over, spongy inside as if he needed to cry or run away. "I don't want any, thank you."

Harry continued to hold the bottle out for another second or two, then he took another swallow and recapped it. "Promise me something," he said quietly. Hugh remained silent. "Okay, Sport?" Hugh nodded. "When you take your first drink of whiskey, take it with me. Okay?"

Hugh nodded again, and Harry rose.

"Stay away from Jonas Wilson."

"Why?" Hugh turned and rose in one movement. He realized for the first time in his life that he was as tall as his father.

"Because your mother wants you to," Harry said as he pulled the screen door open. "That should be reason enough for you."

It was a cheap shot, and both of them knew it. Hugh lowered his head. "What's wrong with him?" he muttered.

"He's a crazy old man," Harry replied. "That's all you need to know. Stay away from him. Edith!" he called, then went inside. "If you've gotten yourself together and finished being hysterical, can we warm up some of this supper? I'm starved."

Hugh skipped the second try at supper and went to his room. He was almost asleep when he remembered a vital detail in his conversation with his father. His father had ordered him to stay away from Jonas Wilson, but, unlike the whiskey, he hadn't made him promise.

CHAPTER THREE

Between seven and eleven o'clock the next morning, Hugh mowed four lawns. He was practically running as he completed Mrs. Thompson's downgrade. She fussed at him as she counted out his money, for in his haste he had come dangerously close to her Chinese ivy. He explained that he feared it would rain later in the week, and he didn't want to fall behind. She nodded grimly and cautioned him to be more careful.

He raced home with the mower, then mounted his bike and pedaled downtown as fast as he could. When he arrived, a fair-sized crowd was gathered in the heat of the day. There was a holiday atmosphere. People passed around iced tea and soft drinks and not a few poorly disguised cans of beer. Some folks sat on lawn chairs under big beach umbrellas while they watched the workers down at the old yellow building. More pickups were pulled in, beds laden with chairs and coolers, all facing the work going on below. Some had erected tarps over the beds to shade their occupants.

Phelps Crane moved through the center of the group, talking a mile a minute. Off by the old Railway Express Office, Grissom, the railroad man, sat in his car and glared at the festivities.

Hugh parked his bike next to the hardware store and walked over the tracks. Tommy popped up along with Ray Marcus, another teammate of theirs and one who also had gone to work for Mr. Hadnought.

"Is it raining?" Hugh looked up at the clear, hot sky overhead.

"Don't be a wiseass," Ray warned. "I got fired, just like Tommy here."

"You eating beans every night, too?"

"What?"

"Nothing," Hugh laughed and took a shadow punch at Tommy, who feinted and jabbed back. "What happened?"

"He claimed I burned out the clutch on his new tractor on purpose."

"Did you?"

"Hell, no." Ray looked hurt. "I mean, I thought about it. That old son of a bitch worked us all day, right up till dark. God, I hated that tractor. He had me on an old sand terrace all overgrown with careless weeds and Johnson grass that hadn't been plowed in about a hundred years. It was just too much for a little 40-20 to pull. I hit a soft spot and sank her right up to the axles. Burned the clutch right out. I had to walk damn near five miles back to the road and hitch to the house. Lucky I wasn't snake bit."

"Lucky you didn't have to take a shit," Tommy put in, and they all laughed.

"So what's happening?" Hugh asked as they moved over to the pylons. Three or four were occupied, and they had to walk down toward the grain elevators to find a vacant spot.

"Not much," Tommy assessed. "They been going at it with a wrecking ball, but it won't hardly dent it. That's a tough old son of a bitch."

Down in the work area, little had changed from the day before. The only evidence of a morning's work was that more of the weeds and grass were driven down, and the crane with the wrecking ball had been moved closer to the building. Hugh couldn't see anywhere in the side facing the crane that the ball might have struck with serious effect. Some of the yellow fieldstones were cracked and broken, exposing the raw concrete underneath, but that was generally true all around the building, so it didn't mean a thing.

"We were thinking about going out to the Four Seasons and going for a swim," Tommy volunteered. There had been no white people swimming in the municipal pool since integration came to town in the late sixties, twenty years before. The well-to-do like the Fitzpatricks went out to the country club. Middle-class families such as Hugh's, steeped in the southern tradition of no mixed-race swimming, paid a twenty-five-dollar-a-month fee for their children to use the motel's pool during the day when there were few paying guests to compete for the tiny blue water hole. Ironically, now, in the late 1980s, there were black and Hispanic people swimming in both refuges, but no one thought to return to the municipal pool or to insist that the city refurbish and restore it to its former splendor.

"Y'all go on ahead," Hugh said. "I want to watch a while."

"We might go over to the field, hit some fly balls after that," Ray said. "You ought to come. You could use the practice." Unlike Tommy and

Hugh, Ray was a big hitter. He had the Civic League record for home runs in their age group. He held down third base and was proud of his natural abilities.

"Naw," Hugh said. "I need to mow a couple of lawns this afternoon, and I really can't take the time."

"Work, work, work," Ray chanted when he and Tommy moved off. "I didn't know he was such a peckerhead."

Some high school boys pulled into the parking lot and sat on the hoods of their cars and listened to music on their stereos until Phelps Crane ran them off. Hugh noticed a knot of girls from his own class moving into the crowd and milling around until they decided that no one would pay attention to them, and they also left. Even though he had no specific interest in any of the girls, he wanted to go on out to the motel and join them in the pool. Just the idea of being around them in their scanty suits excited him. It was a relatively new idea to him, something that had been born the summer before and grown like a weed in his heart.

It made him feel guilty a lot. But it also stimulated him beyond reason.

Down around the building little was happening. Men in hard hats moved around and drove up and down in their pickups and bulldozers. Now and then one would look intently up toward the crowd, but for the most part, things were quiet.

Just as Hugh grew drowsy in the summer sun and had about half-consciously talked himself into the long bike ride out to the motel pool, he heard Phelps shouting.

"They're going at it again, the sons of bitches! C'mon, old gal, give 'em hell!"

The roar of a huge motor aroused Hugh from his stupor. He squinted into the bright sunlit dust and saw the crane lift its arm and move to give the ball a good swing. The large, dark orb angled out away from the building, and a small curve formed in the cable. Then the arm swung in the opposite direction, and the iron ball smashed into the side of Hendershot's Grocery Warehouse.

Hugh expected to hear a loud crash when the heavy ball struck the building, expected to see brick and dirt explode from the point of impact. He couldn't imagine that any structure would withstand such a blow. But when the ball hit the side of the fifth floor, just under a bricked-up, arched window, there was almost no noise at all. The ball smashed into the side, and a few fieldstones flew up and outward, but then it bounced off, struck it again on the rebound, and then hung uselessly.

"Ol' Hendershot was more afraid of moisture'n thieves," Jonas Wilson's voice spoke to Hugh's right. Hugh wasn't at all surprised to find the old man standing beside him. He looked up and learned that Wilson wore the same costume from the day before. If he had slept in it, it looked no dirtier or worse for wear.

"They's seven floors in that building,'" Wilson went on as if Hugh had asked him to explain. "A basement and six stories. The basement's all full of trash, likely. But it's got walls poured four feet thick all the way 'round and lined with stone, just like the outside. Every floor's got two foot of concrete, triple reinforced with steel rebar, by golly, and the walls all the way 'round her is three foot thick." He smiled down at Hugh. "They's forts in the world not built that tough."

"Why?" Hugh asked. "Why did he want it that way?"

"Wasn't no air conditioning in them days," Wilson looked down at the building. "Hendershot hired a man—architect, he was—name of Grady to go all 'round the country and make a study of what would be cool in the summer, warm in the winter. Being anywhere in that building any time of day any time of year, the temperature was the same: sixty-five degrees. You could count on it. He had big thermometers stuck up all over the place to make sure. If one was off a degree or two, he'd call up Grady and have him come down and figger out why and fix it."

"So it kept the food he stored longer."

"Longer and fresher." Wilson smiled. "Back when folks couldn't get no ice, he had fresh vegetables, meat, all sorts of stuff stored in there. Fresh as could be. It wouldn't keep forever, course. But it'd keep a long spell. He was a smart one, ol' Hendershot."

Hugh looked out where the crane was winding up for another try. The workers stood around and watched as the wrecking ball bounced off the building one more time.

"You see," Wilson went on as the ball made its harmless rebound and hung slack and the workers slapped their thighs and threw down their hard hats in disgust, "They's over a hundred thousand tons of concrete poured in for every floor in her. Floors and walls. Solid concrete. Look over yonder." He pointed to the hardware store, where, behind the false front, Hugh could see the uneven brickwork stretching back toward the alley for both floors.

"That's adobe behind fieldstone facade. It's not bad. Pretty good, really, for the time when it was built. Cheap, solid. But it don't last. All them buildings is made of it. All but them they put up in the last fifty years or so." Hugh spotted large cracks running down the sides of several buildings. "Water, wind, every durned thing you can think of eats away at it till it just falls away."

He looked once more down into the construction site. "Hendershot didn't want that to happen. 'I'm building this'un to be here,' he told us when we went to work. He knew, don't you see, that there wasn't another grocery warehouse in a hundred miles. All the little stores in the area, general stores and country crossroads and the like, had to get their foodstuffs from someplace. He wanted his to be that place. Saw a fortune in the making. He brought in cypress trees—not cut lumber, whole durned trees—all the way from east Texas. He had us haul 'em out to Blind Man's Creek and soak 'em for six months 'fore he'd let us use 'em. We nailed 'em in as cross beams while they was still wet. Heavy dickenses, I can tell you. Took a team of mules to haul 'em up. We nailed 'em in place with railroad spikes, and then he had concrete poured all over 'em. Solid."

Hugh nodded. He looked around for Goodlett and spotted her asleep next to the foundation of the hardware store. The gray of the concrete there was mottled, and she stuck out clearly.

"Then he floored each story with sheet iron, covered that with concrete, then laid in second-growth hickory he brought in from Tennessee. Don't have any idea how much all that cost him. Wasn't no regular railroad here, then. Just a spur line. Everything come in by wagon. Cost a fortune. Said he didn't care. Big-time, cross-country railroad was coming, and he knew it. He was building it to be here when it come. And come it did.

"Only thing on that building that comes from this county is the fieldstone and the adobe covering. The stone's granite from down 'round Marble Falls. Hard enough by itself, but we put it on with wet cement, and we held it in place with poles till it dried in place. They're having a heck of a time even knocking that off."

Hugh looked down again and saw the third and final attempt of the morning fail. The crane's motor shut off all at once, and the men stalked in disgust toward the little trailer.

"Them's the bookkeeping offices where they're trying to break in right now," Wilson explained. "But up there on the sixth floor, that arched window was right behind old Hendershot's desk. Had frosted glass in it, till he figgered out it was letting in too much draft. So he had it bricked up the same way as the rest. I was in there once. It was blacker'n midnight in there, like a big ol' cave. He never would light a lamp. Said it made things too hot to have that kind of light. Maybe that's what drove him crazy, made him run off the way he done. Maybe not, though. That'd been back during the war."

"My granddad was in the war," Hugh offered, wanting to keep Wilson talking.

"Not *that* war, boy," Wilson chuckled. "The *big* war. The war in France." His eyes looked into the distance. "The bad war. Course, there never was a good one," he concluded.

"He was in France," Hugh insisted. "During the war. He was in Paris. I have a picture . . ."

"Not *that* war." Wilson reached out and put a hand on Hugh's shoulder. It was the first time he had touched him. Hugh spotted the damaged, twisted fingers coming toward him and fought the inclination to flinch. "World's War I. The *big* war." His voice took on a sarcastic tone. "The war to end all the wars. They wanted me to go off and fight in it. Called up my name. But I wouldn't. Me and Gene Debs, by golly. I'd of gone to jail first. Just like Debs did. Wasn't going to go and die to save a fat man's loans. Wasn't no good reason for that war. Never been a good reason for any war, truth to tell."

"They called you up?" Hugh asked, confused. "You mean they drafted you."

"Yep. But I told 'em I wouldn't go. Didn't matter, though." He lifted his left hand to illustrate the point in his missing fingers. "Wouldn't of took me no how. Big ol' rattler already took these. So I went to Hendershot and asked for a job as a carpenter. Said he didn't need no carpenter, but he put me to work hauling boxes up and down in that building."

"Lots of stairs," Hugh said in mock awe. He couldn't imagine what sort of labor Wilson was talking about.

"Not the stairs," Wilson laughed loudly and caused several people to turn their heads and look at them. Hugh noticed that eating was general up and down the crowd. Many had brought sandwiches and picnic hampers. More folding picnic tables were set up, and several people were cooking over small portable grills. Phelps Crane stood next to a pickup and scowled at Wilson and Hugh over his Thermos cup.

"Elevators," Wilson ignored the stares and went on. "Looky here." He pointed a stubbed finger toward the side of the building. "Right there. You see where them stones is in a different pattern?"

Hugh looked and noticed that just between the biggest doors on the first floor, right where the loading dock had been, the stones were arranged in an vertical pattern as opposed to the crazy-quilt design that made up the rest of the building's outer wall.

"Up on the roof, right at the top of that section, is a bunch of holes." Hugh looked again. "You can't see 'em from here," Wilson snapped. "Used to be cables come up out of them holes and went through some pulleys counter-levered on the roof and then ran down to the yard right there." He pointed to the spot where the semi-trailer with the crane was parked. "Where they was attached to some harnesses for a team of mules."

"How did it work?"

"Well, behind that wall is a shaft with this big ol' platform on it. Elevator. Only Hendershot never called it that. Called it the 'Big Lift.' It ran from the roof all the way down to the basement. Stuff would come in by wagon—and later by truck or on a boxcar from the railroad—there used to be a side track run right by the loading docks—and the men'd wrestle it inside, put it on that platform, and a team of mules'd move it up and down to the right floor. That was my job. Driving them mules."

"Wouldn't an engine have worked better?"

"Only engine they was was a donkey engine." Wilson said. "At first, at least. Later on, they hooked up some kind of big ol' motor to it, but Hendershot said it made too much noise. He liked the mules. 'Sides, hay is cheaper'n gasoline by a long shot."

"So you drove the mules."

"For a while, anyhow," Wilson smiled. "Called it 'hauling boxes.'" He dug into his pocket and pulled out smoke makings. He offered them to Hugh, but Phelps was still watching them, and Hugh shook his head.

"Maybe later," he murmured.

Wilson rolled a smoke and looked down. "Paid two dollars a day during the war. Then things fell off a mite, and he knocked us back to a dollar a day, then fifty cents. I quit at a dollar. Anything less was exploiting, you know what I'm saying? Sweat may be cheaper'n hay, but it ain't free."

"My God," Hugh said and ignored Wilson's sudden frown at the expletive, "I get as much as fifteen dollars for mowing a medium-sized yard. That only takes me an hour. Sometimes less."

"Well, times is changed." Wilson lit his smoke. "Course, man could eat near a week on five dollars back then. Get a place to stay for two bits a night. Good place. Not the hotel, maybe, but a room and a meal thrown in for a dime or fifteen cents more. Working man could get by." He sighed and smoked a moment. "Money meant more then."

Hugh stood up on the pylon behind him for a moment and noticed Grissom's car pulling out. Grissom drove down to the trailer and got out and went inside.

"Seems to me that it means more now," Hugh said.

"Now it ain't the money." Wilson sniffed in disgust. "It's the having of it. More you get, more you want. Never mind how much you truly need."

Phelps Crane could stand no more, and he stalked over toward the old man and boy. "You oughtn't to be hanging 'round here," he snapped at Hugh. "Does your mama know where you're at?"

"Does yours?" Wilson asked Phelps, but he received only a mean look in reply.

Hugh was struck by Crane's audacity. He had known Phelps Crane all his life, but he couldn't remember ever having spoken to him or having been spoken to by him. Hugh was angry, and he looked away.

"Look at me when I'm talking to you, boy," Phelps said. "I asked you a question. Does your mama—"

"Did you snitch on me?" Hugh demanded suddenly. The words tumbled out of his mouth before he could stop them. "I saw you calling somebody yesterday. Did you call my mother?"

"What if I did?" Phelps stepped back. "You got no business down here hanging 'round with . . . with him." He jerked a thumb toward Wilson, who looked calmly at him.

"What's wrong with him?" Hugh demanded. He had never spoken to an adult that way. "My dad knows where I am." The lie struck home in Phelps's face, and Hugh grew warm all over.

"He does?" Phelps rubbed the stubble on his chin. He hadn't shaved, but the whiskers barely covered the broken veins in his cheeks. His eyes were red and small. His breath reeked of tobacco and alcohol. "I can't believe that." He took thought. "I don't believe it. I'm of a mind to call him out at the mill and ask him."

"You do that," Hugh fought back panic and turned away again, unable to hold Phelps's accusing gaze. "He'll just tell you to mind your own business."

Phelps spun on his heel and started back to the crowd, who had all stopped eating and talking to observe the confrontation. Hugh knew he was in deep trouble. At least half the people there knew his mother well, and before supper was half cooked, she would know all the details of the conversation.

"I hear you're getting up a petition of some kind," Wilson spoke up and caused Phelps to stop. The station owner didn't turn around, however.

"That's right," he said over his shoulder. "You want to make something of it?"

"Might want to sign it," Wilson said in his steady, calm voice.

"No, thanks," Phelps took a step and started moving more rapidly away. "They might want to check the signatures, and they don't allow loonies' names to count."

Hugh looked up at Jonas Wilson. Something passed behind the old man's eyes. It was gone in an instant, and he pressed his chapped lips together in a tight smile. He ground his cigarette butt out under his boot heel, sighed, spoke softly. "C'mon, boy. Let's go have us a bite to eat."

"Let me try to explain it to you," Edith said in a quiet, even tone. They were sitting in the living room. They used it only when something serious was happening, and he inevitably associated it with Larry's funeral. Then, it seemed, he spent an eternity sitting on the pink sofa, rising and enduring hugs from women and handshakes from men he was too young to know, to care about. It was a room of tears in his mind, filled with whispers and furtive glances. It was a room Hugh hated. When he came through the door that evening, though, his mother was already seated on the sofa, his father perched uncomfortably on a Queen Anne chair. Both had tumblers full of iced amber liquid that Hugh assumed was whiskey, and both were smoking. Edith's hair was done up high on her head in the manner she wore it when she went visiting, and her makeup was heavy. In between sips of her drink and puffs of her cigarette, she put her hands in her lap and shredded a Kleenex.

Hugh's father slumped—or tried to slump—in the undersized armchair. Hugh knew that he hated the chair and had bought it only because Edith insisted that it matched the pink in the sofa. It was harder than concrete. Harry sipped his drink, puffed his Camel, and looked miserable.

Hugh could smell what had been supper throughout the house: meatloaf. Now it and the mashed potatoes and English peas were growing cold on the stove while they had this family talk.

"We've always brought you up to respect older people," Edith went on. Her hands were now fisted around the wadded Kleenex in her lap. She was working to be strong, Hugh knew, working to put up a good front, but her fragility was showing. He was overcome with guilt for causing her to go through this.

"But this is different," she said. "Jonas Wilson is not a normal person. He has strange ideas. He's a . . . well, he's not a nice person."

"He's nice to me."

"That's not the point," Harry grumbled. "He's probably nice to you because he wants something."

"What could he want from me?"

"Has he asked you for anything?" Edith's eyebrow shot up with a look at Harry.

"No, nothing." Hugh looked at his sneakers. Grass stains covered the white rubber toes. A tear raced across the shredded seam where the sole joined the vamp. They were wearing out. That was new, he idly thought. Usually he outgrew shoes long before they fell apart. "In fact, he gives me things."

"What things?" Harry was alarmed.

"Oh, sandwiches." Hugh frowned with the concealed fact of the tobacco. "Stuff like that. He's got a neat dog."

"That mongrel," Harry sighed.

"You eat with him?" Edith's voice raised, and she forcibly calmed herself and sipped her drink.

"Well, sure," Hugh confessed. "I eat what he eats. Sandwiches."

"Sandwiches made of what?"

"Vegetables." Hugh smiled as Harry rolled his eyes. "Squash, tomatoes, beets, stuff like that."

"You don't like 'stuff like that.'" Edith stared at him with an accusing look in her eyes. "You won't even let me put onions in the meatloaf."

"I never had any onions like Jonas's," Hugh said. "They're not hot! They're sweet. And he puts them in a sandwich with sourdough bread and mustard and beets—"

"'Jonas'!" Edith almost dropped her cigarette on the carpet as her hands groped for the Kleenex strips and her knuckles turned white in their grip. "He calls him 'Jonas,'" she said.

"Onions and beets?" Harry muttered. "That sounds awful. God, Edith, I'm hungry. Couldn't we finish this after supper?"

"He calls him 'Jonas.'" Edith repeated in a rising tone. "I can't believe you're thinking of supper while your son is running around with a psychopath and calling him by his first name."

"What do you want him to call him?" Harry drained his drink. "Jesus, Edith, I think you're making a mountain out of a molehill, here."

"Me! You're the one who called me this afternoon after Phelps Crane called you. You're the one who made me worry all day about where he was, who he was with. You're the one who suggested we might call the sheriff."

"The sheriff?" Hugh shouted involuntarily. His head spun. Phelps Crane had called his father, after all. His hands formed into fists. "Why would you call the sheriff? He hasn't done anything."

"It's not what he's done." Edith settled back on the sofa and took her glass. Her shoe was loose on her foot as she crossed her legs, and she twirled it around on her stockinged toe rapidly. "It's what he might do." She glared at Harry. "I can't believe you think I'm overreacting. After what you said . . ." She trailed off, drained her glass, reached for another cigarette. Her previous smoke still burned in the ashtray.

Harry rose wearily and took both of their empty glasses into the kitchen. "I know what I said," he called from the other room. "And I'm sorry I said it. I was busy when that old fool called me, and I didn't have time to think it through. I shouldn't have called you. It only upset you, and I don't think there's anything to be that upset about. Right now, I think you're scaring the boy." Hugh heard ice clinking. "And I'm not sure there's good reason."

"I think that old man's reputation is plenty of good reason," Edith shot back. She folded her arms and looked at the wall.

"Well, he hasn't done anything, and Hugh seems all right."

Hugh opened his mouth to shout that he was still in the room, to remind them that they didn't need to talk about him as if he were gone. It reminded him of the way they spoke of Larry. It made him feel invisible.

"I mowed all my lawns today," he put in. Actually, he was still three lawns behind, but he was sure he could make them up. Two of the families were on vacation. They wouldn't notice if he was a day or two late.

Harry ignored his comment when he came back into the room, set down the replenished drinks, and took his wife's ashtray back to the kitchen. She remained silent, smoking, staring at the wall.

"I'll admit I was pretty excited when I called," he said.

"Excited! You were in a blue-collar panic," she shouted. Hugh remembered his father explaining that "blue-collar panic" was a Navy term used to describe what happened when things went wrong and there was no officer around to take charge and calm down the sailors.

"All right, Edith. I was in a panic," Harry spoke from the kitchen. "But I've settled down, now. I've thought about it. I don't see that any harm's been done. Hugh's a good boy, and I trust him." He came back in and replaced the ashtray, took up his drink, and tried to settle himself once more on the uncomfortable chair.

"Phelps Crane said—"

"Phelps Crane doesn't know shit from Shinola," Harry said suddenly.

"Harry, watch your language!"

"Well, he doesn't. He's a bitter old busybody and a damned fool besides. He's had a burr under his saddle ever since he retired, and if you ask me, there's more to worry about from him spying on Hugh than there is from some old hermit sharing an onion sandwich with the boy."

"I think he was doing us a favor," Edith sniffed and took up her drink.

"I think he was butting in. Phelps is unreliable and half-crazy. Ask anybody. The only reason he runs the Chevron station is that his brother-in-law owns it. Nobody else would hire him. He's too old and too nuts, and you know as well as I do that he's drunk half the time. If there's anybody we need to tell Hugh to stay away from, it's probably Phelps Crane. I doubt that anything Jonas Wilson might do would be worse than any influence that foolish old drunk would have on the boy."

"I'm still here, remember," Hugh said darkly.

"Don't you smart-mouth me!" Edith yelled at him. She jumped when she shouted and spilled her drink all over her dress. She came to her feet. She looked wild. Her eyes were wide, and her hair came out of its coiffure and sprayed around her head. "You think you're a little big for your britches, don't you?" she shrieked.

"Edith," Harry started, sitting up. Hugh could see fear in his face, and he heard a sharp warning in his voice.

She glanced nervously at him, physically gathered herself together by pushing her hands back over her hair, and lowered her voice. "Well, if you're so satisfied to take nourishment with that filthy old man, then you can just go to your room without supper."

"Seems to me like we're all going to bed without supper," Harry grumbled. He sat back and sipped his drink.

"Go on," Edith ordered. Her painted nail pointed down the hall, but her voice was now calm, her face back to a controlled mask of anger. "I don't want to hear from you until you apologize to your father and me and promise—word of honor—to stay away from that old man from now on!"

Hugh rose and shuffled down the hall. He wasn't very hungry, anyway, and cold meatloaf didn't appeal to him. As he shut the door to his room behind him, he could hear his parents continuing to argue. His father's voice never rose to a yell, but he heard his mother's tones break into tears after a while. They were hurting each other, and it hurt him that he was the cause of it, but he didn't know what he could do.

He wanted to please them, to promise to stay away from Jonas Wilson, but the only way he could do that was to stay away from downtown. The thought of that, he realized with a start, was almost as painful as his guilt for causing trouble in his own house. He had somehow become involved with the attempted demolition of the old warehouse building—personally involved. He wanted to be there when it came down. He couldn't stand the thought of going by there and seeing a clean vacant lot where the old building had once stood, not without having seen it go. It was history, he told himself, and he didn't want to miss it.

He threw himself down onto his bed and looked around the darkened room. Only his closet light was on, and the room was gloomy as the late June darkness descended on the house. Model airplanes—biplanes from World War I and fighters from World War II—dangled from the ceiling, and posters of motorcycles and cars and baseball heroes—Hank Aaron, Mark McGwire, Ken Griffey Jr., Juan Gonzalez, and Nolan Ryan—dominated the wall over his desk. In the center was a small picture of the coveted mountain bike, but he couldn't make out the details in the dark, and he turned over and inspected the rest of the room.

The Rudd house had three bedrooms. When Larry was born, the third was converted to a nursery, but Hugh had been informed that as soon as Larry was old enough, it would be changed into an office for his father's work. Bunk beds were installed in Hugh's room, and his posters and models were shoved off to one side in anticipation of Larry's eventual transition from baby to little brother. It never was to be.

Larry's death had happened seven years before, in July. Hugh still remembered his mother's shrieks when she came running out of the nursery with her younger son's limp body in her arms. Hugh was seated at the kitchen table, mooning over soggy cornflakes, when she raced in and thrust Larry into his lap. She dialed the kitchen phone, screamed out her name and address and a demand for an ambulance, then snatched up Larry's body and raced out the door to meet the vehicle when it arrived. She ran the whole two miles to the hospital before the confused ambulance drivers wheeled up to the Rudd driveway.

Hugh had never eaten breakfast since without feeling his brother's body lying across his thighs. Larry had been dead weight, still and heavy, and Hugh couldn't ever forget the sight of his brother's half-open blue eyes or his head lolling helplessly as Hugh squirmed beneath him. It didn't haunt him. He had no nightmares about it, and it had all happened so quickly that he remembered it as only a bare outline of spasmodic events. But whenever he felt the cool wood of the kitchen chairs on the backs of his bare legs, the images swam up to meet his eyes, and he shuddered.

Hugh's parents had waited only a month after the funeral before selling all the baby furniture from the nursery and the bunk beds as well. Hugh's room was restored to his own personal domain. The third bedroom now had a daybed and a desk with a typewriter on it. They called it an office, but Hugh couldn't recall his father ever going in there to do any work of any kind. When his father had time cards to go over or paperwork from the mill to study, he sat in the dining room.

Now and forever, though, Hugh's bedroom was his own. He had never shared it. Not since Larry's death had he had an overnight guest, although he had spent the night at Tommy's and Ray's and others' houses from time to time. He kept the room neat, his bed made. His father had shown him how to make "navy corners," and he religiously tightened the bedspread across the single mattress every morning but Mondays—wash day.

As his eyes roved from shadow to shadow in the room, though, Hugh began to see his room with different eyes. It didn't seem to reflect his personality at all any longer. The posters bored him, and he wondered what about them made him think that he wanted them on the walls in the first place. He studied the model airplanes as if he was seeing them for the first time. They weren't very good, he acknowledged. The decals on most of them were crooked, and his attempts to paint camouflage patterns on others were childish and awkward.

His eyes roved to his bookshelf. Several model cars were arranged between forgotten toys and paperback joke books, binders full of baseball cards, and other junk. He was disgusted with everything in the room. He got up and glanced down at the quilted bedspread. It showed cartoon characters prancing in typical poses. It, too, repulsed him. He vowed to demand some changes as soon as things in the household cooled off and he was in a position to ask for anything.

He went to his closet and began digging through old clothes, toys, games, and puzzles. He made a pile of discards that grew larger while he worked. Light from the overhead bulb spilled into corners he hadn't inspected in years, it seemed, and he was amazed at how much childish junk was stored in shoe boxes and bags in the nether regions of the walk-in closet.

When he worked through a built-in shelf, ridding himself of boxes of crayons and coloring books and broken parts of toy cars, he discovered a stash of his parents' stuff in a shoe box. He opened it and discovered some pictures of them when they were young. His father stood proudly, muscular and sunburned in a chief petty officer's dress blues, and his mother looked girlish and awkward in a dressy suit with a short skirt that revealed more of her legs than Hugh had ever seen. Her hair was long and straight, her eyes clear. His father's smile was bright, confident. Behind the posing couple was the superstructure of a ship. To his father's right, a palm tree cast a shadow across the seawall at Corpus Christi Bay.

There also were pictures of his grandparents Rudd—dead before Hugh had a chance to know them—standing on the porch of a farmhouse with chickens and some cattle in the background. Next in the stack were grainy sepia-tone snaps of people Hugh didn't recognize, mixed in with shots of old cars that were new when they were photographed, of houses that resembled the ancient unpainted and dilapidated structures that ringed the better neighborhoods of the small town, of railroad cars and engines with proud crewmembers standing out front. There were church parties, weddings, and one photograph of a group of dour people standing in a cemetery in front of a flower-laden coffin. Hugh took the box to his bed, turned on his reading lamp, and was still sorting through the old photographs when the door opened and his father came in.

"How's it going, Sport?" Harry sat down on the bed and arched his eyebrows in surprise at his son's activity. "Where'd you find all that junk?"

"In my closet," Hugh replied. His father smelled of whiskey and to-bacco. It reminded him unpleasantly of the odor surrounding Phelps Crane. Hugh wondered if his father had managed to eat anything. Hugh picked up the picture of the cemetery scene. "What's going on here?"

"That's your great-grandfather Rudd's funeral." Harry picked up the photograph and looked at it. "I'm the kid in short pants, here. I wasn't but six or so."

"Do you remember him?"

"Not much. He was pretty sick by the time I came along. Grandma Rudd, *my* Grandma Rudd, died the summer before him. He never got over it."

"They're the ones buried by Larry, aren't they?" Hugh studied the picture. He saw the cotton compress in the background and now recognized the spot. A small sapling on the left was now a huge shade tree crowding the lot.

Harry nodded briefly. "Your grandparents Rudd—my folks—are in the plot next to them. You know that."

They were silent for a moment. Hugh's father's parents had been killed in a traffic accident when Hugh was still in diapers. That loss was some-thing Hugh and his father shared. Hugh always felt it drew them closer, but the mention of it always made him uncomfortable.

"What's this?" Hugh pulled another picture from the box. It showed a steel suspension bridge spanning two limestone buttes.

"That's the old bridge over Blind Man's Creek," Harry explained. "Look, here," he dug around in the box and found another shot. It was identical to the first, but this time there were small puffs of smoke coming from either end of the bridge. "And there's another one, somewhere." He fished around once more and came up with one that showed the buttes from the same angle, but now the bridge was nothing but a pile of twisted metal.

"They blew it up," Harry said. "I wasn't much older than you when they did it. My dad took these pictures. He said it was a shame for them to de-stroy it, but it was too narrow for modern cars, trucks and all, so they tore it down."

"Blew it up?"

"Well, they tried to dismantle it, but it was rusted up in places, and it was costing too much to take it apart. Some folks had the idea to recon-struct it someplace else."

"Why?"

"It was historical," Harry wrinkled his forehead. "They said it was built especially for Teddy Roosevelt to use."

"C'mon, Dad."

"No, seriously. Back before he was president, Roosevelt came out here on a wolf hunt. He was governor of New York then, and there were all sorts of people with him. Security people, I guess. Press, photographers, that sort of thing. Anyway, the best hunting was in the western part of the county, and there wasn't a good road, no way to cross the creek without getting wet, anyway, so the government sent down some engineers and, I guess, some money, and they built that bridge. They called it 'Wolf Hunt Bridge.'"

"Wolf Hunt Bridge."

"Yeah." Harry stretched his back. "See, Roosevelt hunted wolves from horseback, but all those other people rode in wagons or carriages—or maybe in cars, I don't know. Anyway, they could follow him right out to the hunt across that bridge."

"But they tore it down."

"Blew it up. I remember it. Whole town came out to watch. They put in that concrete job they have out there now. The mill's just the other side of it."

"Right there!" Hugh came up to his knees and pointed to a spot on his bedspread just over the top edge of the photograph.

"Yeah, Sport. Right there." He smiled at Hugh.

"Is there anything left of it? Could we go out there—"

"There's nothing left of it. It was all hauled away years ago. You've crossed that creek hundreds of times."

"But you got to see it go," Hugh said. "The old bridge. You were there when they blew it up."

"Yeah." Harry rose and studied the stack of discarded toys and games on the closet floor. "Say, what's going on here?"

"I'm just cleaning out some stuff I don't want." Hugh looked at the three pictures again. The bridge was gone. Just as if it hadn't been there. He had the disturbing feeling of helplessness. Someone should have saved it, he thought. Someone should have done something to stop them from destroying it.

"You're not doing this to be mean, are you?"

Hugh looked up, confused.

"I mean, you're not just making a big mess for your mother to clean up? Like to get back at her or anything?"

"No," Hugh said. "I'm just getting rid of some old junk I don't want anymore."

"Making room for the new?" He offered a smile.

"Yeah, something like that."

"Guess you're growing up, Sport." He picked up a coloring book, examined it with a sad expression, then dropped it back onto the stack. "Just don't make a mess. And hang onto those baseball cards. Might put you through college, you know. Unless you can learn to hit an inside curveball," he grinned. "Wish I still had mine. I could probably retire."

"Dad?"

"Yeah, Sport."

"You said that when they blew up the bridge, some people wanted to save it."

"Yeah. Don't know much about that. I was too young. There was a committee of some kind. Grandpa Rudd—your Grandpa Rudd—was on it. They tried. Wanted to move it out to the country someplace. Find a spot and rebuild it."

"Why didn't they?"

"Well, like I told you, the Highway Department was in a hurry to get the bridge widened. There had been some bad wrecks. It was too narrow for two cars to pass safely." He thought for a moment. "Guess they didn't have the money, either."

"But it was important. I mean, Teddy Roosevelt and all."

"Well," Harry smiled wanly. "There's likely as much bull in that story as truth. It was sort of a local legend. Don't know of anybody who claimed to have *seen* Teddy Roosevelt go anywhere near the bridge. Matter of fact, I'm not sure he was ever really here."

"But it was still a monument. It was important. Like the old Hendershot building. Right?"

Harry sat down again. "Not exactly. It's not the same thing."

"Why not?" Hugh came up on his knees in the middle of his bed. "I mean, that's one solid building. Mr. Hendershot built it to be there forever. He said so himself."

"Who told you that?"

Hugh hesitated, then almost whispered, "Jonas Wilson."

Harry shook his head. "You can't believe everything that old man says. You can't believe anything. Old Man Hendershot was . . . well, he was crazy, too. The story is that he killed his wife and ran off with a waitress, but all anybody knows for sure is that he and a lot of money disappeared. That was a long time ago."

"But that doesn't change the building," Hugh argued. "The building's important."

"Why?"

"Because it's there. Because it's always been there. It's part of the town. They're just tearing it down because it's old. Somebody ought to try to stop them."

"From what I hear, Phelps Crane and his bunch are doing just that."

"Oh, they're just making noise." Hugh flopped back on his bed. "They stand around and talk and make ugly faces at the railroad man—"

"What railroad man?"

"Mr. Grissom. A guy in a white car who comes over and argues with them."

"Oh." Harry frowned.

"Anyway, they're not going to do anything."

"Well, what do you do down there?"

Hugh scowled and thought deeply. "I just watch."

"With Jonas Wilson."

"Not *with* him. Not exactly. We're just there at the same time, that's all."

"So, you're not hanging around with him?"

"No," Hugh lied. He thought about their dinner that afternoon. It was the second in a row, and Wilson had taken it for granted that Hugh would join him. The period had been quiet, both of them lost in individual thoughts as they munched their sandwiches, had their smokes. Wilson took his shots of whiskey, cleaned up their litter, and they had lain back in the grass and looked at the sky while Hugh scratched Goodlett between her scruffy ears. Then they had gone back to watch the afternoon's continuation of the workers' futile attempts to dent the Hendershot Grocery Warehouse with their ball. The workers gave up at five, just as they had the day before, and the crowd cheered when they climbed into their pickups and drove out to their motel.

"There's a lot of people there," Hugh continued. "Jonas said that he figured there were nearly a hundred in the crowd by the time the men quit today."

"Any other kids?" Harry asked while he pretended to sort through the other photographs.

"No," Hugh admitted. "Tommy and Ray were there for a while, but they went swimming."

"But you didn't?"

"I meant to, but I never got around to it."

"What about your work?"

"I'm keeping up." Hugh avoided saying that he had already made that claim once that evening.

"Well, you need to do that." Harry picked up a baseball card. "Thought you were going to work out some, too. High school's only a few weeks away."

Hugh ignored a quick spasm of guilt. "Then I can keep going down there?"

"I don't like it. I don't like it that you're down there with all those layabouts who have nothing better to do. I don't know why you feel it's so important. And I have to agree with your mother: I don't like your hanging around with Jonas Wilson."

"I don't know why I want to watch, but I do," Hugh mumbled. "I just feel that it's important. You know, Dad, I don't think they're going to do it."

"Do what?"

"Tear it down."

"Of course, they are. Unless Phelps and his crowd can come up with something they haven't tried yet, that building will be gone by the Fourth of July."

"They aren't having much luck."

"They'll find a way. They'll blow it up if they have to."

Panic rose inside Hugh. His father was right. They *would* blow it up. Just like they blew up the bridge in the picture. In his mind he could see the puffs of smoke coming from the glassless windows of the six stories, the hesitation, and then the explosion. The whole thing would just go up. Hugh had watched enough old war movies to know that there was no building that couldn't be demolished by dynamite, by bombs.

"I have to see them do it," Hugh said quietly.

"Why, son? Why do you feel that way?"

"I just do. You saw them blow up the bridge, didn't you?"

"What has that got—"

"Well, it's the same thing. That building is important, and they have no right to tear it down. But they're going to anyway. I want to see it happen."

Harry Rudd studied his son's face and said nothing for a few moments. Finally he stood and sighed. "You're going to have to stay away from Jonas Wilson."

"I can't promise that." Hugh set his jaw. He was defying a paternal order. He had never done that before. He couldn't imagine what sort of storm was about to break.

"For your mother's sake. For her peace of mind." Harry offered one last chance.

"I can't promise, Dad. Don't make me promise."

Harry's face darkened, then the storm passed without breaking. He sighed. "At least promise me you'll be careful. That you'll watch out. Don't listen to everything he says."

"There's nothing to watch out for," Hugh said. He was pushing, but he suddenly softened, pulled back. "But I'll watch out."

Harry's shoulders slumped. "Okay, I'll settle for that."

"Dad," Hugh asked. "What's wrong with him? With Jonas Wilson? That everybody hates him so?"

"He's . . . he's just crazy. Or so everyone says. I don't know him, don't know anything about him. He's just got a reputation, that's all. Some things happened a long time ago. Before we moved here, but even when I was a kid there was talk . . ."

"What kind of talk?"

"Oh, you know." Harry looked up at the ceiling as if searching for help with his explanation. "Gossip. He used to be some kind of socialist, I think. Preached on street corners."

"You mean he's a preacher? A minister?"

"No, not that kind of preaching. When I was a kid, there were stories about how he tried to unionize the farm workers in the county."

"What's wrong with that? There's a union at the mill. You're a member—"

"Times were different, Hugh. It was a long time ago, and there was a depression. And there were other things." He started to say something, then took thought and changed his tone. "He talked about socialism a lot, tried to get people worked up about things." Harry trailed off. "I don't know. It was all before I was born."

Hugh didn't say anything.

"Then," Harry said reluctantly. "There was some trouble about twenty years ago. Something to do with some college kids. But we didn't live here then, and I only know parts of that, too. And I don't believe most of it. Sheriff Anderson says he's harmless enough."

"You *did* talk to the sheriff?" Hugh asked, shocked.

"Just for a minute," Harry confessed with a crooked smile. "I had to check on you."

Hugh looked away. He knew he couldn't argue that point.

"Just be careful, Hugh," Harry said abruptly. "Your mother worries. Be damned careful around him."

"I will."

Harry rose, started to leave. Then he stopped when he reached the door.

"Say," he turned. "I've got to run back out to the mill tonight. I forgot something. Want to come along?"

Hugh sensed that this was an important invitation. "Sure," he said, jumping up and tying his sneakers. "Can we stop by where the bridge was?"

"No." Harry frowned and opened and shut his fist. "That's a lie. I mean, we'll drive out to the mill, and we can stop if you want, but the truth is that your mother fed supper to the disposal and went to bed. I'm starving. How about a cheeseburger from the Dairy Mart?"

Hugh brightened and smiled conspiratorially. "Chocolate shake?"

"Malts," Harry grinned back.

"Let's go," Hugh said.

CHAPTER FOUR

Hugh's Wednesday night trip out to the mill with his father was remarkably uneventful. The sun was already down when they took off from town, and by the time they passed the boxcar where Jonas Wilson lived some five miles from the city limits, it was already too dark to see much beyond the highway. The sturdy concrete structure that had replaced the old "Wolf Hunt Bridge" revealed nothing of the historical significance of its predecessor. After the father and son stood around in the darkness, swatted mosquitoes, and listened to the burping of bullfrogs down on the creek below them for a few minutes, they wordlessly returned to the car and drove back to town.

"Thought you had to go into the mill," Hugh said as Harry swung their Ford around and pointed it east.

"We got close enough," he said and lit a Camel. They went to the Dairy Mart and ate their cheeseburgers in comfortable silence. His mother was asleep when they returned home, but Hugh noticed that the whiskey bottle stood empty on the kitchen counter.

The next two days passed with hot, painful slowness. As always, Hugh beat the sun—and his mother—up every morning. It had for a long time been his one indulgence in disobedience. His mother was a great believer in breakfast—cereal, pancakes, eggs and bacon, if she could get it down him—and only by whining and begging had he convinced her to form the habit of buying snacks that could be easily and quickly eaten on the run. If she noticed that they disappeared with daily regularity, she didn't comment, but she seldom missed the chance to scold him for skipping out of the house before she had a chance to rise and begin serious cooking.

Oddly, though, Harry Rudd's devotion to full meals at suppertime did not extend to breakfast, and during the past two years, he also had formed the habit of rising early and sitting at the breakfast table with the morning paper while he smoked cigarettes and drank cup after cup of coffee in silence.

Each of the next two mornings, Hugh gobbled down a Pop-Tart and drank an Instant Breakfast while his father scanned the newspaper and sipped his coffee, then the boy pushed the Grassmaster off down the driveway to take care of his business.

Although he worked steadily through the mornings, he couldn't keep up with his schedule. The remaining yards on his list were huge, some three lots wide. Pushing as fast as he could, he was unable to complete more than two before noon, whereupon he would quietly—to avoid attracting his mother's attention—park his mower in the garage, mount his bike, and pedal rapidly downtown to join Jonas Wilson and the growing crowd for their midday meal during what everyone, taking their cue from Lydia Fitzpatrick, was now calling "Lunch Break."

When Hugh arrived at the old parking lot on Friday, he was astonished at the size of the crowd. It had been large before, but now, it seemed that more than half the people in town were gathered in and around the area. Watching the building's demolition—or attempted demolition—had become a major civic pastime. In addition to housewives and unemployed men and those whose jobs permitted them time away from the office or shop, Hugh noticed that several of the small city's most important people were comfortably seated in lawn chairs or standing around in the artificial shade of beach umbrellas and other improvised coverings that were often augured down right into the blacktop of the parking lot.

Everyone was chatting amiably, exchanging food and drink and tobacco. Several women were knitting or crocheting while they sat, and some older boys were off to one side tossing baseballs and footballs back and forth. Along the cable-linked pylons, a line of men stood and leaned, their backs to the crowd, their gimme-capped heads pointed down the grade toward the Hendershot Grocery Warehouse.

As he weaved his way out to the pylons where these hardier souls braved the noonday sun in exchange for a "front row seat," he heard Marvin Upchurch say that Henderson's Hardware was ordering more chairs and oversized beach umbrellas and expected the shipment by special truck tomorrow.

"Never sold but three or four a month," Marvin, who was a part-time clerk in the store, averred. "Said that this was the biggest run they'd had on such stuff since they'd been in business."

Tommy and Ray didn't arrive that morning. Ray had called late on Thursday to ask Hugh to join them out at Medicine Lake for a weekend campout and fishing expedition, but Hugh turned them down. It was something they had done several weekends last summer and had talked about doing "every weekend" this year, but now Hugh had no interest in being away from town, even for one night.

"Any luck?" Hugh asked Jonas Wilson, who was leaning against his regular pylon some distance from the crowd.

"Nope." Wilson smiled knowingly, tipped back his fedora. "They're back working on the south side. Ain't going to do 'em no good."

For three days, the crew down around the building had moved the crane from one of the yellow sides to the other. Each move was a Herculean task, requiring them to jack down the trailer from its supporting legs—adjustable steel beams that were set in the ground to support the awful weight of the machine. They then had to bring in the tractor, hook it up to the semi-trailer, and tow the whole thing to another spot, maneuvering around uneven places on the ground around the building until it was in the proper range for the wrecking ball. By the time they unhitched the tractor, replaced the steel legs, and cleared the area to begin operation, hours passed. Most of the workers sat in the shade of their bulldozers and pickups and watched the crane crew's struggles. Then, they rose and stood around expectantly while the ball took the first dozen bounces off the building before they resumed their waiting postures, smoked, and stared up at the growing crowd in the parking lot.

They had tried all four sides of the building during the past three days. Now, they were back where they started. The new idea, apparently, was to adjust the ball so it would strike different stories, searching for a weak spot in the structure to bring it down.

"Each one of them floors is supported by concrete columns," Wilson commented idly. "Solid concrete. I don't recollect how many there is. Not as many up top as there is on the bottom, but they's a lot all the way up. You can't knock nothing built like that down with no piddly little ol' wrecking ball."

"What's that?" Hugh pointed to the top of the building. There, in faded lettering, words appeared.

"That's Hendershot's ol' sign," Wilson squinted. "Sometime 'long about fifty years ago—during World's War II, I think—somebody got the bright idea to cover it up with stone facing. It wasn't put on the same way as the rest. They knocked it off early this morning and thought they had it. Set 'em up a cheer, they did. Didn't do no good. Soon's they got it uncovered, that was all she wrote. They ain't done nothing but stew 'round ever since."

Hugh studied the lettering. Most of Hendershot's name was visible, and the end of the words "Grocery" and "house" could also be seen in faded red letters.

The crowd gathered around Carl's lowboy, preparing for their "Lunch Break." Grissom's car weaved up toward the parking lot, bouncing over the rough ground near the construction site.

"Do me a favor," Wilson instructed. Hugh glanced at him quickly. This was unusual. He had noticed that the old man never asked for anything. He simply stated what he wanted as if it was going to happen automatically. "Skinny over yonder when that young jack shows up here to start hoorahing again, and try to find out if they're fixing to work all weekend or what."

"Aren't we going over to the hotel?" Hugh asked, surprised at his disappointment. The sandwiches in Wilson's bag had grown somewhat stale in the past two days, and the mustard was turning brown, but it was the conversation, the company he dreaded missing. The cool sit-down with the old man was something he had come to look forward to.

"In a spell. Now, get on over yonder and see what you can learn."

The railroad man pulled his car up near enough to the crowd to force several people to back away, opened the door, got out. He had discarded his suit coat, and his white shirt was stained with dust and sweat. A small straw hat covered his head, and perspiration tracks ran down his smoothly shaven cheeks. He scowled his way through the crowd toward a knot of men gathered around Carl Fitzpatrick.

"Listen," he said in a loud, official tone, "I've been on the phone with the home office in Chicago, and you people are just going to have to disperse. You're creating a public nuisance, and you're interfering with the work going on here."

"Just how're we interfering?" Phelps Crane demanded. "We're not doing nothing but watching."

"You know damn good and well what you're doing," Grissom spluttered and pointed at the clipboard in Phelps's greasy hand. Hugh was surprised to see that it contained a large sheaf of papers. "And I'm under orders to put a stop to it."

"Mr. Grissom." Carl Fitzpatrick waved a chicken leg as if it were a gavel and wiped his mouth on a paper napkin. Lydia was just behind him. Their lowboy and its portable grill had become a regular feature of the crowd, a center focus for hibachis, small smokers and charcoal grills, Coleman stoves, and a variety of other types of portable cookers. A small refrigerator in the truck's bed was hooked to the doolie's auxiliary battery, and an electric ice cream maker whirred throughout the day. Surrounding the trailer was a forest of Igloo coolers, grocery sacks, and picnic baskets, left there by the crowd for safekeeping. Four folding tables also were set up around the truck and trailer, all laden with food. Cantaloupe, watermelon, cakes, and pies were sliced and available to be picked up by anyone who knew the Fitzpatricks or wanted to get to know them better. A small, computer-generated banner reading "Carl Fitzpatrick for City Attorney" stretched down the near side of the trailer, and a stack of bookmarks with Carl's picture on them appeared on each of the folding tables.

"I think you're a little confused," Carl said, chewing.

"*I'm* not confused," Grissom insisted. "You're the one who's confused. This is not public property. We've checked and double-checked. We can throw you off any time we want to."

"And we'll just move down to the other side of the site," Carl said. "It's downwind, and the view's not as good. Somebody might even wander in too close and get hurt. But folks want to see this, and—"

"See what?" Grissom demanded. "There's nothing to see. Just a bunch of men trying to get a job done. You're blocking a public thoroughfare. You're creating a public nuisance."

"You see?" Carl bit into his chicken leg once more. "I told you you were confused. You can't have it both ways, Mr. Grissom. If it's *private* property, it can't be a *public* thoroughfare. And if it's private property that has been used as a public thoroughfare for long enough time for it to become precedent . . ." Carl pointed the gnawed leg at Grissom in a meaningful manner, paused, and continued, "then any court in the world would decide that your rights as private owner have been abridged if not totally abrogated."

He let that sink into the glowering Grissom's mind. "I know my law, Mr. Grissom, as well as any Chicago attorney. But this isn't Chicago. This is Texas, and we're particular about the distinctions between public and private land. You'd do well to remember that."

Carl's voice had risen as he spoke, and almost on cue, George Ferguson stepped forward with the same little three-step ladder Phelps had used before and placed it close to the lawyer. Carl smoothly handed his chicken bone to George, removed his suit coat and slung it over his shoulder. He mounted two rungs and placed a well-shined shoe on the top step.

"So, you see, Mr. Grissom." He gestured toward the crowd. "Your rights are in serious question here in the first place." Grissom opened his mouth to speak, but Carl cut him off with a quick wave of his hand across the upturned faces around him. "And as for this silliness about our 'creating a public nuisance.' Well, Mr. Grissom, we seem to be the only public around here, and I don't think anyone here believes that he or she is a nuisance."

He beamed at the crowd, who began a smattering of applause. "Excepting, of course, yourself, Mr. Grissom," Carl concluded. "You seem to have developed a habit of coming up here two or three times a day, trying to stir up trouble and cause a public disturbance. And I believe there *is* a law against that!"

He almost bowed while the smattering of applause became a torrent of clapping and then a flood of cheering. Lydia Fitzpatrick, taking advantage of a lull in the speech-making, brought him another piece of grilled chicken, which he accepted with a grateful smile. She wore tight yellow pedal pushers and a tiny tank top. Hugh tried and failed to imagine his mother wearing such a revealing outfit. She beamed at Grissom when she passed him.

"Can I get you something to eat, Mr. Grissom?" she asked. "Piece of chicken? Potato salad? Maybe a glass of iced tea?" Grissom ignored her.

Carl continued to smile at the railroad man. He bit into the new chicken leg with fervor, almost, Hugh thought, as if it were the railroad man's own limb in Carl's strong, white teeth. Grissom stood steaming in the heat, his tie loose, his shirt sopping with sweat. His cheeks were afire.

"We're going to see about that, Fitzpatrick," he said. "Fort Worth is in Texas, too. And down there in our lawyers'—our *Texas* lawyers'—offices —right now—a brief is being prepared to move you people off to a safe distance where you won't interfere with this project."

"You mean," Carl took up the challenge immediately, "off to where our legal right to congregate and," he pointed the gnawed bone again toward

Grissom's face and spoke in a deep and serious tone, *"peacefully assemble* won't be violated?" He smiled at the crowd, who fell silent. "Our *constitu-tional* right? Is that what you mean, Mr. Grissom?"

There was no applause this time, merely a low undertone of muttering. Tension grew in the crowd. Grissom removed his hat and furiously mopped his brow. His hair was slick with sweat.

"Honey," Lydia shrilled from the lowboy, "do you want some cole slaw with your chicken?"

"Here, just as in Fort Worth or, I suspect, in Chicago, Mr. Grissom," Carl wound up for an exit line, "We practice *American constitutional* law. The same law that not a few of these folks have fought for on foreign soil." He grinned at the alliteration. "The same law that many of these women have sacrificed husbands, brothers, and sons for. That's the law we prac-tice here, Mr. Grissom. Not railroad law. Not corporate law. Not Chicago law or even Fort Worth law. We practice the law of these United States. The Bill of Rights! And you'd do well not to forget that! In the meantime, you're interrupting our lunch, so I'll bid you good day."

Applause exploded upward from the parking lot and rained down on Grissom's sweating forehead. Routed, he turned sharply and marched back to his car. He left gravel flying and rubber burning when he tore out down Main Street and out of sight. Carl Fitzpatrick descended from his perch and endured backslapping and greasy handshakes while he moved over next to his wife and grinned when she handed him a Tupperware bowl full of potato salad and a plastic tumbler full of iced tea. Someone started singing "America, the Beautiful," and it lasted well into the second verse before dying out.

"Reminds me of Clarence Darrow," Wilson whispered to Hugh when he returned.

"Who?" Hugh asked. Someone tried to start up a verse of "My Country 'Tis of Thee," but no one could remember all the words to the first verse. "Dixie" then began raggedly somewhere on the fringes, and when that was done, several high school kids took up "The Eyes of Texas," which was im-mediately followed by "The Aggie War Hymn," offered lustily by a rival group of teenagers. Everyone was standing and clapping each other on the shoulder as they moved around and chanted the verses along with the stu-dents. Then, a small group of enthusiastic singers, led by Brother Mason, minister of music for the First Baptist Church, swung directly into "The Battle Hymn of the Republic," which ran to five sincerely delivered verses.

"Big lawyer. Politician," Jonas said over the songsters while he rolled a smoke. "Heard him talk once. He had big ideas for the common man, the working man, farmers and such. Folks'd come from all over to hear him. Wasn't no flies on him when it come to working up a crowd."

"I hear you used to do some of that yourself," Hugh said quietly.

Jonas lit his cigarette and gave Hugh a narrow look through the smoke. "Who told you that?"

"Well, my father did," Hugh confessed. "He said you used to preach on street corners."

"That a fact?"

Hugh was confused. "Well . . . I don't know. He said it was before he was born."

"That *is* a fact," Jonas said. "But the rest of it's stretched a mite. I didn't do no street preaching, and anybody says I did got his story wrong. I spent some time trying to get folks to see the truth of things, but I wasn't no preacher of any kind."

"Well, Mr. Fitzpatrick's not a preacher, either," Hugh said. "He *is* running for city attorney, though."

"Shoot, boy," Wilson chortled. "Don't let him fool you. He's running for mayor. Least, he is now. He gets off a couple more sermons like that, he'll be running for governor." Sure enough, Hugh noticed that Carl was now standing off to one side, studying the bright red banner on the trailer and frowning as if in deep thought. "Ain't no flies on Carl, neither. Not when it comes to speechifying."

They were silent for a moment. The crowd, finished with singing, now resumed eating and passing food to one another. Voices were merry, laughter general.

"Well, what'd you find out over yonder?" Wilson asked.

"I didn't learn anything," Hugh said.

"You should learn something every time you listen," Wilson growled. "Learn something from everything you do."

"I mean about them working this weekend or not."

"Oh." Wilson rubbed his chin. "Well, get back over there and put out a ear. I'll meet you over to the hotel."

‑≺

Hugh watched Wilson saunter off and Goodlett rise unbidden from her invisible sleeping position near a curb and follow him. Hugh then entered the crowd again and weaved in and out and reluctantly turned down offers of chicken, ham, hotdogs, tuna salad, soft drinks. He was hungry, but he didn't want to spoil his meal with Wilson by eating there on the parking lot.

Finally, he worked his way over by Carl, who was now talking earnestly to several men. Phelps Crane was in the center of the small group, but the rest Hugh recognized as being among that class of citizen his father always called "Civic Leaders." Most of them wore white short-sleeved shirts and ties and small straw hats with colorful bands. They were leaning in, listening to Carl and nodding. Hugh moved closer.

"He's not kidding," Carl said as he fed potato salad into his mouth with a plastic fork. "I'm running a bluff on this precedent thing. He's got one hell of a lot more than the Constitution on his side, and he knows it."

"Well, what you said makes goddamn good sense to me," Phelps said.

"Yeah, but you're not a judge, Crane," Carl shot. "And you need to keep your mouth shut. Let somebody who knows something handle this."

Phelps looked wounded. He still hadn't shaved, Hugh noticed, and his eyes were more red-rimmed than ever. "Well, Mr. Big Shot Lawyer, I suppose *this* don't mean nothing." He thrust out the clipboard. "I got me near five hundred signatures here."

"You can get five thousand or fifty thousand for all I care." Carl put down the plastic bowl and wiped his mouth with a new napkin. "Or for all *he* cares. I'm telling you, you can't stop this thing with talk."

"Well, then, what're we doing out here? You told me to get this thing signed, didn't you?" Phelps demanded. "I've shut down my station to be here."

"Well, nobody told you to do that."

George Ferguson asked, "Is there anything we can do, Carl?"

"We can keep folks coming out here." Carl allowed his eyes to run approvingly over the crowd. "Keep people worked up, and get more out here. Pretty soon, somebody—the press, TV, that sort of thing—will take notice, and then we'll have a shot. Nothing like national embarrassment to change the mind of a major corporation, especially a railroad. Nobody likes the railroad."

"I sure as hell don't," Phelps muttered. "I hate the sons of bitches."

"I'll try to make some calls tonight. I have some connections in the media." Carl said "media" as if it were a holy thing, Hugh thought.

"And we'll save the building?" Harvey Turnbull asked.

"We'll sure try." Carl smiled a sly grin.

"Well, I got an idea or two of my own," Phelps said, and he stumbled off toward downtown.

"Hope it's to go get some Rolaids," Carl belched. "This picnicking is playing hell with my digestion. Never ate so much in my life."

The men broke up and began talking among themselves, and Hugh moved off. He was confused about the men and their motives, but he had seen enough movies, watched enough TV to know one thing: Carl Fitzpatrick was planning to make as much of this as he could. Jonas was right, Hugh thought. Carl could work up a crowd. He might very well run for governor.

Hugh gave up on trying to find out any more concrete information and started toward the hotel, then he stopped and stared. Sitting on a green chaise lawn chair, right beside the Fitzpatrick lowboy, a chicken wing in her long fingers, earphones from a portable CD player plugged into her ears, was Linda Fitzpatrick, Carl's fourteen-year-old daughter.

Hugh's insides hollowed immediately, and he felt himself grow hot and anxious in the cavity that was now suddenly filled with his pounding heart. Since first grade when she had come into Mrs. Schermerhorn's class in a pretty, rose-colored pinafore, her long, blond braids set off by bright red ribbons, he had been smitten beyond logic by this blond beauty. Although he had never admitted to anyone that Linda Fitzpatrick—a girl, after all—was in the least important to him, and although he had never spoken more than ten words to her at a time, it was an acknowledged fact of his childhood that thoughts of her tortured him as much as the sight of her turned him instantly into a stumble-footed, tongue-tied moron.

In the past year, years really, he had dreamed of finding her alone, so he could talk to her without others overhearing. His fantasy had not extended to what he might do when he made such a discovery. The circumstance of getting up to bat alone seemed too impossible to push far enough to visualize what first base might be like. He supposed he would say something to her, something intimate, perhaps, something personal, something to indicate his long-abiding worship of her, something he would never dare to say in front of friends—his or hers—for fear of mortifying rejection.

But now, she was totally, completely alone, only a few steps from him. Hugh could only stand and stare at her.

She finished her chicken, flicked the bone over her shoulder carelessly, and looked with a bored expression around the adults who continued to circulate and eat and talk. She wore short white shorts, and her long, tanned thighs stretched out and crossed perfectly at the knee before tapering to delicious calves that then slimmed down to delicate ankles. Narrow yellow sandals seemed painted on her highly arched feet, and her long, slender toes—the tip of each painted bright pink—rested easily on the purest, whitest insole Hugh had ever seen. Her hair, long, yellow, thick, was pulled back into a casual ponytail and bound with a pink scrunchy. Her cheeks hollowed seductively below the rims of her pink-rimmed sunglasses to frame perfectly full and pouty lips. The sweetness of her throat disappeared into a white-on-white print blouse that perfectly matched her shorts and properly draped across the slight swell of her breasts.

She was, in Hugh's adolescent imagination, the most perfect girl he had ever seen.

Hugh finally realized he was staring and holding his breath, and he emptied his lungs and took in a quick succession of panting gasps to gain a hold on himself. A rapid inspection of the crowd confirmed that no other kids their age—or older—were nearby. The opportunity was too rare, for Linda Fitzpatrick was almost always seen in a crowd of giggling girls who followed her around and, Hugh imagined, hoped to pick up the shreds of attention and popularity she so casually discarded.

Hugh looked down at himself. His Texas Rangers T-shirt was still comparatively white, and his jeans had been clean that morning. But grass stains were here and there, and his sneakers were about shot. Still, he saw a chance to do something he had never before had the courage for. He knew before he started moving in her direction that this time might be the only chance he would ever have.

He was going to do it. There was no hesitation, no turning back. He was afraid and at the same time excited. Linda Fitzpatrick. All by herself. Almost as if she was waiting for him. He swallowed hard to clear his throat.

"Hiya," he said as he sauntered up beside her and leaned against the lowboy's fender in what he imagined to be a casual pose. "What's up?"

Linda pulled her earphones out, turned her sunglasses toward Hugh, and cast a contemptuous glance up and down the grassy-smelling boy who accosted her, looked around the crowd to see if anyone was watching, and then opened her lips into a wide smile, revealing perfect teeth. "Hi, Hugh," she chirped. "What in the world are you doing here?"

His heart thundered in his ears, but Hugh nonchalantly crossed one sneaker over the other and shrugged. "Watching them tear down the old Hendershot building, I guess. You?"

Her hand brushed the air in the direction of her father. "Oh, I *have* to be here. Mother says I have to come and be a part of this. 'Family image' and all that. Daddy's running for city attorney, you know."

"I thought it was mayor," Hugh said before he thought, then winced internally.

"What gave you that idea?"

"Something somebody said," Hugh muttered and looked around. Phelps Crane had returned, and Carl was waving his hands and arguing with him. Their voices were low, but he could almost feel their anger.

"Well, I sure hope not." Linda licked her full, pink-painted lips, and a frown wrinkled the tan above her yellow eyebrows. "City attorney's a big enough hassle." She leaned forward and whispered. "Mother says it's a pain in the butt." She giggled, brought her perfect fingers to her mouth.

Hugh barely heard her. The smell of her hair, her perfume—no, he reconsidered, not perfume, coconut oil—wafted into his nostrils and made him dizzy. He stole a quick glance down the front of her blouse and caught the unbelievable sight of the valley between her breasts before they disappeared into a white brassiere. She looked up and caught the direction of his eyes and narrowed her own.

"You sure have a great tan," he choked out and turned slightly away.

"Yeah," she sounded sad. "I went out to California to visit Megan for a week. She has a beach house right on the ocean, near Malibu. It was great!" She smiled again.

The Fitzpatricks had four children, and Linda was the youngest—and the only one still at home—Megan the eldest and working as a costume designer in California. Rich beyond imagination for the small town in which they lived, they resided in a two-story colonial-style house on the edge of town and kept a fully furnished lake house out in Punkin Center. It was larger than the Rudd family home. They belonged to the country club, kept horses in a stable near their house, owned three cars—all European makes—and two pickups, including the big Ford doolie they used to haul their horse trailers, and a motor home. "Goddamn waste of gasoline," Harry had once grumbled when they drove their ancient Ford station wagon past and spotted all the vehicles parked in the long, circular driveway out front. "Looks like a used car lot."

"Have you ever seen the ocean?" Linda smiled once more with no notion of the effect such a gesture had on Hugh's insides.

"Yeah," Hugh replied weakly. "Well, just the gulf." Somewhere in the back of his mind he recalled someone else saying almost the same thing not long ago. "My grandparents live down in Corpus, you know. We go down almost every year."

"Corpus," Linda repeated idly, again checking the crowd for any as yet undiscovered admirers.

"Well," Hugh frantically sorted through his mind for a topic—any topic—to keep the conversation going. "You really got a great tan." His eyes fell to her tawny thighs. A line of fine, white hair sharply defined where her razor had stopped just below the hemline of her shorts.

"Yeah." She pouted. "But not for long. Even if I go out every day, it'll fade. Texas sun just isn't the same as California sun."

"Maybe it'll last anyway," Hugh said hopefully. He couldn't tear his mind away from the whiteness of her young cleavage.

"You know how to tell?" she asked.

"How to tell what?"

"How long a tan'll last, silly." She pressed her thumb on top of her thigh. The narrow ellipse glowed white for a few seconds, then faded back to light brown. "The longer the white lasts, the shorter the tan duration. Tony taught me that."

"Tony?"

"Boy I met in California. On the beach." Linda said. "Here, want to try?"

She straightened her thighs out on the chaise, and Hugh reached down before he knew what he was doing and pressed his finger against the incredible softness of her leg. He couldn't believe he was really touching her, and if his mind had been able to comprehend that fact fully—which it never could—it would have reeled from the notion that he wasn't merely touching her, he was touching her *leg*, her *thigh*, one of the two matched wonders of his fantasy world, limbs that had sent him into raptures of guilt-ridden dreams for nearly two years, ever since he first noticed that she was shaving her legs and wearing hose to any dressy function.

"Hold it there for a count of ten," she instructed.

He counted slowly, wishing every digit required a hundred thousand beats. Then, when he reached ten, he regretfully raised his finger and studied the oblong white mark that remained.

"Now you count: One, Nevada, two, Nevada, three—it's gone," she giggled.

"Nevada?"

"That's how Tony said to count it. It measures a second precisely. He said that because they did all the gambling in Nevada, you could count on that being precise. Tony's eighteen," she added. "A senior," she whispered.

"So, how long?"

"Three, or two and a half, I guess." she calculated. "That means two months. More or less. Depending on how well I maintain it. You should see Tony's tan. It doesn't last for even one whole count. That could mean six months, and if he stays at the beach all summer, it'll last all year."

"Sounds like he's a tanning expert," Hugh mumbled. He was tired of Tony.

"Oh, you should see his tan." Linda smiled and crossed her legs again. "It's deep and dark. He's *all* muscle. You should see his arms. Muscle tans quicker than fat, you know. He's been improving on it since he was a kid."

"A kid."

"It's all in the contrast," she whispered. "You can't really measure a tan until you see how deep it is compared to the white line."

"The white line?"

"The line underneath." She plucked at her blouse to indicate what she meant. "Like underneath his suit."

"His suit?"

"His bathing suit!" She made a noise with her lips. "Really, Hugh, sometimes you're so dumb. So . . ." she hesitated, licked her lips, and went ahead, "so immature."

He jerked back a step as if she had slapped him. His head was swimming. Images of the two of them in one of the brightly striped cabanas that were always on the beaches in movies about California jockeyed for position in his mind. He saw Tony, tall, blond, tan, muscles rippling as he stood casually masculine, just like the male models in the Sears catalog swimsuit ads, peeling down his suit in front of Linda, her mouth open in lust, her fingers struggling with the straps of her own garment, eager for Tony to analyze her tan's progress. Hugh's stomach suddenly ached.

"Are you all right?"

He realized that he had been idiotically staring off into space.

"Yeah, just hungry, I guess."

"Want some chicken? We have some wings left. Tony says wings are—"

"No." Hugh turned with a sudden startling thought of Jonas Wilson. He was waiting for him. "I have to meet someone."

"Bet I know who," she said with a mischievous lilt in her voice.

"Say, Linda." He looked around. Most people had finished eating and were packing away their picnic gear and replenishing their drinks for the afternoon's session. "You wouldn't know if those guys," he jerked a thumb north toward the Hendershot building, "if they're going to work through the weekend, would you?"

"God, I hope not," she frowned. "Daddy's promised to take me and Mother to Dallas to shop at the Galleria all day tomorrow and Sunday. We're leaving tonight. The new fall clothes are in, and I want to get ready for school."

"School?" Hugh's mind reeled again. It was still *June*, for Christ's sake.

"Yeah, school," she mimicked his surprise. "High school. Remember? Freshman year?" She took a beat, then added with a sly grin, "I may stay out with my sister for the fall."

And Tony, Hugh mentally added.

"Tony's going to UCLA," she said as if reading his thought. "He said if I came out, we could go to all the football games."

"You're only fourteen."

"Fifteen in September, and so what?" Linda sniffed. "You don't have to be such a snot about it."

Hugh suddenly realized she was bluffing. She would be a shoo-in for junior varsity cheerleader next year. There was no way she would miss that, not even for a college boy from UCLA. It also opened up the possibility that she was lying—or at least exaggerating—about Tony. Chances were that he had been some momentary Hello on the beach. Hugh thought he was pretty sure how such things could be blown out of proportion in memory. Linda, suddenly, didn't look nearly so appealing as she had a few minutes before. In fact, he realized all at once what a fake she was, what a liar. He was ashamed of himself for giving in to what she made him feel so easily. All these years he had been afraid to talk to her, to approach her, even as a classmate. Now, she appeared to him as nothing more than a spoiled little girl who made up stories to impress him. She might think he was immature, he thought, but all at once and for the first time in their long acquaintance, he felt much older, much wiser than she, much older and wiser, indeed, than the mythical Tony.

"I'm sorry," he said. "That's not what I meant. I've got to go. You're sure about—uh, that your dad's taking you to Dallas tonight or tomorrow?"

"He'd better," Linda said, and Hugh was amazed at how her face hardened. Her mouth lined into a slit that looked like a crack in plate glass. Even through her sunglasses he could see a ragged edge of ice filling her eyes. "If we miss the fall fashion shows, Mother and I'll make his life miserable."

Hugh glanced up at Lydia, who sat shaded by an umbrella in a chair in the bed of the doolie. Her skinny legs were crossed, her right foot vigorously pumped a sandal that dangled from the ends of her toes, a cigarette jutted from one lip as she flipped through a magazine. Hugh had always thought of her as a pretty woman, almost as pretty as Linda. But now, in that unguarded moment, her features were sharp, almost cruel, her reddish-blond hair tinted orange in the diffused sunlight. She looked something like a crone, a witch, who could instantly transform herself into a charming beauty with a smile and a touch-up of her cosmetics. Again, he contrasted her to Edith, his mother, to her delicate features, her softness, even in anger or frustration. This time, his mother was vastly favored by the contrast.

"Okay. See ya," he said and turned away from Linda with a wan smile and headed at a trot toward the hotel. The two of them were a pair, he thought. They might be the only people in the world who really could make Carl Fitzpatrick's life miserable. Hugh was convinced that Linda was telling the truth about that much at least.

─✕

"I need to go out to the place," Wilson said to Hugh when Hugh arrived breathless and sweating at the chinaberry tree next to the hotel and reported that it was unlikely that any more work would be done that weekend. Hugh hadn't confessed the source of his information, but he did say that he heard that Carl Fitzpatrick would be absent for two days. Wilson agreed that no up-and-coming politician would leave town with something as tempting as a ready-made crowd at his disposal.

"Need some food for me and Goodlett," Wilson went on. "Need a bath, a shave, and other stuff. Garden's going to seed if I don't tear into it. Wouldn't surprise me none if gophers and skunks hadn't run me clean out of business."

Hugh nodded solemnly. He was hungry, but no sandwiches or anything else to eat was forthcoming. Instead, Wilson pulled out his whiskey bottle, took a nip, then began rolling a smoke. He handed the makings to Hugh without a word.

"That'll give Phelps Crane time to get situated, I reckon," he said. "See how big a mess he can make." Wilson smiled and took another swig from his whiskey bottle. Hugh was trying to ignore the upset the cigarette was causing in his growling stomach. "Give that feller Grissom time to think up something to stop 'em."

"Why does he want to stop them?" Hugh asked. "They're not hurting anything. They're just watching."

"Things like this have a way of taking hold," Wilson spoke quietly and puffed his smoke. "They'll start small. There for a while, it was just you and me and a handful of street monkeys standing out there. All by ourselves. Now, it's the biggest show in town. Soon it'll be the biggest in the county, maybe in the whole durned state. You wait. They'll be newspaper folks coming down from New York City and such."

"Think so?" Hugh was overawed.

Wilson nodded. "Chicago, anyhow. That's where the railroad yahoos get their marching orders from." He inspected his pint bottle, then looked up at the sky. There was little more than a swallow left. Hugh wondered how it tasted. It had a different label from his parents' brand. A small layer of amber foam formed on the liquid as Wilson swished it around in the bottom of the bottle.

"Won't make no nevermind. They'll go right ahead on." He tilted the bottle back and emptied it. "But they ain't done, neither one of 'em."

"Who'll win?"

Wilson capped the bottle and stuck it deep inside his sack. "Money," Wilson said, rising and dusting the grass seeds from his dungarees. "Money always wins. That's a lesson it took a while to learn, but I wasn't much older'n you when I learned it. The notion to take that building down was first had by folks who never seen it, never even seen a picture of it, never even been to this town.

"I'll bet you a Saturday off that Grissom feller never seen it 'fore the other day. Folks like that don't care 'bout nothing but saving theirselves." He spat into the weeds and adjusted his hat across his silvery mane. "Take a lesson, boy. Most of the people in this world who have money'll run you into the ground getting more of it, run you into the ground keeping you and anybody else from having it, and the whole time they're doing that, they're running scared their own selves. They don't care 'bout nothing else but that, and every day of their lives, they get up expecting to find their walking papers in their pay envelope. They got no pride, they got no shame, don't care 'bout how good a thing is, 'bout how long it might last, 'bout what it might mean to some folks. They're just getting through the week walking on somebody else's backside, and they'll smash you like a rotten 'mater if you get in their way."

"City people," Hugh said in agreement.

"City people, my eye," Wilson laughed. "They's people like that right here in town, and Carl Fitzpatrick's one of 'em. Bigger one than Grissom. Grissom's just some fat man's dog. But ol' Carl's—well, he's the fat man hisself. Bet on it. That's why he'll make governor one of these days."

The roar of engines from the worksite told them the midday break was over. The men were back at it. Wilson made no move to leave or, to Hugh's disappointment, to eat. He glanced at the old man's sack. It was limp and flat where it lay on the grass. He decided there was no more food to be had. Suddenly, he felt guilty.

"So you're going home tonight?" Hugh asked. The thought made him sad. Two days with nothing to do but catch up on his lawn mowing stretched out before him. He realized how much he was going to miss talking to Jonas Wilson.

"Yep," Wilson nodded. "Got to tend my garden. Take care of business. Be back late Sunday. Get a jump on Monday morning."

Suddenly, Hugh had a thought. "Could I come with you?"

Jonas stopped and stood still. "With me?"

"Out to your place. Just for the afternoon. Or I could come out tomorrow. I could ride my bike."

"Don't think your folks'd cotton to you riding a bicycle out on the highway all by yourself."

"It's the old highway." For the past twenty years, since the bypass was constructed, most cars took the new highway that led around the town and connected to the state route a mile or so beyond the mill. Still, a few people used the old highway, particularly when they were in a hurry to go back and forth to the mill. There was never any cop out on the old highway, a thought that gave Hugh small comfort.

"Don't matter. Lots of speed merchants out there. Big trucks running all the time." He still hadn't looked at Hugh.

"Then let me come with you when you leave. How do you get there?"

"Shank's mare."

"A horse?"

"I hoof it on my own dogs, boy."

Hugh shook his head. "You walk," he concluded.

"Right. Been walking most places most of my life. Never had no break-down, never pulled up lame. I walk. Me and Goodlett."

"And me," Hugh declared. Inside he was quivering. He now felt he *must* go with the old man. The same sense of desperate purpose that had prompted him to refuse to promise to stay away from Wilson now compelled him to make this outrageous proposal.

Wilson cast his faded eyes down on the boy's baseball cap and the tallow-colored hair that shoved out from under it. He nodded. "You check with your folks. If it's all right with them, it's all right with me."

"It'll be all right." Hugh's heart was beating. He wondered just how good a liar he could become.

"Now see here," Wilson set his whiskered jaw. "There ain't no free lunch. You'll have to work off your keep." Hugh nodded eagerly. "This ain't no chicken outfit you're signing on with. Everybody pulls his weight. Even ol' Goodlett."

"I can work."

"We'll see," Wilson nodded. "You check with your folks, and then we'll see." He lay back, pulled his fedora over his eyes, and folded his hands across his chest.

"I seen you sparking that little Fitzpatrick gal," he said. Hugh froze, then was surprised to find himself breaking out in an icy sweat of self-consciousness. It was taboo to discuss girls with anyone, at least anyone other than his friends, who usually did so only amidst shoulder jabs and lewd, speculative comment.

"I wasn't 'sparking' her," Hugh protested weakly. "You told me to find out whether they were going to work this weekend, and that was the only way I could do it."

"By feeling of her leg?" Wilson chuckled. "When I was your age, if I'd touched a girl there, her pa'd of shot me dead as Aunt Rhody's ol' gray goose."

"You're too old to remember when you were my age," Hugh shot back hotly. "Besides, she asked me to touch her there."

"She *asked* you to?"

"It was a kind of . . . of experiment. To test her tan." Hugh realized how silly the whole thing sounded, felt himself grow hot with a deep blush.

"You do everything a girl like that asks you to?"

"Of course not."

"I'll bet next year's crop you do, too," Wilson laughed. "Can't help yourself. I couldn't, either when—"

"I know," Hugh finished. "When you were my age."

"Let me tell you something, boy." Wilson sat up and stared into Hugh's eyes. His voice took on a serious tone. "I blow a lot of smoke 'round, and you shouldn't listen to much I say, but you put a ear on this: Girl like that's no good for a boy like you. Only get you in trouble."

"What do you mean, a 'girl like that'?"

"Rich girl. Daddy's got money, power. Wants more of both. She's the same way."

"That's her daddy, not her." Hugh was uncomfortable defending Linda. His feelings about her were more confused than ever. He was more than half convinced she was going out to California to meet Tony and live happily ever after on the fifty-yard line of UCLA games. But another half of his mind was convinced that she was nothing but bluff, but even when that half was in session, he was convinced that anything he did or said would be measured against some muscle-bound, blond beach bum from California.

He kept telling himself that it didn't matter, that he was nothing to her anyway, only a momentary diversion on a summer afternoon. She had never paid any attention to him before. But the memory of her stretched out on the chaise, her long legs crossed, her pale skin smoothing down into the white-on-white blouse, her blond hair swam up before him and made his throat tight. He hated her for looking like that, but somehow, he was obsessed with her every detail.

"She's the same way," Wilson repeated, settling back and pulling his hat over his eyes once more. "Mark my words. She's just a sprout now. Money and clothes and flash is all she wants. Attention, don't you know. But soon it'll be power, and from the looks of her—and her mama—if that's any sign—and it usually is—she's going to have the right bait to get it all. And soon. Already got you, from the looks of things."

"That's not so," Hugh denied in an irritable voice. "I'm not interested in her—or in any girl."

"And 'maters don't get spider mites," Wilson chuckled.

"You seem to know a lot about women for a . . . a bachelor."

"Hermit, you mean."

"All right. Hermit."

"What makes you think I'm a bachelor?"

"Aren't you? I mean, you live alone."

"That don't make no bachelor."

"Well, are you?"

"Am I what?"

"A bachelor?"

"Am now."

"Did you ever . . . I mean, did you ever get married or anything?" Hugh asked.

"What do you mean by 'or anything'?" Wilson's voice rose slightly.

"Well, you know. I mean, people don't always get married." Hugh thought of a dozen movies he had seen in the past year. It didn't seem that anyone got married anymore, or at least, if they did, they didn't stay married for very long.

"I guess I'm asking if you ever lived with anybody or anything."

"That's none of your durned business," Wilson snapped. His face was still covered. Hugh couldn't judge whether or not he was angry.

"Well, Linda Fitzpatrick's none of yours." Wilson was quiet, and Hugh felt he had won the round on points.

"I guess you get tired of sleeping on the ground," Hugh commented, trying to change the subject and relieve the tension that had grown up during their discussion of women.

"What?" Wilson's voice rose in surprise. "What give you the idea I sleep on the ground? What do you think? I'm some kind of hobo?"

Hugh leaned back on his elbow. "I thought you slept here. Under this tree."

"With the chiggers and ants and skeeters? Lord, boy, you got yourself one big notion of what a man like me does."

"Then where do you sleep?"

"In the hotel."

"C'mon," Hugh scoffed. "The hotel's closed. It's been closed for years. The only one who sleeps there is Mr. Kruickshank, and he's . . . well, I hear that he's—"

"He's drunker'n a skunk three nights out of four," Wilson finished. "Three sheets to the wind and bound for the devil. I know him. Knowed him all his life. Knowed his mama all her life. She liked pansies, I recollect. Never sparked her, though."

Hugh lay down again, grinning. Trying to envision Jonas Wilson decked out in a suit with a bouquet of flowers in his hand and standing on somebody's porch was too much.

"Anyway, there's a loose window-light in the stairwell on the back side. I just open her up and step in. Bring Goodlett right long with me. We go up to the third floor and sort of check in. Got me a room up there. Had it for years. Always stay there when I get caught in town after dark. Bring home the sheets now and then for a wash, and I keep her dusted and swept pretty good. Don't nobody know 'bout it. Nobody except you. Now."

His voice took on an edge. "Don't know why I'm telling you, neither. You'll just blab it round."

Hugh started, and he stared into the darkness above him. "I won't tell, Jonas." Wilson was silent. "But I'll tell you something. Everybody thinks the hotel is haunted." Hugh snickered. "People have been seeing lights up on the third floor for years. Said it's haunted by a murdered girl." Wilson still didn't say anything. "I saw it myself," Hugh lied, trying to prompt a response. Ghost stories were a tradition of the campouts with Tommy and Ray. Still, Wilson was quiet. Hugh wondered if he had fallen asleep while they were talking.

"Front or back?" Wilson asked at last in a soft voice.

"Why, uh . . . front, I think." Hugh was caught off guard. "Yeah, the front. Everybody said it was the front."

"Wasn't me, then," Wilson spoke almost in a whisper. There was a strange, ominous tone in his voice that sent an involuntary shiver down Hugh's body. "My room's in the back."

They said nothing more, and soon Wilson's breathing became raspy and heavy beneath the hat. Hugh sat for a long time watching him, wondering if Jonas Wilson really was the cause of the lights in the old hotel.

CHAPTER FIVE

"I'm all caught up on my lawns, and I want to go camping with Tommy and Ray," Hugh told his parents when his father came in that afternoon. Harry lowered a magazine and stared at him with a long, dark look. His mother turned from the stove, where she was frying steak. She appeared startled to hear him speak. They had not exchanged words since she banished him to his room Wednesday night. He had been eating out on the porch and rising early to escape the house even before his father woke up. When he did see her, the pinched skin around her mouth and strain in her eyes preyed on him. He had misbehaved in a major way, and he believed that was the cause of more misery in her life than she had ever had. He hated himself for it, couldn't stand to add to it, so he avoided her.

He also couldn't stand the sight of the whiskey bottle—or a new one—that stood now openly exposed on the counter next to the sink. Beside the stove where his mother worked, a tall glass full of ice and liquor was beaded with condensation. Hugh had never seen her drink so much or so often. It disturbed him.

"You're just like one another," Harry had told him over breakfast that morning. "Too stubborn to move, too hard-headed to give in. I'm not sure who I want to bend first. I'm sort of enjoying the peace and quiet."

Now, though, she sipped her drink and looked at him with a softer face than she had turned on him in days. Hugh held his breath. It wasn't too late, a voice inside him announced. If she says yes, you can still go with them.

"Tommy and Ray? Just the two of you, I mean three of you? By yourselves, I suppose."

Hugh nodded. "Out by the lake near Punkin Center. Where we always go. Like last summer. We'll stay in the campground. Just like last year."

Edith was silent for a moment, mulling the proposition over. Hugh knew his mother had never been much in favor of these "boys only" over-night fishing trips, even though the campground at Punkin Center was about as safe a place as a bunch of boys could be. Although isolated from clear view of the developed neighborhoods around the lake, it wasn't far from contact or help if it was needed. A caretaker locked up the gate at night, and there was even a pay phone near the fishing dock.

"You're not going swimming?" she asked automatically.

"No, ma'am," Hugh assured her, knowing that unsupervised swimming was forbidden. "We're going to fish. We'll be back Sunday," he added. "Before dark."

"You're all caught up?" Edith asked, a thin eyebrow shooting up, a warn-ing in her voice. "With your mowing?"

"Yeah," Hugh nodded eagerly. Inside he was dying. He was so far be-hind that if he did nothing but mow all weekend, he couldn't catch up by Monday. But he didn't care. He had made up his mind. He held his breath, waiting for her to decide.

"Well, if it's all right with your father," she sighed. Hugh relaxed. Edith hummed suddenly a bright, catchy tune, turned the steak in the skillet, and freshened her drink. "He can take you out right after supper." Harry Rudd nodded briefly and watched his son from the corner of his eye.

"No," Hugh said almost too quickly, panic swimming into his mind. He groped for another lie. "Tommy's dad's going to drive us out. They're wait-ing on me now." Beneath the mask of relief on his father's face, Hugh saw, suspicion lurked. Harry caught Hugh's eye, then abruptly returned to his reading.

"But you haven't eaten," she said. "You don't have anything ready."

"That's okay. I'll fake it," Hugh called over his shoulder as he ran to the garage and gathered together his sleeping bag, fishing rods, tackle box, other junk. When he came back to the kitchen, there was a paper bag on the table where his place was usually set.

"I put the steak in there," Edith said. "You can eat it cold or reheat it. Your father and I can eat tuna fish tonight." Harry groaned, too loudly, Hugh thought. "There's enough for all three of you and some left over for breakfast."

"We'll eat fish," Hugh said. "Save the steak for you and Dad."

"Your father won't mind," she smiled reassuringly. Harry's eyebrows narrowed. Her voice swam in enthusiasm for her son's proposed weekend adventure. "And I know how much luck you boys have fishing."

Hugh looked at his father, who smiled weakly. "Maybe we'll eat some tomato sandwiches," he said in a low voice. Hugh stared quickly, but Harry averted his eyes to a drink he had made while he was in the garage. His mother's glass was full again as well. Third time since I came in, he counted.

They're drinking every night, Hugh thought. That's bad. They haven't done that ever before.

"I've got tuna," Edith insisted. "And there's some leftovers in the icebox. Do you have your mess kit?" Hugh nodded. "Matches, towels, canteen? Change for the telephone if you need us?"

"I've got everything, Mom. I have to hurry. They're waiting."

"Well, be careful and have a good time." She sat down and stirred her drink. She looked weary but relieved.

"Do you want me to drive you over to Tommy's?" Harry asked. He didn't get up, though.

"No, that's okay. It's only two blocks." Hugh pushed out the door, the paper bag dangling from his overloaded arms.

"Be careful, son. Remember to watch out." His father's eyes penetrated his own, and Hugh nodded back.

"See you Sunday night," he called and raced out of the yard, turned toward the highway, away from Tommy's house, and met Jonas Wilson by the Bible Baptist Church.

—<

"Well," Jonas Wilson said and held up the two stubs that used to be his third and fourth fingers of his left hand. "I lost these two when I was just a pup, no older'n you."

"How'd it happen?" Hugh asked. They were walking side by side along the shoulder of the highway, west, out of town. The lights of the small community were already on, although the sunset was still a good while away. They had been walking for over an hour already, all the way from the large culvert by the highway across from the Bible Baptist Church where Hugh had stashed his sleeping bag, fishing tackle, and other camping gear before Wilson showed up. He wanted no questions from the old man about his having his parents' permission for the outing.

"Well, I was working for a feller name of Valdez. Julio Valdez. Hear tell of him?"

Hugh shook his head.

"Well, it was a long time ago," Wilson shook his head. "Valdez was the only Mescan ever to do anything worth a durn in this county. Too many peckerwoods for a Mescan to get a toehold. But Valdez come in early. He took up ranching, and he done pretty good at it. Finally, bunch of ol' boys took a notion to buy him out, but he wouldn't sell. He couldn't get nobody to work for him, and they thought that sooner or later he'd go bust."

"Did he?"

"Heck, no," Wilson said sharply. "I hired on with him. I probably wouldn't of, but I was hungry and needed the work. Like I say, I was young, didn't know no better."

Hugh had a disturbing thought. Wilson was right. Hugh himself was young, didn't know better, and here he was, trudging off with a man everyone thought was crazy to do God only knew what in the middle of the night. He swallowed down his guilt and a slight taste of fear and tried to concentrate on Wilson's story.

"So, anyhow, he wrote down to Mexico and sent for all his family. He already had his wife and kids here, but he sent for his uncles and cousins, everybody. They'd run the durned place, he said. But he needed help till they got there, so he hired me and a couple of other young'uns, who wasn't any smarter'n I was, and we went to work till they come on up."

Hugh forced one sneaker in front of the other. The sky was a mixture of blues and purples overhead, but he was distracted from the sunset by the sole of his left shoe. It was wearing off, and he could feel it flop slightly with every step. Part of the deal about his summer work was that he would keep himself in workclothes. That included sneakers, but right now, this night, he was eight lawns behind and had a payment due Monday on the Grassmaster. He had the money for the mower, but he had no idea where the sneakers would come from. A five-mile walk wasn't going to do them any good, either.

"Anyway, bunch of yahoos decided that the only way to run Valdez off his ranch—which was a big one—covered four sections up in the northeast part of the county—was to start cutting his fences. Which they did. Regular. Valdez saw that there wasn't no way to stop 'em—law paid no more attention to a Mescan then than it does now—so he just went out in a wagon and dropped wire and posts ever so often, and then he sent me or some other feller out to fix 'em when they was cut."

"On a horse?"

"Durned tooting on a horse! How else? Didn't have no automobiles in them days. Never heard of one, let alone seen one."

"So you cut them off fixing fence."

"Not quite. See, my job was to ride along the fence line. When I come to a break or a cut, I'd get down, get some wire and maybe a extra post from where ol' Valdez had dropped 'em here and there, and then make a splice. Well, I reached down for a fresh post one afternoon, and there was this big ol' mama rattler curled up next to it. Never saw her. Never heard her. 'Fore I knew what had happened, she'd bit me. Just like that." He made a set of fangs with the twisted digits of his right hand and clamped down on the thin air where the forefingers of his left should have been.

"That snake took to setting up a rattle then, and 'fore I could kill her with my ax-hammer, my pony shied and took off. There I was, more'n ten miles from the house, dying from snake bite."

Hugh knew what was coming, and he felt a shiver run through his body. He cast his eyes into the weeds in the bar ditch alongside the road.

"I didn't know what to do. Had no more'n a swaller of water, no bandages, just a knife and my ax-hammer. But I was going to die, clear as creek water, if I didn't do something. Found me a rock with a flat top, lay them two bit fingers out like carrot tops, and whacked 'em off clean as a whistle."

Hugh felt his stomach churn, and cold sweat broke out on his forehead while his eyes danced between Wilson's serious glare and the twisted stubs. He had had little to eat that day. By the time they returned to the parking lot, only scraps and a bit of watermelon remained on the folding tables around the Fitzpatrick trailer.

He contemplated Wilson's disfigured fingers again and felt bile rise in his throat. Only with effort did he swallow it back. "Must have hurt," he choked out.

"Hurt!" Wilson threw back his head and laughed at the emerging stars. "Like thunder! You never seen such hurt! I don't know whether I was more scared of snake poison, bleeding to death, or the blaspheming I was shouting up to the sky." His eyes took on a faraway look. "I wrapped 'em up somehow, though. Made me a bandage of my shirt, a arm binding of my braces, and passed clean out. Ol' Valdez found me in a raging fever two days later. Fetched me to a doctor, and the sawbones said chopping off them two fingers was the only thing saved me. Hand swole up size of a cantaloupe, and I was laid up for two months, but ol' Valdez and his family took care of me. Had me a soft spot for Mescans ever since."

They rounded a curve in the highway, and Hugh cast a look back toward the town's lights. Once more, he was consumed with guilt, regret, dread. He had never lied so brazenly to his parents before.

—<

"I'm really looking forward to that meat," Wilson said as they trudged along. They had maintained a steady pace since taking off, stopping only once so Wilson could duck behind a large mesquite tree to urinate. Goodlett stayed right with them, padding along five or six feet behind her master, her long tongue hanging out in a steady pant. Hugh's calves ached with the forced march's pace, but he refused to ask Wilson to slow down. "I ain't had me a good piece of meat in a coon's age."

"How long is a coon's age?" Hugh asked quickly. Lately, he thought with regret at the words, his tongue seemed to work independently of his brain.

Wilson shot him a narrow look from under the ragged rim of his hat. "Don't get smart with me, boy." Hugh thought instantly of his mother's identical words. "It's long enough. When you get to be my age, you'll know how long it is."

"Can I ask you another question?" Hugh's ears picked up the rare sound of an approaching car. Every time he heard a motor approaching, he was certain it was his father—or worse, his mother—coming to grab him and carry him home.

It wasn't that he minded going back home so much. In a way, he confessed internally, he would almost be relieved to be home tonight, or even doing what he said he was going to do, camping with his friends. It was more the shame he knew he would endure when his parents discovered his lying, his sneaking around. All of a sudden, there was never any question in his mind that they *would* find out. It was only a matter of when. His mother could run into Tommy's mother at the store. His father might meet Ray's father at the post office or somewhere. All it would take would be one casual remark. He imagined Harry saying, "Hey, thanks for running the boys out to the lake last night," and Ray's father saying, "Why, Hugh wasn't with us! What do you mean?"

He was sure, dead sure, that something like that would happen, and then there would be thunder and lightning for real.

"Go ahead on. I got nothing but time, but this waiting on you to make up your mind is tiresome."

"Well, just how old are you?"

"Old?"

"Yeah." Hugh took courage from Wilson's apparent confusion. "I mean, you tell me you were a cowboy on the Matador, that you worked for a Mexican I never heard of on a ranch I never heard of. You tell me you could have gone to World War I if you hadn't lost your fingers. You say you did a whole bunch of things. And you tell me you worked to build Hendershot's, and that was built in . . ." Hugh fought to remember.

"Finished in 19 and 10," Wilson concluded.

"That was almost a hundred years ago."

"Durned near it."

"Well, if you were a man then, that would make you over a hundred."

"Might be."

Hugh spat in disgust. He was being put on. "Look," he said, "I'm young, just a kid, maybe. But I'm not stupid. I can count."

"That a fact?"

"Yeah, that's a fact," Hugh dug his heels in with every step. It was ruining his damaged sneaker, but he didn't care. "I asked you a question straight out. Are you going to answer or not?"

"Don't know how old I am."

"Don't give me that," Hugh dug his heels in even deeper. "Everybody knows how old they are."

"No, they don't." Wilson spoke with conviction, and Hugh tried to see his face in the darkness. He caught a whiff of his own body odor as they walked. He needed a bath, Hugh thought. Small chance of that tonight.

"Yeah, who doesn't? Name one person who doesn't."

"I don't."

"How come?"

"Well," Wilson laughed softly in the darkness. "I was too young to read dates and such when I was born." Hugh trudged silently and fumed in frustration. Wilson was treating him like a kid, dodging direct questions, making him feel stupid. Wilson coughed and spoke again. "Ain't you going to ask me how come my folks never told me?"

Hugh remained silent. Heat from his anger flushed his face, and he didn't trust himself to respond. It had been a long day. First the large lawns, then the strange episode with Linda Fitzpatrick, lying to his parents, a five-mile hike in worn-out shoes, and now this. He entertained the thought of turning around and going home. He was dirty, hungry, tired, and, above all, guilty. He remembered the story of the prodigal son from Sunday School. He could go home, confess that he had lied, and then take whatever punishment his parents saw fit, then eat, bathe, and go to bed. This was a mistake.

"Well, I'll tell you why," Wilson said. "I never knew 'em."

Hugh looked up. "Why not?"

"My ma died having me, and my daddy, well, he run off and left me with some neighbors. *Wilson's* really their name. My name's different. I don't truly recollect it. Anyway, they didn't know exactly how old I was, maybe eight or nine, when I come to live with 'em, and they weren't even sure of the year. When my adopted ma, Mrs. Wilson, died, all ol' Mr. Wilson knew to put on her gravestone was the day—January—and he only knew that because of the almanac and looking at the moon. He knew the months, but he never knew the year."

Hugh didn't know what to say.

"You see, when my pa and ma come out here, there wasn't nothing. No people, no towns. Just Indians and outlaws. They fought 'em both, or so the Wilsons told me. They knew, 'cause they did, too. We lived in a cave when I was took to 'em."

"A cave?"

"Down on the creek. Place called Franklin's Crossing."

"I know where that is. I've been there on picnics and things."

"Well, used to be a town there." Wilson looked up into the headlights of an approaching car and moved slightly to his right away from the blacktop. "Can't trust these durned automobiles today. Come racing by at all kinds of speeds. Hit a body and let him drop. Never know it."

"What kind of town?"

"Oh, not a proper town. Nothing you'd know as a town. Just some folks who boarded up some caves and lived in 'em. We lived there till I was near your age. Then we moved into a dugout over yonder," he pointed in the dark off to the southwest. "They's a little ol' run there. Ain't nothing left of it now. Irrigated the heck out of all the creeks and rivers hereabouts. Spoiled 'em for fishing or swimming or drinking water."

"So what happened then?"

"Well, they tried growing some cotton. Done pretty good at it, but I didn't take to farming. I drifted 'bout the country a mite, then I come home looking for work. That's when I signed on with ol' Valdez. That's when I lost them two fingers to that snake."

"And where are the Wilsons now?"

Wilson laughed. "Long dead, son." He stopped and looked across the highway in the darkness, and Hugh found a strange feeling coming over him as the old man spoke. It was, he remembered, the same feeling he had when he looked down at the Hendershot building and thought of what Wilson had told him about how it was built. It was almost as if he could conjure ghosts from the old man's words, see the long-dead people working through shimmering waves of time, ghastly forms of individuals whose names had been forgotten years before Hugh or even his father had been born. Sometimes, he thought, he could actually hear the men calling to one another, cursing the mules pulling the donkey engine, shouting orders and laughing while they worked. Now, peering through the darkness, he imagined the forms of a man trudging through a loamy cotton field behind a mule-drawn plow. He felt rather than heard the "gee-ups" and "whoas" the man wearily shouted at his animal, smelled the newly turned soil, and sensed the early spring heat of planting time.

"I come back to see 'em after my hand healed up," Wilson went on. "It was colder'n a witch's tit, I can tell you. And they was gone."

"Gone?"

"Well, the ol' lady was dead. Died of the fever, folks told me. I found her gravestone, like I told you. Been gone a month. The ol' man'd packed up and moved on. They didn't have no kids other'n me, and I guess they thought I was gone for good. I never did hear of him again."

"Didn't you know? I mean, you were just across the county. That's only a few miles."

"Son," Wilson laughed and started walking again. "In them days, 'across the county' was a considerable distance. Took two days to cross, longer if you didn't have a horse. Wasn't much of a town here then. Folks still lived here and yonder. Word traveled slow. I heard she was sick, but so was I. When I could, I come back, found her dead, him gone. That's all she wrote. I went to work for the railroad then."

"Then for Hendershot."

"That was later. Not much, though, come to think on it. I went down to Fort Worth, then to Houston for a while. I learned to carpenter, then I come home and worked for Hendershot."

Another car buzzed past them, and in the near distance, Hugh spotted the boxcar and fence.

"How long have you lived here?"

"We're almost there, ain't we," Wilson said, surprised. "Time really goes by when you got somebody to talk to." He looked down. "Even if he's got more questions'n a deputy sheriff on Saturday night."

"I'm sorry," Hugh said. "My dad says the same thing."

"Good man, your daddy."

Hugh was startled. "You know my daddy?"

"No," Wilson admitted, quickening his pace now that the boxcar could be clearly made out just off the highway. "But I'm getting to know his boy. Always felt that was as good judge of a man's character as you need."

—≺

They moved up the rutted dirt path from the barbed wire gate and cattleguard that provided an entrance to Jonas Wilson's property. Overhead, stars winked ironically as the two human forms led the dog between piles of rusty junk and the famous garden. The boxcar was a rectangular shadow against one end of the nearly square property. There was no light at all, and Hugh kept hearing ominous rustlings in the junk and plants to his right and left. It was all he could do to keep from reaching out and grasping Wilson's hand as they plodded toward the far end of the residence.

"Place is overrun with snakes, varmints, and horny toads," Wilson grumbled as they reached the boxcar. "Red ants, scorpions, and centipedes. Mind where you reach, boy." He reached up to the overhang and pulled down a lantern, which he lit with a kitchen match. Yellow light spilled out over the immediate area and plunged the garden and surrounding dooryard into immediate blackness. Hugh rubbed his eyes.

Where the sliding door to the boxcar had been, there was a neat tongue-in-groove wall with an inlaid door. Several rusty implements hung there. Lining the porch, or the packed earth under the wooden awning that was also carefully and solidly constructed, was a motley collection of chairs, office swivel seats, soda fountain stools, and bus seats, all covered with a fine dust. Not one was in good repair.

"Don't sit down or nothing till I say," Wilson warned. "Goodlett!" he called, and the dog appeared from the darkness, her teeth already bared and the familiar growl rumbling in her throat. "Critter!" Wilson ordered, and the dog rapidly started moving among the ramshackled furniture, sniffing and growling.

"Hope she don't come up with a skunk," Wilson said and pulled a key from his pocket and unfastened a hefty Yale lock from the door. "Last time she done that cost me a bushel of beans and a bushel of corn to buy enough buttermilk to wash the stink off her."

He opened the door and stood back without entering the dark interior. Without explanation, he pulled out his makings and rolled a cigarette, sharing them at last with Hugh, who followed his example.

"Takes her a bit to clear the area," Wilson explained and squinted out into the darkness. "I like to let the place air out a mite as well."

After a few moments, Goodlett came panting up and flopped down in the dust at Wilson's feet. "Good girl." He leaned down and stroked her head. "Now, inside." She came to her feet. "Snake!" he ordered, and she raced into the darkened room barking and sniffing as she had done before.

"You think there's a snake in there?" Hugh stepped back well into the light and inspected the threshold, which, he noted, was also well constructed and neatly fitted into the packed earth of the porch.

"Once bit, twice shy," Wilson said bluntly. "That's the saying. I don't cotton to hauling your carcass back to town tonight."

"Aren't you afraid she might be bitten herself?"

"You can always get a dog," Wilson remarked and dropped his butt into a coffee can that was nailed to the awning support. "I found out I can't grow me no more fingers."

Goodlett came running out with the same enthusiasm with which she entered. There was nothing in her jaws but her long tongue, and Hugh followed Wilson, who took the light and stepped inside.

As often as Hugh had passed the old boxcar squatting at the far end of Jonas Wilson's place, he had never tried to envision what it might be like inside. He merely guessed that it looked pretty much like any other empty boxcar, although he had seen the insides of those only in movies and on television. When the lantern's light opened up the darkness to his inspection, he discovered he would never in a million years have guessed that it was anything like what he saw.

The walls of the boxcar were finished with a collage of different patterns of paneling. All of them, mismatched as they were, reflected the lantern's light in a bright shine. At the far end of the car were two bunks, one atop the other, that momentarily reminded Hugh of his brief experience with a similar arrangement before Larry died. An ancient overstuffed chair sat next to a solid table with an oil lamp on top, and a shelf of neatly arranged but soiled paperbacks stood against the wall in arm's reach. Other heavily laden shelves and open cabinets were neatly lined along the sides of the room. A braided oval rug covered the whole area, and a footstool was stacked with magazines about farming, gardening, plants, and other matters of husbandry. None of them looked newer than his first birthday.

"These are kind of old," he said, picking up *Gardener's Life* and noting the twenty-year-old date.

"They'll do. I don't guess they've found that much news 'bout growing stuff in the last week or so. If they do, I'll hear it soon enough."

Wilson busied himself lighting lamps all around the boxcar-house, and Hugh noticed that in the other end behind a huge piece of metal that came up almost head high on him was a small wood-burning cookstove. A neat stack of split wood rested against the door in a box, and a handsome set of large cabinets dominated the opposite wall.

"Cast iron," Wilson said as he went about the car throwing open windows. They had been cut right into the sides of the car and were held open by locking hinges that responded to Wilson's pushing them out with a lever that came through to the inside. Each was heavily screened, and a surprising, cool cross-breeze soon swept inside. Hugh ran his hand up and down the polished edge of the dividing iron screen that separated the kitchen area from the rest of the car.

"Got it off a boiler from a locomotive they cut up down at the ol' yards. Keeps the rest of the place cool when I'm cooking in the summer. Wintertime, I haul it out of doors. Need the heat."

"This is a neat place," Hugh could hardly contain his admiration. Everything was in place. The woodwork was fitted and spliced and finished expertly. "You must be some great carpenter."

"Oh, I can cut a chalk line and drive a nail straight." Wilson was, to Hugh's surprise, flattered and embarrassed. "Ain't no proper profession. Never did make no money at it."

"Carpenters make good money," Hugh protested. "Dad says the carpenters at the mill don't do much but stand around until something needs fixing, then they don't do it but half right. That way they keep their jobs."

"Them's not union boys," Wilson grumbled and began to snap kindling and thrust it into the stove. "Yankees, for the most part. You get what you pay for." He pushed some scraps of newsprint in after the kindling and set a match to it. "Go out and fetch some water. They's a bucket on the porch, and the well's straight back by the fence."

"In the dark?" Hugh was frozen for a moment. He remembered that back in the culvert, rolled in his sleeping bag kit, were two flashlights.

"Well, take a lantern, then." Wilson snapped. Hugh picked up one of the heavy kerosene lights. "But if you can figger how to carry both it and the water, power to you. I been trying for years, and I ain't got a notion of it yet."

Hugh went out onto the porch and peered into the gloom. He started out on the path that led to the back of the boxcar, but the lantern's glow was so bright that he found he could see only a few inches in front of him at a time. Finally, he returned it and hung it where it had been before, then took the bucket and groped his way out to the well.

The well was covered with a wooden housing. Like everything else built of lumber on the place, it was tightly seamed and solidly nailed. Hugh fumbled with the handle and lifted the top, then pulled up the rope hand over hand. Crickets and katydids sang wildly around him, and overhead the stars winked and blinked through the darkness.

"Don't take the first bucket," Wilson called from behind him. "Might be a snake in it."

Hugh had almost brought the bucket all the way up, and he quickly dropped it. It splashed in the distance below him. After taking a deep breath, he started his hand-over-hand motion again, careful to hold the well bucket away from him as he transferred the water to the carrying bucket for transport back to the house. It sloshed all over his legs and sneakers. He never imagined that something as clear as water could be so heavy.

"Don't spill it," Wilson admonished him when he sloshed through the door. "Out here, water's precious. It's work to get, work to keep. Take care of it."

Hugh set the bucket down gingerly, walked over to the chair and collapsed.

"Come on," Wilson said. He had put on an apron that was splattered with flour. "Dough's rising for biscuits. I'll show you the cellar."

He pulled back a small rug in the center of the kitchen and revealed a trapdoor. Once opened, it showed a set of even steps leading down into darkness. Wilson reached for a lantern and led the way down the steps.

The cellar beneath the boxcar was a miracle. Lining the paneled walls, floor to ceiling, was shelf after shelf of jars and cans, all filled with various vegetables, fruits, and other foods. Two small flour sacks occupied one shelf, and a crock stood next to them. "Milk" was scrawled on the crock. Mayonnaise, mustard, and other commercially manufactured condiments lined another shelf, and a variety of spices and herbs were on another. Hugh walked around, speechless.

In spite of the cross-breeze above, it was still warm in the boxcar-house. But here in the cellar, it was cool, almost cold, he realized. He reached behind some empty jars and felt the walls. They felt normal, but the atmosphere was still cool.

"Lined with cotton," Wilson explained while he observed Hugh's inspection of the walls. "A foot thick all 'round. Upstairs, too, behind the paneling. Went 'round and picked it up 'longside the road. Combed it, cleaned it, stuffed it in tighter'n a rich man's mattress."

"Wouldn't concrete have been better?" Hugh asked, reminded of Wilson's description of the Hendershot building.

"Concrete costs money. Roadside cotton is free."

"Paneling costs money."

"Not off a garbage pile, it don't." Wilson held up the jars. "I got every one of these jars out of a trash barrel someplace. Some of 'em was chipped a little, but I sanded it out, and they're all fine. I got the lumber, all of it, by just asking here and there where they was building something. That's why none of it's a match."

"The chair and the stove?"

"Same thing," Wilson nodded. "I see something somebody don't want, and I bring it home. I generally find a use for it sooner or later."

"This is a great place," Hugh announced. "It's really neat. Really."

"It keeps the food good year 'round. You'd be surprised what folks'll trade for a jar of good squash or black-eyes or a can of garden sweet 'taters in the middle of a January norther. I get stuff that away, too. Smokes, even my whiskey when I need it." His obvious pride in his lifestyle began to embarrass him once more, and he replaced the jar and straightened the empties Hugh had disturbed.

"Wish I had me a peach tree or two," he said sadly. "Freestones put up real nice." He gestured for Hugh to go up. "Dough ought to be ready," he said.

—≺—

The meat was prepared on a flat-iron skillet, and Wilson matched Hugh's mother's cooking with a bowl of smooth white flour gravy and the fluffiest biscuits Hugh had ever tasted. A can of honey complemented the bread, and Hugh's serving of fresh potatoes, boiled and nothing more, along with crisp, steamed snap beans soon rendered both diners almost helpless as they sprawled out in the dilapidated furniture on the porch.

"You'd get along with my dad," Hugh sighed and breathed in a lungful of smoke. It was the best job he had done rolling his own yet, and the fat cigarette was burning slow and evenly. He was relieved to discover that his feelings of regret and guilt were completely banished from his mind.

"Why you say that?" Wilson nipped liberally at a fresh bottle.

"He likes a good meal better'n anything. He would have eaten himself to death tonight."

"Good food is worth a day's work, I always say," Wilson said, looking up. "The stars is blue. Look yonder."

Hugh leaned back and studied the firmament. The stars did look blue. All of them. He remembered his science classes and tried to spot some red ones or yellow ones or white ones, but tonight they were all blue.

"Matter of fact," Hugh thought out loud on the same track as before, "that was his steak we ate tonight."

"That so?"

"Yeah. He had to eat tuna fish."

"Power to him," Wilson said. "I like to get me a can of tuna now and then. I cut up some onion, some chives, celery when I can get it, sweet pickles if I've got some open, maybe squeeze in a little lemon juice if I have some, then roll the whole thing in biscuit crumbs and fry it in a little grease."

"That sounds good," Hugh sat up. "I'll have to remember that. Mom usually just dumps in some mayonnaise and serves it on lettuce."

"I like mayonnaise," Wilson mused. "Might try that sometime."

"Dad hates it. I hate it. It tastes like raw fish."

"Never ate a fish raw. Been hungry enough to, but didn't have no fish at the time."

"Maybe if you ever do, you could try some mayonnaise on it."

"Yeah."

"You need a refrigerator," Hugh opined.

"Need 'lectricity for that."

"Well, there's a pole right out there," Hugh pointed toward the highway, where a semi roared by. He was surprised by how quiet it was after the truck passed.

"Costs money," Wilson said. "Won't take nothing else in trade."

Hugh shut up for a moment.

"You ever hear of a man named Thoreau?" Hugh asked and fumbled in the darkness to roll another smoke.

"Live 'round here?"

"No." Hugh finished the roll and reached for Wilson's match box. "It was a long time ago. Henry David Thoreau. He lived sort of like you live. All by himself. Raised some beans. He wrote a book about it. We had to read parts of it last year in English class. I thought maybe you read it."

"Nope. Never heard tell of him. White man?"

"Yeah," Hugh answered too quickly. "I think so. Why?"

"Oh, sounds like a colored man's name," Wilson said. "Colored people're fond of giving a man two or three first names like that."

"What's your other name?"

"Don't know as I ever had one."

"Well, anyway, this Thoreau, he had an idea that a man was a slave to his money, to his possessions." Hugh wrinkled his brow trying to remember. "He said that he knew men who went through their whole lives dragging around barns and fields and stuff they really didn't even want to own."

"Sounds like a smart feller."

"Yeah, well, maybe." Hugh smoked and thought. "I just thought maybe you'd read his book. I saw your books."

"That's just trash people throw away. I find 'em here and there. Sometimes right out on the highway." He was silent and took two quick drinks. "I can't read all that good," he finally admitted. "Oh, I can make out what I need to know in a newspaper or magazine, but I can't read proper. I tried to teach myself for a long time, but it never took good."

"I could teach you!" Hugh cried, surprised at how loud his voice was. For a moment all the crickets fell silent.

"Simmer down, boy. You'll scare off the toad-frogs. They eat the bugs, and I need 'em." Hugh settled back. "I don't need to know how now. It's too late to do me much good. I can get through them magazines and make an order for the store if I have to. I can make my way through a bill of sale or a deed of property, and I can sign my name. That's all I need to know."

Hugh fell silent and finished his cigarette. He thought about rolling another, but it required too much effort to move. He found himself growing sleepier and sleepier. Holding his head up was almost too great an effort, and he wanted to doze.

"You 'sleep?" Wilson asked after a long while.

"Nuh-uh," Hugh muttered. He had been lightly dreaming, he realized. He wondered idly what his parents were doing, what Tommy and Ray were doing, what Linda Fitzpatrick was doing. Probably writing a letter to Tony, he decided, telling him how immature Texas boys were. He put her out of mind and tried to recapture the elusive dream.

"Good," Wilson's voice cut through Hugh's reverie like a knife. "You wash, and I'll dry."

"What?" Hugh was confused.

"Time to clean up. We ain't got no washer-woman on this here plantation. You wash, and I'll dry. I know where everything goes. My turn to get water, I reckon." He rose and relit the lantern.

"Okay," Hugh sighed and hoisted himself up. He was almost too full to move, groggy and irritable.

"I guess 'okay,'" Wilson muttered. "We got to clean that garden out quick. Going to rain in a couple of days."

"How do you know?" Hugh looked up at the clear sky and a couple of million tiny lights blinking at him.

"I told you, boy." Wilson went inside to fetch the bucket. "The stars is blue."

⤙

It took more than an hour to clean up. Then Hugh had to fetch more water for them to wash themselves in. He was surprised at the care with which the old man brushed his teeth with baking soda, and he wished he hadn't forgotten his own toothbrush.

"I got all my teeth," Wilson bragged when he observed Hugh trying to scrub his own molars with his forefinger. "Hadn't been to a doctor in thirty years. Last time I went, he wanted to cut me open and take out something, but I wouldn't let him, nossir. You eat right, work hard, take a little whiskey —when you're old enough—a little smoke, then—when you get some older —get you a good woman when you need one, and you'll live as long as me."

"Even if you don't know how long that is?"

"If she's a good enough woman," Wilson grinned shyly, "you won't be worrying 'bout it."

They washed off with the harsh bar soap Wilson provided, and soon Hugh lay back on one of the lower cots and pulled a stiff, white sheet over him. Wilson took the lower berth. It was surprisingly cool in the box-car-house, and the breeze seemed to increase once the lights were out and they were lying down.

CHAPTER SIX

Confident of his ability to do hard work, Hugh rose with Wilson, ate a full breakfast of biscuits and gravy, fried tomatoes, and the remainder of the steak from the night before, and washed the whole thing down with well water that was sweet, cold, and pure.

"It's artesian. Only sweet-water well in this part of the county," Wilson explained when Hugh commented on it. It carried a faint, metallic taste from the bucket, but otherwise, it was delicious. "Fact is, it's one of the reasons I got this place. Likely, the only reason I'm still living on it."

Wilson explained that he had been hired to pull a water well for Good-night Harrison, the owner of the land that surrounded Wilson's place on three sides.

"That was back 'fore World's War II," Wilson explained, looking out into the darkness that covered the mesquite-grown pasture surrounding his property. "Me and a feller named Diamond Jack Jackson—worthless son of a buck—went to work for Harrison one summer and pulled wells all over his property. Come in dry or too gyppy for cattle to drink everywhere we tried.

"Finally, he decided that he was going to beat it or kill us trying. He bought this boxcar and had it moved here, and me and Diamond Jack lived in it while we went 'round trying to find sweet water. We must of dug forty wells. Drilled all year till first frost, when Harrison was ready to call it quits."

Hugh dried the last of the breakfast dishes and peered out through the screen. It was still dark outside. There was no indication at all that the sun would be up that morning. He glanced down at his wristwatch. It was not yet five o'clock. They'd been up an hour.

"So what happened?"

"Well, we was sitting 'round talking 'bout it one day, and Diamond Jack said he reckoned he could find sweet water if he really wanted to, and Harrison laughed at him and said he was fixing to give up the whole shooting match, let the place go to seed. Well, sir, that made Diamond Jack mad, and it kind of scared me, 'cause it was coming on to snow, and I didn't fancy the idea of being out on the road—which is where we'd of been if Harrison'd called the whole deal off and throwed us out. I'd counted on working for him all winter, don't you know."

Wilson rolled the first cigarette of the day and offered the makings to Hugh, who shook his head. He wasn't fully awake yet, and he discovered that his throat and tongue were swollen and burning from all the smoke the night before.

"So, I jumped up and said if Diamond Jack said he could find water, he could, and I bet Harrison the cost of our wages for the whole month that he'd do her."

"And did he?"

"Heck, no," Wilson grinned. "We stomped 'round these pastures for another two weeks, sank three more holes, and durn near froze to death. Come up gyp every time." He laughed. "One morning I woke up, and Diamond Jack was gone—took ever cent I'd saved with him."

"So what happened next?"

"Well, I figgered that Diamond Jack reckoned there must be some sweet water 'round here, but he just couldn't find it. I poked and prodded 'round another week or so, then I called in Delvin Castro."

"Delvin Castro?"

"You never would of heard tell of him. He's a water-witcher."

"A what?"

"Water-witcher. Got him a divining rod—some folks call 'em witching sticks—little ol' forked willow stick it was, and he walks 'round with it till it points down to the ground where the water's at."

"You can't do that."

"I know *I* can't," Wilson snapped. "I told you I done tried. That's why I called in Delvin. He was a ol' man. Older'n I am now. Folks said he was a witch of other kinds as well, but I never took no stock in them stories."

Hugh's mind flew to the tales he had heard all his life about Jonas Wilson. It seemed funny to hear him talking about another old man and the rumors that surrounded him.

"What kind of stories were they?"

"Oh, the same sort of stuff folks tell 'bout me." Wilson smiled grimly and studied his cigarette's coal. Hugh flushed and turned away. "Seems people're likely to say anything that comes into their heads when they're scared of something or when somebody don't exactly fit their notion of what's right. They was scared of Delvin 'cause he always found water where everybody said there wasn't none."

Hugh wondered why people were scared of Wilson. The night before he woke up and had trouble remembering where he was. Once he recalled, he lay awake for a long time being frightened all over again of the old man, who snored softly in the other bunk. Now, in the bright yellow glow of the morning's lanterns, his fears seemed silly, unfounded. But he wanted to know the cause of the fear.

"Anyhow, ol' Delvin come out here of a Sunday morning and tramped up and down with his witching stick, then he told me he knew where they was water."

"Where?"

"Right out yonder where that well's at." Wilson hooked a twisted thumb toward one of the dark screens. "He said everything on the whole place run through gyp rock except a artesian spring he could feel way down in the ground. But I had to go right down there and get it."

"So you did."

"Not right off. You see, I seen opportunity knocking. I hadn't had no place to live regular for years, and I was getting older. Too old to be out on the road. I went to Harrison and told him I wanted to double our bet. He wasn't ready for it, since Diamond Jack'd run off and all, but it was wintertime, and there wasn't much going on, and he needed fresh water for his cows, so he thought on it a spell and told me that he'd do her, but he wanted me to put up a full year's work without wages as my part of the stake."

"And you did it?"

"Didn't see no choice. He sort of caught me off guard, and I'd already promised Delvin fifty dollars if the well come in sweet. But 'thout thinking, I told him I'd do her, but I also told him I wanted him to put up this piece of land, give me the time to fence her off, let me have the boxcar to live in, and deed it to me inperpetally."

"What?"

"Forever. Long's I wanted it."

"And he agreed?"

"Not right off. Said he wanted to think 'bout it. But it blew up a blue norther that night and froze the only windmill on the place with good water, which meant he didn't have nothing but the cistern by the house to work with, so he come back and said he'd do it, but he wanted the mineral rights to keep."

"Why?"

"Well, they was just starting to find oil 'round here, and the way his luck'd been going, I guess he reckoned it'd be just right for him to give me the land and have 'em find oil on it. Never did. But it turned out to be a smart move on his part."

"Why?"

"'Cause the place was right on the same piece of property where the water was!" Wilson almost shouted. "Gosh-darn it, boy! Don't you pay attention? Water's a mineral just like oil is. Least it is in Texas."

"I see." Hugh's eyes widened. "If you owned the land for finding the water, you'd also own the water."

"Well, not exactly. What I wound up owning when the well come in sweet was the land the water sat on. I didn't own the water. Harrison was madder'n a jammed thumb. Said I'd tricked him."

"Well, you sort of did."

"Naw, I didn't. I never done a dishonest thing in my life . . ." Wilson's eyebrows drew together. "Not often, anyhow. But that deal was straight."

"Did he keep his word?"

"Well, you see me living here, don't you?"

"And he did without water?"

"Naw, he had the mineral rights, like I said. So I had to share it with him. I piped it out with a windmill and ran it out to a tank other side of the fence. His cows could water there, and I had plenty for my needs, and we got 'long."

"I didn't see any windmill."

"Blowed down in a cyclone twenty, thirty years ago," Wilson said. "Harrison lets his boy run the place now, and he don't run no cows, just oil wells. They did find oil, you see. Loads of it, all over the durned place. Them's rich men, now, and they don't worry 'bout ol' tumbleweeds like me." He crushed his smoke out in a cut-off can. "They leave me 'lone, and I leave them 'lone. Let's boil some coffee and get to work. It's going to be dinnertime soon."

Hugh peered out once more. A dim gray light was visible atop the mesquite trees on the eastern horizon. "The sun's not even up yet."

"Will be," he said, rising and placing a black coffee pot full of water on the stove. "And 'less I miss my guess, you'll be wishing it'd go down again soon enough, too."

The water boiled, and Wilson placed a fist full of grounds on top of it, grumbling all the while that Goodlett wouldn't tolerate chickens because aside from the eggs and table meat he missed, he also could have used the shells, he said, to settle the grounds when the brew was ready. After a bit, he poured half the black mixture into an old, rusty Thermos and halved the rest between their two cups.

"I like me some milk and sugar in my coffee, but I'm out of both," Wilson frowned as he sipped the scalding liquid.

Hugh held his cup under his lips and blew on the surface of the nearly boiling ebony. He had tasted his mother's brew several times but had never had a cup of his own. He had found it too bitter and hot and usually settled for cocoa. He didn't want to offend Wilson, though, who had taken it for granted that he would want to share the coffee, so he finally took a slight sip. It was like drinking boiled dirt, he decided, sour dirt with a strong aromatic kick to it. He, too, longed for sugar or milk or even the courage to put in some cool well water to cut it. It had the color of motor oil, and Hugh imagined it tasted about the same.

"You can put some honey in it if it's too strong for you," Wilson muttered. He took his like medicine, Hugh noticed, sipping it slowly, but taking it all finally, even though steam still rose from the cup.

"That's okay," Hugh gagged slightly and sipped. "It's fine."

"Well, c'mon." Wilson stood and rinsed his cup quickly. "We got weeds to tend to. They's a hoe out back."

—≺

Hugh thought the midmorning break would never come. Sweat ran off of his forehead in canals that cut through the red clay dust rising from his hoe's action. There seemed to be an infinite variety of green weeds at the vegetables' bases, and every time he stood to stretch or rest, Wilson called to him that they would never finish if he kept loafing.

Hugh's back ached. He developed blisters that had already burst before his watch told him it was eight o'clock—time for ordinary people to go to

work. His arms turned to rubber, and his legs became heavy and almost unable to lift his dirt-encrusted sneakers from one position to another as he
chopped, cleared away, chopped some more. When he moved from the
thick stalks of corn, which seemed alive with gnats and other tiny flying
creatures, to the smaller, wiry plants that held okra, bell peppers, and
other vegetables, he discovered that he could see beneath their leaves only
by stooping over and then hoeing with the edge of the instrument's blade.
That was bad enough, but when he moved on to take care of the squash,
cucumbers, watermelons, and cantaloupes, he had to squat down and pull
each tiny seedling weed out by its root for fear of damaging the tender
vines. Some of the stalks were hairy and stuck to his hands and forearms,
and soon he was stinging and itching all over.

"Take care over yonder," Wilson called from the onion patch. He had
taken on weeding the beans and tomatoes, radishes and beets, and while he
worked, he also harvested, bringing the fruits of his labor to the back of the
boxcar, where Hugh discovered a huge collection of baskets, boxes, and
cast-off laundry hampers into which Wilson carefully laid his produce.
"You might run up on a snake or scorpion in the sandy patches," he
warned.

Wilson's garden ran the full length of the acre and a half of his property
and was half again as wide. He had hand-plowed the whole thing, Hugh de-
duced by looking at three separate hand-push cultivators leaning against
the house. The soil on the surface was red and sandy, although the sun had
baked it to a hard crust where it was exposed, and when Hugh's sneakers
broke through the top, he found that he sank to his ankles in a gummy tex-
ture that smelled rich, fertile, fecund. His only previous experience with
horticulture had been trying to grow some bean plants as a part of a science
experiment in school, but it didn't take an expert to recognize that a
well-planted, well-cultivated garden existed here amidst the junk and
weeds of Jonas Wilson's property.

By midmorning, Hugh had made ten full passes down the rows and was
exhausted. He went over and leaned against the boxcar-house and decided
he didn't care what Wilson said, he was going to rest.

"Ready for a break?" Wilson grinned at him when he came up to the
house with an armload of red onions. Hugh was too tired to speak. "Reckon
so," Wilson nodded. He studied the sky. It was clear, but the blue was covered with a white haze that Hugh decided was nothing but raw heat. He
had never been so tired, he thought, not even on a day early in the month

when he had "overdone"—his mother's word for it—and tried to mow ten lawns in one day.

Wilson left him leaning on his hoe and went around to the front of the house. He quickly returned with a newspaper wrapped around four cold biscuits from breakfast. He produced the butcher knife, sliced a fresh onion, put it between a biscuit, and handed it to Hugh, who was too exhausted to do anything more than take it. Wilson prepared a similar snack for himself, then he uncorked the Thermos and poured them each a half-cup of coffee.

"I don't want any coffee," Hugh protested weakly. He wanted water. Loads of water. Buckets. Tubs.

"Drink it anyhow." Wilson bit into his biscuit. Juice from the onion ran down his chin and mixed with his gray whiskers. "When you're hot on the outside, you got to put something hot on your insides. That way, your outsides feel cool."

Hugh slouched down and sipped the coffee. It was still hot, and it burned his tongue. He bit into the biscuit and winced with the acidic taste of the onion. Hot coffee, biscuits and onions, he thought. Some snack.

"Following that theory," Hugh said in his best imitation of his science teacher's voice, "in the wintertime you must drink iced tea and eat Popsicles."

"Don't be a idjet," Wilson frowned at him. "Where in the world would I get a Popsicle?" He stuffed the rest of his biscuit into his mouth, washed it down with a swallow of the hot coffee, and made himself another small sandwich. "Eat up, boy," he said. "We ain't got a good start at it yet."

Hugh's heart sank, then rebounded in anger. He came out here on his own, maybe, but the old man was taking advantage of him. They were more than half through with the weeding, and it wouldn't hurt to slack off a bit.

"I didn't know you were going to work me to death," Hugh mumbled. His eyes ranged beyond the garden to the piles of rusty junk stacked opposite the cornrows, and he wondered what other chores might be on Wilson's list once the garden was in shape.

"Don't recollect inviting you out here," Wilson said. "Come of your own accord, you did." Hugh stared at him, and Wilson continued, "This is what I do. And if you think I'm going to do her while you sit up in the shade and eat my food and smoke my tobacco, you can think again. Now, eat up your biscuit, and let's hit her another lick."

Hugh continued to stare at Wilson with growing anger in his young eyes. Wilson smiled at last and finished his coffee. "Course, if you're going to let a ol' coot like me work you into the ground, then maybe you ought to take a rest in the shade. Get you a sugar tit, and I'll sing you a lullaby."

Hugh answered him by stuffing the remains of his biscuit into his mouth. He swallowed the rest of the coffee in a gulp and rose to his feet. Somehow, he had to admit, he did feel cooler on the outside, but the heat inside of him had nothing to do with the spice of the onion or the warmth of the coffee. He picked up his hoe and followed Wilson back into the garden.

In a half-hour, he was convinced that the real story of Jonas Wilson was not that he lured kids out to his house, stuffed them with sweets, and then killed them. He simply worked them to death, then buried them in the garden for fertilizer. The pair labored steadily without speaking until they broke for their noon meal.

"Dinnertime," Wilson called when Hugh stepped out of the last row. Hugh looked back over his shoulder at the neat, clean lines of vegetables and the large piles of weeds that he had cleared away and dumped along the edge of the cultivated ground. His whole body was stinging, aching, hurting, and his hands looked like raw meat, but he had to admit to the sensation of a certain accomplishment in his work. He felt superior to each driver who whizzed by spraying gravel and raising dust out on the highway and was amused when one slowed nearly to a stop and spent some time watching them. Hugh wouldn't give him the satisfaction of stopping, of looking up. The rubbernecker, whoever he was, didn't know the satisfaction of a morning's work—a day's work, he mentally corrected when he studied his watch and realized they had been hard at it for nearly seven hours—all he had to do was drive around and be surprised to find men hard at it in the noonday sun.

Hugh fetched well water while Wilson prepared fresh tomato-and-cucumber sandwiches—with mayonnaise this time, from a jar brought up from the cellar—and supplemented them with the last of the biscuits and honey. The bread was older than the original meals Wilson had fed him, and the old man explained that he couldn't waste daylight by cooking. He would bake that night. They ate in silence, mostly, as Hugh tried to imagine what sort of labor lay ahead in the afternoon.

As soon as the plates were washed, fresh coffee brewed, and a smoke finished, Wilson pointed a crooked, stubby finger toward a corroded implement and picked up a long-handled shovel. "They's a wheelbarrow over yonder. Get it and follow me."

Hugh numbly obeyed. They walked the barrow out to the highway, where Wilson paused briefly and tied a bright yellow cloth to a pole that stuck up in the dirt next to the cattleguard. Hugh wasn't going to give him any more satisfaction by asking dumb questions, so he followed silently as they crossed the blacktop and walked down about a hundred yards, where the neighbor across the highway had set up a windmill and watering trough for cattle.

"This ain't gyp, either. I reckon it's fed by the same spring that does my well," Wilson said with a worried frown. "Bothers me. He pulled it 'bout ten years ago, and I noticed my level dropped some. So far, they's enough for both, but if it gets bad, I might have to do something."

"Like what?"

"Well." Wilson winked. "We get some bad windstorms out here, time to time. Could be a windmill just couldn't stand up to 'em for long."

A prickle of fear climbed Hugh's neck when he realized what the old man was implying. "I thought you never did a dishonest thing in your life," Hugh reminded him.

Wilson gave him a long look, then winked again. "Ain't nothing dishonest 'bout protecting your holdings, boy," he said. "'Sides, we do get some bad windstorms out here."

The lot around the tank was void of cattle for the moment, but they had clearly been there recently. The ground was strewn with mounds of smelly, black manure, most of which were covered with blue and green flies that swarmed every time Wilson's shovel scooped up a pile and dumped it into the wheelbarrow.

"It's good you come out this weekend," Wilson said, leaning against his shovel. "I wasn't sure I could do this all in one day. Usually takes me near two whole days. With you here, we can get her done 'fore supper."

Hugh set about the task with a firm resolution not to protest or shirk from the work until his body gave out entirely. Somehow, it didn't quit, and he soon had lost count of how many barrows full of hot, smelly cow patties he pushed across the neighbor's cattleguard, guided down the soft shoulder of the highway into Wilson's property, then dumped into compost piles. Hugh tried to count, but he never could keep up. If he paused to number the piles, he found he couldn't recall whether Wilson had instructed him to put three or four barrows' worth in this one or that one, and soon Wilson's voice would call him to follow him while made his way back across to collect more.

His arms were rubber soon, and it took conscious effort for him to keep the barrow steady and moving to ease the strain on them when he stopped. He came to resent the occasional vehicle that came by, each pass forcing him to stop and wait to cross the highway. He kept his head down, focused all his will into keeping the barrow level and ready to roll again when the superheated slipstream whirled around him in a truck's or car's wake. He particularly hated those who slowed down and delayed their passing.

"I wouldn't care if you did run over me," Hugh said when one motorist slowed to a crawl when he passed him. Death, he thought, might ease the pain in his hands, arms, and shoulders.

After several hours, the cattle lot was swept clean of fresh droppings, and Wilson led Hugh back with the half-full barrow. They then worked with rakes and hoes to mix the manure with the compost, then carried it to the garden rows, one shovelful at a time, and mixed it with the earth that had been loosened by the weeding. They pushed it high against the base stalks of the vegetables, even lifting the green fruit and allowing it to rest gently on its new bed of natural fertilizer.

"The man's plumb crazy," Wilson commented after what seemed like three or four hours of silent, backbreaking work. "Feeds them cattle pure alfalfa hay and mixes in some kind of cottonseed oil and other junk. I can't say whether it makes better beefsteak, but it sure as heck makes good vegetables. Look at them 'maters."

Hugh had to admit that he had never seen produce from any garden to match Wilson's. It was magnificent, and he didn't see one vegetable that had been victimized by disease or insects. The corn was juicy and plump, bursting from its shucks, and the tomatoes and other vegetables were also enormous and colorful. But none of it was worth his exhaustion. His arms felt like soaked sponges, and his knees wanted to buckle under his weight every time he took a step. His head ached, and his hands had been blistered so badly they seemed to glow with tingling pain. By the time Wilson announced that it was suppertime, Hugh was almost staggering.

He fell into one of the ragged chairs near the boxcar's door and took deep breaths as if he had been running hard for a long way. Wilson observed him briefly, then went to get water. It was a good thing, Hugh thought. He couldn't have roused himself with a stick of dynamite, and the thought of the bucket's handle across the ragged flesh of his palms made his fists close in painful agony. His watch told him he had just put in almost fourteen solid hours of hard labor. He was now ready to die, he told himself. He couldn't have cared less what Wilson might do with his body.

The smell of cooking food revived him, though. They dined on corn-bread and fresh green beans flavored with onions and bell peppers. Hot corn and boiled beets complemented the meal, as did dill pickles and steamed okra.

"Wish we had some more of that meat," Wilson commented as he cleaned an ear of corn and reached for more okra. "You just can't do much with vegetables all by theirselves." The two were covered in dirt except for their hands and forearms, and Hugh wondered when the old man was going to take his promised bath. They were both pretty rank.

Wilson fed Goodlett from what Hugh guessed was the last can of dog food and then began washing up. Hugh saw his duty and told himself to rise from the chair where he had placed himself after dinner and waved off another smoke. He was too tired to roll it. Wilson finished his bottle of whiskey and went to work washing the pans, and Hugh knew he was waiting for his help. He commanded his legs to lift him, his arms to push him upward, but his mind kept postponing the action. The next thing he knew, Wilson was shaking him.

"Biscuits is on, boy," he said. "Sun'll be up direc'ly. We got work to do."

Hugh was still in the same chair. He had slept there all night.

They began work that dawn by hauling buckets of water from the well to the garden and dumping the water into the newly cultivated furrows so it would run down the rows. The bucket's wire handle opened the light scabs that had formed over Hugh's blisters, and he had to wrap a rag around it to keep it from cutting too deep. The garden's northern end was higher than the end by the road and gate. Wilson explained that he had de-signed it that way to minimize the distance he would have to tote water from the well. Hugh's arms and shoulders sang a renewed chorus of painful protest as he sloshed bucket after bucket into the head of each row, and as the ground became saturated, the water flowed farther and farther down.

"Thought you said it was going to rain," he complained breathlessly when he passed Wilson, who carried two buckets at a time to Hugh's one.

The boy noticed that the old man rarely spilled any, while Hugh's trails back and forth had grown muddy in his clumsy wake.

"Will. Stars was blue again last night. Reckon it'll come on tomorrow. Trouble is, this time of year, you can't tell if it'll be a cat splatter or a frog floater. If it rains hard and short, it'll do more harm'n good. If it comes a good soaker, then we're wasting our time. I won't be here, so I don't want to take no chances."

"Besides," Hugh muttered while he filled another bucket at the well, "you've got me to help you." But if Wilson heard him, he said nothing, and the pair kept up their bread-and-butter passes for nearly four hours until Wilson called for the morning break.

Hugh grabbed the only biscuit and cucumber sandwich Wilson prepared and left the two onion snacks for the old man. He had noticed six fresh loaves of bread cooling inside when they had gone out that morning, but he didn't ask Wilson about it. The old man must have been up half the night working, Hugh thought, yet he continued to keep step with Hugh, even outstripped him in every department involving physical labor.

After their break, Wilson took up an old pump sprayer and filled it with a mixture of dish detergent and cold water. He moved up and down the rows, spraying all the vegetables' leaves with the concoction, pausing only to replenish his supply.

"Keeps the bugs off," Wilson explained when Hugh asked if he was washing the vegetables before he picked them. "They eat this stuff, swell up, and die. It's cheaper'n them fancy chemicals." Hugh took over after a while, and Wilson returned to the house, where Hugh heard him banging around and sweeping and generally setting things in order. His watch told him it was nearly noon, and they'd need to set out for town soon if he was going to beat Tommy and Ray back to town and prevent his parents' discovery of his secret visit to Jonas Wilson's place.

They finished their vegetable sandwich dinner and were smoking and sipping coffee, saying little to each other now that the work was all but done, when a horn's honking brought Wilson to his feet. Guilt and fear swam up from inside Hugh and banished his exhaustion at once. He almost crawled under the chair he sat in. He was certain that his father was driving up to Wilson's gate, and Hugh was already preparing himself for the singeing he figured he was in for. Then he heard shouting and good-natured banter coming over the noise of an old truck lumbering up the path between the junk and Goodlett barking and growling in defiance of her master's orders to get down.

Hugh peeked around the side of the house and discovered a rusty bob-tail truck. Two dark men stood on the opposite running boards and lifted their feet away from Goodlett's snapping jaws. Wilson ran up with a stick, with which he tried to swat the dog every time she came within reach. Hugh stepped out and called her without thinking, and she stopped so suddenly that she almost bowled over before racing up beside him and took up a defensive position, her body quaking and her long tongue panting in the noonday heat.

"Well, I'll swan," Wilson said. "That mongrel's took a liking to you, boy." He shook his head. "That's not usual for her."

The two men stepped down and shook hands with Wilson. Hugh moved closer—Goodlett following right behind him—but he learned nothing other than that Wilson apparently spoke fluent Spanish. The truckers spoke quickly and gestured toward the garden. The driver, whom Hugh recognized as the proprietor of a fruit-and-vegetable stand that set up every summer in the parking lot of a burned-out bowling alley on the edge of town, grinned at him and spoke cordially in Spanish. Hugh nodded back. The man had three gold teeth that caught the sunlight when he smiled, and his white shirt and khakis were stained with sweat and dirt.

The other man said nothing after greeting Wilson. He was much younger, Hugh noticed, and stood off to one side and eyed Goodlett warily.

Wilson paid no attention to Hugh or the other man as he led the driver around behind the house where he had boxed and crated the produce from his garden the day before. The two seemed to speak at the same time, their words running into each other in rapid Spanish that sometimes sounded angry, sometimes joking as they picked up a tomato here, a bunch of radishes there, and hefted them gently.

Finally, Wilson and the driver began walking back to the truck, their arms full of the produce. The driver called instructions to the other man, who pulled a rusty scale from the cab and hung it from a beam attached to the vehicle's bed. For half an hour they weighed and haggled in Spanish, and Hugh finally squatted in the dust and wished for Wilson's tobacco makings. Cicadas and grasshoppers sang in the mesquite and switchgrass all around him, and the heat seemed to rise by the minute. He wondered how he had ever worked so hard for so long at such a temperature, and he was about to retreat inside and boil some more coffee, which he was surprised to find that he wanted, when the last of the produce was weighed, and the driver reached up into the truck's cab and pulled out an account book.

He and Wilson argued a bit more, but finally, he held the book open for Wilson's inspection, and the old man nodded. With that signal, the younger man moved to start loading the baskets onto the truck, and Wilson came over and sat down.

"Shouldn't of drunk all the whiskey," Wilson said and sat heavily in a chair and gestured to the driver to join him. "He's easier to get on with when I get him a little juiced."

Hugh realized Wilson was speaking to him, and he smiled and joined them.

"Manuel Ortega," Wilson waved toward the space between them, "*Mi amigo, Señor* Rudd."

"*Mucho gusto,*" Ortega flashed his gold teeth and grasped Hugh's hand and shook it. Embarrassed, Hugh muttered a hello and sat down.

"Manuel here's my regular summer buyer," Wilson smiled at Hugh. "When he sees I'm ready, he'll take all I can sell him. Course, the price changes every time. Man's a bandit just like his granddaddy."

"Who was his granddaddy?" Hugh asked, smiling at Ortega, who grinned back and fished a pack of cigarettes from his pocket. He broke off the grin to yell something in Spanish at his fellow, who was still loading vegetables into the back of the truck.

"Why, Pancho Villa," Wilson smiled, and Ortega looked quickly around at the mention of the name and smiled broadly and pointed at his hairy chest.

"*¡Mi abuelo!*" he grinned at Hugh.

"C'mon," Hugh said. "That's im—"

"You believe what you want, boy," Wilson smiled back through tight teeth. "But it don't do to call a man a liar. I happen to know he ain't, and friendly as he looks, he'd cut your gizzard out soon's look at you."

"But that was a long time ago," Hugh muttered, remembering to smile. "And this guy just runs a fruit stand."

"*Sí,*" Ortega exclaimed. "Fruits and vegetables. Fine stuff. You bet. Best price in the whole damn county."

"He's been coming 'round here for years," Wilson explained. "Runs up from the valley with a load of citrus in June, and when that sells out, he picks up what he can from local truck farms, sells it, and when that runs out, he hauls back. He laughed and addressed Ortega. *"¿Cuántos hijos tienes, Manuel?"*

Ortega wrinkled his brow and held up both hands. *"Once,"* he said. *"Dos más este año."*

"¿Pablo, también?" Wilson pointed toward the younger man, who was completing his loading and sweating profusely. Hugh knew he should be helping him, but he didn't want to leave the shade. He thought he could almost see the waves of heat rising from the ground around the truck.

"No," Ortega shook his head. *"Él tiene solamente tres hijos. Dos hijas, pero ellas no cuentan."*

"Poor Pablo," Wilson shook his head and grinned slightly. "Mescans put a high regard on sons, especially when they're in this kind of business."

The men chatted briefly in Spanish for a while, and Hugh found himself beginning to doze. Pablo completed his loading chore, came up to the shade and took a drink from the bucket, then squatted in the dust and smoked a while. He said nothing while his father talked to Wilson. After a bit, they rose, shook hands. After a few more words, the two Mexican vendors climbed back into their truck and backed it down to the gate. Hugh watched Pablo climb down and lower the yellow flag before they drove out onto the highway and headed west.

"I didn't see him give you any money," Hugh commented.

"Don't ever carry none," Wilson frowned. "Some smart aleck would just knock me in the head and take it when I wasn't looking. He'll go and put what's due me on my account at Grayson's Store, and next week, he'll fetch what I need out to me. That's the way we work it."

"That's a pretty good deal," Hugh nodded. "But you need dog food for Goodlett, now."

"Oh, I'll go by and get some," Wilson said. "She's good till morning anyhow."

"Time for the wash," Wilson said when the men had disappeared from sight, and he went into the house and added wood to the stove to start heating water.

―✕

Two hours later, both workers and every cloth, rag, and stitch of clothing they owned were clean. In a large metal tub near the well, Wilson first laundered the sheets and pillowcases from their bunks, then he added more hot water and pushed in the towels and cloths from the kitchen. After that, the old man insisted on washing Hugh's T-shirt, jeans, socks, and underwear along with his own soiled clothing. And while the clothes dried in the sun, more boiling water was added to the sudsy tub, and Hugh was ordered to bathe himself. He did, and then while Hugh sat naked on one of the porch chairs, Wilson himself entered the steaming water.

The solid build of Wilson's body belied his age. The old man's skin was milky white from his neck all the way down to his feet. His hands were scarred and burned red, and his neck, wattled and leathery as it was, also showed the ravages of the sun and weather. But his torso was as pale as the underside of one of his melons. He removed his hat only to pour hot soapy water over his head where his hair was silvery gray and thick. Then Wilson carefully scrubbed himself with a coarse cloth. Heavy muscles roped up and down his arms and legs, and his chest, though old and slightly concave, was still sturdy and crossed with well-defined ribs and stout pectorals. There was no doubt about it, Hugh thought, Wilson was still a strong man no matter how old he was.

Finally, Wilson used an old straight razor to scrape off his whiskers while he sat in the tub and awkwardly studied his face in a cracked hand mirror. He looked younger without the week's growth of beard, but his cheeks were still sunken and aged, and the creases in his facial skin seemed like canyons in comparison to the smooth stretch of brown leather that covered his jutting jaw.

When he finished, Wilson dumped the dirty water out, ordered Hugh over to the well, then he doused both of them with bucket after bucket of icy well water. Hugh had gone from too hot to move to comfortably cool to freezing cold in the space of a few minutes. He couldn't believe he was shivering when he drew his damp jeans on before helping Wilson take in the sheets and other laundry and remake the bunks.

Hugh's watch told him it was nearly four when they shut up and locked the boxcar-house and started down the path toward the highway. Clean and well fed as he was, the boy dreaded the five-mile walk back to town. At the earliest, it would be nearly dark when he arrived at his house, and if Tommy and Ray ran true to their normal schedule, they would have been home by five at the latest. They almost never stayed out on the lake on Sunday any longer than it took to guarantee that they would miss evening church services.

As Wilson refastened the barbed wire gate, he stood and looked approvingly at the garden and junk piles that paralleled the path up to the boxcar. He had two tow sacks filled to bulging. One, Hugh knew, held a stack of freshly made sandwiches and some implements the old man needed. The other Wilson had filled while Hugh bathed, and its contents were a mystery to the boy.

"We done a good job of work," Wilson said.

"Well, it's good to be clean," Hugh remarked with a grin. His body ached horribly, and his hands continued to sting and burn. His legs were unequal to the task of the walk back, but he knew he would have to make it without comment. He doubted Wilson would suffer complaint.

"Bathe every week," Wilson advised. "Always have. Much more'n that'll give you the ague. Now, where's that Mescan?"

Almost as if his words summoned him, Ortega's bobtail hove into view on the western horizon. It chugged to a stop, and Hugh followed Wilson up onto the bed, where they nestled themselves between baskets and boxes of fruits and vegetables. Hugh was too relieved to ask how or why, but since the truck was now full to bursting with produce, he decided that the two men were out making the rounds of other farms and gardens in that part of the county, and Wilson had a regular ride arranged.

As the truck ground through the gravel back onto the shoulder, Hugh spotted Goodlett slinking down the fence line. Just as the vehicle hit second gear and began to pick up speed, Wilson whistled, and the dog came bounding up and leaped high into Wilson's arms and was lifted aboard.

"Ortega don't mind riding me to town," he yelled over the wind that threatened his hat as the truck ground through its remaining gears and roared out onto the highway. "But he don't like Goodlett for nothing and won't give her a ride. I let her stow away, though."

In minutes, they arrived at the city limits, and Ortega pulled over. Hugh realized they were but two blocks from his cache of camping gear, but he didn't want Wilson to see him retrieve it. He stood on the side of the street and held Goodlett out of sight as the old man spoke again to Ortega, and the Mexican's truck pulled out.

The old man and boy sat under a bois d'arc tree and enjoyed one more smoke. They said little to each other. Despite his aching muscles, Hugh felt better than he had in his life. If they started talking about things, the mood would be spoiled.

After they finished, they rose and walked along for a few blocks generally in the direction of downtown. Hugh needed to break away and go home. He was too tired to think about going off too far and having to return for his sleeping bag and tackle. Even so, he paced himself beside Wilson and strolled along.

"Was Mr. Ortega really the grandson of Pancho Villa?"

"Claims he was. Course, they's probably a couple thousand old boys down on the border says the same thing. Villa had him a mess of wives—during one spell there, he married one a day for two weeks."

"How—"

"Don't ask me," Wilson cut Hugh's question off. "He just done it, that's all. Story was more of them padres spoke the vows down the barrel of a six-gun than not, but that was the story at the time."

"Next you're going to tell me you knew him. Pancho Villa."

"Naw," Wilson smiled. "I chased him with the army a spell, but I never seen him. Not that I know, anyhow. I was at Columbus, New Mexico, when he come across the border and raided ol' Blackjack Pershing's headquarters. Made that little feller madder'n a scalded dog."

"Who?"

"Pershing. Called him 'Banty Rooster.' Most of us did."

"I thought you weren't in the army."

"Wasn't. Wouldn't take me, like I told you."

"So why were you there?"

"Hauling salt."

"Salt?"

"They wasn't no salt in Columbus, so we had to haul it from some salt flats about a hundred miles away. I'd just come in with a load the night before. When they hit, they burned my wagons and run off with my horses. So I went with the army tracking him. But they never caught him. No, sir."

"Seems to me like you've done a little of everything." Hugh couldn't keep the skepticism from coming into his voice.

"I told you," Wilson grumbled down in his throat, "you oughtn't to call a man a liar."

Hugh shut up and studied the old man walking along beside him. He couldn't believe everything Wilson said, but at the same time, he spoke with so much conviction it was hard not to accept it.

"Well," Hugh said after they strolled another block and he realized that he was about to follow Wilson all the way downtown, "I suppose I ought to be getting home. My folks will be worried."

"Reckon so."

"Will you be downtown tomorrow?"

"Yep."

"I guess I'll see you there."

"Doubt it." Wilson looked up into the afternoon sky.

"Rain, right?"

"Right."

"So they won't work."

"Right."

"So you'll be in the hotel?"

Wilson's face darkened, and he rubbed his chin. "Now look, boy," he said. "I had me a drink or two too many of that whiskey, and I told you some things I oughtn't of. You tell anybody 'bout that or let on you know anything 'bout it, and ol' Jonas's going to be in trouble with the law."

"I won't tell anybody. I swear I won't," Hugh protested. "I mean, you can trust me." He thought of all the work he had done over the weekend. His hands were raw, open sores, and his shoulders and legs cramped every time he sat or stood still. Weariness hung all about him like a fog, and he realized that subconsciously he had been looking forward to nothing more than going home and crawling into his bed and sleeping through until morning—something he often did after a camping trip with his friends.

"Well." Wilson looked up and down the street. It was a humid Sunday midafternoon, and there was little traffic. People were shut up inside their houses watching ballgames, napping, enjoying the air-conditioned privacy of a steamy day. "Trust is a funny thing. Used to be if you worked shoulder-to-shoulder with a man, broke bread with him, shared your smoke and whiskey with him, you could trust him. We done all that—except the whiskey—and I got to allow you stood up to it better'n I figgered you would.

"You got grit, boy, I'll tell you that. You're nigher on to being a growed man than you know. You don't ask a lot of nonsense questions, and you know when to keep your mouth shut. Most boys your age would of drove me crazy. But saying all that don't mean we got trust tween us."

"Why not? I trust you."

"But you don't respect me, boy. Maybe you never will. You don't believe what I say most of the time, and you think I'm odd. I think you're a little scared of me, too."

"I am not!" Hugh exclaimed to hide the guilty memory of lying awake and worrying about Wilson and the lights in the old hotel.

"Well, that over to the side, you ain't always told me the truth."

"I have, too." Hugh blushed with anger. He was hurt that Wilson doubted him. He had thought they were getting along well. "You said to be careful who you call a liar."

"I ain't calling you a liar." Wilson looked down at the extra sack. "Just telling you what I think."

"Well, I'd better be going," Hugh said bitterly. "Maybe I'll see you, and maybe I won't."

"Maybe so," Wilson said. Then he lifted the second sack. "Here." he handed it out to Hugh's hand. "Take this to your mama. Maybe it'll make things go easier on you."

"What do you mean?" Hugh accepted the sack to prevent it from falling from Wilson's twisted fingers.

The old man turned away. "Maybe you can get somebody to help you carry it home with the rest of your stuff." Hugh looked backward through the shimmering waves of heat toward the church and thought of his stashed equipment and blushed again, this time in embarrassment. "Just see to it you don't drag it on the ground. Bruises the 'maters," Wilson said, then he whistled and sauntered off with Goodlett following in his wake.

CHAPTER SEVEN

Hugh wasn't able to sleep late the next morning at all. Predawn thunder awakened him early on Monday, and his plans to start catching up on his lawn mowing that morning were automatically canceled in the first flash of the thunderstorm's lightning. It was just as well, he thought with a shake of his head that made his neck ache. Wilson had almost worked him to death. But the experience had taught him a lot about the old man even as it had raised questions about why Wilson had taken such an interest in him.

Along with the physical pain in his joints and muscles, Hugh discovered in himself an enormous capacity for guilt that seemed never to be satisfied by any justification or excuse.

When Hugh arrived home the afternoon before, weary and nearly staggering under the weight of his unused camping gear, Harry was using the Grassmaster to cut their lawn. Edith, standing by the front window, made a point of noting the time on her wristwatch and giving him an approving nod when she spotted him coming up the sidewalk. Hugh packed his stuff back into the garage, and he had no more than seated himself at the kitchen table with a bowl of frozen yogurt than his father came in, poured himself a large glass of iced tea, and ordered him to come out and finish the job. In the meantime, his mother was unpacking the tow sack full of fresh vegetables that Jonas Wilson gave him. She had guilelessly believed his story that he and the other boys helped one of the lake residents harvest his garden in exchange for the produce. She actually beamed when she saw the size of the tomatoes, squash, and okra that the bag produced. When she discovered a dozen plump roasting ears in the bottom, Harry chimed in with congratulations for Hugh's enterprising way of increasing the family larder.

But his father's anticipation of a good meal did not distract him from his purpose. "Hurry up and get on that yard," Harry warned him. "It'll be getting dark soon, and supper'll be ready." Hugh trudged outdoors and took up the chore.

He tried to ignore the burning, burst blisters on his palms and fingers while he pushed the mower up and down the family yard, completing the job Harry had just barely begun. By the time he swept the clippings into a bag and cinched it up, he was so tired that he could hardly drag himself in to clean up to eat. But he made it to the table, shoveled pot roast and mashed potatoes into his mouth along with an ear of Jonas Wilson's excellent corn before he was permitted, mercifully, to shower and fall into bed.

During the meal, his parents kept up a running series of questions about the camping expedition he had supposedly been on all weekend. He made noncommittal responses, but Harry was unusually persistent, it seemed, in his hunger for details of his adventure, asking specific questions about people they might have seen, places on the lake that might have changed since he was out there last. Hugh soon found that open and forthright lies were all that would satisfy his father's casual third degree. He shocked himself with his ability to manufacture elaborate, even humorous anecdotes out of thin air. Meanwhile, Edith ate very little, merely sat there sipping her fourth drink—by Hugh's count—and smiling weakly at him as she listened to his creative responses.

As chocolate cake was served for dessert, he managed to detail the number and kind of fish caught, even estimating individual weights and lengths, and invented wonderful new stories about Tommy's ineptitude with a skillet on an open fire for his parent's nodding heads and too wide smiles.

"So where are they?" Harry asked, forking the last morsel of cake from his plate. Hugh stopped and stared. "The fish?" Harry asked. "Where are all these trophies? Sounds like some good eating there."

"Oh," Hugh said, casting crazily about his mind for something to say. "Uh, we gave them to the guy who gave us the stuff. The vegetables." Harry's eyebrows raised. "It was too hot to keep them fresh," Hugh added. "We didn't take an ice chest."

His audacity amazed him. He couldn't believe the ease with which lies rolled off his tongue or the sincerity in his tone. He discovered that he more than half believed what he was saying the whole time he was inventing it, and he was shocked at his capacity for deception. It was as if he was born to it. For a moment he saw himself as a stranger, someone older and more casually dishonest than he ever thought he could be. He wasn't pleased with the image.

After he went to bed, he lay and listened to the distant hum of his parents' conversation and clinking of ice in cocktail glasses over the muffled canned laughter from the television. He wondered just how much they suspected, how much they knew about where he had been and what he had been doing. If they knew much at all, he said to himself, then they knew what a liar he had become. Guilt welled up in him. He promised himself that this was an end to it. If he got away with this series of lies, then he was done with lying forever—at least insofar as his parents were concerned.

Further, he vowed, he would rise early the next day and begin catching up on his lawns. He didn't dare think about how many he was behind, but it didn't matter. By the end of the week, he swore, he would be up to date and able to defend himself honorably against any other charges.

The early morning rain short-circuited that, just as it had prevented the demolition crew from returning to work on the Hendershot building. Over an inescapable full breakfast that morning, Hugh groggily muttered responses to his mother's too cheerful questions, then he took advantage of a temporary break in the series of thunderstorms that was rolling across the area to ride his bike downtown and install himself on the stool at Central Drugs. Now, at eleven o'clock, he was still there, and he was sipping his fourth lime Coke of the morning and wondering what he should or could do next.

Being in the drugstore was hardly relaxing. Instead, it jerked him back to the more immediate problems surrounding the old building. Up toward the front were Phelps Crane, George Ferguson, Harvey Turnbull, and a half-dozen other men, who were sipping coffee and glaring at the row of booths in the back of the store where four hard-hatted men also sat and poured cup after cup of coffee and spoke in low tones. To make matters worse, Linda Fitzpatrick came behind her father and now wandered up and down the cosmetics aisle. Carl picked up one of the chairs and moved slightly away from the circle of townsmen by the Serve Yourself counter. He turned it backwards and sat down astraddle of it. Hugh noted that he was there, part of the discussion, but he was also outside the group, and he said very little.

In the mirror behind the soda fountain, Hugh could see Linda moving slowly, inspecting item after item briefly, and stealing glances at him when she thought he wasn't looking. Her surreptitious attention brought forth the old tugging inside him, but there also was something new, a sort of warning that echoed Jonas Wilson's cautions about the girl. It was confusing and frustrating, but he enjoyed the idea that she was paying attention to him, and he wondered what he would do when she decided to "find" him seated at the counter.

The men in the front of the store weren't saying much of anything, but the men in the back were keeping up a steady stream of conversation and were occasionally looking up to see if anyone was listening. They were nervous and unhappy, Hugh could tell between sips of his drink, and the weather was probably the reason. He sympathized.

Hilda Brestwood, the counter girl, was kept busy refilling the Serve Yourself pots and chasing back to the booths to slosh fresh coffee into the demolition crewmen's cups. When Hugh ordered another lime Coke, she frowned at him. "This ain't free. Coffee refills are free, but Cokes are pay as you go." Hugh nodded and placed a dollar bill on the counter and kept dividing his attention between watching Linda move up and down the aisles and monitoring the men in the rear of the room.

After a few minutes, Hugh wasn't paying much attention to anyone but Linda, and soon his thoughts began to wander away from her as well. He calculated that he had enough money to make a payment on the lawnmower that was due the next day, but if he didn't catch up on his work this week, he would never raise the following week's payment. It worried him more than a little. He was trying to figure out exactly how much he would have if he started mowing the next afternoon—as soon as the grass was dry enough—when he was startled by the smell of Linda's perfume and the sight of her in the mirror as she climbed up onto the stool next to him.

"Which one do you like?" She held out three postcards for his inspection. One showed a jackrabbit fitted photographically with a huge pair of antlers. The caption said, "Texas Jackalope." The second showed a weary family standing beside a jalopy that steamed and sat raggedly on two flat tires in the midst of cactus and sandy desert. It read: "The sun has riz. The sun has set. But here we is in Texas yet." The third showed a beautiful and busty cowgirl mounted on a horse and wearing a skin-tight western suit and gaudy boots. She was lifting her hat and straining her breasts against her yoke shirt while she offered a bright smile. She had a 1940s coiffure, and her lips and cheeks were unnaturally red against the paleness of the sky behind her. Also in the background were the towering formations of Monument Valley, Utah, dotted with large sequoia cacti, native to Arizona. It simply read: "Greetings from the Lone Star State."

"I don't really care for any of them," Hugh muttered. He was no less bamboozled by Linda Fitzpatrick today than he had been before, but there were weightier things on his mind at the moment, and he surprised himself by half hoping she would just go away. "Who're you going to send them to?"

He knew the answer before he asked the question, and he wished he had the words back, but she smiled a sly smile and pretended to examine the cards closely.

"Why, Tony, of course."

"I thought, maybe, your sister or somebody." Hugh sipped his drink.

"Why in the world would I want to send a postcard about Texas to my sister?" Linda's eyes widened in horror. "She's *from* here. She knows all about Texas."

"Are these about Texas?" Hugh fingered the card with the Jackalope. "These are older than I am. We are," he quickly amended.

"Well, they're as close as this old drugstore has. I should have bought some in Dallas, but there wasn't time. We ate at La Fontaine's, by the way. It was very elegant. I had lobster and real French wine."

"I don't think I'd send any of these to some guy who doesn't know anything about Texas."

"You're just jealous." Linda batted her eyes and mocked him. "You just wish you had someone to write to."

"Yeah." Hugh frowned. He didn't want to argue with her, and he certainly didn't want to discuss Tony.

"Well, I like the one with the cowgirl." Linda picked it out and held it up. "It's kind of cool."

"It probably was, about a hundred years ago," Hugh growled.

"Boy, *you're* in a mood today." Linda leaned back and looked at him. "What's the matter? Somebody steal your bike?" She said "bike" sarcastically, and Hugh suddenly remembered that in school she had made a big deal out of the fact that she was too old, now, to ride a bicycle when they were trying to organize a "bike hike" out to Medicine Lake for a picnic. He also realized that his dreams of the Yosemite Mountain Bike seemed less important than they had before.

"No," Hugh said. "I'm supposed to be working today, but I can't. Rain." He pointed out the front windows.

"What work?"

"I mow lawns," Hugh explained in a tired voice. He now desperately wanted her to go away and leave him alone. "I have a lot of lawns to mow. I can't work when it's raining."

"Isn't that kind of kid work?"

"Kid work?" Hugh was irked. He saw himself sweating and grunting while he shoved the mower up and down lawns. All the physical pain of the heat and agony of his regular labor came to him at once. "I make pretty good money at it."

"Well, Tony works in a cycle shop." She fingered the postcards with her long nails. "A motorcycle shop. Harley-Davidsons. 'Hogs,' they call them. Or 'choppers.' You know?"

"Yeah, I know," Hugh looked away. The men in the back were becoming more and more animated in their conversation. The men in the front were becoming more and more sullen in their silence. "But you said he's older, right?" Hugh probed this point of vulnerability. "A lot older, right?"

"Yeah," Linda was uncertain of his meaning. "He's going to college next year. UCLA—"

"Right." Hugh watched Linda's eyes in the mirror. "So he probably needs a lot of money. I mean, he'll be dating college girls in the fall, right?"

Linda's eyes flickered to the invisible distance for a moment. "I suppose."

"Well, motorcycle shops pay a lot for trained mechanics. Is he—"

"I don't want to talk about it anymore," she said, pushing the cards away down the counter. "Why don't you buy me something to drink?"

"I'm having a Coke," Hugh said. He had wounded her. He couldn't believe it. He won a round with Linda Fitzpatrick. He was elated. "A lime Coke."

"Diet Coke's fine," she muttered, then she brightened. "I'm just waiting on Mother to finish at the beauty parlor. She got this permanent at Neiman Marcus on Saturday, and you ought to see it." She lowered her voice. "Her hair is green," she whispered, "Daddy said he was going to sue, but he can't."

"Why not?" Hugh fought back a grin. The prospect of Lydia Fitzpatrick with green hair seemed funny, but Linda was deadly serious.

"Well, they said that it was because she went swimming at the hotel right before, and there was chlorine in her hair when they put the rinse on it, and that's what turned it green." Linda was speaking so low that Hugh had to bow his head to hear her. "She didn't wash it out, see. We just went right over to the beauty shop there, and it was still wet, so they just put the dye right on it, and pow!— green hair." She dropped her sober frown and giggled.

Hugh didn't fully understand the process, but he got the picture.

"She's furious!" Linda went on, straightening her face. "She went around wearing this turban all day Sunday, and she wrapped it up in a towel before she went over to Viola Ledbetter's beauty shop to see if there's anything they can do. Daddy says—" Linda checked her father's presence. Carl was still seated, smoking a cigar and sipping coffee. "—Daddy says they might have to shave her head to get rid of it." She burst out in a loud laugh.

"That's pretty funny all right." It was, and Hugh laughed. He ordered two drinks from Hilda when she passed by. She scowled briefly, then brought them over.

"Well, Daddy doesn't think it's funny at all," Linda magically recovered her composure in seconds. "He said if he heard me telling anybody about it, he'd ground me," she confided as she completed her first sip. "He said there was this big meeting tomorrow night, and he didn't know what he was going to do if she couldn't come. He said a man in his position needs his wife right beside him. He also said that . . ."

Hugh's attention wandered. Grissom's car cruised by slowly.

". . . it's about that old building," Linda tried to steer Hugh's concentration back toward herself.

"What old building? The Hendershot building?"

"Right."

"A meeting?"

"That's what I'm talking about. I swear, Hugh Rudd, talking to you is like talking to a brick wall."

"A meeting about the building? What kind of meeting? A town meeting?"

She smiled. "That's what Daddy said. He said they were going to put a stop to the demolition or he was 'going to die trying.' That's what he said. He said it's a 'famous historical landmark,' and we have 'to do everything in our power' to save it." She lowered her voice into another conspiratorial whisper. "He called the governor last night."

"The governor?" Hugh was stunned. "Of Texas?"

"That's right," Linda sat up straight, proud of her factual knowledge. "Called right from our kitchen phone. He said he was the head of the Committee to Save the Hendershot Building."

This was news, Hugh thought. He wondered where Jonas Wilson was. He ought to tell him. He then thought of his own father with a spasm of guilt. He would want to know, also.

"When's the meeting?" Hugh asked. "Can anybody come?"

"It's in the lodge hall." Linda pointed out the windows. The empty second floor over Sanderson's Fine Furniture and Appliances served as a meeting hall for four of the small town's lodges and the Eastern Star. "It's tomorrow night, but I don't know what time."

"Are you going?"

"Who wants to go to some stupid meeting?" Linda sniffed. "I was thinking about having a pool party out at the country club. If Mother's in a better mood after while, I'll ask her."

Hugh was torn. Here was almost an invitation to Linda Fitzpatrick's pool party. She surely wouldn't have mentioned it to him if she hadn't been planning to invite him. Jonas Wilson was right about her: She was a flirt and spoiled and self-centered, but she was still Linda Fitzpatrick, and the old fantasies again filled his mind. The prospect of frolicking in a pool with her and her friends was deliciously inviting. He also sensed that as much as she liked to tease him, she would never allow her sense of social grace to slip far enough to snub him so openly. It was something he would have been able only to dream of a week ago, and now, all of a sudden, here it was in tempting reality, as close to him as this sweet-smelling blonde beauty on the next counter stool.

At the same time, Hugh's mind raced, there was the prospect of a town meeting to try to save the Hendershot building. He couldn't say why he wanted to be there. Whatever happened would happen with or without him, and he would hear about it soon enough. But he couldn't bear the thought of its taking place and his missing it.

"Well?" Linda was looking intently at him, and he turned on his stool and stared at her, as if actually seeing her for the first time that morning. Her yellow hair spilled down over her shoulder and found its end against her right breast, which moved ever so gently up and down as she breathed. Her long, tanned legs thrust out of the light green shorts outfit she wore and crossed delicately at the knee, and her blue eyes seemed to draw him inside her.

"Well what?"

"Well, if I have the pool party, do you want to come?"

"With you?"

"Well, not *with* me," she said with a slight frown. "Mother won't let me date till next year."

This announcement surprised Hugh. From all her talk about her California beach boy, he assumed she was going and coming pretty much as she pleased.

"But you could come," she said. "I'm inviting you. I don't know who else. It's going to be sort of short notice, and a lot of kids are on vacation."

"Or working," Hugh offered.

"Or working," Linda said uncertainly.

"I'll have to see," Hugh said, but when outrage began to take form behind her eyes, he amended, "I mean, I'll have to check with my folks." She relaxed her expression and nodded with a wink as she returned to her drink. "It might be raining," he added.

"If it's raining, we can stay in the clubhouse's youth room and play games." She smiled slyly. "We played Western Union last time."

"Western Union?"

"Sort of like post office, only faster," she smiled more broadly and reached down to flick her hair behind her shoulders. Her long finger rested briefly against her breast, and Hugh felt an invisible fist strike him hard in the solar plexus and leave a hole filled with raw heat. He stared at her for a moment, but she quickly spun around to see who was entering the drugstore.

Grissom, the railroad man, came in slapping water from his hat. Right behind him another man dressed in khaki workclothes followed closely, but as they passed the knot of disgruntled coffee drinkers at the front of the drugstore, they were accosted by Phelps Crane, who stood and blocked Grissom's path. Hugh noticed that the old man hadn't yet shaved. He also wore the same overalls and shirt he had on all the week before. Hugh imagined he could smell him, even from a distance.

"You know, Grissom, you got one hell of a nerve just sashaying in here like God Almighty," Phelps said.

"I just came in to see my people," Grissom fired back and made his way past Phelps's burly form. In the back, Hugh noticed, several of the construction workers were standing. He had the feeling that they wanted to hit someone.

"Well, seems to me like you could meet somewheres else." Phelps grabbed Grissom's arm and spun him around. "This here's for local folks."

"I didn't see any sign that said 'private club.'" Grissom jerked his arm free and turned to face Phelps. "You're the ones who've been trespassing all this time. This is a public business, and I've got as much right to be here as you do. That's your line, isn't it?" Phelps reddened. His small eyes darted around. Grissom turned away, saying when he turned, "Don't you have a job?"

"Don't you worry none 'bout me having a job," Phelps roared at Grissom's back. "Don't none of you railroad people need to worry 'bout none of us having jobs," he bellowed at the collection of men at the rear of the store. "We *had* jobs. Good jobs! But you took 'em away. Now, we're getting along just fine, thank you very much, but you come in here and want to make things worse. I ought to fix your wagon."

Phelps was shaking, his jaw working in pure rage as Grissom pushed his companion down the aisle toward the booths where the construction workers awaited them. Carl Fitzpatrick, who had watched the entire exchange from his seat with a slightly amused expression on his face, finally rose and put a hand on Phelps's arm, and the older man sat down. "Had jobs," Phelps muttered. He pulled the pint bottle from his pocket and downed nearly a third of it in three giant gulps. "Had good jobs," he concluded.

As if they were embarrassed by the display, George and Harvey rose and went out the door, and in a few moments, Carl followed them. Carl called out that Linda was to wait there for her mother, and she frowned back at him.

"I think I'll eat a sandwich," Hugh said and mentally tabulated the money in his pocket. That would leave him exactly enough required for the mower payment this week, he thought. The last thing Hugh wanted was food, but his intention was to find a reason to move back to a booth. Grissom and the others were now talking in a low, intense discussion, and he wanted to know what was going on.

"I'd like one, too," Linda chirped. "You can treat. I have no money with me at all. But let's move back to the booths. I hate to eat at the counter. Mother says it's so vulgar."

There went this week's payment, he thought. But on the other hand, he welcomed her company. Two kids sitting and eating together looked natural, he thought, and if she wouldn't talk so much, he could hear what was going on. He ordered two tuna fish sandwiches from Hilda and escorted Linda back to the open booth nearest the men. So pleased was he with the arrangement and the appearance they put up strolling back to the booth that he completely ignored the significance of the fact that he was about to share a meal with Linda Fitzpatrick until they sat down and he was stunned to realize where he was, what he was actually doing. He looked at her as if she had just materialized in front of him. He could hardly believe it. Once again they were alone. Together. The heat in his chest returned.

Linda settled on her favorite topic: shopping in Dallas. Hugh left his eyes on hers but paid her only scant attention. Instead, he trained his ears on the men in the booth behind them. They were almost whispering, and from time to time Grissom would lift his head and glare toward the door and the rain outside. He ignored the two youngsters, though, and Hugh always managed to nod or say something to Linda every time he looked over his shoulder past where they were sitting. He had no idea what she was talking about, but somehow, she didn't seem to notice. Their sandwiches came with another round of Cokes, and Hugh strained his hearing to listen to what the men were saying.

It wasn't clear. There was talk of the "damn weather" that had delayed work on the old building for another day at least, and Grissom was trying to get a commitment from them as to when they thought they could finish the project at the earliest. The word "lawyers" was mentioned more than once, and he heard Judge Parker's name evoked with disgust, along with the governor's. Grissom wasn't happy, that much was clear, but with Linda going on and on about the awful fall colors and how the new shoe styles made her legs look too skinny, Hugh couldn't pick up a whole thread of any series of thoughts.

"So what do you think?" Linda's voice penetrated Hugh's concentration, and he was startled to realize that she had asked him a question that required something besides a nod or shake of his head in response.

"What?"

"Are you even *listening* to me, Hugh Rudd? I swear, sometimes I think you're just deaf and dumb."

"I'm sorry," Hugh looked down at his half-eaten sandwich, "I was thinking about something."

"Well, you should pay attention to the person you're talking to." She pouted quickly and then set her mouth back to its former prettiness. "I asked you if you thought a string bikini was too mature for someone my age?"

Hugh's eyes drifted involuntarily down toward Linda's body. The image of her bare stomach and abdomen exposed to view emerged vividly and momentarily put to rout thoughts of demolition and old buildings.

"Uh, no, I don't," he said. "I think it's in style. I saw some in some magazines."

"What magazines?" Linda's eyes widened. "Did you really? On girls my age?"

"Uh . . . I don't remember," Hugh's mind raced for titles that were proper for him to mention. He remembered seeing some pictures somewhere. "I couldn't tell how old they were. Maybe it was in the Sears catalog or somewhere."

"Are you looking at girls in swimsuits in the Sears catalog?" Linda's voice rose to flirting level as she nibbled at her sandwich.

"Who me? No," Hugh responded automatically. "I mean, yeah . . . I mean, I don't know."

"You're blushing, Hugh Rudd." She grinned at him, and Hugh's face burned even more. She was utterly beautiful. Once again the unseen but terribly solid fist of heat struck him in the middle of his chest.

"Well?" Linda's eyes narrowed playfully and pressed her advantage, "you don't think a string would show too much?" She raised her body high in the booth's seat and ran her hands down to her waist and indicated the area slated for future exposure. "It's cut to here," she spaced her long fingers down to the insides of her thighs and spread her thumbs up to flank her crotch.

Hugh instantly grew intolerably uncomfortable, and he looked away. Grissom was standing. Hugh tried to direct his attention on what the railroad man was saying. The man who had come in with Grissom also rose, and he was speaking in a louder voice than before.

"I'd like to see you in it," Hugh stammered. What were they talking about? he demanded of himself.

"I'll bet you would," she chastised him in a scolding voice as she seated herself again. "You just have a dirty mind, Hugh Rudd."

"What about the, uh . . . top?" Hugh asked her absently. The words "rail crane" and "Beaumont Hotel" came to his ears.

"Well," Linda warmed to the topic and brushed her blonde hair behind her as she graphically illustrated the cut of the new suit's bra. "It's cut sort of low here, but it doesn't show anything. Not that I have much." She giggled. "Yet. But it's goes up behind my neck like this." She folded her hands under her hair. "And it ties, but it might come loose when I dive."

They were talking about some big crane on a rail car, Hugh determined, like the one they had used to demolish a big hotel in Memphis. He strained to hear more. The man in workclothes was illustrating the action of the machine with his hands, holding out one fist and moving his arm in a wide arch before slamming it into the palm of his other hand with a loud smack. He did it three or four times while he spoke. When his fist struck the base of his palm, his extended fingers collapsed.

"What would you do if it came loose?" she asked, now exasperated with his wandering attention. "What do you think would happen?"

"When it hits the foundation, if there's nothing to support it, both sides will collapse," Hugh said aloud.

"What?"

"I mean," Hugh lowered his voice, "if there's nothing to hold it up, nothing to support it, it'll just fall down."

"I've got plenty of 'support'!" Linda insisted in a hot voice. "Wouldn't you like to know!"

Hugh woke up. "Oh," he looked around and almost shook his head. "I'm sorry. What were you saying?"

"Never mind, Hugh Rudd! You're just a hopeless child. I don't think you'll ever grow up." She rose from the booth and left her sandwich with one tiny bite gone from a corner. "I don't know if I'll invite you to my pool party or not. You've got a dirty mind, did you know that?"

Hugh was not listening to her at all. He now could hear clearly that the big crane was expected by Wednesday and that the men were hoping the rain could clear so they could clear track down beside the building so it could work on it. He had to let someone know. A big crane like that could end the job all at once by knocking out the building's corner supports for the foundation. It would just fall in on itself. He joined Linda in coming to his feet.

"I got to go," he explained and dumped a five-dollar bill onto the counter. He didn't know where he was going or why, but this news had to be communicated to someone.

"What? Where? What's wrong with you?"

"See you, Linda." He waved and ran out, leaving her to stare at him with a look of indignation and bewilderment, and not a little anger.

—≺

The rain, if anything, was heavier than it had been all morning. Heavy sheets of water poured off every downtown awning, and downspouts flooded the streets. Cars and pickups crept through windy, wet gales showering down from low clouds, and ripping claps of thunder echoed off the buildings.

Hugh's bike was sheltered in a doorway. He mounted it and ducked his baseball cap against the slamming downfall as he rode up the street toward the depot parking lot.

The area was deserted, but scraps of paper and other debris from Friday's crowd were blown up against the pylons and the sides of the hardware store, where they were being washed by the incessant rain. Hugh splashed through a puddle and guided his bike up beside a pylon. He peered down into the worksite, but aside from the abandoned bulldozers, pickups, and the wrecking ball and crane, there was nothing unusual. There also were no railroad tracks leading down to the building. Hugh determined that it was at least a hundred yards from the established railbed down through the weeds and forgotten piles of gravel and sand the railroad had piled up and ignored years before to the side of the building where the loading docks had been.

He relaxed and lowered his head against the falling water. No crane, no matter how big, could reach the building from the tracks up by the parking lot. For the moment, at least, the Hendershot Grocery Warehouse was safe.

He mounted his bike again and steered it toward the old hotel. This was something worth sharing. He hoped to spot Jonas Wilson somewhere nearby and tell him of the latest development in the demolition of the building.

Hugh rode around the hotel three times, but Wilson never appeared. It was illogical that the old man and his dog would be sitting outside in the rain, but Hugh thought he might be camped in a nearby doorway. Hugh's inspection of any number of potential shelters, though, yielded nothing more than deepening rain, and by the time he completed his third circuit and pulled his bike up under an alley door's awning behind the Chic Boutique, his clothes were thoroughly soused. They hung on him like great wet weights.

He gave the area around the hotel one more inspection, then his eyes lifted to the third floor of the old structure. The windows that weren't boarded up were covered by torn yellow shades. Those that still had glass were long ago rendered opaque by dirt and fly specks. They looked like a long series of blind eyes peering out of the abandoned floors' blackness. Hugh wondered how many people had found a night's lodging up there, how many wild parties might have been staged on the third floor before the building was closed and sealed, awaiting the city's apparently futile attempt to find the money to refurbish it. He also wondered about ghosts.

The old building had been closed all his life, and he had always just taken it for granted that it always had looked as it did. But now, staring up at it through the rain, he saw it differently. He remembered that from time to time the local paper would run photos of the hotel during better days along with old photos of other structures in town. He remembered seeing old cars lined up out front, people in fine dress posing in front of the big front doors—now closed and sealed. It was billed as one of the "most elegant" places to stay in that part of Texas, and during the war, Hugh had always heard, it was the site of dances and parties held for soldiers passing through on their way to combat. He had never been inside it, not even in Coach Kruickshank's office.

As his eyes drifted from window to window, he thought he saw brief movement on the third floor. He squinted through the rain, but he couldn't tell if it was a trick of the watery light or, perhaps, a gust of wind through a broken pane that might have caused the tattered shade to waver. Once more, he thought of the mysterious lights that kids had reported coming from the abandoned structure. The stories had circulated among his friends for years, but all the kids knew that they weren't the first generation of youngsters to retell them with convulsive shudders.

A murder. That was the horror of it. There had been a party up on the third floor, a group of kids, the story went, but reports of their ages varied. There was drinking and dancing, and things got out of hand. A girl—her name lost to legend—was pushed from a window. Or she jumped. Some said she was running away from someone. Embellishments ran the full gamut from the girl's having had her throat slashed before she was heaved out the window to her living long enough to write out the name of her murderer on the sidewalk using her finger for a pen and her own blood for ink. But someone accidentally—or on purpose—smeared the message before anyone else could read it. The spot where she hit was theoretically around front, and Hugh was one of several hundred youths who claimed to be able to identify the darker shade of concrete on the sidewalk where her body struck and she died in a bloody heap.

There were other versions of the story, of course, and there was little consistency among them. There wasn't even a consensus about when the incident was supposed to have happened, but everyone—old or young—who related the story swore that he or she had been by the hotel at night and had heard noises, seen lights where there shouldn't be any, and suspected that it was the ghost of the girl, roaming the ancient hallways and seeking revenge against her unpunished killer.

The tales always provided a chill whenever they were told. Even Hugh had claimed at one time and another that he had seen the ghostly lights, but if pressed for the truth, he would have admitted that he made it up. He also would have had to deny being able to identify any spot on the sidewalk out front as being any different from any other.

Now, however, standing in the dark gray early afternoon rain, he found the old structure to appear even more ominous than it was at night. The heavy thunderheads seemed to hang right over the building's roof, and gust after gust of wind assaulted the structure's sides. Its heaviness was like a weight sitting on the street corner, holding down the very concrete and mortar beneath it.

Suddenly, Hugh realized where Jonas Wilson was. There was no doubt. He mounted his bike and pedaled into the rain, circling warily around to the back of the hotel after a pass by the lobby, where he saw Mr. Kruickshank sound asleep inside the tiny gift shop. His feet were propped up on a desk, a magazine was open across his stomach.

The alley behind the hotel was overgrown with weeds and piled high with construction debris from the lobby's remodeling. Hugh leaned his bike against a tree and walked through the mud up to the small window next to the huge, overflowing Dumpster. The glass panes were opaque, blocking any view of the inside.

Hugh worked his fingers around the window and tried to push it up, but it wouldn't budge. He decided that Wilson had misled him or simply had lied to him about the window's being open. Then he discovered that it wasn't a sash window at all. It pulled out on a stiff, rusty hinge, and when he tugged at it, it slipped open just wide enough to climb through.

He looked up and down the alley one time to make sure no one was watching, then scrambled inside and pulled the window to behind him. He stood as still as he could. Water ran from his clothing and cap down onto the floor. It was the rear stairwell, he thought while he peered into the gray darkness above him. The rickety, wooden steps led upward, and a door to his right indicated the way down into the basement. Hugh inspected the narrow space of the landing and tugged lightly at another door to his left. It parted silently and revealed the dark and shadowy kitchen of the hotel. Dust and cobwebs covered everything. An ancient stove was humped against one wall, and a pair of oversized sinks dominated another. A big wooden table was in the center, and suspended from the ceiling was a rookery of black, odd-shaped cooking implements, all dripping dirt and dust into the darkness below them. The only light in the room came from the painted-over windows. Hugh decided he would never want to enter the kitchen alone.

He looked again up the stairs, but there was no sound other than the beating of the rain against the windows. On the landings overhead, he could see sparse light from the windows. With a decision that it was sufficient, he stepped up and started his climb to the third floor.

Dirt and grime attacked his hands and stuck to his clothing at every turn. His clothes were still soaked, and his sneakers squeaked and squished with the water they carried, but he was determined to find Wilson and tell him about the railroad's plans. He was also fascinated to be on the "haunted third floor" of the hotel. Fear buzzed around his head like a swarm of bees, but he swallowed and entered the dark third floor hall.

The shaded window at the far end of the hall admitted only enough dim light for Hugh to make out the row of doors on either side—each shut tightly—and the faded flower pattern in the ratty carpet beneath his sodden sneakers. The hallway split into a T at the window, and he tried to get a mental picture of the interior of the hotel while he stepped toward the window shade. Wilson had said his room was in the back. Hugh decided to raise the shade to admit more light, then try the doors back there. He wondered if he should knock.

He walked down the hall, listening to the old building creak and moan. Rain slammed against the outside walls, and thunderclaps seemed to rattle the entire structure. Finally, he reached the shade and tenderly fingered it. It was rotten, he realized too late, as part of the paper covering came loose in his hand, and the rest slammed upward like a lightning bolt. Its flapping din filled the hallway and echoed up and down the main staircase to his right, and Hugh instinctively threw himself down onto the floor and crawled into a protective ball.

After a few moments, he realized that, apart from the rain and continuing thunder, the only thing he could hear was his own heart beating, his breath pounding out of his lungs. He forced himself to calm down and sit up. The stench of the moldy carpet stuck to his face where he had buried it in the ragged floor covering, and he pulled his wet Cardinals T-shirt loose from his jeans and scrubbed his cheek and nose. In one or more of the rooms a scratching noise indicated that he had disturbed mice—or rats, or bats, he thought with a shudder.

He peered out the wide window. Below, the street was beginning to flood as high as the curbs, but Hugh's elevated position permitted him to see the tops of all the buildings on Main Street. Hendershot's massive presence dominated one edge of his vision, its stubborn familiarity refusing to be diminished by the storm. He thought of how small the town really was, of how tiny it must look from an airplane.

He then spotted two boys, Tommy and Ray, standing still as posts under the brick cover of an old gas station on the corner across from the hotel. The station had been closed for years. It had been a garage and then a bus station before it was completely abandoned. Now, the two boys sheltered themselves from the rain and were staring, mouths open, up at Hugh's window. Beneath the brims of their ball caps, their eyes were wide with shock.

He almost waved before he caught himself and jerked back. He realized what they had seen. They couldn't recognize him through the filthy window. All they saw was the shade slapping up, maybe a hand reaching for it as it escaped, and then a face peering out at them. They had been doing what they always did when they had occasion to bike by the old hotel: stop, take a look, and tell another version of the ghost story. Now, though, they really had seen something: Hugh. Only they didn't know it, and they were likely trying to convince themselves that what they had witnessed wasn't a trick of the storm. Hugh grinned. He couldn't wait for them to find him and tell him of the latest chapter in the story.

He peeked out at them two or three times more, each time exciting gestures and opened-mouthed gapes from the pair. Finally, he tired of the game and decided he needed to find Wilson. He turned and started back down the hall. The former ominous ambiance of the floor seemed to have dissipated after the incident with the window shade, and Hugh strolled almost casually down and knocked lightly on the last door on his left.

There was no answer. He tried the door across the hall. Again, silence was the only response. He then knocked on several other doors, but if Wilson was behind one of them, he didn't respond. It finally occurred to Hugh that even if the old man was there, he wasn't going to just open up and greet whoever might be calling in the middle of the afternoon. Wilson was trespassing in the first place, and in the second place, there was no telling who else might be trying to find a secret hideout in the old hotel.

Hugh tried several knobs, but all the rooms were locked tight. Finally, just as he reached the first door where he had knocked, he heard something behind him and swung around to see the thick silhouette of a large man at the opposite end of the hall. Mr. Kruickshank was standing by the window, and he was carrying a long gun.

Hugh crouched down and held his breath. The caretaker was peering out the window into the street and muttering curses. He had his back to Hugh, hadn't seen him. It was a good ten feet to the rear stairwell door, and Hugh would have to cross a shaft of light that shot from the now-raised window shade down the hall. Panic seized him.

He looked up at the doorknob over his head, and with a silent prayer on his lips, he reached up and tried it. To his shock, it turned slowly. The door cracked open. As silently as he could, he rolled backward into the room and closed the door behind him. The old hinges were silent, and the door went to with a barely audible click.

From the other side of the door, Hugh heard Kruickshank's heavy footsteps marching down the hall in his direction. Doorknobs were being rattled, and Hugh could hear the jangle of keys. He didn't think twice. He reached up and thumbed the deadbolt to lock the door.

The room's windows were shaded, and it was as dark as a cave inside, but he fidgeted the lock until it turned and secured the room. He expected that Kruickshank had a key to all the rooms, but it would take time to open both locks on the door. Hugh scurried on his knees across the musty rug to another door—the bathroom—which he opened and scooted behind. A dark shower curtain raggedly concealed a claw-footed bathtub, and he climbed inside, drew the curtain to, and lay breathless against the rust-stained porcelain.

CHAPTER EIGHT

"So, you paid me a visit," Jonas Wilson said to Hugh.

The boy could see that the old man was less than pleased to find him climbing out of the stairwell's window and back into the alley. Wilson's appearance, as it most always did, startled Hugh and almost caused him to cry out when he heard the voice right behind him.

"Yeah," Hugh gasped and tried to catch his breath and compose himself, "but you weren't home."

"Well, you could of got me caught." Wilson looked beneath the window and then shut it firmly. Goodlett sat off to one side and ducked her head against the rain. The wind had decreased, and the water now fell in a steady downpour onto Wilson's battered hat. The brim was turned down, and water sluiced from the crushed crown and flowed in an even pour onto his shirt.

"I almost got caught myself." Hugh moved against the building and tried to shelter himself. "By Coach Kruickshank. I guess he heard me."

"Ain't likely," Wilson said. "More'n likely, them two young'uns got him up and moving."

"Who?" Hugh looked around.

"I seen them two come a-running into the hotel a while ago, then after a bit, they come out."

"Where were you?"

"That's none of your nevermind," Wilson snapped. "I told you something that was a secret, and you done all you could to ruin it for me." He stepped away. "Now, c'mon away from there. Let's get out of this rain."

Hugh found his bike and pushed it behind Wilson down the alley and around to an old icehouse that, like the hotel and the Hendershot building, was abandoned and sat ruining just across the tracks. It crossed Hugh's mind that every third building in town seemed to be in the same derelict condition. He'd never noticed that before.

The old icehouse was a long building with a high, deep loading porch. It hadn't been needed since the advent of efficient home refrigeration and, like the hotel, it had been sitting idle and empty since before Hugh was born. Insofar as he knew, though, there had been no interest in trying to salvage or save it. It was a genuine eyesore. It was constructed with walls made of corrugated tin, long since gone completely to rust, and the heavy planking of the front dock was rotting. Still, the overhanging roof offered shelter from the rain. They climbed up next to the padlocked front door and squatted and watched the rain falling off the roof in a steady cascade.

With Goodlett curled up at Wilson's feet, they sat in silence for a long time. Finally the old man reached into his pocket and pulled out his tobacco and papers—both wrapped in wax paper—and offered them to Hugh. Hugh reached for them and began rolling a smoke. He was nervous doing so in such plain view of the street, but between the rain and the shadow of the icehouse's porch, he felt relatively safe.

"So, what'd you learn up there?"

"Learn?"

"I told you to learn from everything you do." Wilson started a cigarette of his own.

"Not much," Hugh admitted. As soon as he had heard Coach Kruickshank's footfalls leaving the floor, Hugh had climbed out of the tub and looked around. The room in which he had taken refuge was dark and musty. The bed was covered with burlap bags that had been split and stitched to form a kind of blanket over a naked mattress. There was a single kerosene lamp on a dusty bedside table, but no other evidence that anyone had been in the room in years. Still, he felt uncertain if this was Wilson's secret hideout. For sure, it was someone's.

"What were you thinking of, boy?" Wilson breathed smoke out of his nostrils and gazed out into the rainy streets. "Going up where you had no business."

"I was looking for you."

"Well, I told you I only go up there at night. Not every night." They sat and smoked a moment. "You see anything?"

"No," Hugh shook his head. "Mr. Kruickshank showed up and scared me, and I hid out in this bathtub."

"Bathtub?"

"In one of the rooms. I snuck in and hid out until he looked around and left."

"Did he come in?" Wilson's eyes were set.

"Naw. I could hear him rattling the knobs on some rooms. Cussing a lot. He left after a while."

Wilson smiled. "Bet he scared the peewaddle out of you."

Hugh matched the old man's grin and nodded. "No kidding. I turned around, and there he was. He had a rifle."

"Shotgun," Wilson corrected. "Old twenty gauge. He keeps it in case some critter gets loose up there."

"What?"

"Oh, possum or skunk or some other varmint sneaks in from time to time. Never know what might be tromping 'round a ol' building like that."

"Maybe that's what he thought I was," Hugh speculated. "He was asleep when I snuck in."

"Them two boys woke him up," Wilson said again. "I seen 'em. One minute they was just looking up the way they do, and then they jumped like they seen the devil hisself. Durn near drowned coming 'cross the street."

"That was when the shade snapped up," Hugh explained. "I just touched it, and it flew up. Scared me, too."

"They kept looking a spell, then talked 'bout it for a spell, then they skedaddled over to wake up ol' Kruickshank. I guess he sent 'em on their way, 'cause they come running out with him cussing 'em."

"But he came up there anyhow."

"Had to. That's his job."

"Boy, wait till I tell them," Hugh's eyes brightened.

Wilson reached out and took a firm grip on his leg. "You can't tell 'em," he said, his pale eyes suddenly hard, focused on Hugh's. "Now, you promise me that." His crooked fingers bit into the boy's leg painfully. "You give me your word on that."

"All right," Hugh gasped. It took all his strength to keep from wrenching his limb away from the old man's viselike grip. It was incredibly strong. Tears came to his eyes. "I promise," he said.

Wilson released him and leaned back. "Now, you keep that," he said, "and you promise me you won't go prowling 'round up there no more. You're just going to mess me up."

"I'm sorry," Hugh muttered. Wilson was treating him like a child once more, and it made him mad. "I just wanted to find you to tell you—"

"You let me do the finding," Wilson spoke sharply. "That ol' hotel's no place for a boy like you to be hanging round. Bad things happen there."

"What sort of bad things?"

"It was all a long time ago." He flicked his butt out into the rain behind Hugh's. "Best forgotten."

"Does it have to do with that girl? The murdered girl?" Hugh suddenly realized that Wilson—more than anyone else he'd ever met—was old enough to know the truth behind the legend. He might even have been there when it happened.

"Bunch of durned nonsense," Wilson grumbled. He watched Hugh's face fall but set his jaw. "Best forget it. Just stay away from there." Hugh sat silent for a moment, disappointed, but Wilson changed his tone. "Now, what was it that was so all-fired important?"

Hugh explained what he had heard in the drugstore. Wilson's eyes narrowed while he let the boy finish telling what he knew, then he rubbed his chin.

"And there was this new guy with them," Hugh concluded. "He was dressed up to work, but he looked like some kind of boss or foreman. I know—my dad's a foreman, and he wears clothes like that. Lots of pens and pencils in his pocket. You know?"

"Engineer, likely."

"What would an engineer be doing here? I mean, this crane's coming by train, but—"

"Not that kind of engineer. Structural engineer. Builds buildings and such. Tears 'em down, too. He's probably some kind of expert."

Hugh repeated what he saw and heard and even illustrated it by smashing his fist into his palm as he had seen the engineer do.

"That's a big ol' railroad crane they're talking 'bout." Wilson rolled another smoke. "I seen 'em before. Come in on a flatcar. Too heavy for a truck to pull. They're pretty durned big. Could just do her."

"I don't think so," Hugh said with a smile.

"Why not?"

"Well, they've got to get it down to the side of the building," Hugh was proud of his investigation. "But there aren't any tracks down there. They won't be able to get it close enough."

"They's tracks there, all right," Wilson nodded.

"No," Hugh stood up and pointed off toward the old building. The top two floors were just visible as the rain began to taper off to a light, dripping drizzle. "I went and looked. There's nothing there but weeds and piles of dirt and stuff."

"And under the dirt and weeds and stuff is tracks. I know, boy. I helped lay 'em."

"Maybe they took them up."

"Too expensive. Steel was cheap in them days. They're still there. Bet your Saturday off on it."

"Well, then, that's it," Hugh's face fell, and he slumped against the building. "That's what he said. Hit the foundation hard, knock out the corner supports, and the sides will just cave in." He imitated the hand motions he had seen in the drugstore. "Give me the tobacco."

Wilson ignored the request. "Maybe. But I doubt it. They're likely to wound her up some, but they're not going to have anything like a easy time of it, rail crane or no rail crane."

"You think it won't work?"

"We'll see, boy," Wilson smiled to himself and reached out and scratched Goodlett's ears. "We'll see."

—<

"There's a meeting tomorrow night, and I want to go," Hugh announced over the roast beef leftovers on Monday night. He was already in trouble, he knew, for coming home dripping wet and tracking in all over his mother's kitchen. She told him he would have to mop the entire floor right after supper. He couldn't imagine the kind of punishment he would receive if she knew half the truth of what he had done that afternoon. He soon had an idea, though. Her whole body instantly tensed with his announcement.

Harry spooned a helping of Jonas Wilson's squash onto his plate and leaned down to take in the aroma of Parmesan cheese that covered the vegetable. "What would you do down there?" he asked.

"You'd just be in the way. It's going to be boring," Edith offered in a high, false voice. She sat down and began overfilling her plate with salad. Hugh's weekend labor and the payment therefor had provided the Rudd household with a surplus of fresh vegetables. The main dish—leftover roast—was barely touched as steamed beets, swimming in real butter for a change instead of margarine, crowded the plate next to the squash and fried okra. "It's just a bunch of busybodies getting together to talk about something they know nothing about." She gave Hugh a forced but serious smile.

"Well, I know something," Hugh said quietly, and both his parents stopped eating and looked at him.

"Well?" Edith demanded. "What?"

Hugh told about the rail crane, the buried tracks, and the plans he was certain the demolition crew was making for the destruction of the building. He left out Jonas Wilson's assessment of their potential success, but he did add what he had overheard about lawyers and Judge Parker.

"I heard Parker all of a sudden decided to stop cooperating with the railroad," Harry offered.

"This is turning ugly, Harry," Edith sighed when Hugh finished. "I don't like Hugh hanging around downtown eavesdropping on adults' conversations in the first place, and all this plotting and bickering is not a good sign."

"I've also heard Phelps Crane's been drinking more and more," Harry said around a mouthful of food, "causing more and more trouble." Edith concentrated on her plate and said nothing. An empty highball glass sat next to her plate, Hugh noted with some relief. At least she was eating something, not just drinking her way through supper. "My God, the man must be seventy-five," Harry went on. "I don't know how his system stands it. They say he hasn't been sober ten minutes since all this started."

"I don't think we need to discuss that here," Edith said with a quick, nervous glance toward Hugh.

"I saw him today," Hugh said. "He looks half crazy. I thought he was going to fight with—"

"You see what I mean?" Edith said sharply. She rose and went for more iced tea, although no one's glass needed replenishing. "Hugh's down there all day hanging around and picking up all sorts of things. The next thing you know—"

"He just sees what everyone sees, Edith," Harry Rudd said in a soft but firm voice. "He's getting older."

"And what's that supposed to mean?"

"You know what it's supposed to mean," Harry replied more sharply this time. "This is a small town, Edith. There aren't many secrets. Sooner or later, he's going to hear . . ." Harry trailed off, but Edith's eyes widened. She turned away and placed her hands on either side of the sink and stared down into it. "He's going to hear all about this business," Harry continued awkwardly. "About who's crazy, who's drunk, and what's going on. It's his town, too."

"That's why I want to go to the meeting," Hugh put in. Once again, he had the irritating feeling of being discussed as if he wasn't sitting right there in front of them.

"I don't know, Edith." Harry resumed eating and spoke with encouraging confidence. "In a way, it could be sort of educational. Democratic process and all that. Get it all out in the open. Better than hanging around and eavesdropping on people," he added.

"I wasn't eavesdropping," Hugh lied, amazed at how easily he slipped back into the habit. "I was sitting with Linda Fitzpatrick in a booth, and they were just talking right behind us. I couldn't help overhearing."

"Linda Fitzpatrick!" Edith jumped up and spun around as if she had been touched by a live wire. "Lydia Fitzpatrick's daughter?" Hugh nodded and concentrated on his plate. "Since when do you run around with her?"

"I don't run around with her." Hugh blushed.

"How old is she?" Edith demanded of Harry. "I thought she was in high school."

"We're the same age. We're in the same class."

"Well, I know that!" Edith exclaimed in a confused tone. She wiped her eyes with the knuckles of her hand and took a breath. "But isn't she . . . well, isn't she a little . . . uh, fast for you?"

"What?" Hugh was confused.

"I mean, she's a part of that country club crowd, isn't she?"

"Well, uh . . . yeah." Now Hugh was confused. "Maybe. So what? Lots of guys belong to the country club."

"That's not what I mean." She went over to the counter, but she could find nothing to do there and turned to face her husband and son. "I mean, well . . . Carl Fitzpatrick is running for city attorney."

"Mayor," Harry corrected between mouthfuls.

"Mayor?" Hugh's question was automatic. "I thought Pete Thompson was mayor."

"He is." Hugh's father looked up at his wife. Her face was a storm of confusion. He then shrugged slightly and went on. "One of the things that's going to happen is that Pete is going to resign. Tomorrow night."

"What?" Edith was stunned. She reached out her hand, groped for the kitchen chair, and took her seat. Her supper sat untouched in front of her.

"At the meeting, tomorrow night." Harry looked at his son, then took a breath and went on. "You're right about one thing, Edith. This is turning ugly. I'm not sure what's causing it. It's not just the building. It's something else, something about the whole damned town. Anyway, since neither Pete or anybody else could stop them from tearing down that old pile of bricks out there, the City Council is going to hold an emergency meeting tomorrow night. Pete will be asked to resign, and . . ." He hesitated, then plunged on. "Carl Fitzpatrick is going to be elected mayor pro tem. Or at least, that's the plan."

"Pro tem? What does that mean?" Hugh asked.

"It means," Edith answered, "that Phelps Crane and that bunch of crazy old fools is ganging up on the only good mayor this town has ever had." She rose, picked up the highball glass, and moved to the refrigerator's freezer for ice.

"You only feel that way because you and Loretta are . . . uh, good friends," Harry put in.

"Well, she's not part of that . . . that country club set," Edith returned. She pulled the whiskey bottle over, poured a generous dollop over the cubes.

Hugh suddenly realized what was wrong. He had no experience in the situation to back up his opinion, but his mother's reaction to the news that he was chummy with Linda Fitzpatrick, her attack on the town's well-to-do families—something that had always been vicious—and her dismay at learning that Pete Thompson was about to be ousted from office all pointed to some problem that went deeper than the Hendershot building or anything else they were discussing. He was surprised to see tears forming in her eyes.

"It's not fair," she yelled suddenly. "Loretta Thompson is a decent, good woman, and Pete is one of the few men in this town with an honest bone in his body." She wiped her eyes with a napkin, sat down with her drink. Mascara ran down her cheeks. Hugh was shocked to see how ugly she was becoming right in front of him. "They've worked hard for this town, treated everyone right, and now they're throwing them to the dogs because of this silly old building. I don't think he should be blamed because of something he couldn't do."

"It's not quite that simple," Harry said quietly. "It's not so much a question of what he could or couldn't do." He paused and glanced at Hugh once more, took a deep breath, and then continued. "It seems that Pete had a chance to have the building declared a national historical landmark a year ago. A committee came through here and offered to put a plaque on it, just like they did for the hotel. He turned them down flat. Practically ran them out of town, or so I hear."

"So?"

"Well, Carl Fitzpatrick, or so I also hear, has done some checking, and he discovered that Pete . . ." he trailed off once more, took another deep breath, and went on. "Well, it seems that Pete owns stock in Burlington Northern. A lot of stock. And, as a shareholder, he stands to benefit—"

"It's not true!" Edith's hand smacked down hard on the table and rattled the glasses. "Pete Thompson doesn't own a single share of stock! Not a share! Loretta would have told me."

"Maybe she didn't know."

"She knows! She knows everything about him. She's proud of the fact that he worked at the mill all those years, that they haven't piled up their money and lived like kings while the rest of us have . . . have—"

"Sometimes wives say things—"

Edith stood up and finished her sentence, "—have done without and supported one of our own kind—people just like us—working people—to lead this community." Hugh was shocked. His mother was drawn up to her full height and had thrust a finger high into the air as if she were giving a speech. "He is not a shareholder in any railroad company! In *any* company! He doesn't own a single scrap of stock in any—"

"Look," Harry's voice cracked like a whip across the kitchen. Edith deflated at once, almost collapsed, and had to hang onto the chair's back for support. Her eyes darted around the room, as if she expected someone to come from an unseen corner and attack her.

"I don't know," he said. "I'm not the one saying all this. It's all over the mill. From what I hear, it's all over town. A lot of people who don't care one way or the other about that old building are mad about it. There's talk of impeachment or something, even if they don't do anything about the building. It seems . . ."

Edith collapsed into the chair and emitted a long, low moan all of a sudden. She started rocking back and forth, holding her head. Harry looked at Hugh, alarmed. "Go out on the porch, Sport," he said quietly.

"I haven't finished eating." Hugh couldn't bear to leave.

"*Go out on the porch, Hugh.*" Harry's voice seemed to rattle the glasses and china in the cupboards. Edith flinched as if he had hit her.

Hugh rose. "Can I go to the meeting?"

"You most certainly *cannot*," Edith said, coming to herself all at once, matching Harry's volume and glaring at Hugh as if he were a stranger. Her face was pale, her lipstick smeared. She looked like a monster.

"Go on," Harry ordered in a softer voice, and Hugh grabbed up his plate and left the kitchen.

—<

The rain had stopped, and the evening sky was clear, washed deep in purple and orange. Mist rose from the garden and grass, and the air was thick with humidity. It would be baked completely away by noon the next day. He would be able to mow some tomorrow. He picked at the cold food on the plate. He'd better be able to, since he was now well short of having the mower payment due on Wednesday.

From the slide on the porch he heard his parents' voices rising and falling. His mother's sharp cries were matched by his father's angry shouts. Through the window, he could see both adults through the curtains when they paced back and forth in the kitchen. They both were drinking now, smoking and drinking furiously. After a while, things went quiet, and his mother went across the living room and toward her bedroom.

Harry soon came out, a drink in his hand. He wearily sat down on the porch.

"Damn shame to waste that food." He glanced at Hugh's plate. "Best meal we've had in months. And these days, I don't even get to finish the average ones." He smiled. "Did you get enough, Sport?"

Hugh nodded. "I want to go to the meeting, Dad."

"Well . . . I expect I'll go, so I guess you can, too."

"You're going?"

"Yeah. Guess so. Your mother wants me to go down and lay it all on the line for Pete Thompson." He shook his head.

"I didn't think you really liked Pete Thompson."

Harry sipped his drink and looked out into the gathering night. It seemed to Hugh that such back porch talks were becoming a tradition, and not a pleasant one.

"I don't, Sport," he admitted. "He was foreman before me, and I didn't like the way he treated the men who worked under him. He's a nice enough guy, I guess, but he was always using us to cover his own mistakes. You know, laying the blame on us for stuff that was really his responsibility. I don't know. He didn't do it a lot. But he did it when it really mattered. Maybe it *was* our fault. Maybe that's the way a foreman's supposed to be. I'm not that way, but I came up from the bottom out there. I've always believed a foreman owes his first loyalty to the men who work under him, not to the front office." He smiled again. "Maybe I'm just a sucker. Maybe Pete's all right. He has worked for a living. It's just that when I worked for him, I just always thought he was sneaky."

"A crook?"

Harry gave Hugh a sharp look. "No, just sneaky. Kept things to himself, things he needed to share. I was glad when he moved up into sales and got out of our hair."

"Is he a good mayor?"

"Your mother thinks so." Harry sighed deeply. "She and Mrs. Thompson have been friends a long time. When we first married, your mother felt all alone here. She was used to being in the military, moving to new places every few years, being a stranger and having to make new friends. But here, in a small town like this, everyone knows everyone. She was on the outside, I guess, and we didn't make the kind of money that would put us in with what she calls 'the country club set.'"

"Like the Fitzpatricks."

"Yeah, something like that. Anyway, they snubbed her, I guess. Made her feel poor and trashy."

"We're not trashy!" Hugh's ire rose again. Linda's silly prating about shopping at the Galleria and eating in fancy restaurants with names he couldn't remember or even spell crossed his memory, and he involuntarily made a fist.

"No," Harry spoke rapidly. "Of course not. I'm a working man. Always have been. So was Pete Thompson. Once," he added softly. "Anyway, Loretta—Mrs. Thompson—she sort of took your mother under her wing. When we were expecting you, they were like sisters. She was over here a lot, every night, in fact. The night you were born, Loretta stayed right with her, right through delivery."

"Where were you?"

"Oh, I was there, too. But—" He stared off again. Hugh was embarrassed. "Your mother didn't want much to do with me. She just wanted Loretta." He coughed and sipped again. "It was kind of a female thing. Something you'll understand when you're older. Anyway, when your brother . . . when Larry died, it was Loretta all over again. Half the time I slept on the sofa, and they . . . well, they were just very close."

Something dark and slimy quivered in Hugh's stomach. "What do you mean, Dad?"

"Oh, nothing," Harry said. "Loretta's just one of those women who always gets her way. She thought she knew what your mother needed. Maybe she did. That's what the shrink said, anyway."

"Shrink?" Hugh asked as if the word were a foreign term.

"I shouldn't even be talking about this with you," Harry said. He lit a cigarette. "But you might as well know. Your mother went to a psychiatrist. She was in therapy for a long time after Larry died. I was, too. With her. Same shrink." He waved his arm in the evening's air as if to ward off the past. "The thing is," he went on, "your mother's kind of high-strung. Delicate. You know."

"Fragile." Hugh recalled the word his father most often used.

"Yeah. Fragile. She can't take a lot of pressure."

"But you—" Hugh broke off. He wanted to say that he had seen his father putting pressure on his mother, snapping at her about supper, sometimes, Hugh thought, being mean to her. "I mean, you say things to her."

Harry looked at his son. "Hugh, it's hard to explain. I'm know I say things to her, 'fuss' at her, I guess you would say. But she needs that. That's what the shrink told me. That's what he said she got from Loretta, what she didn't get from me, I guess. I just try to do what he—what I think is best. I'm not mean to her. I treat her all right. Hell, son, I love her. I love you. More than anything."

"I still don't see what the Fitzpatricks have to do with anything," Hugh pressed the point. "I mean, Linda's just a kid in my class." Hugh thought how much more she was to him than "just a kid in my class," but he had his father talking. He wanted to probe more deeply.

"Back when your brother . . . when Larry died, well, there was some trouble. You were too young to pay any attention to it, but . . . well, Lydia Fitzpatrick sort of started it all."

"What kind of trouble?"

"Rumors." He looked at Hugh. "I shouldn't tell you this. Promise you won't tell your mother what I'm going to tell you." Hugh nodded eagerly. "Larry, your brother, as you know, just died." Hugh nodded again. "He had his morning bottle, and he was asleep. Your mother checked him, just like we do you, even now, and he was fine. Then she went in to check him again, and he was just gone. Just like that. That's all there was to it."

"I know all that," Hugh was again embarrassed. "I was here, remember?" When his parents talked about Larry, it made him feel unaccountably guilty, as if it were his fault his brother had died.

"I know you know. I know you were here. What you don't know is that someone—your mother believes Mrs. Fitzpatrick—started a rumor that she, well . . . that somehow it was her fault that Larry died."

"How could it have been?" Hugh was shocked. "He just died. They called it 'crib death' or something like that."

"That's what it was," Harry spoke sharply. "The doctor said so, and the medical examiner said so. Everyone knew that. But someone didn't know it, or didn't want to know it, or for some reason wanted to hurt your mother—and me—and . . ." Harry wiped his eyes hard as if his head was aching. "Anyway, Carl Fitzpatrick's law partner, Otis Simpson, was county attorney, and he filed charges against your mother."

"Charges?"

"They tried to say that she . . . that she killed your brother."

Hugh's jaw fell open. Anger filled him. He came to his feet. "That's a lie!" he shouted. He wanted to run to her, hug her close.

"Sit down!" Harry ordered. "She doesn't want you to know all this."

Hugh stood defiantly for a moment, but finally he gave in part of the way to his father's glare and squatted beside him.

"How," he began, "how did they say she . . ."

"Negligence." Harry squared his shoulders and then let them sag once more. "They said she was drunk, not paying attention to him. That she had too much to drink and passed out in the living room and didn't hear him, didn't check him."

"But it's not true."

"No, it's not true."

"I was here."

"I know. But you weren't much more than a baby yourself. But you probably knew more about it than anybody who was going around talking about it. It was all based on rumors, gossip, lies. People want to believe the worst about people, I guess, especially if they're hurt, wounded somehow. Pretty soon, the rumors are more believable than the facts, and then it becomes a federal case."

"So what happened?" Hugh searched his memory and came up with no help. "She didn't have to go to jail or anything?" He ran his mind through a hundred cop shows where suspects were arrested, booked. He couldn't visualize his mother going through that.

"No, it never came to that. Loretta—Mrs. Thompson—heard about it, and she—and Pete—went to the sheriff and then to Judge Parker. They dropped charges the same day they made them. There wasn't any cause for it in the first place. They stuck up for her completely, for both of us, really. They were right here through the whole thing, practically moved in. Don't you remember that? I think they would have if the doctor—the shrink—hadn't told them to move out." He sighed. "That was one thing he was right about."

Hugh did remember the funeral and all the people who came and went through the house. Now that he thought about it, Loretta Thompson was there a lot—day and night, in fact. He had never much cared for her. She wore thick, heavy perfume that seemed to settle and stick on everything it touched, and she always seemed at the time to insert herself between Edith and anyone else who wanted to approach her, especially Hugh himself. "Your mother's sick," she would lecture him. "She needs to sleep, so you be a good boy and play quietly."

Hugh furrowed his brow and tried to recall more about those days. He couldn't remember his father being around the house much when Loretta was there. In fact, Hugh thought, he couldn't remember his father being around at all from the time Larry died until later, much later. He must have been there, of course, Hugh told himself. He was only at work, gone during the day when Hugh was awake. But Loretta, Hugh now remembered, was always there. He now thought of how often he associated the detested living room with her presence, her scowling face and heavy cheeks, her stern lessons on the need for him to be a "good boy."

He sat silently beside his father as the crickets and katydids began to sense the darkness and began their night songs. "So that's why she hates the Fitzpatricks?"

"That's part of it. There's no reason for her to believe that Lydia Fitzpatrick—or Carl—had anything to do with it, although they may have. Rich people get bored sitting around and playing golf and bridge or whatever they do out at the country club. Pretty soon, rumor can become fact if it's repeated enough. Everyone likes to gossip. When the true stuff ran out, it's possible they just made it up."

"Why?" Hugh was amazed at the truth behind his father's words. He knew that kids did that sort of thing, just to get attention or to try to work themselves in with a new crowd. But was it possible that adults did it?

"It's hard to say why, Hugh," he said. "One thing was your mother's attitude about things."

"Like what?"

"Well, drinking, for one. She was used to a place where you could have a drink or two in public, where, when people entertained in their homes, they put out a lot of booze."

"They don't do that here," Hugh noted.

"This is a dry county," Harry explained. "Always has been, since before I was born, anyway. Lots of drinking goes on, of course, but it's all kept under wraps. Everyone pretends they're against it, then they have a drink to celebrate their hypocrisy. But your mother didn't understand that. She had a little too much to drink from time to time, and people started talking."

"I don't get it," Hugh said. "There's a bar right in the country club. Heck, Mr. Fitzpatrick's got coolers full of beer right downtown, and Phelps Crane—"

"I know, I know," Harry shook his head. "It's all so silly and stupid that it stinks. But there are ways of doing things here, and your mother had a hard time adjusting to that. She never could understand how mean people could be when their way of doing things is upset by somebody who doesn't play by the rules."

"So, just because Mom had a drink or two—" Hugh started.

"Hugh," Harry's voice was low and even. "You might as well know it. When we got married, even when we came here, your mother had a drinking problem, and so did I." He paused for a moment. "We weren't alcoholics or anything. We didn't drink every day, even every week. But when we drank, we drank a lot."

"A lot," Hugh said, a numb fear growing inside him, thinking of how much they had been drinking lately. What, he wondered, was his father's definition of "a lot"? He felt something collapse inside him. It was as if he didn't know his parents at all, he thought. As if the people he thought were his parents had somehow been replaced by these strangers with mysterious pasts about which he was totally ignorant.

"I mean a lot," Harry said, as if he was reading Hugh's thoughts. "I'm not bragging about it. Just telling you. We were young. That's not an excuse

I'd let you get away with. But we were foolish, too." He gestured to the glass in his hand. "Sometimes, we went out after we'd had a few drinks, and we were loud and probably obnoxious. We both got a couple of tickets for drunk driving, and—"

"But—"

"Let me finish. When you were born, about two years after we moved here, we stopped drinking. At least in front of anyone. I mean, we knew about all the talk we'd caused, and even though we pretended it didn't matter, we didn't want it to go on. I mean, even now, we keep a bottle here, and we have a drink or two from time to time. But we don't drink like we used to, nothing like that, and we only drink at home."

"I see," Hugh said. He couldn't think of any other words, but he knew that their drinking had escalated well beyond "from time to time" over the past week or so.

"I thought all the talk had died down. But when Larry died . . . well, that's what was at the bottom of all the rumors."

"So they thought you were alcoholics," Hugh said. "And that Mom—"

"I don't know," Harry sighed. "And I don't know if Lydia had anything to do with it or not. To tell you the truth, I kind of doubt it. I don't think she knows we're alive. But when Otis Simpson died of a heart attack last year and Carl announced that he would run for city attorney, Loretta and your mother decided that it was the Fitzpatricks who were behind the rumors about Larry's death from the start. Maybe they were. Maybe they weren't." All at once, Hugh realized that Harry was no longer talking to him. He was talking to himself. "It doesn't make any sense, but none of it ever did. It was all a lot of bullshit. Just pure, mean bullshit."

Harry glared now at some invisible object. "They always hated her because she was better than they are. Hell, she's turned down membership in fancier clubs than that damn country club. Her father, your grandfather, was an officer, a navy captain. He commanded an aircraft carrier, and your mother was raised in a different kind of place from here. A place with a whole different attitude."

"What do you mean?"

"Oh, you know. She was the head honcho's little girl. When they lived in Norfolk, she was a deb, you know."

"A deb?"

"Debutante. She had a coming-out party with lots of society people around. She went to one of the best finishing schools in Virginia." Harry sighed. "Then to Bryn Mawr. She grew up in high society. She had a lot of nice things: money, a big house. You know the kind of place Grandpa and Grandma live in down in Corpus."

"Big house," Hugh confirmed and thought of the Ocean Drive house with its large lawn and palm trees surrounding a big circular driveway. His grandparents owned two Cadillacs and had a Land Rover with four-wheel drive they took to the beach. They had a large swimming pool, a boat they could take out into the ocean, and they also had a Vietnamese maid and a Mexican gardener. He had never thought of them as rich. It was just the way grandparents lived, he imagined. The way city people lived. That his grandparents Rudd had never enjoyed such luxuries did not seem to contradict that logic. They were country people, farmers. It seemed natural for them to live in an old house, to appear the way they looked in the old photos. It always just seemed normal. Until now.

"So, when your mom married me—a hick nobody from hick nowhere—and moved here to Hicksville—the smack-dab middle of nowhere—she had to give all that up."

"High society," Hugh commented softly, thinking of a movie he saw on the late show once.

"Something like that. We couldn't afford the country club, but we get out from time to time. We just drive that old Ford wagon, but it gets us around. And we have a pretty nice house, which we mostly own, I'm proud to say. But compared to the Fitzpatricks, we're not doing so hot."

"We do all right." Hugh wanted, suddenly, to put his arm on his father's shoulder. But he folded his hands in his lap.

"I know we do. I make good money. We've got a lot in savings, and," he whispered conspiratorially, "I *do* own some stock." He smiled. "But not in the railroad." He put his hand on Hugh's knee and patted it. "You're guaranteed a chance at college, maybe even a new car to go in—that's not a promise," he inserted with a false cough, "and while we don't shop at Neiman Marcus, we do a little better than Wal-Mart." Hugh nodded. "But sometimes, that's not enough."

He stood, drained his drink, and moved to the slide. "It's not money, not even how much you make or how much you have. It's what you do with it, I guess. In a small town, it's what they'll let you do with it."

"What do you mean?"

"Well, your mother always thought she was . . . well, pretty hot stuff. When she came here with me, she found out that the 'hot stuff' around here didn't think she was worth the freight."

"Huh?"

"The Fitzpatricks—the 'country club set,' as she calls them—didn't want to treat her as if she was good enough to be a part of their crowd, and your mother thought—she knew—that in another place, Corpus, for instance, they'd be nothing but a bunch of hayseeds, and she'd be top drawer. It's kind of in the way you look at it. You see, it's not her. It's me—who I am and what I do. Here, what a man does for a living says everything about what sort of people he is. What class he belongs to."

"Class? You mean, high class, low class, like that?"

"Yeah, I guess. I'm working class, a working man. Not a lawyer or a doctor or a big politician. I didn't go to college—well, I took some courses while I was in the navy, got a two-year degree in industrial management, but that doesn't count. I married your mother, came back here, and took the best-paying job I could find. But it's a job—not a profession. I punch a clock, say 'yessir' to men I know I'm smarter—and better—than. That makes me a working stiff. Not a big deal. Hell, even ranchers and some of the farmers around here are pretty high-toned."

"So we're low class?"

"No," Harry spoke sharply and then retreated again into his low voice. "We're just middle class. Working middle class, they call it. But that's not good enough for the Fitzpatricks and their crowd. But I'm in middle management now. We can afford the country club, if we wanted to belong—which we don't—and we're doing all right. I might make a promotion to the front office if I don't screw up."

"Like how?"

He took a beat. "Like getting involved in this building mess." He shook his head. "This is a big push going nowhere. There's nothing to it."

"I think the building is important."

"The building's got nothing to do with it." Harry pointed a finger at Hugh's chest. "This is a power play, nothing else. Oh, a couple of those old idiots like Phelps Crane and the rest mean well enough. They're pissed off at the railroad, and this is their way of getting some payback. But for Carl and the rest of that crowd, this is a way of getting Pete Thompson kicked out of office and putting somebody like Carl in."

"I don't see how that will help them." Hugh shook his head and was surprised to find himself feeling exactly the way his father looked.

"It won't. Not just now. But mayor is only a step away from state representative or senator. Who knows? Carl could do a lot of them a lot of good down in Austin. He may be a class-A prick, but he's a sharp lawyer, and he knows politics."

Hugh did not react to his father's language, although he'd never in his life heard him be so vulgar. "So, what about Mom? Is she all right?"

"Oh, yeah," Harry smiled. "She'll be fine. You know how high-strung she is. She's gone to bed, and you and I can wash up, maybe dig into that peach pie she baked for dessert."

"I mean about . . . about Larry and all?"

"Oh, that. Yeah. I mean, she'll never get over Larry's dying, and she'll probably always remember what it was like to be blamed for it. She blamed herself enough anyway. I blame myself. But it's probably best not to mention the Fitzpatricks around here much. I wouldn't. I don't."

Hugh's mind filled with Linda's golden image. "She's awful pretty, Dad," he admitted in spite of himself. It seemed like an evening for candor, and he was again surprised to discover how comfortable he felt talking to his father like a friend.

His father smiled. "I said the same thing to my father about your mother, once. Your grandpa Rudd was worried that I was marrying too far above myself, that she would ruin me."

"But she didn't?"

"No." He rose and put his arms around Hugh once more. "She hasn't yet. The truth is that she's the best thing that ever happened to me. Second to you, of course."

Hugh lowered his eyes. "Linda wants me to come to a party tomorrow night. At the country club. At the pool."

"No kidding?" Harry thought for a moment.

"I'd rather go to the meeting."

"I don't know for sure," Harry chuckled, "but given a choice, I suspect your mother'd rather the same thing." He studied Hugh across the dark back porch. "You know, you're growing up. I don't know why, but I'm just now seeing it in a way. You know, having a talk like this: man to man, I guess you'd call it. I'm feeling it."

"So, I can go?"

"If you keep quiet and listen. Try to learn something."

Hugh spoke with more cheer than he felt, "I try to learn something out of everything I do."

"That'a boy."

CHAPTER NINE

Hugh's attempt to digest all his father had told him the night before provided him with a sleepless, fretful night. He rose and left the house early to avoid both his parents, checked to confirm that it was still too wet to mow that morning, then pedaled downtown and spent money he couldn't afford on a breakfast he didn't want or even finish at the drugstore's counter. It was nearly the last of his cash, and he was more worried than ever. He hoped to hear more news, but the store was nearly empty, so Hugh left the eggs and hash browns cooling on his plate and took a long bike ride around the small city's perimeters, tried to clear his head, put things into perspective.

He had little luck, and the lack of sleep and latent exhaustion from his weekend labors combined to make his legs sore and heavy as he pushed the old bike against a light breeze. The sweat he worked up felt good on his back, though, and strengthened a resolve to stick by his father, no matter what. He didn't want to add to his troubles. Nagging thoughts about the mower payment crept around his mind, but he planned to mow all afternoon and most of the next day to make up for lost time and money.

When he circled the city and arrived once more downtown, he discovered a larger crowd than ever gathered on the parking lot. It was too muddy for the men to do too much real work on the building, but the bulldozers were busily pushing back the weedy piles of wet gravel and sand to make a clearly defined pathway that, Hugh presumed, would soon expose the old railbed and buried tracks Jonas had mentioned. The roar of the machines' engines soon attracted people from downtown, and well before noon, over two hundred had gathered to watch and speculate as to what was going on. More seemed to arrive every few minutes.

The holiday atmosphere of Friday had worn out, Hugh noticed. Now, the people just milled around and talked among themselves in low tones. They seemed apprehensive and a little confused, as if they were waiting for someone to start the party, but they were uncertain about whose party it was.

Three or four newspaper reporters from Wichita Falls, Amarillo, and Fort Worth had arrived. They wore plastic badges identifying themselves as "Press," but it was hardly necessary. They moved through the crowd asking questions of everyone, jotting down notes on pads, peering down at the worksite as if they expected something big to happen right away.

Grissom drove up and parked his car beside the old Railway Express Office. He stood beside it, glowering at the growing crowd while he ignored the shouted questions of reporters. The REO was a squat red-brick building perched on the worksite side of the railbed, across the street from the depot parking lot. It had been closed since passenger-mail service was suspended.

Grissom had apparently ordered it reopened. Two workers from the site came up and pulled the plywood away from the large front window. From time to time, he paced back and forth by his car and talked angrily into a cellular phone. In a while, a crew from West Texas Utilities arrived and turned on power.

Grissom's new companion, the engineer, also soon drove up in a Jeep. He was accompanied by another man in white coveralls. They conferred with Grissom, then began traveling back and forth from the worksite for consultations with Grissom. Another small travel trailer arrived and was parked close to the REO. Men unfurled an awning and set up tables with walkie-talkies on them outside the vehicle's open door.

Hugh moved through the growing crowd, watched the activity, and kept his mouth shut, his ears open. Jonas Wilson, who was back beside his regular pylon, caught his eye when the crew down by the building broke for lunch, and he gestured. Hugh went around the block and met him under the chinaberry tree.

Hugh didn't have much to report that Wilson hadn't seen, but he was bursting to tell him some of the things his father had said. He just didn't know how to bring it up. For a while, they sat silently, shared tomato sandwiches and hot coffee from Wilson's old Thermos. Hugh waited for Wilson to break the silence, to create some kind of opening.

"They'll have the tracks cleared up by nightfall," Wilson finally speculated. "If it hadn't rained, it'd take 'em longer, but the ground's soft 'round there now, and them dozers're having no trouble."

"They're working hard at it," Hugh agreed. He slipped Goodlett a scrap of bacon he had taken from the refrigerator.

"If they back her up all the way from Wichita Falls, they'll be here early in the morning, and then they can set her down, rig her up, and have at it by noon."

"Maybe." Hugh smiled.

"Ain't no maybe to it." Wilson's bushy eyebrows narrowed. "What'd you learn, boy?"

Hugh sighed with relief. He thought he'd never ask. He told Wilson about the planned town meeting, the ouster of Pete Thompson, and with some satisfaction in corroborating the old man's prediction about Carl's rising ambitions, he announced his father's assessment that Carl Fitzpatrick would soon be running for higher office.

"I don't doubt it, boy," Wilson agreed and cut a slice of cheese away from the heel he produced from his bag. "People're like a bunch of snakes 'bout half the time. They'll bite anything that moves. Other half, they're like sheep. Follow any judas—or any jackass—that'll stand up and walk in a half straight line."

"My dad's going to try to stop them."

"Stop 'em from what?"

"From getting rid of Mr. Thompson. They're sort of friends." Hugh wasn't ready to discuss the deeper relationship between the two families.

"Heck, boy, that won't do no good. It'll only fly back and get his britches' leg wet."

"What do you mean by that?"

"Pete Thompson's no durn good!" Wilson declared. "His daddy was a thief. Died in prison."

Hugh gave him a shocked look.

"Over to Oklahoma. McAlester State Penitentiary. That was back during the Depression. Stole a bunch of turkeys from a poultry farm up near Chickasha. Oklahoma state troopers chased him down, and he shot one of 'em 'fore they quickgrabbed him and threw him in jail for life. Ol' Pete was just a little bitty thing then."

Wilson chuckled. "Shoot, boy, it runs in the family. He had a uncle used to run cockfights up near Altus. His granddaddy was a horse thief, as I recollect. Hung him right down there on the courthouse square. That'd been aught-two or aught-three. I remember 'cause it wasn't but a month later I seen my first automobile on the same spot."

Hugh gaped at the old man. "They hanged him?"

"Right down yonder. I seen the whole thing. I wasn't much older'n you when it—"

"C'mon, Jonas," Hugh scoffed suddenly. "It seems like everything you've ever done you did when you were my age. I thought you were a cowboy then. When you lost your fingers, remember?"

Wilson looked wounded. "That's right, Mr. Smarty-pants. I was cow-boying, and I lost my fingers to that rattler, just like I said." Wilson gave Hugh a sideways look. "You can believe it or not. Makes no nevermind to me."

"And then you walked back to the Wilson place and found that grave, the place where your real mother was buried?"

"That's right. Was the same year."

"C'mon, Jonas," Hugh laughed. "I'm just a kid, but I'm not stupid."

"What's stupid 'bout it?"

"Well, in the first place, you can't have done everything at the same time, and in the second place, you don't have your times straight. You said you were a cowboy back before the Hendershot building was built, and that was just after the turn of the century." Hugh gave him a steady look. "I can count, Jonas."

"Well, I might not have the times right, but I remember it anyhow."

"Yeah," Hugh giggled and reached for the tobacco sack and rolled him-self a cigarette. "Tell me another one."

"You calling me a liar?"

"I'm saying you're pulling my leg. That's different." Hugh leaned back and lit his smoke.

Wilson sulked and wrinkled his brow under his hat. For a moment, Hugh was uncomfortable, for the old man looked suddenly mean, and his face darkened. He sat and pouted.

"What part of the county did I say I worked in when I was cowboying?"

Hugh thought for a moment. "Northeast."

"And where was it I told you the ol' Wilson place was?"

"West."

"Well, just how in heck you expect me to get from out yonder," he pointed northeast, "to over yonder," he pointed toward the west, "'less I come through town?"

"Well . . ." Hugh sat up and thought about it.

"They wasn't no courthouse there, then. Just a big ol' empty square. Fact of the matter was, this here'd only been the county seat for a while. They was handling business—holding court and the like—in a tent."

"What'd they hang him from?" Hugh warily baited the old man. "There aren't any trees on the square."

"Wagon," Wilson set his jaw. "Put a singletree in the ground, and made him stand in a wagon, and whipped the horses to make him run. Hung there two days 'fore they let his family cut him down and bury him. I remember now. It was sleeting."

Hugh leaned back again. He wasn't going to swallow everything Wilson said any longer. He knew him well enough now to tolerate his tall tales.

"Well, it doesn't make any difference what his grandfather or father did. He's mayor, and they want to get rid of him, and Dad's going to try to stop them."

Wilson shook his head. "If he sticks his hand in that mess, he's like to jerk back a stub."

"Why?"

"I told you why."

"That's not good enough," Hugh came up on his knees. "What else do you know?"

"Well," Wilson studied the boy, then shook his head. "You're too young to know 'bout this." He turned away.

"I'm not." Hugh was frightened again, the way he felt the night before, talking to his father. "Tell me."

Wilson averted his eyes away from the boy, but Hugh scooched around and searched the old man's face, forced contact. Wilson finally sighed.

"Well, you're going to hear 'bout it sooner or later. We've broke bread together, worked side by side. Traded secrets. Traded smoke. I guess I might as well be the one to tell you."

Hugh once more thought of how often Jonas and his father said the same things to him. He wondered if they would like each other if they met.

"It ain't just Pete," Jonas said slowly. "I mean, he's probably a thief just like his daddy and granddaddy, but he ain't never done nothing bad enough to go to jail for. Not yet, anyhow."

"So what is it?"

"It's his wife."

"Loretta? Mrs. Thompson?"

"Yeah," Wilson rubbed his chin. "She ain't . . . well, she ain't a whole woman."

"What does that mean?"

"Well, you ever hear of her being a schoolteacher?"

Hugh thought for a minute. "Yeah, so?"

"Well, they fired her."

"So? What did she do?" In Hugh's mind, all teachers could be divided into categories: good and bad. The good ones usually got married or moved on. The bad ones remained in the classroom to torture students.

"Well, she taught the girls their exercises in the high school."

"You mean P.E."

"Yeah, I reckon." Wilson rolled a cigarette, and Hugh was surprised to see the old man's hands shaking. Hugh began to get the same nasty, sick feeling from the night before when his father spoke of Loretta Thompson. He sensed that if he would tell Wilson to forget the whole thing, it would go away. He couldn't.

"Well, anyway," Wilson continued, his voice halting. "It come out that she was sort of . . . sort of sweet on a couple of the girls."

"Sweet on them?" Hugh's mind couldn't register the complaint. What could Wilson mean? "Sweet on them?" he repeated.

"You know. Queer for 'em," Wilson said angrily. "Ain't that what you young'uns call it? She ain't a whole woman. She's a woman who likes women more than she likes men. Or so they say." He lit the cigarette and flung the match away. "There, I told you. I didn't want to, but you made me."

Hugh's mind was spun once, then settled hard. He sat down on his hams, held the cigarette away from him. It wasn't possible. It was stunning. His next thought was how much he would relish telling Tommy and Ray, maybe even Linda—no, his thoughts recoiled from the prospect—not Linda, not ever Linda. Then his memory kicked in: "It was kind of a female thing," Harry had said, "Half the time, I slept on the sofa . . . they were just very close." Hugh remembered the look on his father's face, and now he heard the pain in his voice, the pain behind his eyes. His father. His mother. Hugh's insides collapsed, as if he was a balloon that suddenly deflated. He was suddenly very sick.

"It's a lie," he gasped a mouthful of air. "It's a goddamn, son-of-a-bitching lie!" His words tumbled out just ahead of his stomach's contents, and he raised himself up, hunched over, and vomited in great heaves. He was barely conscious of Wilson's twisted fingers across his brow, holding his head up and away from his chest as the convulsions seized him completely.

"Let it out, boy," Wilson's voice reached his ears. "Let it all out."

Hugh gained control over his body at last and lay back on the grass and weeds. "It's a lie," he croaked bitterly. "You're a liar! A goddamn liar!"

"I never said it was a truth," Wilson muttered. He reached out and stroked Goodlett's ears. "I said it's what people say."

"It's still a lie! And it's wrong to repeat it. I don't care who says it."

"Let me tell you something, boy," Wilson said softly. "My telling you that wasn't in the nature of gossip. I'm just pointing out something that was there all the time. You need to see it, elsewise you'll run right smooth into it and hurt yourself. Worse'n you're hurting now. Bet on it."

"But my dad—"

"Your daddy knows it's there. He's seen it. If he's bent on taking a run at it, power to him. But he'll lose, likely. You can't knock down granite with a baseball bat. It's all of a piece, I'm telling you. You're old enough to learn that much."

Hugh lay still and said nothing. Thoughts of his mother and the red-headed older woman who had sat so often in their living room, her thick arms around Edith, her hugs and cloying perfume filling the atmosphere of the house like noxious gas, her insistence on her love for "Edith and Edith's family," all came flooding out of his memory in strong, pulsating images. Wilson was right, Hugh thought: His father knew. He knew all along what was happening, what was going on, and there was nothing he could do. Nothing but leave, and that wasn't something Harry could do, either.

That kind of thing wasn't talked about openly, Hugh understood. It wasn't like drinking or getting caught doing something by the police. It was worse than murder. People talked out loud about that sort of thing. But they didn't talk about . . . about what? Hugh wondered. What was it called? Love affairs? Queers? Lesbos? They snickered about it in school and on campouts, talked about "spinster sisters" who weren't related, about "old bachelors" who never married and preferred the company of men, about their schoolmates, male and female, who chose classes and activities more suited to their opposite sexes. They called the boys "pansies," "fairies," and other names. The girls they called just "tomboys" or, if they wanted to be mean, "butch." It was the kind of thing that happened in movies, on television, maybe. It happened in New York, in Hollywood, but it didn't happen here. Not really. It was all campfire and boy's lockerroom chatter.

This was different. This was serious. And it was real.

Hugh's eyes closed against the sky. His stomach heaved again, and his throat closed. He clenched his fists and wanted to cry. He wanted it to be yesterday when all he had to worry about was how many lawns he could mow in a day. He wanted it to be last week, when a Yosemite Mountain Bike was the only thing in the world he desired. He wanted to be a baby again, totally dependent on the goodness of his parents, his teachers, his friends. He threw one arm over his closed eyes and sighed. He prayed that all this was a dream, a nightmare, that he would soon hear his mother's voice calling to him that it was getting late and that he needed to rise and get out and start mowing. His mind reeled back and forth, and he felt an ant or something biting him beneath his shirt. He ignored it. The bite wouldn't be there when he awoke, he told himself, and he would be awake soon.

Hugh drifted off into a fitful, hot sleep and didn't awaken until he felt more ant bites on his arms and back. He leaped up, stripped off his T-shirt, used the battered Yankees cap to swat away the insects, then the shirt to wipe his sweaty body clean. The old man and dog were gone, and his watch told him he had lain under the tree for more than two hours. He put on his shirt and made his way groggily back to the parking lot, where the crowd was larger than it had been before. It all did seem like a bad dream, now, or at least most of it did. He refused to think about it anymore.

"I'm sorry," he muttered and eased through the crowd and moved up beside Wilson. "I didn't mean to call you a liar."

Wilson turned his dark eyes toward the boy and stared at him. "It's a mean thing," he said quietly. "But you're young. You'll learn to live with it. Or you won't." He pulled up his sack, removed the Thermos, poured a cup of coffee into the cap, and thrust it out toward Hugh. He accepted it and sipped. When Hugh finished, Wilson passed over the tobacco, and Hugh, unmindful and uncaring of who might be watching, casually rolled a smoke and allowed Wilson to light it.

"Right now, you're going to have to find us somewhere else to go to eat," Wilson said. "You ruint that spot." He then turned back to the workers' efforts to uncover and restore the buried railbed. They stood there together, side by side, all afternoon.

PART II: THE MAN

CHAPTER ONE

The town meeting began promptly at eight, and Hugh and Harry Rudd arrived after things were already well under way. Harry had also had a long day, Hugh learned over a desultory supper of soup and sandwiches during which Edith said very little but merely looked at both of them with a drawn, severe expression. He had been called into the front office and grilled for twenty minutes about his attitude regarding what was going on in town. The mill's corporate management was worried that too many of the workers were showing an interest in blocking the railroad's demolition of the structure, a worry that was compounded by the sudden appearance of bumper stickers that read, "Save the Hendershot Building" on several cars and pickups in the mill's parking lot.

The rumor was that Carl Fitzpatrick was behind the bumper sticker campaign. Another rumor suggested that a half-dozen employees who called in sick were seen hanging around the old depot parking lot, watching the proceedings.

Harry explained to his son and wife that he disavowed any interest one way or another in what might be the fate of the Hendershot Grocery Warehouse, but when he admitted that he planned to attend the meeting that evening, his boss, Gary Riley, an enormously fat man with a crewcut and bulldog's expression, cautioned him that he might be putting his job in jeopardy.

"I told him to go to hell," Harry confessed to his family. "Probably set myself back on the promotion list five years, but I couldn't let that slob sit there sucking his cigar and telling me that I couldn't exercise my right as a free citizen. I mean, who the hell is *he* to tell me I can't attend a town meeting?"

"You are absolutely right!" Edith agreed. "It's awful! The nerve of the man, trying to tell you what to do on your own time. What did he say when you told him off?"

"Well, he calmed down some. He didn't exactly apologize or anything, but he asked me not to wear anything with the mill's name on it—you know, a cap or anything. Then he wished me luck, and that was all there was to it."

Hugh noticed that his father's casual manner was belied by a tightness around his lips. His parents had had several rounds of drinks before supper. His mother's mouth remained a tight thin line, and the wrinkles around her eyes seemed unusually pronounced.

"I spoke to Loretta today," Edith sighed. Hugh's attention was immediately arrested at the mention of her name. "She said that there was nothing to all of this talk about Pete's owning stock. I told her I would go down and try to talk some sense to them, but she begged me not to. I can't understand it."

She glanced nervously at Hugh. "She just insisted that I stay away. She and Pete are coming over here after."

"Here?" Harry's eyebrows shot up.

"Yes, here," Edith said. "She—both of them—were there for us when we needed them, and we're going to be here for them. They're coming over here, and that's that."

"I hope they don't stay late," Harry muttered with a sideways glance at Hugh. "Some people have to work tomorrow."

"They'll stay as late as they like," she stated, sat down. The rest of the meal passed in uneasy silence.

When Hugh arrived at the meeting with his father, his thoughts were a wall to shut out the things Wilson had told him. Still, his father looked weary while he shook hands with a number of men and threaded through the chairs that had been arranged in front of a long table set upon a platform. Nine other chairs were pulled up behind the table, and Judge Parker, Pete Thompson, Carl Fitzpatrick, and the rest of the City Council members were already seated, banging their fists on the table for order while the people stood around the room and talked in tones varying from gossipy humor to angry declarations.

Between May and September, the various lodges that used the hall removed their meetings to the pavilion at Medicine Lake, and the room was not ordinarily used for summertime gatherings. A creaky old air conditioner tried to keep the evening's humidity at bay, but men were already sweating. Tobacco smoke filled the high ceilings and was not entirely dispersed by the half-dozen fans that turned in slow, rusty protest.

"I told you people if you don't sit down and be quiet, we won't get anything done!" Pete Thompson yelled at the crowd.

Judge Parker kept banging a book down on the table and yelling, "Order!"

Finally the hubbub died down, and people—mostly men—took their seats. Harry sat next to some men Hugh recognized as being from the mill, and the boy walked to the back of the room and stood in a corner. He passed Phelps Crane on his way. The stench rising from the old railroad worker filled his nostrils and made him gag. The only change in his appearance was a gray and white striped railroader's cap perched on his balding head. He gave Hugh a nasty look when he passed, but Hugh was distracted from the old conductor's appearance by the sight of two of the newspaper reporters, who sat quietly against the far wall, next to the kitchen door, their notebooks on their knees.

"The first thing is that this is an extraordinary meeting of the council, and the rules are suspended," Elton Matthews, chairman of the City Council, said. "You can't introduce any new business, and we can't take up any old business. Minutes will be kept, though." He nodded at Gracie Gholston, the junior high school principal, who sat primly in front of a small table with a legal pad open in front of her. She smiled briefly and began jotting down everything Elton said.

"We're here to decide one thing, and one thing only," Elton continued, "and that's what to do about the continuing demolition of the Hendershot building." He smiled all around and seated himself. "The chair recognizes the mayor, His Honor, Mr. Pete Thompson."

The mayor stood up and gave a nervous smile to the crowd while he unfolded a sheet of paper. Hugh spotted Loretta Thompson standing in a corner by herself. She was old, Hugh realized suddenly, much older than his mother. Her hair was dyed and cropped close to her forehead, but he would bet that it was gray beneath the henna color. She looked like a man, he thought with disgust. Her hands were large and hammy with blunt, stubby fingers, and her nails, unlike his mother's brightly polished and well-manicured fingertips, were cut short and square. She wore thick-soled shoes, white stockings, and a suit over a white blouse with, Hugh winced with the recognition, a man's necktie knotted tightly around her neck.

Dyke. The word took shape in his mind, and his stomach tightened once again.

"I want to put a few items to rest, here," Thompson said. His hair was cut stylishly, and his suit was expensive. Still, Hugh thought, he looked as if he would be more at home in a pair of dungarees and a work shirt instead of a white shirt and tie. He probably was more comfortable working at the mill than standing up and trying to be somebody so important.

"There've been a lot of rumors lately about my having personal stock in the Burlington Northern Railroad Company." Murmurs filled the hall. "And I want to go on record right here and now by saying that all of that is an out-and-out lie. I personally do not own one single share of Burlington Northern stock. Personally, I have no vested interest in that corporation."

"No, you don't, Pete," Carl Fitzpatrick came to his feet, amidst shouts that he was out of order, that Pete had the floor.

Pete, however, was surprised and obviously delighted to see Carl standing in his defense. With a wave of his hand, he yielded and sat down. Loretta smiled hopefully at her husband.

"What you own at the moment, Pete," Carl said deliberately as he removed a paper from his coat pocket and donned a pair of reading glasses, "is approximately—well, exactly—two hundred thirty thousand twenty-four dollars and nineteen cents of hard cash which you received this morning about ten o'clock by electronic transfer from the Wells Fargo Bank in Dallas."

"How—" Pete came to his feet, then he looked at Loretta, who scowled at him. His face went from a burly red to pale, and he sat down and studied the tabletop in front of him. The room was completely silent.

"Those funds were deposited to your account in the First Security Bank here in town as the direct result of your liquidation of your entire portfolio, which was being managed by Carlton, Wayne, and Hoggard, a brokerage firm in Las Colinas, Texas," Carl read carefully. "A portfolio that consisted up until this morning of nothing other than shares of Burlington Northern stock." Carl held his paper up to the crowd's stunned silence, which suddenly broke wide open in a mixture of applause and angry shouting.

"Aside from those assets," Carl concluded, replacing the paper in his coat pocket, "you have a retirement policy from the mill, a savings account with about forty thousand dollars in it, and a Christmas Club account with a little over twenty-four hundred saved up."

Carl turned to address the crowd. "But, no, right at this moment, you don't own a single share of stock. Not personally." Carl removed his glasses, spun and pointed them at Pete, who continued to stare at the tabletop. "But this time yesterday, you could be described as a *major stockholder* in the Burlington Northern Corporation."

The crowd exploded, the newspaper reporters began writing furiously, and Carl sat down. Hugh could see the smile on his face as he adjusted his cuffs under his coat sleeves. Jonas was right, Hugh decided. People would follow Carl Fitzpatrick anywhere.

Judge Parker was banging his book again for order, and Elton Matthews was shouting. The other council members sat in silent wonder. Hugh spotted his father sitting helpless among the standing, shouting men around him, and he wondered what Harry would do now.

"Objection!" Toby Atwell, the owner of the town's Ford dealership and husband of Pete Thompson's sister, shouted again and again over the crowd.

Finally, Judge Parker rose. "This is not a court of law!" he yelled, and his voice, old and creaky as it was, seemed to silence the crowd. "You cannot object, and no charges have been filed. You people watch too much television."

"Well, I want his head on a fence post," Phelps Crane shouted back. "I say let's impeach his sorry ass and get on with business." Another chorus of shouting rose at Phelps's suggestion, and it was almost a full minute before everyone was quieted and seated again.

Pete said nothing. Loretta stood, her hands clasped in front of her, her mouth a brittle line of hate directed toward Carl, who continued to grin and accept handshakes and slaps on the back from those around him.

"We cannot impeach anybody here," Elton Matthews patiently explained. Pete Thompson stared down at his lap. "That calls for charges, a trial, and so forth, right, Judge?" Parker nodded sagely. "We're not even here for that," Elton continued. "No inquiry into what Pete's done or hasn't done is within the bounds of this meeting."

Carl Fitzpatrick rose again and with a wave of his finger received a nod from Elton, who sat down again. "I am a lawyer," he said unnecessarily, "and a pretty danged good one. I know we can't impeach old Pete, and I'm not sure we want to." He beamed at everyone, and even Pete looked up, again astonished by Carl's smooth handling of the angry crowd. "Hell, he's our neighbor and our friend. But I do think," he winked at Elton, who looked away in embarrassment, "that it would make things go a whole lot smoother if ol' Pete'd just step down."

"Resign?" Pete Thompson exploded at last. Loretta stepped forward to join him. She worked her way between him and Carl, as if she were protecting one from the other, but it was unclear to Hugh whose safety she was more concerned for. "Never, you son of a bitch! I haven't done one thing wrong, not one thing! There is nothing illegal or unethical about anything you say I've done."

Carl turned to face him and found Loretta's angry face almost level with his. Hugh hadn't realized what a large, tall woman she was.

"Am I talking to you or your wife?" Carl asked.

"You're talking to me!" Pete yelled. He banged his fist down on the table. "And I'm waiting for you to say something. Just what do you think I've done wrong?"

"Well," Carl smiled at Loretta, who stepped aside and cleared his view of Pete. "We could start with what you just said a minute or so ago. That was an 'out-and-out lie,' as you put it. Maybe you'd like to start these proceedings over again. Gracie can amend the minutes . . ."

"That won't be necessary," Pete said with a sharp look at Gracie, who smiled weakly and continued scribbling.

"Well, then . . ." Carl said. "What about it?"

"All right." Pete opened his hands. "You're right. I did own some stock in Burlington."

"Quite a lot of stock," Carl corrected.

"All right. A lot of stock. I don't know how much there was. I didn't ask. To tell you the truth, I didn't even know I owned it until last week. Then all these rumors started, and I ordered a broker to sell it for me—for us. I didn't know how much it was worth. I'm sure Mister Fitzpatrick has all the correct figures. Like he says, he's a lawyer."

"And a 'danged good one,'" someone called. Laughter was general.

"But owning stock in a railroad—even on purpose—is not a crime," Pete went on, "and however much you people may not like what they're doing out there, it's not even a violation of ethics."

"No," Carl admitted. "You're absolutely right there, Pete."

"Mr. Chairman?" Hugh's head snapped back to his father's position. He stood, hand in the air like a schoolboy. Even though he was a large man, he seemed small and shy in the crowd. "Mr. Chairman, uh . . . Elton?"

Matthews nodded, and Harry cleared his throat as every head in the room swiveled toward him. Even the reporters stopped writing, stared at Harry Rudd. Hugh remembered Wilson's warning that his father might get hurt if he interfered, and fear gripped his abdomen, climbed up his back, closed his throat. He almost shouted for his father to sit down. But his eyes were nailed to his father's back, and his hands opened and closed in fists as his father's voice wavered briefly and continued.

"I've known Pete Thompson for a long time," he started. A murmur rose behind him, already agreeing with what they imagined that he was going to say. "He's been a good friend and . . ." Harry paused briefly, "and he was my boss. He was a good man to work for." Hugh wondered just how much it hurt his father to say that in public. Pete beamed at the unsolicited testimonial.

"I don't know anything about all this building business," Harry said. He took a breath. "But I do know that for the past two years, Pete's been as good a mayor as we've ever had." Elton Matthews winced, and Hugh remembered that Elton had been mayor before Pete and had been defeated by only "a cat's hair," as his father put it. "And, anyway, I just think we ought to think this thing out. I don't see that it's wrong to own any stock in Burlington or anything else. Most of us own some in something." One or two people around Harry nodded. "That is, if we have anything saved at all, we'd be foolish not to make investments if we can." Again there was a murmur of agreement rippling through the crowd.

"I just think we ought to slow this thing down. Think about it. That's all. I don't see that we need to hold Pete responsible for what the railroad might or might not do. If he owned some stock, so what? That doesn't mean he's running the show or even telling the company what to do. Let's cool off and think this thing through."

Harry sat down. The back of his shirt was soused with sweat. He ran his hand through his thinning hair and shot a quick guilty look toward his son. Hugh extended a thumb upward, and his father smiled thinly, then turned back toward the front of the room.

"I couldn't agree with you more," Carl Fitzpatrick stood again, smiled, and matched Pete Thompson's grateful look while he spoke directly to Hugh's father. "Mr., uh . . . Rudd, isn't it?"

Hugh was embarrassed when his father nodded briefly. Carl knew his father by name. He knew everybody in town. "You've certainly made a good point." Carl spoke to Harry as if he were a little boy, an idiot. Hugh hated the man right then worse than anyone he knew. "And, speaking as an attorney—and a candidate for city office—I can tell you that you're absolutely right. There is absolutely nothing illegal, immoral, or unethical about owning stock—even in the Burlington Northern—the one company that has done more to ruin this town than any other corporation or vested interest I can name."

Carl's voice rose to the familiar speech-making tone, and Hugh was astonished by how people began muttering agreements. It reminded him of being in church when the minister would say something, and members of the congregation would respond, "Amen."

"Jackass," Hugh whispered, thinking of Wilson's comment.

The man next to him chuckled. "Judas goat's more like it," the man said and lit a cigarette. Hugh stared at him for a moment.

"Even so," Carl continued, holding up his hand for silence, although no one was talking, "I do believe that Pete might like to tell us—if he decides to remain in office and put the entire town through the embarrassment of a trial and impeachment, that is—how it is that a man who has never made more than thirty-five thousand dollars any year of his life has managed to acquire over a quarter-million dollars worth of anything!"

"I inherited it," Pete said quickly. "Or, actually, Loretta inherited it. From her mother. I told you, I didn't even know we owned it until last week."

"That's right," Loretta spoke up. "My mother left us the whole 'portfolio,' as Mr. Fitzpatrick calls it, along with her house, her car, and two Siamese cats. Does anyone here have a problem with our having kept the cats?" Sarcasm dripped from her voice. She advanced on Carl, who didn't retreat at all. "Maybe you'd like to come out and count the droppings in their litter boxes, Carl," she hissed at him. "You seem to be more at home digging around in other people's mess than in taking care of your own business."

"Of course," Carl said, ignoring her and turning again to the crowd behind him, "I'm perfectly willing to believe that Pete inherited every certificate and that he had no idea what the extent of his mother-in-law's estate was. When was it she died?"

"Five years ago—" Loretta started.

"Five years ago," Carl repeated meaningfully and with a slight arch of his right eyebrow. "And, again speaking as a lawyer, I'm prepared to believe that you never inquired as to the nature of her holdings in the stock market." He brushed imaginary lint from his lapels. "Then, also as a law-yer, I'm used to believing whatever my clients tell me. But as a future elected official—if such is my fortune—I would have to ask you—should this all come to trial—just how you managed to remain so ignorant of what you owned while, at the same time, you ordered your brokers to improve on it! In short, to purchase more stock with more money than you have any right to have, based on Pete's earnings."

"I . . ." Loretta looked at Pete. "It's my money, my inheritance. Not his. I never told him," she said. "I was keeping it a secret, a surprise for when we—"

"This is a community property state!" Carl insisted. "And Mrs. Thompson has no job, no earnings of her own. No man, no elected representative operates in a vacuum. It is entirely possible that you improved your portfolio with Pete's money, without Pete's advice and consent, but to ask us to believe that you had no hand in his decision to reject the historical designation of the Hendershot building and to clear the way for its razing is . . . well, ridiculous. Such a move is directly in the interest of the company in which you were a stockholder. It was also, then, directly in your personal interest."

He spun on Pete. "Are you going to tell us you didn't consult with your wife about that?"

The crowd erupted in an angry demand for answers.

Pete was deflated. He dropped slowly to his chair and put his head in his hands, and Loretta, her stance between the two men eroded, went to him and put a hand on his shoulder. The noise and shouting in the hall were deafening. Finally, she turned and addressed Carl in a loud but calm voice that seemed to penetrate the din and turn every head in the room in her direction.

"You're a first-rate, silver-plated son of a bitch!" she said to Carl. He looked at first stunned, then wounded, then proud of the accusation. "He's a good man," she continued. "Look at him! What did he ever do to you?"

"It's not *I* who have been wounded by his treachery and political back-door shenanigans," Carl cried, ignoring Loretta and addressing the crowd again. "It's this city, and the historical preservation of its landmarks! Sold down the river for a handful of dirty, filthy shares of Burlington Northern Railroad stock!"

"Impeach the son of a bitch!" Phelps Crane bellowed. "Ride his ass out of town on a rail, a Burlington Northern rail!" A number of men leaped to their feet as if their intention was to follow the angry old conductor's advice. Only Judge Parker's rising and shouting along with the rest of the council brought the room to order once more. When things settled, Pete raised his hand and received a weary nod from Elton.

"*I* called this meeting," Pete said in a low voice. He stayed seated, Loretta continuing to hold her hand on his shoulder. "This was my idea. I wanted to stop them. God help me, I did! I didn't sell anything to anybody. I—we—held some stock, I guess. So what? I didn't buy it. I didn't even know about it until last week. When I found out, I didn't even ask how much there was. When I realized how all this would look, when the rumors started, I—that is, Loretta—ordered it sold. I had no idea how much there was. It's my wife's business, not mine. It's her money, for Christ's sake. Look, Carl, you're a lawyer, and you know as well as I do that an inheritance is exempt from community property laws in Texas."

"The profit from it isn't," Carl shot back. "Not in practical terms."

Pete started to argue with Carl, but instead he took a breath and looked up at Loretta. "Anyway," he said, opening his hands, "none of that had anything to do with my decision not to accept that stupid plaque from the historical society. They wanted the town to put up two million dollars to restore the building. *Two million!* Where in God's name were we to get that kind of money, just to save a useless old building? The wye they want to build would bring in some jobs, do everybody some good. I was doing what I thought was best."

He pulled out a handkerchief and mopped his brow. "You people have gone crazy," he said and took his wife's hand. "I don't know you anymore. Half of you voted for me. Half of you go to my church. What the hell do you want?" His voice trailed off. "To hang me on the courthouse lawn?"

Jonas Wilson's story of Pete's grandfather's end rang in Hugh's ears, and a chill ran through him.

"I think we ought to hold on," Harry was back on his feet. His shirt was now completely soaked, his voice shook. "We're taking your word for an awful lot, Carl."

"It's all right here in black and white," Carl waved the paper in the air. "I've had two detectives and an accountant going over it for nearly a week, and there're affidavits and depositions in my office, signed and sworn by the brokerage firm and Wilda Tillman over at the bank. Judge Parker's seen it all."

Parker nodded grimly.

"Still, that's not what we're supposed to be meeting here for," Harry argued weakly. "That's not on the agenda."

"Mr. Rudd, uh . . . Harry," Carl smiled. "This isn't pleasant for me. It's no delight to me to rip this town apart, to hurt Pete. But if he refuses to do the right thing—the honorable thing—and step aside and allow someone who genuinely cares about this town and its history to take the lead in saving it from the ravages of corporate greed, then what can I do? I have the facts, and I'm honor bound to use them."

"It seems to me you worked your ass off to get them." Harry's voice lost its quaver suddenly. The boy was proud to hear a familiar tone of toughness emerging. "What's in this for you?"

"Well," Carl narrowed his eyebrows and pursed his lips a moment. "I can't say that *anything's* in it for me." He refused to look Harry in the eye. "But I think we all know what's in it for you, Mr. Rudd. Or for your wife. Isn't that right, Loretta?"

Something inside Hugh plummeted, like an elevator falling down a shaft. He waited for it to hit bottom, to explode, for his father to leap across the chairs between him and the smarmy attorney and hit him. But Harry didn't move. He stood, slightly wavering, grasping the back of the chair in front of him and staring at Carl's wide smile. No one looked at him. No one said a word. Loretta's eyes shot pure acid in Carl's direction, but his smile didn't flinch from his lips while he waited for a reply that would never come.

Harry sat down again, and Hugh could see how red his father's neck and ears were. There was nothing more to be said, nothing more to be done. Wilson had been right. His father had dipped his hand into a mess, and he had pulled back something bloody and painful.

Finally, Pete struggled against his wife's staying hand and rose. "Very well," he announced in a voice that was misleadingly deep. "A mayor—any elected official—serves at the pleasure of his constituents. I'm not an idiot. I know I can't be thrown out of office by a mob of loudmouths. But if you all want to follow this horse's ass—" he pointed at Carl, who continued to smile, "—to believe everything he says, and to let him tell you what to do, that's fine. There's more people in this town than that.

"But I have a pretty good idea of how this is going to go, and by tomorrow morning I won't have a friend left anywhere in the county. I'm not going to let you do it. You people want me out, I'm out. I'm sorrier'n hell I was ever in. I should have just stuck to what I know and left the politics for tin-plated sons of bitches, liars, and cheats."

He paused, looked at Loretta, then again addressed the crowd. "To hell with all of you. But especially," he bowed deeply in a gesture of false sincerity, "to hell with you, Carl. You can have the goddamn job. I'm retiring."

With that, he took Loretta's arm, and they walked out of the room toward the kitchen, smiling and speaking to a few people on the way. When they went through the swinging door, the reporters were right on their heels.

Hugh stood with his back to the wall, sweat causing his shirt to stick to the plaster. His father sat upright, as stiff as if a steel rod was running down his spine. The redness was gone from his neck and ears, but Hugh knew he was hurting. He, too, was hurting, and he turned and left the room, stumbled down the steps and into the night air.

CHAPTER TWO

Hugh found Linda Fitzpatrick sitting on the steps in the doorway that provided a separate sidewalk entrance to the second floor above Simpson's Fine Furniture and Appliances.

"What are you doing here?" he exclaimed before he thought. She was the last person he wanted to see. Today had been too painful already, and he had gone through too much to fence and flirt with her.

That was what she expected, though. Her face brightened when she turned and saw his form descending the stairs into the pool of darkness that spread between the outside streetlamps and the dim bulbs over the narrow stairs.

"Hugh!" She scooted over and patted the wooden step, indicating that he should sit next to her. "How neat! I thought I was the only kid in town tonight."

"I thought you were having a party." He stepped down past her level and looked across the dark, empty street. No one was about. All the stores and shops were closed. A mannequin in the boutique window across the street pouted and pointed a long wooden finger in their direction. He realized that he wanted a smoke, and he wished Jonas Wilson and his makings would suddenly appear.

"I *was* having a party, but Mother canceled it." Linda's voice matched the look on the store dummy. "She said none of my friends were in town, and there was no one to invite."

Hugh thought that there were likely a couple of hundred kids who would have loved to have spent the evening swimming in the country club pool and eating and drinking on the Fitzpatrick tab, but he said nothing.

"She's such a snob, Hugh," Linda confided. "She said that if you have too many people who aren't members out there, they charge too much.

But I think that she just didn't want me inviting my friends who aren't members."

"Like me?" He sat down next to her and continued looking out onto the emptiness of Main Street. Even the hot, humid air of the summer night was cool after the steamy enclosure of the room above.

"Sure, like you." She smiled at him and thrust her long legs out and pointed her sneakers' toes at each other. She had on another of what Hugh had come to suspect was an endless supply of short and top sets. It was deep red, and it fit tightly around her waist and breasts. The muscles in her thighs contracted as she stretched, and she smiled more broadly when she saw him looking at them. "You think I have nice legs?"

"I think you have nice legs," Hugh repeated in a flat statement. His thoughts were miles from Linda Fitzpatrick's legs.

"I think I have *great* legs," Linda confirmed and ran her long fingers down as far as she could reach, past her knees, and massaged them. "I'm so glad I'm a natural blonde and don't have to shave so much. Some women have to shave every day. Did you know that?"

Hugh, who had begun scraping the fuzz from his cheeks every three days only last Easter, just nodded. It was funny, he thought. He knew girls shaved their legs, but he didn't think of it as a big deal. It just went with being female.

"When I was out at my sister's, I had to shave a lot. But my tan was getting deeper, and I was wearing a swimsuit every day. Did you know there was a beach right down from my sister's house where people don't wear any suits at all?"

Hugh gaped at her, disbelieving. He had heard that such places existed in far-off, exotic places like France or South America. But California? "Right," he snorted.

"I swear it's true! We snuck down there and spied on them one afternoon." She arched her back. Her hair spilled down in a long ponytail onto the step behind her. "You wouldn't believe how hard it was to keep from laughing. These old, fat, ugly women with their big boobs hanging down to here," she pointed to her waist. "And the men! I mean, you absolutely wouldn't believe some of them, Hugh. I don't know how they can walk! Tony said—"

"Tony?" Hugh couldn't help himself. "Tony went with you?"

"It was his idea," she laughed. "You didn't think I went down there with Megan, did you?"

184

"Uh . . . well, I didn't know."

"Well, of course not. Megan's an old prude. She didn't even like me hanging around with Tony. But anyway, we went two different times. It was awesome, I can tell you."

"Neat," Hugh said. Linda's words brought back the old hot feeling of jealousy. "What else did you do? Just watch?"

"Yeah," Linda leaned back again, and her eyes took on a dreamy look. Suddenly she sat up. "Tony wanted us to take off our suits and go down and join them. I mean, that's the only way we could do it. Nobody was wearing anything. But I chickened out. I couldn't do it."

Hugh couldn't think of a thing to say.

"Tony took off his suit, of course, and started out, but I hid behind a sand dune and wouldn't look."

"I'll bet," Hugh coughed nervously.

"I didn't," she insisted.

He looked up at her. A loud explosion of yelling and noise mixed with applause and boos came from the hall above them.

"It was pretty rough up there." He nodded back up the stairs, where more yelling was going on.

"Mother said it would be. She would have come, but her hair's still green. She's getting it cut and dyed tomorrow." Linda frowned and then whispered in a low, secret voice, "She said Daddy was going to cut Mr. Thompson's balls off."

Before Hugh could think of anything to say in return, he heard people coming down the steps behind him. It was Pete and Loretta Thompson. Hugh remembered that they had exited in the direction of the kitchen behind the room. This was the only way out since the store below was closed for the night.

Pete was tight-lipped and looked as if Lydia Fitzpatrick's prediction had come true in a painful, physical way. He held Loretta's arm, but it was she who was providing the support, Hugh could see, as they descended to the sidewalk and past the two youngsters.

"Good evening, Mr. and Mrs. Thompson," Linda chimed as they turned to walk away down the sidewalk.

The pair stopped as if a net had been dropped over them. They were directly under the streetlamp, and Hugh held his breath as Loretta slowly turned to see who had spoken to her. Pete continued to stare vacantly down the sidewalk.

Loretta's eyes took a moment to focus on the crimson-clad girl, who had reseated herself and was smiling pleasantly at them. The older woman's face became a stone mask as her mouth cracked slightly into a cold smile.

"Good evening, Linda," she said. Every word hung frostily in the night air. "Hugh," she added when she made out his form as well.

Hugh mumbled something, and the Thompsons resumed their walk. He and Linda remained silent until the Thompsons entered their Cadillac and pulled out and drove off. Loretta was behind the wheel, and Pete was slumped down on the passenger side, as if afraid someone would recognize him.

"Did you have to do that?" Hugh demanded.

"What? What did I do?" Linda's eyes widened, and she looked at him in a mockery of being shocked. "I was just being polite! That's more than they were. They walked right past us as if we were parking meters or something."

"You know, Linda," Hugh turned to start back up the stairs. "One of these days you're going to have to decide whether you're going to be a spoiled little girl or whether you're going to grow up."

She opened her mouth to reply, but he held up his hand. "It takes more than shaving your legs to make you a grown-up, and it takes more than a country club membership to make you cool. Right now, you're about the most uncool person I know, and I don't know if you're ever going to stop being such a rich bitch." He slammed his foot down on the step and marched up to the hall before she could think of a comeback.

—≺—

If anything, it was hotter upstairs than it had been when Hugh left. Most of the heat, however, was being generated by large groups of men who had gathered and were talking angrily and loudly in various corners and along the walls. Judge Parker, Elton Matthews, and Carl Fitzpatrick were at the center of the largest group gathered around the table in front, all talking at once.

One reporter stood nearby and scribbled furiously as the men talked. Another moved from group to group, listening and writing while he walked. Phelps Crane was in another corner. Hugh could see a bottle wrapped in a paper bag being passed around among them. His father sat alone and stared at the floor. Hugh went over and sat down next to him.

"I guess we ought to go, Sport," he said when Hugh arrived. "I'm trying to think of what I'm going to say when we get home."

Hugh shook his head in sympathy. Harry put a hand out and touched Hugh's knee. "I'm sorry you had to hear all that."

Hugh tried to smile. "It's like you said, Dad. I'd have heard it sooner or later." He put his hand on his father's, and for a moment there was a tight squeeze between them.

"Yeah," Harry said and looked into his son's face.

Hugh wanted to tear his eyes away from his father's, but he couldn't. "I'm glad we had that talk last night, Dad," he said quietly. "It makes this easier to understand," he said.

Harry continued to look into his son's face and finally smiled and gripped his knee tightly. "It's not true," he said softly. "I mean, what they said about your mother. It's a goddamn lie."

"I know that, Dad," Hugh said. "You don't have to tell me that."

Harry nodded once. "Well, let's go."

Before they could rise, Elton Matthews started yelling for order once more, and the knots of men broke up and resumed their chairs.

"Just a minute," Hugh whispered. "Maybe they're going to talk about the building."

"I don't give a damn about the building."

"But that's why we came. I mean," he looked down, "that's why I came."

Harry's eyes were sad, but he settled back a moment and crossed his arms. A couple of men returned to the seats they had abandoned next to him, and Hugh took that as a cue to move off. He went back to stand near the rear of the room where he had been before.

"As all you people know," Elton shouted, then gradually lowered his voice as the hubbub in the room died down and he could be heard, "we can't do one thing about the mayor's office here, tonight."

Judge Parker nodded in agreement, but Carl Fitzpatrick looked upset.

"If Pete Thompson goes through with his resignation," Elton continued, "then we can add it to the next election's ballot, but for the moment, what we've got is nobody sitting in the mayor's chair and an awful lot of hard feelings."

"I don't see why we can't elect a replacement right now," Carl said. "I mean, it's not regular, but this is an extraordinary situation. There's a crisis at hand."

"There's not going to be any such a thing as an election," Elton said. He glared briefly at Carl. "You know better than that." Then he turned and faced the crowd. "There's not enough people here by a long shot to do anything official. But since I'm the chairman of the City Council and the senior member, I'm taking over the mayor's office, pro tem." He glanced down at Judge Parker, who nodded again. "Unless there's some objection."

Carl slapped his folded paper against his leg and sat down. There was a good deal of muttering, but no one said anything aloud. Finally, Elton sat down.

"All right. Now, what we're supposed to be doing here is discussing what might be done about that old building out there. Does anyone have anything to say on that subject?"

Carl stood, but Elton ignored him and cast his gaze around the room. When no one else spoke up, the mayor pro tem was forced to nod in the lawyer's direction.

"You go on and say what you came to say, Carl," Elton warned. "But I warn you, if you get off the subject again, I'll declare you out of order and have Grady over yonder throw you out."

Grady Cartwright was a sometime deputy for the sheriff's department and the sergeant-at-arms for all City Council meetings and had been for ten years. Old and arthritic, he was neither strong nor physically impressive, but he carried both a pistol and a nightstick. From time to time, he had been known to use the club when anyone protested his authority.

Carl beamed a grin at Elton, and then he turned his smile on the crowd. "Ladies and gentlemen," he began, and Hugh was reminded of a circus ringmaster. "Fellow citizens," Carl continued, and Hugh thought of every politician who had been on television during a campaign. "Friends and neighbors," Carl lowered his tone to a serious level, and Hugh incomprehensibly wanted to laugh. Carl seemed to be acting out a part, Hugh thought, like a TV comedian in a skit. "I want to go over the history of this affair, so we're certain of all the facts."

And so he began. He started with the razing of the depot years before and seemed to have in his notes the dates and facts concerning every building that had been torn down, burned, or simply allowed to fall back into the dust its bricks and lumber came from. He lamented the "decline of our native city and county businesses" and outlined the population decrease year by year. When he began citing statistics supporting tourism as an enterprise for any city in the country that had any historical interest to passing motorists on their way to the ski slopes of Colorado and New Mexico, Hugh tuned him out, folded his arms across his chest, leaned against the wall.

A large, fly-specked sash window was behind Hugh's right shoulder, and he suddenly realized that it was open, forcing the weak air conditioner to work even harder. He turned to put it down, then, to his surprise, saw the figure of a man perched on the ancient, rusty fire escape platform outside. Startled, Hugh stepped back. The figure gestured with the flat of his hand for the boy to crouch down to the opening. It came as much less of a surprise to Hugh to hear Jonas Wilson's voice whispering through the six-inch opening next to the sill.

"They're fixing to get down to it, boy," Wilson whispered. Hugh smelled whiskey on the old man's breath. "What're you planning to do?"

Hugh shook his head, but he didn't know how Wilson could see through the layers of dust that opaqued the window.

"I mostly came to listen."

"Well, you heard a earful tonight," Wilson rasped.

Two men leaning against the wall turned and frowned at Hugh.

"I thought I'd tell them about the big railroad crane," Hugh whispered.

"That ought to light 'em up," Wilson chuckled.

"Why don't you come inside?"

"I'm fine where I'm at. Shush, now. Look there."

Hugh turned to see Grissom and two men, the engineer and his white-coveralled companion, entering the hall. They stayed against the far wall by the door and worked their way back into a corner. Several men moved away to give them all the space they wanted.

Hugh forgot about Wilson and studied the trio. The engineer still wore his green khakis and hard hat, and he looked uncomfortable beneath so many angry gazes. The other man Hugh recognized as being from the worksite. Grissom had on a suit and tie. Aside from Carl, he was the only one so attired in the whole room.

Carl had moved his history of the town up to the present, completed his statistical analysis of just how many tourists he believed could be lured away from the bypass and into town if there were enough bona fide attractions for them. He now threw open the discussion to the floor. He might have failed to seize the mayor's chair from Elton, but he was in charge of the meeting nevertheless.

"And, so let me tell you what I've done today, and then I think it's up to you people whether we save one of the town's oldest most important landmarks, or whether we just go home and forget the whole thing."

There was a murmur again in the room. People sat up in their chairs. Hugh's father was still slouching.

"Today. This day," Carl raised his hand for silence, "I've been on the telephone with both the governor and the state attorney general." His hand became a fist. "And even though both assured me of their concern and their interest in seeing the Hendershot building preserved, both of *those elected officials*," he sneered, "also assured me that there was absolutely nothing they could do to save the building."

An angry buzz began low in the crowd. "Of course," Carl's voice dripped irony, "if it were a beer joint in Fort Worth or a whorehouse in San Antonio, that would be different! But a grocery warehouse, the repository of food and sustenance for an entire community for lo these many years is of no historical importance to our esteemed, elected officials down in Austin!"

A pious nodding in the crowd quickly turned to anger, and Hugh heard several people shout "Amen."

Carl's face reddened, and sweat bathed his high forehead. "That the Hendershot building is a virtual shrine to hard work, free enterprise, and everything that's decent and law-abiding in this community is of no significance to those elected officials who, doubtlessly, are gathered in the ginmills and fleshpots of the state capital to laugh and scoff at a bunch of rednecks up here in the sticks, men and women—voters and taxpayers, mind you—whose only concern is to preserve the integrity and maintain the decency represented by that monument to the American way of life: the Hendershot Grocery Warehouse!"

The crowd was on its feet, stamping and whistling in a combination of anger and applause. Most were too confused to know how to feel, Hugh thought, and he himself wasn't certain where Carl was going. He could sense that the man had the crowd behind him all the way. Hugh had played in too many close games when a championship had been on the line where there was less enthusiasm than he could feel all around him. The floor beneath him vibrated with the noise and stamping. Grissom stood and scowled. The railroad man's two companions looked bewildered and a little dazed.

After a brief crescendo, the demonstration subsided, and people found their chairs again. Hugh's father moved to the opposite wall and grimly watched the proceedings.

"But," Carl's voice rang out over the dying voices, "let me tell you what I *have* been able to do today! I have also been on the telephone with the attorney general of these United States, and I was able to receive considerably greater satisfaction dealing with a man whose political ideals and ethics are somewhat elevated from that bunch of self-serving good old boys down in Austin."

A brief cheer was followed by intense silence. Everyone leaned forward, and even Grissom, Hugh noticed, stared at the front of the room in expectation. Carl took advantage of the moment to pull a huge handkerchief from his coat pocket and towel his face. Beneath his coat large sweat rings showed under his arms. His shirt clung to his body like a wet rag.

"The man in Washington," Carl said in a softer tone, "told me that if we, the good citizens of this town, could find *any reason whatsoever*, any legal cause, however minor or circumscribed, to delay the demolition of that great monument out there, he would *personally* see to the issue of a federal restraining order to force the Burlington Northern thugs *to cease and desist* until a full Department of Justice investigation could be conducted into the recently revealed payoffs of our former mayor, His Honor, Pete Thompson."

Hugh was disappointed. He had hoped that the lawyer would have some trick up his sleeve, something no one had thought of to prevent the building's destruction. All he had done was say what everyone had said all along: If there were a way to stop them, they'd be stopped. There was no way, so the building was a goner. Hugh wondered if he was the only one in the room who understood that.

Judging from the crowd's reaction, he was. People were shouting at the table now, and Carl resumed his chair. He was panting and smiling and nodding in agreement with every charge ranging from the danger involved in tearing down the building to the results of losing an important windbreak for the grain elevators that sat several hundred yards south of the Hendershot building. People groped for any shred of evidence that the removal of the building would harm the town, but no one was coming up with anything meaningful.

Hugh squatted down by the window's opening. He wondered what Jonas Wilson was thinking, but he didn't want to ask. In a moment, the old man's whiskey voice told him anyway.

"That's a dangerous man," Wilson whispered. Hugh nodded. "You going to tell 'em 'bout the big crane?" Wilson asked.

Hugh didn't answer but stood up and leaned against the wall again. There didn't seem to be much point in it, he thought. No one was listening to anyone. Judge Parker's head was down on his chest, but Hugh couldn't see if he was asleep or what. Elton Matthews was pointing at different people to give them the floor, but no one was paying any attention to him, and Gracie Gholston had given up trying to keep the minutes and just sat and glowered at her pad.

Grissom was in conversation with his two companions. Finally, he stepped away and moved forward toward the table. Carl saw him coming and rose to his feet.

"All this is well and good," Carl said, putting out his hands to subdue the rapid-fire, useless suggestions that seemed to have no end. "But does anyone have any legal or moral reason—*legal or moral*—why that building should be saved?"

"Mr. Fitzpatrick," Grissom spoke before anyone could resume thinking out loud. "I'd like to say something if I could."

"Why, certainly, Mr. Grissom," Carl smiled, "but properly, you should address the chair."

Elton waved his hand. "Why the hell should I care? I should've stayed home and watched TV for all the good I'm doing here. It's your show, Carl."

"We've been over all this before." Grissom moved out in front and flanked the table opposite Carl. "Your people, your city attorney, *your* Judge Parker," the old judge's head snapped up when his name was called, "and *our* lawyers and representatives have all been over this with a fine-toothed comb. This issue is settled, and all this talk about politics and Washington and 'the American way' isn't going to change that."

The crowd mumbled angrily, and Grissom, who also was now sweating profusely himself, wiped his forehead with a pocket handkerchief and continued.

"I understand how you must feel. We tried for years to sell that building, but no one wanted it. We have found a use for the land now—an important use. Years of planning and details go into that kind of thing. We aren't just ripping it down for the fun of it."

"Looks to me like you ain't ripping it down at all," Phelps Crane piped up hoarsely. "Looks to me like she's got you buffaloed. What're you fixing to do now?"

"We're going to build a wye out there," Grissom ignored Phelps and went on. "And that's important. It's good for us, because it gives us a chance to use this point as a turn-around for mill traffic. It's good for you, because it means a switching crew will be stationed here. That's jobs, and jobs—"

"How many jobs?" Phelps came to his feet and stalked forward to meet Grissom. His pace was uneven, and he almost tottered when he stopped and put a grubby finger in Grissom's face. "Ten, maybe? How many from local folks? Two, three?"

He turned and faced the crowd. "Don't let him flimflam you! If they put three men in here, it'd be a wonder. If they hired two high school boys summers it'd be all we're going to get. It's the goddamn depot all over again. Railroad's out for the railroad. Fuck anybody who gets in the way."

"Watch your language!" Elton piped up.

Grissom glared at Phelps. "It's all we're prepared to do, and I can assure you that it's more than we have to do."

He turned to Carl. "Mr. Fitzpatrick, you have a flair for working people up, but you may be misleading them. I don't care what people in Washington or Austin or anywhere else have told you, there is no legal way you can stop us from tearing that building down."

Carl smiled confidently and stared back at the railroad man. Phelps stood his ground as firmly as his wobbling legs would allow. His tiny eyes ping-ponged between the two men while his fists opened and closed. The crowd seemed to be holding its collective breath. But then, from the most unexpected place, the tension among the men was snapped.

"I think maybe there is," a voice from the side of the room came up quietly and drew every eye once more toward Harry Rudd. When Harry moved away from the wall, Hugh could see a wet spot where his back had touched it.

"I'm no lawyer," Harry said, "and I've got no love for Carl Fitzpatrick —most of you know why, and the rest of you will know before morning, unless I miss my guess. But he's the one who can tell you if anybody can whether or not the railroad has to have a permit to cross city property."

"A permit!" Grissom exclaimed and laughed. "We have all the permits we need. Your own county clerk signed them himself."

"What city property?" Carl asked. His hand rubbed his chin in confusion.

"The street between the Burlington Northern tracks and the building is a city street, isn't it?"

Carl looked more bewildered than ever. He looked at Elton, who shrugged.

"Well," Harry went on, "if they have to bring any equipment across that street and disrupt traffic on it for any reason, don't they have to have a permit? A special permit?"

"What street?" Grissom yelled. "There's no street there."

"Yeah, there is." Harry smiled weakly. "It's just a dirt road, but if I remember right, it was called 'Market Street' when I was a boy."

"That's right!" Phelps Crane's grizzled face spread into a wide, satisfied grin. "I remember that." Several older people also nodded and muttered their agreement with the recollection.

"It's not a street!" Grissom insisted. "It's just a dirt path, overgrown with weeds."

"A street is a street!" Phelps yelled. George Ferguson and Harvey Turnbull rose to join him.

"We can check the town plat," Carl said carefully. "If it's on the books as a street, then it's a street. It doesn't have to be paved or even graveled." He turned to Hugh's father with a quizzical expression on his face. "But I have to confess, I don't see your point, uh . . . Harry. What difference would it make? They're already at the site. They've already begun work."

"But they're not getting anywhere, or so I'm told." Harry opened his hands, and Hugh glanced at Grissom's two companions. They looked nervous and uneasy. The engineer was eyeing the exit door.

"So?"

"So, well, they're going to have to bring in . . . Well, let it come from the horse's mouth, so to speak." He looked around and found Hugh against the back wall. "You tell them, Sport," he said. "You're the one who knows."

Every head in the room swiveled around to face Hugh, who at once was the victim of distressing sensations. His stomach dropped like a roller coaster. His heart started pounding, and his breath left him. It seemed like an hour of silence and expectant looks passed before he heard Jonas Wilson's voice whispering loudly from beneath the open window.

"Go on, Sport. It's your show, now."

Hugh swallowed and licked his lips. "They're bringing in this big crane," he started, swallowed hard, then continued. "It comes on a flatcar. Too big for a truck . . . uh, trailer." He was almost stammering, but Harry's eyes were full of pride. He took heart. "It's coming tomorrow, and they're going to bring it right down to the side of the building, and—"

"And cross a city street!" Phelps Crane cried triumphantly. "And they can't do it without a permit! That's heavy equipment, and they ain't got no goddamn permit."

"And they ain't going to get one, either," Harvey seconded.

The crowd applauded. Every smile in the room warmed Hugh's face to the point where sweat flowed out of him in oceans. Several men near him jumped up and began slapping him on the back, but he wriggled away and went over to where his father stood grinning down at him.

"How did he know that?" Grissom demanded. "Have you people been sending your kids out to spy on us?"

"Why was it such a secret?" Carl rejoined, clearly glad to be back in the fray. "Thought you could just pull an end-run on us. Now, we've got you where we want you!"

"I don't think so." Grissom fought for composure. "We already have a permit to block traffic on city streets. Even an *intellectual* such as Mr. Crane here knows that. And if we can get the equipment across in the allotted time—" He looked at the engineer, who nodded in agreement. "Then I don't think you have a leg to stand on."

"Oh, yeah, we do!" Phelps Crane smacked his hands together. "You forgot one little detail, Mr. Grissom, something your fancy-dan lawyers down to Fort Worth probably thought was just a minor thing. You might can use that permit to block a city street, but that only covers Burlington Northern's crossings."

"So?" Grissom wasn't yet worried. He could smell a final card, but he believed he was still in the catbird seat.

"So, them tracks, that spur running down from the main grade don't belong to Burlington Northern." Phelps looked at Carl, who shrugged in confusion. "That there spur was laid by Hendershot hisself! All that belongs to you now, I guess, but there's a good twenty-five, thirty yards of steel out there, that part you been uncovering. That's on city easement, and you can bet your ass that you ain't going to get either permission to use 'em or permission to cross Market Street, which is right where they go."

"I think he's right," George Ferguson said. He stepped out from behind Phelps and addressed the room in general. "We carry the policy for the city, as you know. And that path—Market Street or whatever it's called—is on city property. So's the easement, which would include those tracks. If the tracks are there. I wondered about that when I saw them working over there this morning. You see, we have to know about things like that whenever we have a renewal or rate increase. You see, the State Board of Insurance—"

"We got you by the short and curlies now," Phelps interrupted and chortled. He danced a little jig. "Your tit's in a wringer, railroad man, and there ain't one goddamn thing you can do but pull it out and suck off the bruise."

Grissom stood fuming for a moment, and then he turned to Carl. To everyone's surprise, all the anger was gone from his voice when he spoke.

"You realize that this is only going to delay things, prolong this whole ugly affair. It's only going to make things harder. I don't know what else to say."

"You could quit," Phelps hooted. "Cry uncle, tuck tail, and get on back to Chicago or wherever the hell you come from and tell 'em the Hendershot building stays where it's at. You been hoofed, hided, and horned."

"I doubt very much, Mr. Crane," Grissom pulled out his handkerchief and wiped his face carefully, "that you have any idea of how small you and this whole town are, of how little my employers in Chicago—or even my immediate superiors in Fort Worth—think of this whole affair. This isn't even a footnote at a board meeting. They don't give a damn, and . . ." He looked over and nodded at his two companions, who, with wondering looks at Hugh, started moving toward the door, ". . . and if they consider it at all, I suspect they just get a good laugh when they wonder why in the hell you do."

He turned sharply and smiled at the crowd and left.

Hugh let the air out of his lungs and believed it was the first breath he had consciously taken in ten minutes. His father stood next to him with his arm draped over his shoulders. Harry's hand gripped him with a firm but affectionate hold.

"Is it true?" Elton asked Carl Fitzpatrick, who still had a puzzled expression on his face. He was outwardly pleased, but Hugh sensed that he was also upset about something. Probably, Hugh thought, he was disappointed at how easily his spotlight had been captured, and by Hugh's father, no less. The boy looked up and grinned at his dad.

"Well, I'll have to look at the plats, the maps, the books," Carl frowned suddenly. "I'll know by tomorrow." He realized that everyone was looking at him. "Grady," he ordered, "you tell the sheriff to come out to the worksite tomorrow morning early. If what that kid said is true, then we've got to be ready."

"I'll tell him," Grady grumbled. "But I can't promise he'll come. He don't take orders from me. Or from you."

With that, Elton Matthews declared the meeting adjourned. People rose, said their good-byes, and started filtering out the door, down to the street. The reporters followed Carl and Elton out, firing questions as they moved down the stairs.

"Why'd you do that, Dad?" Hugh asked quietly as they continued to stand against the wall and watch the crowd recessing. "You said you didn't give a damn about the building." Hugh was careful to get the words right.

"Oh, I don't know," Harry smiled again. "You think it's important, and that ought to be enough." His smile faded, and his mouth lined itself into a serious expression. "That's a lie," he said. "The truth is that I wanted to get Carl Fitzpatrick's goat, and I saw a way to do it." Hugh looked confused.

"You see," Harry said, "Carl's a lot like a banty rooster. He struts and fluffs his feathers and makes a lot of noise, but when you come right down to it, he's still nothing but a capon, what your granddaddy Rudd would have called 'a peckerless wonder.' A hawk or a coyote'll still scare the piss right out of him."

"I don't get it."

"What your old man's trying to tell you, boy, is that Carl Fitzpatrick don't care a pitcher of warm spit for that building." Jonas Wilson raised the window high and stepped into the room. His plaid shirt and worn trousers and battered hat seemed to be even shabbier when he stood next to Hugh's father, sweaty and drawn as he looked.

"Old Carl thought all he had to do was talk 'bout it for a while, and everybody would come to see what a good old boy he was and cast him a vote come next voting day. The building could go to the devil for all he cares."

Harry gave Wilson a steady, even look. Hugh sought contempt or disapproval in his father's expression, but there was nothing of the sort there.

"So, what you and your daddy here did was put the dog on his yard, and he's either got to run him off, or he's going to have one heck of a mess to clean up."

Wilson stuck out his hand, twisted, chopped fingers and all, in Hugh's father's direction. "Jonas Wilson." Harry didn't hesitate. He took the old man's fist and gave it a firm shake. "That's one heck of a fine boy you got there, Mr. Rudd."

"I'm proud of him, Mr. Wilson," Harry returned. His eyes were locked into Wilson's grin. Hugh glanced around. Most everyone had gone. Grady was moving about, turning off lights.

"I see where he gets it," the old man said. "You took a load of manure your own self here tonight." Harry didn't reply. Wilson pulled out his pint bottle in its paper bag and handed it to Hugh's father. Harry glanced over to make sure Grady was not looking, then tilted it back and took two quick swallows. He handed back the bottle, and Wilson followed his example and then restored the cap and stuck it away. "It's going to get a whole lot worse 'fore it gets any better," he said quietly. "Phelps Crane's going to win or die trying." Harry nodded agreement.

"What about the others?" Hugh asked.

"Phelps is the one bears watching." Wilson glanced at Harry with an appreciating look. "They's trouble brewing. Knowed him all his life, and he's never been much account since he come back from the war with all them medals. Troublemaker. Now, he's near the end of his rope. Question is, will he just let go or hang from it?" Wilson turned and pulled his famous tow sack in after him. "See you tomorrow." He winked at Hugh, and then went toward the door and out.

"I'm still not sure I understand," Hugh said as they followed in the old man's wake down the steps. When they reached the street, Wilson had utterly disappeared. No one was hanging around. Except for Grady, they were the last to leave, and the streets were deserted.

"There's something I need to tell you," Harry said quietly. "Carl embarrassed me tonight. He embarrassed your mother, and he embarrassed this town."

"Because of what he said about Mr. Thompson?"

"That, and a whole lot of other things." Harry's jaw tightened again. "He stuck his neck out, begged for someone to put a noose around it, but nobody had one ready." He looked down at Hugh and smiled widely, "At least he didn't think anyone had one ready. He didn't count on you."

"Or on you."

"Or on me. Now, he's made promises he can't keep, probably, and he's in all the way. If they go ahead and tear down that building now, he's dead politically. Before you spoke up and told them about the crane, there wasn't anything he could do, really, except make a lot of noise and get some votes out of the deal. Now, he's got to act."

"But what about the building?" Hugh asked. "That's what I thought all this was about."

"Son, it never was about the building. The building will come down one way or another, sooner or later. This was about something entirely different."

"Mom?"

The question filled the night air, and Harry stopped. Their car was sitting all alone in the slant parking, and the dead emptiness of the downtown area was like a weight.

"About that," Harry's voice was heavy. "You heard some things tonight. You may have guessed at more than you heard."

"I don't believe any of it," Hugh said.

"Good." Harry rubbed his mouth with his hand, as if he had tasted something bad and bitter. "It's not true."

"You told me that, and I believe you," Hugh said too quickly.

"But that's not the point. The point is," he reached down and turned Hugh to face him. "The point is that she loves you, and she loves me. And we love her. She's a good mother, and she's a good wife. It's exactly the same thing I talked to you about last night. There are some mean people in this town who would say nasty, cruel things about her just for the hell of it."

"Things about her and Mrs. Thompson."

"Yes. But it's not true." Harry's voice underscored the words in a soft, firm way that made Hugh think of his teachers' dark red pencils when they corrected his essays. "It never could be true. Not about her. Believe me, I would know if anyone does."

"What about Mrs. Thompson?"

"Believe none of what you hear and half of what you see," Harry spoke angrily, and his fingers dug into Hugh's shoulders. "I learned that the hard way, and it almost cost me her . . . and you. Your mother is a good woman, and a loving woman, and . . ." His eyes narrowed with the pain of what he was saying. "A normal and moral woman. Don't let anyone convince you of anything else."

Harry's grip on Hugh's shoulders relaxed. He turned and wordlessly opened the door and got behind the wheel, then he looked at his son.

"Your mother's had trouble in her life. Lots of trouble. More trouble than most women ever dream of having. But that's not for you to worry about. The important thing is that we love her, no matter what."

Hugh nodded.

"Are you all right?" Harry asked after a moment.

"I'm all right," Hugh said. "But I think I want to walk."

"It's after ten. C'mon, the Dairy Mart's still open. We'll stop for a cheeseburger."

"I don't think I'm very hungry," Hugh muttered. "I want to walk. See you at home."

Harry nodded, lit a cigarette, and stared off down the empty street. Finally, he started the engine, pulled out, and drove off with a hesitant, half-wave at his son. Hugh waited a beat, then trudged off down the sidewalk.

It didn't surprise him when his steps took him two blocks out of his way to pass the old hotel. Behind the yellowed shades of a rear room, he could see a dim light. Things had moved too far in the wrong direction that day, he thought, and with that thought, he saw the light go out. With a shudder and a quickening of his pace, he moved off toward his house and wondered just how far they might go tomorrow.

CHAPTER THREE

The next morning, momentum increased. By first light Wednesday morning, television crews arrived from stations in Amarillo, Wichita Falls, and Lawton, Oklahoma, along with reporters from Dallas and Fort Worth. Word of what happened at the meeting spread, and a large group of early birds gathered on the old depot parking lot. Their number multiplied rapidly, and Phelps Crane bragged to each newcomer that there would be thousands there "to see the show." Rumors ran through the town that a big movie star—maybe Robert Redford or Jane Fonda—was on the way to add support to the "Save the Hendershot Building" movement. No one but the TV reporters seemed to take such stories seriously, but word was spreading anyway. Every news correspondent seemed to have two or three cellular phones working all the time, and the pay telephone adjacent to the parking lot was jammed with coins and rendered out of order before nine o'clock as everyone was trying to alert friends and relatives that major celebrities were apt to appear at any moment.

The day before, the construction workers had managed to clear and completely expose the rusty rails that ran from the main Burlington line across the forgotten hump that was once Market Street. They now worked to clear the rails all the way to where the old loading docks had been, directly beside the Hendershot Grocery Warehouse. The crowd now openly jeered at the men, while Grissom ran from his makeshift headquarters in the abandoned Railway Express Office to his car and drove down once or twice an hour, or whenever he spotted the workers standing around, their hands on their hips, frowning from under their hard hats up at the swelling mob on the raised parking lot.

Tension grew. Everyone seemed to expect something important to happen, and conversations were unnaturally restricted to whispers and low, ironic laughter as the events of the evening before were rehearsed and embellished. When anyone caught Hugh's eye, he received a bright smile or, sometimes, a thin look of disapproval, depending on who observed him. He ignored both and wished he could just fade away, forget all about the Hendershot building, Jonas Wilson, Linda Fitzpatrick, and, most of all, his father and mother and their problems.

The night before, the walk home from downtown seemed to take only seconds. Although he was in no hurry, his mind was swirling so rapidly, trying to absorb the meaning of all he had seen and heard, especially of what he had heard from his father, that he was shocked to find that he was turning into his own sidewalk so soon. It normally took a half-hour or more to make the journey on foot, but that night he believed he had taken only a few steps, and there he was.

He stood for a while on the front porch, looking through the windows at the bright lights from the living room, wishing with all his heart that when he went inside, he would find that none of this had happened at all, that it was only his imagination that had led him along such dark paths, suggested such horrible things. But when he finally trudged up the porch and through the front door, he found his parents and the Thompsons sitting forlornly in the living room, and he knew that there was nothing imaginary about it.

That they had been drinking heavily was verified by the nearly spent bourbon bottle sitting next to an empty bowl of ice on the coffee table. Ashtrays overflowed, and smoke swirled in the ceiling fan overhead.

Hugh spoke softly to everyone in the room—a greeting that garnered him only the barest flicker of recognition from anyone, including Harry. Edith sat on the edge of the sofa, a drink in her hand, a cigarette burning down in her long fingers, and a sad, almost mournful expression on her face. She didn't move at all when Hugh's father rose to make himself another drink, then sat down next to her, lit a cigarette, and rejoined them in silence. The scene reminded Hugh of the days following Larry's funeral. He shuddered.

He moved down the hall to his room, and even after he had showered and crawled into bed, he heard no conversation coming through his walls. They apparently had completely talked out the events of the evening long before he came in, and now they were reduced to just sitting and drinking and smoking, sharing their individual, silent misery with each other as if it were the warmth of a fire in winter.

That morning, he had risen early and raced downtown to see for himself what would be the results of his handiwork the night before. He would have been looking forward to it, eager to see it arrive, if not for the disturbing images of his mother and Loretta Thompson creeping around his mind and painfully inserting themselves, like fingers in an open wound every time he let his guard down. To Hugh, the prospect of a major standoff between Carl and the town and Grissom and the railroad seemed nothing more than a sideshow.

The huge crane was already there when Hugh pushed through the mob, reached his pylon, and took up his familiar position next to Wilson. He accepted a Thermos cap full of coffee from the old man, who pointed out the huge piece of machinery. It rested on an oversized flatcar pushed by two diesel locomotives. In the rear of the engines were two other cars. One looked like another locomotive of some sort, only there was no cab, no front or back. Wilson explained that it was a generator that would provide extra power for the big crane when it began work.

After an hour or so, the railroad crew finished working on a switch, and the train pushed the huge machinery car into position to shift it onto the siding that led down by the old grocery warehouse. This took nearly another hour, and the crowd continued to grow while the TV crews maneuvered for position. Grissom kept racing back and forth from the crossing to the Railway Express Office. He occasionally glared at the growing mass of people, steadfastly ignored reporters' questions, and constantly talked on his cellular telephone.

Finally, the train began inching its way slowly down the grade toward the Hendershot building, but when it arrived at the old street crossing, the crew stopped. Blocking the way was Sheriff Jim Anderson—who had called in two highway patrolmen to back himself up—and a tight knot of townspeople, including Carl Fitzpatrick, Elton Matthews, and a handful of other council members, who drove up in cars and trucks across the newly exposed tracks. Phelps, George, and Harvey, along with several other men, marched down to join them on what had once been Market Street, a slight rise of dust and weeds that was unrecognizable as any sort of thoroughfare at all.

A larger group, mostly high school kids, followed the men down about halfway and began cheering and shouting at the turmoil. Some of them brandished hastily made signs reading "Save Our Town's Heritage" and "Railroad Go Home," among other brightly lettered slogans. The TV vans bounced across the uneven ground. Their crews scrambled atop the vehicles and began taping while the reporters moved through the crowds, blocking people's view and asking questions.

"This is the showdown," Wilson chuckled softly.

The town's representatives, official and otherwise, joined forces and stood in the dust and weeds with their arms crossed over their chests, feet spread apart. The train's engineer shouted from the lead locomotive and blew the diesel's whistle several times, but the men didn't move. Sheriff Anderson stood off to one side, smoking and chatting with the highway patrolmen. Hugh noticed that Anderson carried a shotgun casually across one arm. The helpless trainmen climbed down from the lead locomotive and were officially refused right-of-way. Carl brandished several papers in Grissom's face while the railroad man stamped back and forth through the dust and argued with him.

By noon, it was over. Carl and his cronies apparently won, at least for the time being. The sheriff and other officers departed. The huge crane sat atop its flatcar, still limbered and covered with blue tarpaulins. It was hauled back and pushed off onto a nearby siding. Grissom and Pruitt retreated to their temporary office, and the workers down at the building went back to their older, smaller machine and continued to flail away uselessly at the solid sides of the Hendershot building.

The day grew warm and humid. Shortly, the TV crews packed up and left, and the bulk of the crowd began to drift off toward their homes.

Hugh joined Jonas Wilson in the sparse shade of the rotten porch of the old icehouse for a noon meal—beet and onion sandwiches—but they said little to each other. They had come, Hugh suddenly understood, to a point in their relationship when each other's company was comfortable without the necessity for small talk. Hugh was glad for the gentle silence that floated between them. He was afraid that the old man would bring up the topic of his mother and Loretta Thompson, but, at the same time, he found a terrible urge to bring it up himself, get it out into the open and talk it out with Wilson. He was afraid of the subject, though, so he said nothing, waited for Wilson to speak first.

The old man munched his sandwich in silence, scarcely making eye contact with the boy. Goodlett curled up and took a nap while the two continued their wordless companionship and shared tobacco after they ate. Wilson made a pillow of his hat and lay back on the porch, and Hugh finally gave up trying to reconcile the conflicting emotions inside himself.

He stretched out for a while and studied the large white clouds over-head, wondering idly if the rain was over for a while. The afternoon was steamy, so he sat up, hoping to catch any breeze that might happen by. Tommy and Ray pedaled their bikes around a corner a few blocks away. They had bat bags slung over their shoulders. They were heading in the di-rection of the high school, obviously going to get in some practice. A pang of guilt struck him. He should be going with them, he thought, not lazing about in the shade with some old man. But the thought of going home, grabbing his mitt, and spending the superheated afternoon chasing down fly balls seemed too heavy to lift. As they wheeled out of sight, he sighed.

"You play a little ball, don't you, boy?" Wilson said. Wilson's ability to comment on things Hugh was merely thinking about unnerved him.

"Yeah, a little," Hugh said.

"You any good at it?"

"I'm okay."

Wilson cracked an eye and squinted at him. "You any good at anything?"

Hugh felt a prickle of anger, but he forced it down. False modesty was not the right tack to take with Wilson, he decided. "I'm better than aver-age," he said. "Tommy and Ray—my friends—they're really good. Coach Kruickshank says they're phenoms. Naturals. They both want to play in the majors." Wilson didn't reply. "I have to work at it," Hugh added when Wilson didn't comment. "I'd settle for a scholarship, maybe. Someday." The prospect of college seemed far away to him, like talking about getting married and having children of his own. It was something that would hap-pen, he knew, but he had more immediate things on his mind.

And there was high school, and the high school team. Again, his thoughts drifted painfully to the field where his friends were practicing. He ought to be with them, he thought.

"Never played no ball, myself," Wilson said after a moment. "Wanted to. When I was a pup, that is. Always wondered if I'd of been any good at it. Not many is." Hugh nodded, though Wilson wasn't looking at him. "Used to have these barnstorming teams come in. Traveling teams, they was. They'd show up in a bunch of ol' jitneys and jalopies and such. Take on all comers. Made for some exciting Sunday afternoons, I can tell you."

Hugh knew a little about that. He had even heard that long ago the town had a team of its own.

"Them ol' boys was something," Wilson went on. "Not like these young feather merchants today with all their fancy uniforms and such. Then, they was a rough lot. Foul-mouthed bunch."

"I've heard about them," Hugh said, wanting to change the subject. His promise to himself to practice all summer felt more neglected with every word.

"Once in a while, a colored team would come in," Wilson mused. "Now, they was something else again," Wilson said. "They was polite as could be, but they could play. They'd beat our boys like a tin drum, right up until the last inning or two, then they'd quit."

"Quit?"

"Oh, yeah. It didn't do in them days for a bunch of colored boys to beat up on a white team too much. So they'd lay down, make lots of mistakes."

"Errors," Hugh corrected.

"Yeah. They'd be whomping that ball all over the place, then just couldn't hit it no more, all of a sudden. But they was making some money off it. Reckon that's all that mattered."

"I 'reckon' that's all that matters today, too," Hugh offered, thinking of what he'd heard so often about professional ballplayers.

Wilson grinned. "You're learning, boy. Some things never change."

The blast of the engine's whistle caught Hugh's attention. "You think they'll try to sneak that crane in when no one's looking?" he asked.

"Naw," the old man coughed slightly, sat up, and began cleaning his knife on a piece of waxed paper. "Not 'less they can get it to grow wings and fly her in. They won't cross that street. They got too much savvy for that. That'd play right into ol' Carl's hands."

"So what'll they do?"

"Don't know. They'll pound on her a while, but I count near thirty men working down there. Figger they're making upwards to twenty a hour, some of 'em—them's union boys, don't forget—and pretty soon some ol' boy in a suit and tie's going to get wind what this little shindig is costing. That'll be a end to her, one way or 'nother."

"What'll happen then?"

"Well, it's hard to say." Wilson rolled another smoke and tipped up his bottle. "Dang that Mescan," he frowned. "I told him to get me a good whiskey. This stuff's cheap. It burns."

Hugh thought of his father's sharing a drink with Wilson the night before. The image played across his mind like a summer breeze.

"Anyhow, I reckon that prissy little feller—"

"Mr. Grissom?"

"Right. I reckon he'll lose his job—'less he's married to the right woman—and that engineer and the foreman down yonder'll be give their walking papers, too." He drank again, cursed again in his innocent way. "They ain't union, you see."

"But what about the building?" Hugh asked, sitting up. "I mean, will they just walk away, leave it alone?"

"Ain't likely." Wilson lit a new cigarette. Hugh accepted the makings to roll himself another. "They got theirselves tween a rock and a hard place. Can't tear her down, can't leave her standing. Sort of like ol' Pancho was when Carranza sold him out."

Hugh looked narrowly at the old man. "Did you really . . . I mean, were you really . . ."

"Go on, boy. Ask me straight out. Did I ever go down on the border and chase 'round after that greasy little dickens?"

"Well, did you?"

"I told you I did," Wilson snapped. "That ought to be good 'nough. When you going to learn to stop calling folks liars, boy? I chased after him, and I dang near caught up with him. But I was kind of like ol' Carl's going to be here in a spell. I didn't know what I'd of done with him if I'd of caught him. Whether I'd of kilt him or joined up with him. Times was different then. 'Revolution' was a word people respected. They wasn't so afraid of it as they are these days. Trouble was, I never could decide whether that fat little dickens was a real revolutionary or just a bandit. Hear Carranza and that bunch tell it, he was nothing but a thief, a outlaw. Federales said the same durned thing. Hear the peons talk, though, you'd of thought he was the next best thing to the Second Coming."

Wilson's eyes took on a dark, faraway look, and almost a minute passed before he spoke again. "Course, Carranza sold him out, and he stayed 'mongst the people right to the end. They loved him." He nodded his head once. Now, anger and pain filled his voice. "You got any more questions you want to ask 'bout my truth-tellin'?"

With that, the old man sulkily gathered his things and stalked off. Hugh sat up and watched Wilson's back when he turned the corner of the Railway Express Office and disappeared. Every time Hugh believed they were becoming friends, Wilson would snap at him and make him feel like a fool. Where did he come from? Hugh wondered. Just how much truth was there in what he said about himself? Even an idiot could figure out that he couldn't have done all he claimed. He wasn't that old, Hugh insisted to himself. Nobody was that old.

Hugh jumped down from the porch and strolled toward downtown. As he paced up the tracks between the REO and the northernmost structure of the official business district, he noticed for the first time the huge cracks running up the masonry to the roof. The building was one of the oldest in the downtown area. It had once been a harness and tack shop, he remembered his father telling him, but Wanda Kilroy rented the front portion, remodeled it, and opened a children's clothing store there. That lasted four years before she became bored or went broke—depending on who told the story—and now it, along with so many other buildings, sat empty, forlornly contemplating the bustling front door of Henderson's Hardware across the street.

Henderson's building also had cracks, Hugh noticed, and there was more than one. Some were large enough for him to stick his hand into. Now that he strained his eyes against the midday sun to study all the buildings of downtown, he realized that not one was without structural faults, some running jaggedly up from their foundations and opening wide, ugly tears in the concrete and brickwork all the way to the sky.

It was as if the whole town was crumbling under the ineffective blows the construction workers leveled against the Hendershot building, as if their efforts to take out one building were rippling across the whole community. The sidewalks and streets looked old, used, in need of repair or patching every few feet. Some parking meters stood at odd angles where careless motorists had rammed them. Three or four storefronts were boarded up with "For Lease" signs in their fly-specked windows.

Hugh suddenly had the impression that instead of looking at his own downtown, his hometown, the place he had been born and was planning to spend at least the rest of his boyhood in, he was looking at some sort of grotesque cemetery, with adobe brick headstones and ornate, false fronts.

He shook his head and stared again into the crowd gathered on the depot parking lot. Where did Jonas Wilson fit into any of this? he asked himself. Then he knew. Wilson fit just fine. He was an old man, out of his time, living in the past, slowly crumbling away in the heat and wind. The town, Hugh thought, seemed to be more a part of Wilson's life than anyone else's, particularly Hugh's. And, Hugh realized, compared to Wilson, he didn't know a thing about it, about the town or its history or why it even existed. He suddenly felt like a stranger, a visitor who had just dropped in and discovered himself in a strange and alien place.

Instead of going back to the demolition site, he went to the County Memorial Library. He wanted to find out what he could about the town, about Jonas Wilson. He was tired of being treated like an idiot, of trying to guess at answers.

Miriam Lawless, the librarian, was delighted to see a boy of Hugh's age in the library on a summer afternoon. Without a question about what he was up to, she settled him behind a desk and happily surrounded him with large volumes of county and city histories. He learned very little about the old man, though. Wilson's name didn't appear in any of the records, such as they were. The Hendershot building also was a mystery. What little official materials the library had on the structure, Miriam told him, were all over on Judge Parker's desk, where they had been "sent for."

"They wouldn't wait for copies," Miriam sniffed. "Lord only knows when I'll have them back."

There were pictures enough of the building, though. Hugh discovered it had long been a principal feature of the town's skyline. No photograph, rendering, or description of the city omitted it. He studied the grainy shots of it reprinted in newspapers and the two official histories of the community. It always seemed to be a center of activity. Pictures of it surrounded by Model T's, trucks, and heavy wagons were on page after page. He saw the mule teams hauling the freight elevator and, later, a proud crew of dirty men standing around the donkey engine that replaced the animals. If Jonas Wilson was among any of the figures photographed, Hugh couldn't spot him. He tried to imagine what the old man looked like when he was younger, but no clear image would form, and he had to content himself with squinting at the several heavy figures who stood around and grinned at the camera's lens from beneath the deep shade of their hats and caps.

After the forties, photographs of the building all by itself began to disappear, and finally, by the time Hugh's research arrived at a point where photographic quality was clear and sharp, the only pictures that included the building were focused on other structures, often the whole skyline of the town itself.

By five-thirty, the time the library closed in summer, he had learned exactly nothing about his mysterious friend. Hugh went home and sat through a desultory supper of pork chops and black-eyed peas with his silent parents, who had consumed a good portion of a fresh bottle of bourbon before sitting down to eat. What few words passed between him and either of them were of a perfunctory, formal nature. It was as if his home had been invaded by strangers, people who were courteous to one another, but who hardly knew each other anymore.

The only thing he looked forward to was returning to the worksite and watching the continued efforts of the crew, the continuing ebb and flow of onlookers in the parking lot. He gave no thought to anything else.

As he hit the door on Thursday night, his mood wasn't much lighter than on the previous evening, even though Jonas Wilson had apparently forgiven his questions of the day before. They had spent a pleasant noon hour laughing about developments, not down on the building's worksite, where nothing had changed, but on the parking lot, where the number of spectators continued to swell. Still, the tension between the town and the railroad continued to escalate.

Someone had gotten the bright idea to go out to the high school football stadium late Wednesday night and load up four sections of the end-zone bleachers and haul them downtown. Hugh heard that it was Phelps Crane's idea, but no one would take the credit—or blame—for the deed, which had been accomplished in the wee hours and must have taken a large crew and an industrial forklift to manage. Each section was twenty-five feet long and had ten rows of seats. How anyone managed to move them without breaking them apart occupied the whole crowd's conversation as people filled the seats while they shared drinks and snacks in the spirit of any other civic event. The holiday atmosphere of the previous week had returned and, if anything, grown stronger.

Sheriff Anderson and Coach Lefty Crawford joined with the high school principal, Joe Percy, in deploring the act and in trying to find out who did it. No one would own up to it. Every inquiry they made was met with a knowing smile and the question, "What does it hurt? Football don't start for months yet."

When it was recalled that Randy Truman, owner of the largest automotive repair service in town, owned a crane-and-lift rig mounted on the back of a semi-trailer, which he used to haul wrecks from his shop to the salvage yards in Wichita Falls, Coach Crawford and Joe Percy started yelling for the sheriff to arrest him. They tore off toward Randy's shop, but he was up on the top row of the bleachers sharing an ill-concealed cache of beer with Becker Fallworth and Dub Tyler. By the time they got back, everyone was saying how it was impossible for Randy to have done it by himself in the first place, and in the second place, no one was about to give up a seat so someone could haul them back out to the football stadium.

The coach and Joe Percy gave up, made three high school kids move over, and joined the rest of the crowd.

With the festive mood returned, and with Grissom continuing to sit in his temporary office and steam at the mob on the depot's parking lot, people milled about and ate and drank and kept the party rolling while the workers down by the building continued to batter and slam the smaller wrecking ball against the building's impervious concrete sides. All they managed to do was raise clouds of dust and jeers from the crowd. Meantime, the big railroad crane sat on its flatcar like some great, wounded bird covered in bright blue bandages.

Even so, some progress was being made in the building's destruction. All of the stucco and adobe facing had been knocked away from the concrete walls, and in places holes had been gouged out by the ball's incessant swinging and one or two perfunctory attempts with pneumatic hammers. Pieces of the roof's edge and parts of some corners were beginning to crumble, and Hugh worried aloud to Wilson about the building's power to continue to resist.

"Oh, sooner or later they'll make a dent in her that'll hurt," Wilson nodded over a double cheeseburger that Hugh had brought to that day's luncheon. Hugh decided that all his sponging off the old man needed to be repaid, so he had left the party downtown and pedaled out to the Dairy Mart for the burgers and a pair of chocolate malts. He had told Wilson he would meet him in their old spot next to the hotel.

Hugh wanted to make amends to Wilson, and he was taking pleasure in watching the old man lick mustard and a chocolate mustache from his whiskered lips, even if it did completely deplete all of Hugh's cash.

"Even a well-built place like that can't stand but so much shaking," Wilson said.

"I thought you said they'd never break her down." Hugh bit his lip as soon as the words left. Here he was, trying to apologize for his mouth, and he was calling Wilson a liar once more. But the old man seemed not to notice.

"I never said 'never.'" He bit into the cheeseburger and let the grease run down his wrist and under his sleeve. "What I said was . . . Well, I tell you true, I don't remember exactly what I said. But it don't matter one way or 'nother. What I know is that it's going to take a whole lot more time'n them boys of got to bring her down to rubble, so it don't make no nevermind."

"I hear there's a pool going. Randy Truman and the boys are taking five-dollar bets on the exact hour they tear it down."

Wilson's eyes narrowed. "What'd they mean, 'tear it down'?"

"I don't know." Hugh hadn't thought about that.

"I mean, do they mean right down to the ground?"

"I don't know," Hugh repeated. "I mean, I just heard about it. It's not something they're advertising."

"No, guess not." Wilson finished his burger and carefully rolled the paper wrapper into a ball. "I'd like to get in on that," he said. "Wished I had some money. Maybe I'll pay Grayson a visit, take some of my credit out in cash."

"When would you pick?"

"Have to look at it. They probably fixed up a chart of some kind. Tell you this much, though. I wouldn't take no time this week. Not next week neither. It'll be a good two weeks anyhow, even with that big ball. Depends on what they mean by 'tore down.'"

Hugh thought for a moment. "I was hoping that they wouldn't tear it down at all. I had kind of hoped there for a minute that they'd stop them."

"They can't stop 'em, boy."

Hugh looked up in shock. "I thought you said—"

"I don't know what you *think* I said, but what I *meant* was that sooner or later, it'll come down. If them fellers can't do her, it'll just fall down on its own. That's the way of things. Ain't nothing built forever."

"But Mr. Hendershot said—"

"Well, that's true enough," Wilson interrupted. "But not even a tough ol' son of a gun like him *meant* 'forever.' Sooner or later this whole town'll be gone. This whole county'll go back to prairie, and we'll all just be a bad memory in the mind of some varmint or other."

Hugh recalled his observations of the dilapidated condition of the town's buildings. "They could fix some of these buildings up," he said.

"Could," Wilson noted, "but they won't." He looked around sadly. "Time was this was a fine town. Biggest town in the whole county."

"Only town, you mean."

"No, still is that. I said 'biggest,' I meant 'biggest.'" Wilson gave him a narrow look. "You ever heard of Fargo Wells?"

Hugh shook his head.

"How 'bout Hoolian, Pease City, Naples?" Again Hugh acknowledged his ignorance. "Well, all them was towns, and there was more besides: Goodlett, Franklin's Crossing, Squaw Creek Store, Medicine Lake, Milltown, Apex, Piss Ellum Church."

"What?"

"Piss Ellum Church," Wilson laughed. "It was a joke, kind of. Piss ellum's a kind of tree. Hard as hickory, folks say. That place didn't last long, though. Tent city, boomtown. Thought they had 'em some oil found. Didn't. Still, time was this whole county was overrun with little towns and settlements. Some lasted, some didn't. Now, most is gone. But when I was your age, why, you didn't have to walk but a few miles 'fore you run up on a store or a mill or a church or something."

"Well, those weren't towns."

"Not proper towns, I don't guess," Wilson admitted. "But folks lived there. Some was good-sized. Pease City, Hoolian. Had 'em a general store, a smith—later a automobile garage—sometimes a drugstore, saloon, a church or two, maybe even a school."

Hugh wracked his memory for any mention of these ghostly places. "Where are they now?"

"Gone, boy," Wilson said. He removed his bottle and took a quick sip. "All gone. Some was tore down, some just disappeared. Folks moved here, or they moved somewheres else. Sooner or later, folks'll move away from here, too. Sooner or later, this'll be just a wide spot in the switchgrass, and then the mesquite'll come in and take it over just like it done all them other places."

A hollow feeling struck Hugh. "When?" he asked. "I mean, do you think I'll see that?"

Wilson laughed. "Well, it ain't likely to happen tomorrow or next week," he said. "But it'll happen. You'll see it happen, likely." His mouth turned down in a crooked frown. "Day of the small town is done, boy," he said. "When I was your age, most boys just stayed right where they was. I reckon your daddy did the same."

"He was in the navy," Hugh said, anxious to find a flaw in Wilson's logic. "He went away, and he came back."

"Well, that's what I'm talking 'bout!" Wilson said. "He went off and saw all kinds of things. Pretty places. Good places. But he come right on back here after a spell, 'cause that's what folks his age did. This was still a pretty good place then."

He pointed a finger at Hugh. "But you young'uns, you're diff'rent. You grow up, get out and away, and you don't come back. Not never. Oh, you might sashay back to show off what you done, and you'll come back to visit your folks so long as they're 'mongst the living. But sooner or later, you won't come back. Too far, too much trouble, too many memories."

"I don't think I'll really ever leave," Hugh said softly. "I mean, I'll go to college, sure, but then . . ." He trailed off, once more lost in the frightening prospect of the future.

"But then you'll stay wherever you're at, and that'll be it," Wilson said, swigging once more, then recapping the bottle. He looked hard at Hugh. "Don't be fretting over it, boy," he said. "Places like this was good 'nough for folks once upon a time. But that time's done. 'Bout all that's left anymore is places like that ol' building down there. They're sort of like signs saying that what was 'round here was worth something. Maybe that's why they're worth trying to save, even if the trying's a long way from the doing, and even if the doing don't make no difference, one way or other."

Hugh lowered his eyes and studied the toes of his worn-out sneakers. The sole of his left shoe was wearing completely off. He could feel it flop slightly with every step he took.

All at once, he wanted to cry. It was as if he found out a part of himself was dying, as if something he had counted on always being there was going and he could not stop it. He didn't understand all Wilson was telling him, but he sensed that the old man was somehow right. The world was passing him by while he sat under the chinaberry tree and watched the town crumbling down around him. But somehow, some way it was all connected to his mother and father, to his being their son, and to their relationship to the whole town.

Wilson studied the expression on Hugh's face, then laughed and sloshed his melted malt around in the bottom of the cup. "It ain't over yet, boy. Not by a long sight. You'll be a sight older 'fore you'll even stop and worry 'bout it, and even then, it'll be a while 'fore it's happened. By then, likely, you won't care."

"I think I'll always care, Jonas," Hugh said.

"Maybe so, boy. Maybe that's one thing you are good at." He stood and stretched. "C'mon," he said. "Time we got back to see the matinee."

214

✕

The afternoon grew overcast after that. A renewed promise of rain filled the air with electricity while huge white thunderheads grew gray, then purple and green in the southwest. The threat of a violent storm had no effect on the crowd's enthusiasm, though. As the sun disappeared and temperatures cooled, more people than ever joined the mass on the old parking lot. Kids from the motel pool showed up in swimsuits, and golfers from the country club, driven off the links by the threat of lightning, came by and sauntered through the crowd in their brightly colored pants and shirts.

A portable snow cone stand from the rodeo arena had been towed in and set up. The Methodist Women's Alliance was selling sandwiches, cookies, and cakes from a table in the shade of the feedstore's awning, competing with the First Christian Women's Auxiliary, which was hawking brownies, fudge, and freshly cooked funnel cakes across the way. A Coca-Cola truck towed up a portable concession stand around three o'clock, and Hugh learned that the Odd Fellows were going to bring their barbecue pit the next day to compete with the Elks, who were talking about unlimbering their chili cooking booth as soon as they could remember who took it home to store.

The rumors of bigger and better food and drink sales spread through the delighted crowd and soon reached Grissom, who immediately lodged a protest with the sheriff. Anderson, however, suggested Grissom try some of the lodge's brisket, which was famous throughout the county, or the chili, which had several cookoff awards to its credit, and sent him on his way.

Grissom stomped around and fumed, but few paid him any attention at all. Finally, he returned to the Railway Express Office with a sandwich from the Methodist ladies and a Coke from the trailer concession stand and stood in the doorway, glowering and eating at the same time.

"That feller's going to get hisself a dose of the fantods," Wilson chuckled. Hugh wondered what that might be, but he kept his mouth shut.

For a while, they leaned against the familiar pylon that people had instinctively, somehow, deeded to Wilson and Hugh whenever they arrived. From time to time, Wilson would suggest that Hugh scout the crowd to pick up any news that might have come through, but for the most part, they just talked. Tommy and Ray arrived, once again carrying their baseball gear, but they left Hugh to himself, and few of the other kids approached him. He was vaguely distressed by being ignored, especially by his teammates, but he stayed around the adults, listening and trying to learn something of value.

"That there," Wilson pointed a crooked finger down toward the almost invisible Market Street, "used to be one of the busiest streets in town. Back 'fore automobiles was common, old Hendershot used it to ferry freight from the railroad up to the building and then out again for distribution."

Hugh stared and tried to make out the road. It wasn't clear where it intersected Main Street or where its termination might be. Only a raised line of withering brambles and tumbleweeds marked it as particularly different from the eroded ditches on both sides.

"He laid them tracks down to the side of the building in aught-eight or aught-nine. Never used 'em much till after the war, when 'frigeration come in and he needed to move stuff in from the iceboxes, vegetables mostly. Anyhow, he built them tracks, paid for 'em hisself, but they've been covered up for a coon's age. I doubt they's many folks here ever seen a piece of rolling stock on 'em. 'Fore yesterday, that is."

Hugh scanned the crowd. A number of faces turned away when he caught them staring at the two of them, but Hugh noticed that there had been a gradual breakdown of the open hostility shown toward Jonas Wilson in the past couple of days. Hugh wasn't sure whether people were just getting used to Wilson, or whether the mood on the parking lot was so happy that no one wanted to think about him.

Even Phelps Crane was ignoring them, except for once, when he gave Hugh a sly wink as he passed by, his thick petition stuffed into his greasy overalls' bib pocket. A pint bottle stuck openly from Phelps's hip pocket, but Hugh never saw him drink from it. No one was left to sign his papers, but he asked everyone all the same. Most people stepped back from him a space when he approached in his unsteady, weaving stride, and several men suggested openly that he go home, take a bath and a shave, change clothes, sober up.

Phelps shrugged off such advice and moved on to bother someone else, often getting into shouting matches if anyone suggested that he was wasting his time. More than once, Hugh heard Phelps's voice raised, his insistence that he and the "whole damn town" had been "screwed in the ass" by the "goddamn railroad" and that no one but he and Carl Fitzpatrick was doing anything to stop it.

People avoided Phelps when they could and gave him pitying, sometimes fearful glances of contempt. It was as if he had replaced Jonas Wilson as the town loony. Hugh wondered why Sheriff Anderson or Grady Cartwright, who moved through the crowd with one hand on the grip of his nightstick, a fierce expression of authority on his face, didn't arrest him.

Hugh was glad that Phelps was behaving so obnoxiously, though. It turned the crowd's attention elsewhere from him and Wilson. The only face that still showed open hostility toward them was the plainly beautiful countenance of Linda Fitzpatrick. She had been there Wednesday and since the earliest arrivals that morning. Thus far, she had stayed close by her mother and, except for white hot glares of hate, ignored Hugh. Lydia's hair was cropped shorter than Hugh's, and it was now dyed a kind of bright red that glowed orange in the diffused light of the approaching storm. They didn't bring their trailer and barbecue grill again, but now they sat under umbrellas just outside their large motor home and read magazines. Carl moved through the crowd and talked to everyone, especially reporters. Aside from Hugh and Wilson, the only person Carl ignored, Hugh noticed, was Phelps Crane.

"What happened tween you and that gal?" Wilson asked late that afternoon just as the workers began piling up their tools and making ready to depart for the day. The sun broke suddenly from behind the storm clouds, caught the western side of the building, and made the facing glow red.

"What—?" Hugh looked at Wilson. "Oh, that. Nothing. We just . . . sort of had words." He used an expression he'd heard his mother use to describe a falling-out with someone.

"Words, my hind leg," Wilson spat out a piece of tobacco that stuck to his tongue. "More to it."

"Are you allowed to call *me* a liar?" Hugh asked hotly.

"Only when you're lying, boy." Wilson didn't look at him. "Y'all was kind of sweet on one another. I seen it. You looked like a calf in a new moon whenever she come 'round smelling of jasmine and new lace. Now all I see is that she looks at you with something sharper'n a Dutchman's razor. You better fix that, boy. It'll blow back on you."

Bitterness came out before Hugh realized he was speaking. "She's a spoiled little bitch and a pricktease." He spat in imitation of Wilson. "All she does is . . . well, all she does is try to get me horny and—"

217

Wilson's hand snaked out and slapped Hugh across the cheek in a quick, backhanded motion. Hugh was stunned, shocked more by the shock of the blow than by the pain that now spread across his face.

"What the—"

"You watch your mouth, boy," Wilson growled in a thin, hot whisper. The rebuke was so quick that only a handful of people around them turned to look when the sharp slap reached their ears. They clearly weren't sure what happened. Neither was Hugh. He knew only that suddenly he was facing Wilson and had tears in his eyes.

"I'll not have you talking trash 'round me 'bout any woman." Wilson turned away, folded his arms, and leaned against the pylon.

"You're the one who told me about Loretta Thompson," Hugh protested furiously. His cheek was tingling. "You said—"

"I know what I said."

"Well, that was—"

"That was rumor, not fact. *And* I told you that for a reason. What you was saying 'bout that gal wasn't no good, no good at all. You talk nasty like that just to make yourself look big. You say a thing like that, and pretty soon, you'll come to believe it's true."

"It is true."

"No, it's not. It can't be true 'bout no young'un like that." Wilson's tone softened, and his frown turned up on one side. "I know how she tries to get you," he chuckled. "And I know how it feels to get your motor all revved up only to have her shut it down. But that's okay, boy. That's the way women is, and it don't make 'em nasty or trashy. Take a lesson, boy. You can't go blaming that gal for how you feel 'bout her."

"What do you know about it?" Hugh wiped his eyes. The shock of the slap was gone, but he could still feel the sharp sting of Wilson's twisted hand across his skin.

Wilson glanced at him from a corner of his eye. "I know 'nough," he said. "I'd tell you what I know, but you'd just call me a liar, and," he winked, "this time, you'd likely be right." Hugh lowered his head in spite of himself.

Wilson went on, "But what I ain't lying 'bout is that you and her got something tween you. I wished you didn't, for your own sake and for hers. It may not be good, and it probably ain't right, and it probably won't last till the coffee water boils, but it's there. You best fix it up for now, or you'll spend a lot of years regretting it."

He turned and looked seriously at Hugh. "Regret's a lonely bed partner, boy. Take it from somebody who knows."

Hugh started to reply, but Wilson waved him off with a gentle motion of his hand, and the boy remained silent. He glanced around and found, to his surprise, that no one was looking at him. Then he looked again over toward Linda, who had moved to a bleacher seat. Lydia Fitzpatrick sat like a bored sentinel outside the motor home. She had a small hand-held TV in her lap and was glancing at it while she read a magazine. Inside the open door of the RV, Hugh could see Carl, Elton Matthews, Judge Parker, and another man Hugh didn't recognize. They were sitting around a table piled high with sandwiches, listening to the stranger and picking their teeth and chatting amiably. A bottle passed among them as they talked.

"Go on," Wilson said without looking around. "Talk to her. Make it right. This dog-and-pony show ain't fixing to last forever. You got a lot of life ahead of you yet. Time you learned a bit of something that'll do you some good."

Hugh pretended not to hear the old man's raspy voice, walked over toward Linda, who sat on the bleachers and applied polish to her toenails. She looked up to check his approach and gave him a quick scowl before returning to her chore.

For a moment, she pretended to ignore him. He stood there, weaving in the sun, desperate to find something to say that would break through the frost that encircled her like a protective Arctic moat. She focused her entire attention on one nail, carefully brushing the polish on, tilting her head, and studying it from various angles.

Finally, he could stand her deliberate ignorance of his presence no longer. "Uh . . . Linda," he started.

"What do you want?" she shot back at him. She capped the polish and stretched back, staring at him through her sunglasses.

"Uh . . . do you have to come down here every day?" he asked stupidly.

"No," she said, her voice dripping with sarcasm, "I just *love* coming down here every day. I can't think of *anywhere* I'd rather be than sitting on some splintery bleacher in the middle of town, getting hotter and hotter while my friends are all out at the country club or riding their horses, or going shopping, or just staying home and watching TV. You seem to know so *much* about me. Can't you tell what a great time I'm having?"

She gave him a vicious smile that made her pretty white teeth look like sharpened fangs, but before Hugh could turn away, she went on.

"I'm here because Mother says *I* have to be here." Singsong mock patience replaced the sarcasm in her voice. "Mother says *I* have to be here because *she* has to be here, and *she* has to be here because *Daddy* has to be here, so we *all* have to be here to make sure that the family is 'well presented.'

"I'll tell you something, Hugh Rudd: If you've a brain in your head—which I doubt—you'll never go into politics. It's hot, and boring, and absolute *hell* on your family. I never thought I'd wish my sisters were still living at home again, but I do. At least we could take turns."

Hugh smiled, but she wasn't ready to crack yet. "But then that wouldn't work, probably. Daddy'd just want us *all* to come down here. This way, only one of us has to be miserable." Now she smiled.

"Linda . . . I'm sorry—"

"I am, too. I'm sorrier than you can imagine," she said in a voice loud enough for her mother to hear and scowl back at her. "This is most definitely *not* the way I planned to spend my summer vacation. For about ten cents, I'd get mono or something. At least that way I could stay home in bed."

"What I mean is, I'm sorry for—"

"This is the most *awful* summer of my entire life, and from what I can tell, it's only just beginning. Daddy's talking about running for every office in the country. I may spend my entire high school career living in a motor home and talking to nerds like you."

Once more, he started to turn and leave, but she was far from done.

"And another thing: I have to tell you that you say the most appalling and indecent things. Some people said you were nice, and I was beginning to think so, but after the other night, I have an entirely different opinion of you. You were mean and spiteful, and I didn't do one thing to deserve it."

She looked out over Hugh's head and seemed to take thought. "I was sweet," she confirmed. "And generous, and I tried to be nice to you. And another thing," she wiggled her toes and waved her fingers over them to encourage the polish to dry. "I think you spend entirely too much time with that old man over there."

Hugh spun around and looked, but Wilson had slipped off and was now almost two blocks away and fading into the haze of the late afternoon. "Why, uh—"

"People are beginning to talk, you know," she said with a serious, maternal mask now overtaking her features. "You know he has a reputation. A lot of your friends—or so-called friends—are beginning to talk."

"Yeah, but I don't know why," Hugh muttered. "He's okay. He's just old. I—"

"Well, you ought to spend time with people your own age," she admonished him, now slipping her delicate feet back into her sandals. "Those two dorks, Tommy and Whatshisname—"

"Ray?"

"Whatshisname," she insisted. She stood up and flexed her leg muscles in a series of dancer's poses. Hugh's eyes followed every precise movement. "Well, they said you won't even speak to them half the time. They think you're in love with that old man," she continued.

Hugh was stunned. Then, as the import of her words sank in, a sick sweetness invaded his throat. What did she mean by that? What did they? "What did they say?"

"Well." She softened her look. "Nothing, really. But they think it's weird. You can tell by the way they look at you. I think it's at least odd. And I can't have any oddball taking me to the Midsummer Dance at the country club."

Hugh's head spun while he tried to follow her logic. "What? Who's taking you to what dance?"

"You are. If you want to go." She smiled and changed her mood once more. "I don't ordinarily ask people to take me anywhere," she lectured. "And, as you know, I can *not* date until next year. So it is *not* a date. Your mother or father—or mine—will have to pick us up and take us out there. The other's parents can come get us when it's over."

Hugh's mind would not stop reeling. He had the impression she was talking about someone else. When had all this been arranged? He was trapped. It wasn't altogether an unpleasant feeling, but he was too confused to sort it out. "When . . . uh, did I . . . uh . . ."

"You did not. You could not. You're not a member, and, naturally, you could not ask me to go to a country club dance." She smiled cannily. "So I'm asking you. This is a new age," she quoted. "It's time for women to take charge of their own destinies. Megan says . . . well, never mind."

Hugh stuck his hands into his jeans pockets. "Well, okay. Uh . . . sure, why not?"

"I can give you a couple of hundred reasons 'why not,' Hugh Rudd, starting with all those nasty things you said to me the other night. But Daddy always says that 'actions speak louder than words,' so I am going to show you that I am not what you think I am. I am also going to show you how a woman of the new age acts. The dance isn't until next weekend, so we have lots of time to plan. I think, though, that I will wear white, so make my corsage red or blue or both—the theme is patriotism. Do you have a suit?"

"Uh, sure," Hugh stammered.

"Well, get it cleaned or something. You may not need it. It's always been semiformal, but last year there was talk of making it casual. And if it's still this hot, we may go swimming. I'll wear a corsage, no matter. I'll let you know what time later."

She flounced down from her perch and stood next to him. It was the first time he had actually stood so close to her, and he was surprised to find that she was almost a head shorter than he. In his mind's eye, he had always looked up at her. Now, she gazed up into his eyes, and, to his shock, he wanted to kiss her. The urge was overwhelming and came as such a surprise to him that he almost started leaning down to do it before reason seized him and froze him in place.

As if she perceived his desire and restraint all at once, she glanced around to make sure that neither of her parents was watching and then pertly rose on her tiptoes and pecked him on the cheek. Then with a mischievous grin on her lips just revealing a flash of her perfect white teeth, she fixed a pout on her face and bounced away toward her mother with a demand to be taken home "this instant."

Hugh never felt the tires of his bike on the pavement. He was riding far too high to feel anything. He was almost two blocks away before he decided the old bike wasn't behaving properly, looked down, and discovered that the rear tire was completely flat.

CHAPTER FOUR

After Hugh fixed the flat and made his way home through the begin-
nings of what he dismally realized was going to be another heavy rain, his
mood had soured. Because the downtown Chevron station—Phelps Crane's
station—was now permanently closed, with a sign taped to the door that
read, "Closed Until the Goddamn Railroad Backs Off," Hugh had to walk
the bike all the way out to the highway to get the tire fixed. The long, slow
side trip gave him time to think, but he was unable to come to any lasting
resolutions about how he would solve or even approach his problems. He
was numb inside, confused, and at the same time apprehensive. Linda's
forward behavior bewildered him, and it otherwise complicated an already
complex series of feelings about his mother and her relationships to the
Fitzpatricks and others in the community, particularly Loretta Thompson.

He also thought of what Tommy and Ray had said—according to Linda,
anyway—about him and Jonas Wilson, understanding better than he ever
thought he could how vicious rumors could begin, grow, and spread. That
led his thoughts back to the confrontation at the railroad crossing, the bitterness in Grissom's eyes every time he spotted Hugh, the mania the people seemed to have for watching all this, for taking delight in another's
misery.

Rain began pelting him hard two blocks from the house. He was more
bewildered and depressed than ever when he arrived home, late for
supper.

With his usual "I'm home" echoing through the house, Hugh slammed
through the front door and started toward his bedroom to change. He was
quite late, more than an hour past the family's regular suppertime, but he
had not seen his father's car in the garage when he pedaled up through the
now driving rain.

Now in dry clothes, he sailed down the hall, his mood growing lighter with each step. Maybe he was making too much of all this, he thought. Maybe everything would work out. Linda's invitation to the dance was the only real cloud he could see on the horizon. It was a small one, though, and he now began contemplating it with far more thrill than dread. He knew his mother wouldn't like the idea of his going anywhere with Linda Fitzpatrick, particularly to a country club dance. But he believed he could convince her that it would be all right. Once all this political nonsense was settled, he was sure she would relent. Besides, Linda wasn't Lydia or Carl. She was just a girl, a classmate. That was a different thing. Still, he resolved to do nothing to start any family arguments. He wanted things to return to normal so badly that he could taste it.

But when he banged happily into the kitchen, he was confronted with a harsher version of reality than any he had imagined. He knew immediately that things weren't going back to normal for a long while to come, might, indeed, never be normal again.

"What, young man, is the meaning of this?" Edith's voice brought him down to earth in a jarring, tearing crash that rattled his teeth and brought an instant pang of fear and dread to his temples. Her brightly painted forefinger's nail—the same shade, he hazily realized, that Linda was applying to her toes—was thrust down in a sharp point onto a spiral notepad that was lined with carefully listed names. With a guilty start, he recognized the list: his lawn customers.

"I have been on the phone all afternoon," she said. A full glass of bourbon sat next to the pad, and another fresh bottle was now one-third down. No supper was cooking or, Hugh realized, had cooked that afternoon.

"Actually, the first call came this morning. The Blankenships returned from Florida to find their yard knee high. Fred thinks it will take a bush hog—whatever that is—to get through it now. Then I heard from the McCartneys, the Mineshafts, the Trailors, the Hatchers, the Mewshaws, the Andersons . . ." She paused, sipped her drink, lit a cigarette. She had been rehearsing this all afternoon, Hugh understood. It was going too fast, and she wanted to slow it down.

"The Earlys, the Fischers, the . . . oh, it goes on and on, Hugh! After several calls, I started calling all your regular customers. I have more than fifteen names here. Most of them asked if you've been sick. You haven't mowed a lawn in almost two weeks."

"It hasn't been two weeks," Hugh offered weakly.

"It's been too long." She brought the focus back where she wanted it.

"It rained Monday."

"It snowed in Idaho," her voice remained steady. "I saw it on the news. But that's not an excuse, either. I want to know what's been going on. Where have you been? What have you been doing? Where do you *go* every day?"

Hugh sat down and searched for a way to stall this until his father came home. He knew that he wouldn't be any easier on him, but if he could hold her off, he wouldn't have to go through it but once.

"Well, things just sort of piled up."

"Piled up! Hugh. *What's* piled up? You leave here before breakfast, you don't get home until almost dark. You told me you were all caught up. I couldn't believe this was happening. I went out into the garage and looked! That mower hasn't been moved in days. Where do you go? What do you do?"

"I just hang around," he muttered.

"Hang around?" There was no explosion. Hugh began to dread it even more than whatever else might happen. She was too cool, too composed. She had barely spoken to him or his father in two days, and now—in a way he had never hoped for—she was at last "back to normal."

"Hugh, we've always trusted you. We don't follow you around or worry about you because you're—you've always been—a good boy. A responsible boy. But now—" She glared at him. "Where do you go?"

"I don't go anywhere." He worried the sentence out, careful not to lie too openly. "I watch them downtown some."

"Downtown." She stalked to the sink and tapped her ash off and spoke to the window. "He watches them downtown." He noticed all at once that she was all dressed up: heels, stockings, perfume, makeup. Her hair was done, too. "And with whom, may I ask?" She spun on him and pointed a finger in his face. "Careful what you say, Hugh. I've spoken to Ray and Tommy, and I've called two or three others. Don't make things worse by telling more lies. You've never lied before, and I can't believe you're doing it now. With whom were you 'hanging around' downtown?"

"I'm not really *with* anyone. I'm just hanging around down there."

"I hear," Edith kept her voice calm, her tone soft, "that in spite of your promise, you're hanging around with that old man." Hugh flinched. "That nasty, filthy old man." Hugh should have known it was coming. The pattern on the tablecloth suddenly seemed intense, and he stared at it. "You broke your word to me, Hugh."

"I did not," he said suddenly. "I didn't promise. Dad tried to make me, but I didn't. I couldn't."

"Don't lie to me, Hugh! Don't lie to me anymore!" she shrieked. Hugh winced as if he had received a physical blow. "He's a pervert, a radical, a drug addict, crazy as can be!" She ticked off Wilson's supposed faults on her fingers. "He leads young people astray. Ruins their lives. That's what he does!"

"Mom," Hugh said softly, but her hands went up and fluttered around her throat until she stopped them, folded them under her arms in front of her breasts, forced calm on herself. She took a deep breath and began again in a lower, calm tone. "He is a dangerous, dirty, filthy old drunk, Hugh."

"No, he's not!" Anger swarmed around his head, and he rose to Jonas Wilson's defense. He was on his feet before he thought about it, his fists clenched. She blanched, stepped back, and he froze. For the second time that afternoon, he was standing taller than someone he had always imagined he looked up to. The realization buoyed his ire. He was furious with her. She, of all people, should know what it was like to have rumors and gossip spread about her. She, more than anyone he knew, *should know* how people could be harmed by what people said about them. He knew what people said about her, but he also knew the truth, because his father had told him.

Now she was unwilling to give the same benefit of the same doubt to someone else, so it was up to him to tell her, and to tell her in a way that would make her believe him, make her understand what kind of pain could come from saying such things.

He was trembling all over with defiance, breathing heavily, prepared to do battle for Wilson's reputation, just as he would have for hers. In his mother's eyes, though, there was no fight, only fear. She looked at him as if he were a monster, and all at once terrified of the effect he was having on her, he came to himself, relaxed his stance, and softened his voice.

"I mean, he's not what you say. He doesn't take a bath every day, if that's what you mean. And he lives with his dog out in the country, all alone, and his clothes are all worn out—but he's not dirty. Not in the way you mean."

"Hugh—"

"And he's not dangerous or filthy, either." He was speaking rapidly, earnestly. "Not in the way you mean. He's just old. He doesn't even cuss. Not as much as Dad does. And . . ." Hugh took a breath. Edith's cigarette had burned down to the filter, but she stood transfixed, unable to resist the quiet logic that flowed out of him. He sensed that he had the momentum, so he threw her his best pitch. "And he doesn't drink as much as you do."

Her eyes shot to the cocktail glass, the bottle, then came back to him. He had surprised her, he realized, but not enough. He was ahead in the count, but she was still in the box. He breathed out, emptied his lungs, and with the air came all of his internal resolve. He sank back into the chair. "I don't hang around with him much, anyway. I only see him a little, talk to him a little. That's all."

"That's all?" Her voice was shaky but cold. Disbelieving. She was regaining control. He could feel it.

"That's all. He doesn't try to 'lead me astray,' or make me do anything I wouldn't do anyway." Thoughts of the illicit tobacco drifted across his mind with the gray smoke from her cigarette, but he banished them. That wasn't what she was talking about, he sensed, and he'd gone far enough in that direction. "Sometimes . . ." Hugh's hand came up and touched his cheek. "Sometimes he keeps me from doing things I shouldn't do."

"Like what?" Her voice was small, almost childlike, but there was a firmness beneath it.

"Like spreading lies about people," he said softly. It was another good pitch, low and inside, but it missed, she didn't swing, didn't flinch or seem to take the deeper meaning he so desperately wanted her to understand. Ball two, he thought.

"So, what else do you do all day?"

"Nothing," Hugh said. "That's it."

"And what about this?" She tapped the list again. She was still angry, but the fire within her was banked, and the fear was now gone. She sounded more weary than furious, more frustrated than afraid.

Hugh said nothing. There was nothing to say. She had him there, and he knew it. He had blown it. He hadn't given more than a second's thought to mowing a lawn all week. He tried to count how many lawns he was behind. More than the fifteen his mother knew about, that was for sure. The rain had made things worse, and outside, he heard the wet slam of the storm against the house and thunder rattling off in the distance. Full count, he thought. She was too smart for him.

"And what about that mower?" she asked as she ground out the dead smoke and sat down and finished her drink. "That *expensive* mower you just *had* to have? Your father co-signed the note for that. Have you made a payment this week?"

He hadn't, and after buying the cheeseburgers, he didn't have more than two dollars left in his pocket. He shook his head.

"And how are you doing for next week's installment?" He had no pitch left. Now, she was waiting to hit or walk, he thought. He couldn't even offer to start catching up the next day. It would be noon at the earliest before it was dry enough to cut even those lawns with no trees to block the drying heat of the morning sun. It would have to be a walk. He shrugged.

"I don't know what to say, Hugh." She shook her head and replenished her cocktail. Straight whiskey, Hugh noticed, no ice, no water, and nearly a full glass of it. Her hands were steady again, her composure was restored. Beneath the surface, though, she was boiling. Veins in her forehead stood out, and the muscles of her neck were taut. "Your father will *not* take up those payments. And these people are counting on you."

She lowered her head into her hands, and he realized she was about to cry. "Oh, Hugh," she whispered. The rebuke was sharp, painful. His face suddenly burned where Wilson's hand had struck him.

"Mom," he said softly. "I'll make it up. Somehow. Maybe Ray or Tommy can help—"

"No!" She looked up sharply. Her mouth was an ugly tight line across her face. Mascara ran in a tear down one cheek. "You will *not* drag your friends into this. It's your responsibility, and *you* will deal with it."

"Yes, Mother," Hugh said.

She stood, then turned and faced him with a new concern on her face. "Hugh," she said quietly. "Tell me one thing. Truthfully, now. I mean it. I know I'm angry, and I know things have been . . . difficult around here lately. But you must tell me the truth." He nodded and swore that whatever she asked, he would answer. "Does this have anything to do with drugs?"

That was it, he realized in a torrent of relief. That was the bottom of it. That was the big worry. His face broke out into an involuntary grin. He shook his head vigorously. "No, Mom," he spoke happily. "Not that. Never that. Never worry about that."

"Well, I *do* worry. And don't blame me for thinking that way. You read about these things, and all those TV ads . . . well, about the symptoms . . . And there's Jonas Wilson . . . ."

"No, Mom. I don't even know anybody who has anything to do with drugs. Especially Jonas. He's never even mentioned drugs."

She sat again, but her mouth fixed itself once more into a red lipstick scar across her face. "This is still serious. And your father and I will have to decide what to do about it."

"I think—"

"You will have no part in our decision," she said grimly. "We've had a bad week, Hugh. A very bad week. You can't imagine how bad it is. The phone has been ringing off the wall. I've heard the most awful things about . . . about a lot of nonsense. I thought the worst was behind us years ago, but it's not. Now we have this to deal with."

She reached across the table and took both of his hands in hers. Hugh felt something hot and heavy drop inside him. "I just don't want to lose you, Hugh. I don't think I could take another loss like that." He couldn't either, he thought.

At that moment, Harry came in.

Hugh and Edith both rose and stared open-mouthed at Harry Rudd when he literally blew through the kitchen door. The gale outside invaded the relative peace of the kitchen and seemed to vault Hugh's father into the room in a shower of water and wind. He was sopping, his clothes hung off him like great, wet drapes. His hair was matted down on his forehead, and water dripped from his chin. He flung himself into a kitchen chair, wrung water out of his shirttail.

"Cats and dogs out there," he gasped. "Lucky I didn't drown. God-damn, Edith, pour me a drink."

"What happened?" She fumbled with a glass and ice as he pulled a paper napkin from the holder and mopped his face.

"Goddamn Ford broke down again. Just died and wouldn't start."

"Where?"

"Out by the compress. I had to walk in. Wasn't so bad until it started raining. Jesus, that cloud came up quick." He gulped his drink.

"Go and change. You're making a mess here. You'll catch your—"

"Christ, Edith, give me a chance to get my breath. I ran the last six blocks. I don't know what was worse: the hail or the lightning. You know I ran right past Cullen Nicholson's house. He was out in his garage, but when I started for it, he put the goddamn door down. I know he saw me, too."

"I never did like Cullen Nicholson," Edith said. She took a tea towel from the rack and began rubbing Harry's head. Annoyed, he brushed at her hands but said nothing to stop her. Hugh noticed that she also wiped her eyes once or twice, took deep breaths, and gradually regained the image of her normal self.

"What's worse," Harry said into his glass, drained it, and held it out for a refill. "I left the goddamn window down in the car. Probably afloat by now."

"I'll call Randy Truman and have him—"

"Oh, leave it," Harry accepted the refill and sipped it. "Goddamn thing's shot anyway. It's got over a hundred thousand on it. What the hell? Who'd want it? I sure as shit don't."

"Harry," Edith's voice took a rising pitch to match her elevating eyebrows and a nod in Hugh's direction.

"Sorry," he said automatically.

"Well, go and take a hot shower, and—oh," her face fell.

"What?" He looked around and noticed the empty table, the cold stove. "What's going on? Where's supper?"

"We were going over to the Thompsons'," she said. "They were having some people from out of town for dinner, and we—"

"Oh, Edith." Harry shook his head. "Not tonight. Really, not tonight."

"Well, it doesn't matter now. I mean the car . . ." she looked around. "I could call Loretta and ask them to come pick us up—"

"Really, Edith," Harry repeated, "not tonight." He looked at her clothes, her heels, her hair. "It's been a shitty day, Edith," he said softly. "A real shitty day."

"Hugh." She shifted her eyes toward him, sensing that more was amiss than a broken-down car. "Go to your room."

"No." Harry held up a hand. "Stay right there. You may as well hear it from me. You were there when the old ball got rolling."

"What are you talking about?" Panic swelled in her eyes, and she grasped her drink so tightly that Hugh worried that the glass would shatter.

Harry pulled a soused pack of smokes from his pocket, crushed it to soggy pulp, then reached over and removed a cigarette from her pack, broke off the filter, and lit it dramatically. Then he drew the smoke into his lungs and leaned back with a crooked smile on his face. "I'm now among the ranks of the unemployed."

"You quit?"

"Got canned."

"What?!" She stood up. "They can't—they wouldn't!"

"They did."

"Harry. Twenty-two years! You've been out there twenty-two years."

"Twenty-five. Don't forget where I was before I joined the navy. I had a watch coming this October."

"And they let you go?"

"No," he smiled and took another puff. "They fired me. Shit-canned me. Showed me the gate. Gave me the old pink-slip-don't-let-the-door-hit-you-in-the-ass-on-your-way-out-heave-ho." He leaned forward and spoke steadily. Water still dripped from his clothes in a steady splatter onto the linoleum.

"I was *fired*. Get used to the word. Don't go around telling people anything else. I wasn't laid off, let go, or part of any 'general reduction in personnel.' I was *fired*. Don't let me hear anything different out of either one of you."

"But why? They must have said why." Her voice was cracked. Hugh kept his eyes fixed on her, expecting her to fall completely apart. To his amazement, though, she seemed to grow stronger, to gain power from this latest disaster.

"Oh, they said *why*. They said all kinds of whys. Mostly, they said I was a troublemaker and not a 'team player.' That's how Riley in the front office put it. You know, I think his wife must cut his hair. He has a fresh crewcut every goddamn day."

"It was because of that meeting the other night, wasn't it?" Edith accused. "It was because of what you said about Pete Thompson."

"That was part of it, but that wasn't all of it. I mean, they like Pete. Pete's one of theirs. He's on a leave of absence, or was, while he served as mayor. I guess they knew about Loretta's inheritance, whether Pete did or not." Edith's back stiffened. "Anyway, it didn't have much to do with what I said about Pete. It had to do with what else I said, about Market Street, if that's what it is, and with what Hugh here said."

"Hugh? What did Hugh say?" Her eyes narrowed.

"It doesn't matter. It was true, and that's what matters."

"So they fired you."

"Well, that's not the reason they gave. They couldn't do that. There's still a law against firing somebody for what he says or thinks." He glanced at Hugh. "Right, Sport?"

"So what reason did they give?" she demanded.

"Well, mostly it was because I'm the oldest foreman in the mill." Hugh's father crushed out his smoke and sipped his drink. "Mostly it's because I never went to a regular college and never will make the front office."

"But you were in line! You said yourself—"

"I said a lot of things, Edith. I even believed a lot of them. But today they announced that Milton Brady was retiring, and Terry Eubanks was going up to the top, vice president for production, and when I called them a bunch of sons of bitches for passing me over, they fired me."

"But Terry Eubanks is just a kid. He's not much older than Hugh. I remember when he was—"

"He's twenty-three and has a degree from A&M and is engaged to Riley's daughter. He doesn't know squat about wallboard, and he never will. But he gets Pete Thompson's old office, Milton Brady's old secretary, and my job, or at least what I thought was my job."

Silence fell with the same intensity as the rain outside, and Hugh slowly found himself rising. His problem with the lawns was forgotten, at least for the moment, but his guilt was now pushed aside in hollow regret. If he had never insisted on going to that meeting, even on staying long enough to become involved, none of this would have happened.

"I'll talk to Pete," Edith said confidently. "There must be something—"

"No!" Harry's hand smashed down on the table and upset both of their glasses and the ashtray. "We will not talk to anyone, especially Pete Thompson. This is my hole. I dug it, and I'll either climb out or make a grave of it."

"Harry!"

"I mean it! I don't want any help from Pete Thompson or anyone else associated with the mill or the corporation that owns it. They fired me, Edith! I wouldn't work for them now, no matter what." He sat back. "That's not pride talking. I couldn't work for them, now. I couldn't look this boy straight in the eye if I went back even if they begged me."

"Well, what'll we do?"

"We'll make it. I can do something else. Hell, I've been bossing men for years, and somebody always needs that kind of talent. We've got money saved, and I'm vested—s.o.b.'s didn't think of that. It's cost them over a hundred thou to see my butt walking out for the last time." He laughed dryly. "I'll say one thing for them: They've got one hell of a retirement plan."

"But you're too young to retire."

"I'm not. But I'm not going to become a monument to butt-kissing. Hugh deserves more than that for a father. You deserve more than that for a husband. And I deserve more than that for myself. Now, get some supper on. Soup's fine if nothing else. I'd say let's go out and celebrate," he smiled at Hugh, "but we ain't got wheels. I'm going to take a hot shower, eat something, and see what damage I can do to that bottle. Tomorrow's coming, no matter what happens tonight."

With that he rose dramatically, bowed, and left the room. Hugh sat still while his mother stared after him. She seemed to be in shock.

Almost a full minute went by before she rose, went to the pantry closet, and came out with a mop. "Don't say anything to him about this other business," she said while she attacked the muddy puddles. "I think it might break him." Hugh nodded, and he rose to go. "Help me," she ordered. "There's some tomato soup in the cupboard. You put it on. I'll make some sandwiches."

"It'll be all right, Mom," he said as he found the Campbell's cans and took them to the opener. "He'll pull us through it."

"I know that," she said, sitting down and staring at the kitchen door. Her hand idly brought the glass to her lips.

—≺

Friday dawned gray and overcast. Hugh rose early and went outside to inspect the weather. The air was laden with water. The rain had continued most of the night, and at dawn a thick layer of clouds boiled overhead and threatened to resume thunderstorming at any moment. At the very least, Hugh thought as he scooched around on the front porch of his home, it won't be dry enough to mow until sometime tomorrow, maybe not until Sunday. His mother had forbidden him to work on Sundays—"It just doesn't look right, Hugh"—and he wondered if she would relent under the present circumstances.

He calculated that he still owed over two hundred dollars on the mower. At twenty bucks a week—the agreed-upon rate—he should have had it paid for by the first weekend in August. Missing a payment wouldn't ruin that plan completely, but it would delay it, and it meant that he would have to go down to the hardware store and confront Mr. Bryant and explain why he hadn't come by on Wednesday with the installment. It also meant—Hugh lowered his chin into his chest—that he would have to go around and deal with all those folks whose lawns were overgrown and waiting on him. Some hadn't been cut in two weeks, others in three, and with all the rain, they would be hard going. Some, he remembered, had big berms and inclines, which meant the mower would stall a lot, and it also meant he would have to buy extra bags—part of the arrangement—to sack up all the clippings. The more he thought about the problem, the more depressed he became.

Hugh's attention was distracted by a movement in the heavy dim stillness of the early morning. A figure turned the corner under the streetlamp a block away and walked briskly toward their house. Hugh watched him idly. Somebody out for a morning jog, he guessed. He had vowed to run every morning all summer, and he hadn't once. It went with the batting practice, the fielding he'd promised himself to work on, too. And hadn't. The prospect of exercise seemed impossible. He was weary. He hadn't been able to sleep all night.

After he had cleared away the supper dishes, he had gone to his room and listened to music on his earphones, afraid of what he might overhear from his parents, whom he had left sitting silently in the living room. Harry had barely touched his soup and sandwich, and as soon as everything was cold or wilted, he rose, left the kitchen, and enthroned himself on his mother's antique chair with his bare feet up on her delicate, Victorian ottoman. He turned on the television but muted the sound. Then he opened the paper, but he didn't read it. It rested on his lap while he sat and stared out the window at the rain and smoked one cigarette after another.

After a while, Edith quit fussing about the way Hugh was loading the dishwasher, and she took a glass, a bowl of ice, and the bourbon bottle and went in to join him, and that's the way Hugh had left them.

It seemed, Hugh thought, that he had been leaving them that way a lot lately.

Now, though, he was up again, facing a new day. Worries followed him out onto the porch and buzzed around his head. He wondered what it would be like with Harry out of work. It was hard to imagine. The wondering soon gave way to what it really meant for his father to be out of work, hanging around the house. Or would he start looking for a new job right away? Hugh had trouble seeing his father doing anything else, working for anyone else. He wasn't entirely sure what Harry Rudd's job consisted of at the mill, but there was no other plant or industry like that anywhere around. That might mean that they would move away, go to another town or even state. Hugh's thoughts swirled in the gray morning light.

Briefly, he recalled the confrontation with his mother the afternoon before. It frightened him, now, the way he had stood before her, argued directly with her, looked into her eyes, not as a son, but as an adversary, the same way he might have stood up to Tommy or Ray or anyone his own age. But the image didn't fit his idea of himself, didn't seem like him at all. It was some stranger: taller, stronger, somehow more confident than Hugh had ever believed himself to be. Oddly, though, when he contemplated it, he felt those things inside, as if they had been there all along and were only now being realized. He shook his head violently, trying to disperse the discomfort they caused.

Shifting mental gears, he spent a while going over the list of the unmowed lawns, adding names of those who had been too polite to call about his negligence and then listing those whose lawns were just coming due that week. He had agreed to do twenty-two a week on a regular basis, and there were almost a dozen "specials," people who were out of town or sick or otherwise temporarily indisposed to mowing. On top of that, he had less than two dollars left in cash—no money for gasoline or bags—and what he had in the bank was out of reach unless he took his passbook down and faced Mr. Goodwell, who, he knew, would immediately telephone his mother to report that Hugh was "robbing his college account."

Of course, he could start collecting fees when he started mowing again, but given the weather, that wouldn't happen until tomorrow. If it didn't rain any more. His mood was as low, dark, and unsettled as the clouds overhead.

The figure—the jogger—coming up the street toward him was now recognizable, and Hugh was startled to see his father approaching. Harry did indeed have on a gray jogging suit, a Christmas gift from two years before. After trying it on, Harry smiled and put it back into its box. It had not been worn since that Hugh knew about, and it looked somehow strange and misplaced on Harry's portly frame.

"Morning, Sport." Hugh's father raised his hand and waved in a cheery tone to match his greeting. "Up kind of early, aren't you?"

Hugh nodded and scooted over to make room on the concrete front porch. His bare feet were cold in the wet grass that he nestled them in. Harry smelled of sweat and tobacco. He jauntily vaulted to the porch and turned and sat down next to Hugh in one motion. "Mom up yet?"

Hugh shook his head. "I didn't see her. I've been out here a while. Couldn't sleep."

"Know what you mean." He pulled off a sweaty headband and wrung it out. A few drops of moisture joined the heavier water on the grass. "Humid out here, this morning." He smiled and stretched out his arms. "I've been promising myself to get up and take a long walk before dawn for years. This morning, I heard the rain stop, and I decided: What the hell, it's Friday, and I've got no place to go, nothing to do for once in my life. So I just suited up, and there I went."

"Was it fun?" Hugh asked flatly.

"Oh, it was good, I don't know about fun," Harry replied and pulled a pack of Camels and a lighter from the suit's pockets. "And I was only able to run about two blocks before I gave out." He grinned and lit the smoke. "When I was in the navy, I always liked being up early. Didn't have much choice. I seemed to draw the dog watch more often than not. I didn't mind. There was something peaceful about the sun coming up over the sea. It was sort of like seeing the first sunrise ever, you know?"

Hugh didn't reply.

"That's what I was doing when I met your mother. Did I ever tell you that story?"

"No," Hugh said. He wished his father wouldn't talk so much. He had other things on his mind. Hugh wanted to tell him about the unmown lawns, about the trouble he was in financially. It wasn't a good time for stories.

"Well, she was a student at UT in Austin, you know, doing some postgraduate work. They were all down in Corpus—Aransas Pass, really—for spring break. A big storm came up, and they came back into town and sort of camped out on the bay. That morning, she and a bunch of friends were walking down the seawall, looking for a doughnut shop, of all things, when I came into the pier with an admiral."

"An admiral?" Hugh asked in spite of himself.

"Yeah. Admiral Benstock. I was on the *Hornet* then, and he was doing an inspection. We'd been on maneuvers in the gulf. We made port the night before, and we were bringing him in the gig for a breakfast meeting he was having with some other officers somewhere downtown. He always liked me. Said I reminded him of his son." Harry coughed briefly on the smoke, then continued, "He was killed in Vietnam. Anyway, he knew your mother. Her father, you know, was captain of the *Enterprise* then, and she was docked in Corpus, too. Anyway, when I helped him onto the pier, she spotted him and came over, and he talked to her a while, then he introduced us and went on to his meeting."

"Love at first sight?" Hugh asked.

"Naw," Harry said. "But we did spend the rest of the morning talking while I waited on Benstock. Anyway, I had a liberty coming, so we made a date. Two years later, we were married."

"Were you in Corpus the whole time?"

"Nope. All over the world. I sailed the Pacific, the Med, Persian Gulf, and even got up to Iceland once. But we wrote back and forth. She finished her college work, and I finished my hitch, and we hitched up."

Harry smiled weakly. "Her father never did take to her marrying a common seaman, even a petty officer. He thought she should have held out at least for a lieutenant. Still doesn't much like me for taking her so far from the sea, either, I don't think. But if I hadn't had the gig that morning, I wouldn't have taken Benstock in, and I wouldn't have met her, and you wouldn't have come along. All in all, I'd say mornings have been good to me. Come to think of it, you were born about this time of morning."

And Larry died in the morning, Hugh thought darkly. "Where did you go? On your walk, I mean."

"Out to the eastern edge of town. Right down Oak Street, all the way out to Old Man Southern's house."

"That's a long way."

"Used to be nearly four miles, there and back." Hugh's father laughed and pulled another cigarette from the suit's pocket. "They might have changed it, though. Lots changes when you're not looking."

"Yeah." Hugh thought again of the lawns.

"So, what's on your mind?"

"What?"

"C'mon, Sport. I may be a 'loudmouth and a troublemaker,' and I can spin a boring sea yarn before the sun comes up, but I'm not stupid. I know when something's bothering you. Any other time, you'd be sleeping till noon. Rain means no work for you young outdoor types."

"Dad . . ." Hugh looked off.

"You're not worrying about *me*, are you?"

Hugh shook his head.

"Well, don't. Hey, we're going to be just fine. I've got quite a pile saved up with my retirement and all, and we've got some time. I was thinking we might just take a vacation. You and me. How'd that be? Maybe go up to Colorado. Do some camping, fishing, that sort of thing. God, I used to love to fish. Haven't been out in years. What'd' you say, Sport? Want to go out and drown some worms with your old man?"

"Uh, maybe," Hugh started.

"Oh, that's right. You're a working stiff! You're not footloose and fancy free like me." Then he turned serious. "You know, Sport, except for the hitch I did in the navy, I think I've punched a time clock or been on paid vacation or a weekend every day since I was seventeen. Even at sea, there was somebody telling me where I had to be, what I had to do. It's a good feeling not having to go or do anything all day long. I think I could get used to it."

"Dad—"

"I mean, you've got the right idea. The rest of those yo-yos working out on that farm may be making good money, but hell, Sport, you're your own boss. Work when you want to, don't when you don't."

"Dad, I need to talk—"

"I've been thinking about doing the same thing. Maybe go into some kind of business. Maybe what you're doing, only large scale. Landscaping. I used to be pretty good at that sort of thing—planting, arranging flower-beds, putting in those little creosote timbers, concrete stepping-stones, trimming everything up, bagging leaves . . ."

"Dad, I—"

"Mowing lawns." Harry finished and took a long drag off his cigarette, and they both fell silent.

Hugh knew it was up to him to speak. "Mom told you?"

"Didn't have to, Sport," Harry said. "Three guys at work have been ragging me about it all week. I made some calls, did some checking. I found out you 'forgot' to make your payment this week. Wasn't part of our deal, Sport."

"I know."

"So, how bad is it?"

"It's bad. I figure I'm behind more than thirty-five yards, counting to-day and this weekend." Hugh gestured toward the sky. "Most of them will

line up somebody else, I guess, or they'll just be too mad and do it themselves." He looked at his father. "Guess I blew it, Dad."

"Guess you did, Sport. I took care of the payment on the mower, next
week's, too. There's a full can of gas in the back of the Ford, so that should
get you started. Soon as it clears up, you're going to have to get going, see
how much you can salvage, and work your young ass off catching up."

"I will," Hugh promised. He never meant anything more in his life.

"And no more lies." Harry spun the butt off into the wet grass. "I know
where you were last weekend, Sport." Harry looked up and pretended to
inspect the clouds that now began to offer a drizzle. "And I know what you
were doing." He looked at Hugh steadily. "I have to tell you I don't see
much harm in it, although why you would want to do it is beyond me."

"I'm not sure, either." Hugh's sore muscles reminded him of the work.
"He's a neat guy, Dad."

"I guess you think so. For you to lie to me and your mother that way, he
must be about the neatest guy in the world."

"You wouldn't have let me go."

"Probably not. Your mother sure wouldn't have. But she doesn't know
where you were, and she doesn't have to."

"How did you find out?"

"C'mon, Hugh. Guys I work with drive by there all day long. The sight
of you pushing a wheelbarrow full of cowchips around attracted quite a bit
of attention."

Hugh bowed his head. How stupid. Of course. Every car and truck that
passed down that old highway was on its way to or from the mill. He was a
fool to think he could expose himself that way and not be recognized.

"Well, it turned out all right." Harry stood and stretched. "You're not
dead, mutilated, or kidnapped. From all I could see when I rode out that
way with Homer Dubose, you might have been in danger of being worked
to death, but that's about it."

"You've got that right," Hugh confirmed. Then he started. "You came
out there?"

"Sure, Sport," Harry laughed. "You're still my kid. My responsibility. I
drove by a couple of times, but I didn't see any problem."

"You came out there," Hugh said, shaking his head. He didn't know
whether to be pleased or angry.

"Anyhow, I talked with Ortega out at the fruitstand. Did you know he's been doing business with that crazy old fool for years? Seems that's how he gets what he needs. That must be some garden."

"It's wonderful." Hugh's eyes brightened. "It's full of stuff. Those vegetables I brought home came from there." Harry nodded, and Hugh plunged ahead. "He's got a neat house, too. That old boxcar might not look like much, but inside, it's clean and neat. You wouldn't believe it."

"I'll take your word for it." Harry sighed. "But in the meantime, we'll just keep it all between ourselves."

"Aren't you going to tell me to stay away from him?"

"Would you?"

Hugh looked up with a hard, searching stare. Then he shook his head.

"Then I won't tell you to. I don't want any more lies."

"There won't be any." Hugh stood and accepted a firm handshake from his father, who took the occasion to spin him around and put an arm over his shoulder and gave him a brief, firm hug. "I still don't know what's wrong with him, why people hate him so," Hugh said.

"Well." Hugh's father dropped his arm from Hugh's shoulder and rubbed his chin. He needed a shave. "It was like I told you before. It was a long time ago. Before I was born, I guess. But even then, he was something of an outcast. Then, about twenty years ago, little more, before we came here to live, some things happened."

"What sort of things?" Hugh asked.

"You get in this house right now!" Edith's voice came through the front door as it swung open to reveal her standing there, her hair in curlers, her hand clutching her robe tightly to her throat. "It's raining out there! Doesn't anyone around here sleep?"

"Tell you later, Sport," Harry whispered. The father and son exchanged sheepish grins, hung their heads, and filed in past her.

"Harry, you smell like a wet dog! Go take a shower. Hugh, go put your sneakers on! You'll catch your death sitting out there like that. I'll put some coffee on."

In a half-hour they sat around the table to an old-fashioned breakfast—something that Hugh's father had been mockingly demanding for years. Flapjacks and eggs, sausages and gravy, and hash-browned potatoes filled their plates. His mother buzzed around the kitchen looking like an absurd robot with her curlers catching the overhead light and surrounding her head like electrodes. Her eyes were bloodshot, there were large bags under them. Her skin was splotchy, and Hugh noticed that her hands shook until she downed three tumblers full of orange juice.

That she laced each with a generous dollop of whiskey didn't surprise him in the least. He was growing accustomed to the smell of alcohol on her breath.

Hugh shocked both of them by asking for coffee, but Edith insisted he drink an extra glass of juice as well. He could see that her anxiety was just under the busy surface, and he and his father chatted about sports and other items of small interest to either of them while she fussed and cooked. Finally, she shooed them out of the kitchen, and Hugh went out and got on his bike.

For a moment, he didn't know what to do, where to go. The drizzle had stopped, but more rain threatened. He rolled out to the end of the drive-way and sat and thought. Then, without much more than a look over his shoulder to where Harry stood and smoked and watched him from the house's window, he pushed off and headed downtown, wondering idly as he pedaled why he was so lucky to have been blessed with such a father.

CHAPTER FIVE

Hugh heard the word "implode" for the first time later that morning. The clouds broke up as he turned the corner of Main Street and parked his bike in front of Central Drugs. He was glad. The sparse change he had in his jeans wouldn't have kept him in lime Cokes for very long that morning, and he had no other place to go. Down by the tracks the crowd was already gathered for the day's festivities, so when he went inside, he wasn't surprised to find the place nearly empty.

Grissom and his engineer friend were in a booth in the back, and Hugh eased down the aisle adjacent to them and pretended to inspect suntan oils and insecticides while he listened to their conversation.

"I got back about six," Grissom said. Hugh could see through cracks in the shelves' stock that Grissom's suit was rumpled and his hair was tangled into spiders' nests. Hugh had previously thought of him as a young man, barely older than Randy Truman or some of his cronies. This morning, though, Grissom looked older than Phelps Crane, and no less worn out.

"I didn't get out of here until after nine," he said. "It's no mean thing to fly to Chicago and back before anyone knows you're gone. They weren't exactly thrilled about the Christless midnight meeting, but they're happy this is going to be over soon. If they hadn't let me use the company jet, I'd still be in the air. God, I'm worn out."

The engineer nodded, and Hugh watched his head dip when he leaned over his coffee. "So, are we set?"

"The stuff's coming in from Kansas City tonight. The team you asked for."

"Exactly what are they bringing?"

"Uh, I don't know. TNT, I guess. They're bringing enough for four charges."

"That won't do it."

"What do you mean? We took out that grain elevator in Fort Worth with less than that."

"On the third try." The engineer spoke so softly that Hugh had to move down to the sunglasses display and pretend to be trying them on in order to hear him. He remembered the concrete grain elevators in Fort Worth. It had made the network news. They had set charges inside the building to bring it down in one blast, but the dynamite—or whatever they used—went off, and except for some puffs of smoke, nothing happened. It took three days and three tries to demolish it. On the final try, the concrete tower sat there for a moment, and then it just collapsed into itself, like a paper bag full of dust suddenly deflated.

Hugh's stomach suddenly went cold. What the wrecking ball couldn't do, explosives could, eventually.

"Then, we'll get plastic," Grissom said. "I'm authorized to get whatever it will take. Just so it works."

"Look." The engineer's voice rose. "I've been trying to tell you for a week: That's no ordinary building down there. It was built to stay. I've torn down gun emplacements down on Galveston and out on the Coast that weren't built that well. Shit, I did a SAC bunker up in Kansas City that the governor had built back during the Cold War, and none of them were built half that good. I've never seen anything like it. I could go in right now and do two months' restoration and turn it into a better structure than the command bunker under the White House."

He sipped his coffee. "I'd say that you can set high-quality *plastique* or whatever the hell you want, but unless you have the right stuff, and the right amount in the right place, nothing short of a nuclear warhead's going to faze that structure. Maybe not even that."

"I thought you said you could do it." Grissom's voice was tired, cold.

"I *can* do it. I *will* do it. But I'm not guaranteeing that it'll go on the first try. Or even the second. Not with TNT or standard demolition HE . . . high explosives. I need gelatin, C-1209, at least four tons' equivalency for each—"

"Shit!" Grissom sat back and tortured his hair some more. "You know damn well I don't have authorization for *that*. That's experimental stuff. Dangerous as hell."

"We used it in Fort Worth."

"That was different. Dow wanted to see if it would work for this kind of thing."

"Well, it did, didn't it?"

Grissom rubbed his chin. "That stuff scares me. It's not stable. The god-damn army won't even use it. It's not reliable."

"Tortelli can handle it. He says it's the best stuff around for a job like this. I'll go with that."

"I'll have to call Chicago." Grissom sighed. "Again. God knows what they'll say."

"Well, I can try with what you've got," the engineer said wearily. "But it might be a popcorn fart. In my opinion, it's going to take the gelatin and a lot of it. That building should be preserved as a monument to the construction industry a hundred years ago. They don't build them like that anymore."

"You sound like you're on their side." Grissom looked out the drug-store's window. No one else had come in, but outside, a steady and grow-ing flow of people was moving north, up the street toward the old parking lot. Many had lawn chairs and plastic coolers in their hands.

"I'm not on anybody's side." The engineer sat back and put his fists on the booth's table. "I like old buildings. I can't help it. That's what I became an engineer for in the first place. I'd rather put them up than tear them down. Lots of times, it's just a waste. There was this one structure on this college campus in Tennessee. I went in, just like now, worked my people for a week or so, finally had to implode it."

"So?"

"So, the goddamn floors were eight feet thick and had quadruple rein-forcement. Concrete was so dense, I couldn't even drill through it for the charges until I brought in diamond tips. There I was, drilling holes and stuffing HE into a structure that for half the money they were paying me to take it down could have been refurbished and restored and would still be standing a hundred years from now."

"I don't get it. What's it to you?"

"Nothing. Not one goddamn thing. But I tell you, every time I drive by on I-40 and see the cheap brick gymnasium they put up there, it makes my colon hurt."

"Progress," Grissom said. "You can't get in the way of progress."

"Progress, my ass," the engineer's voice came up once more. "That gym won't be there ten years. They spent nearly three million bucks on it, but the foundation's already cracked, and half the windows leak." He paused and reflected. "They ain't won a basketball championship since it was built, either. I root against them no matter what."

"Seems like you're rooting against me right now."

The engineer took a moment to light a cigar, and Hugh leaned over and pretended to inspect himself in the mirror. The sunglasses he had on were too large and too feminine.

"You pay my salary—or your company does—and all I'm supposed to do is consult. Give you my expert opinion. Then, I'm supposed to engineer the job, if that's what you want. Now, part of my opinion is that you don't have sufficient or the right kind of high explosives to do the job, and there's no other way short of investing a whole summer's work to bring that building down. But my opinion also is that this is a bad mistake, a big deal over nothing. You're creating a lot of hard feelings here, stirring up a hornet's nest. You and the goddamned railroad should put your wye some-place else and give the whole damned thing to this sorry bunch of hicks to turn into a curio shop or something. Would have bought you more goodwill and cost you half what you've spent already.

"But that's just my opinion, and you didn't pay for that one. Only other thing I know is that you better bring it down in one fell swoop. Remember what happened in Fort Worth with that grain elevator. There must have been ten thousand people there by the time that bunch of concrete fell. NBC, CBS, ABC, and CNfuckingN. Local TV's already all over this. If peo-ple around here get wind of what we're planning now, chances are they'll find some ordinance or other—"

"You let me handle PR," Grissom growled and stood. "And the god-damned ordinances. We'll have all the permits we need, for high explo-sives or anything else we want. I've seen to all that. And I'll handle the lo-cal yokels. That's not what you're paid for. That's what I'm paid for."

"And you're doing one hell of a job, Grissom." The engineer waved at Hilda for more coffee. "Where'd you work before this, Beirut?"

"Fuck you," Grissom shot. "You just do your job and let me do mine. There's more cooking here than that building or the wye or anything else."

"That's just my opinion," the engineer said.

"All right," Grissom said. "You've given me your opinion, and I've heard it. Now, I'm calling the shots, and the first shot is going to be to bring that son of a bitch down and quick. You need C-1209, you'll get C-1209, but I'm warning you, if one person gets hurt, if anything goes wrong, then it's your ass that'll be in a sling, not mine."

He looked at his watch. "Shit. It's Friday. They probably won't even come in on a Friday, especially after being up half the night with me last night. I want that building down by Sunday—Hey!"

Grissom spotted Hugh, jumped out of the booth, walked over, and spun him around. "Just what the hell're you doing, you little sneak? You've caused me enough trouble."

Hugh tried to wrestle free of the man's grip, but Grissom had a fistful of his T-shirt and was trying to lift his face up close to his own. "Lemme go!" Hugh yelled.

"Hell I will, you little shit! I've been wondering how everyone knows what I'm going to do before I do it, and I guess you're the answer, you sneaky little bastard."

"Hey, let him go," Hilda called from behind the booth. She waved the half-full coffee pot menacingly. "Claude!" she yelled for the druggist, who peeked over his counter and frowned.

"What's going on out there?" Claude Cutter hollered. "I won't have you kids rough-housing in here."

"I wasn't doing anything," Hugh said to Grissom, who continued to grip his T-shirt in a fist and to breathe his bitter coffee breath all over him.

"You were spying on me," Grissom yelled. "There's a law against corporate espionage in this country."

"Oh, for the love of God." The engineer put his head in his hands.

"I was just looking at the sunglasses," Hugh insisted.

Claude approached, yelling at both Grissom and Hugh—but mostly at Hugh, whom he recognized as being a member of the greatest class of enemies he had ever known—kids—and Hilda joined them, coffee pot in hand, to try to explain what she had seen. The engineer rose and walked to the front of the store, where the Serve Yourself counter's pot rested. He passed Jonas Wilson, who was coming in at the same moment.

"I'm going to take this sneaky little bastard over to the sheriff's office!" Grissom declared to Claude. Hugh twisted ineffectually in the railroad man's hands. "He's fucked me over once too often."

"Think I'd let the boy go, if I was you," Wilson said in a voice so low that Hugh was instantly reminded of every western he had seen.

For a moment the three of them—actually five, counting Hilda and Claude—formed a tableau in front of the sunscreen and beach toys. Grissom stared defiantly into Jonas Wilson's unshaven face and kept his hold on Hugh's T-shirt.

"And just who the hell's going to make me?" Grissom asked.

Hilda backed away at last, and Claude, sensing bigger trouble than he bargained for, scooted back down the aisle toward his telephone.

"Think I'd let him go," Wilson repeated. "An' I'd watch my language, if I was you."

"And just who the fuck are you?" Grissom finally breathed out in Wilson's direction, and his eyes ran up and down Wilson's raggy exterior. "The town bum?"

"Just let the boy go." Wilson's voice was deep and even. Hugh couldn't believe he was standing there. Where had he come from? The old man had a bad habit of appearing when Hugh least expected it, but this time, he was thrilled to see him.

"Oh, yeah, now I remember you," Grissom sneered. "You're the town loony, aren't you. Heard about you."

"Last time." Wilson's eyes were set. "Let him go." His fedora was pulled down on his forehead and shaded his face from the overhead fluorescents. Hugh could hear Claude talking excitedly into his phone behind him. He was pleading with someone to "come quick."

"I'm taking this sneaky little piece of shit to the sheriff," Grissom growled and jerked Hugh up even higher. He was tall, and Hugh's sneakers left the tiled floor beneath him. The shirt cut into the back of his neck.

"Well, I asked you polite," Wilson said without changing his expression. The old man's twisted fingers were closed into fists. "You remember that."

Wilson's right fist came up so swiftly that Hugh couldn't remember seeing it move. There was only a flash of sun-baked flesh as it passed Grissom's jaw. The railroad man's head snapped back on his neck. His hand opened and released Hugh, who stumbled backward and upset the sunglasses display behind him. Grissom dropped like a sack of old laundry, crumbling to the floor, his eyes glazed. Blood spurted from his lip. His arms collapsed like empty bags as they folded themselves across his chest.

"You okay, boy?" Wilson put the same hammer hand on Hugh's shoulder to steady him and looked into his eyes. ". . . Uh, yeah," Hugh muttered. The engineer moved down the parallel aisle and around to stand over Grissom. He looked down at him, and then he raised his eyes to Wilson.

"Somebody's been needing to do that for a while," he said. He stood upright and stuck out his hand. "C. W. Pruitt," he said. "Pleased to meet you."

"Jonas Wilson," Wilson said, grasping Pruitt's hand and shaking it. Two of Wilson's knuckles were red. Grissom moaned. "You're the man going to take down the Hendershot building?"

"I'm the man who's going to try."

"Power to you," Wilson smiled. "I helped put her up."

"Well, you did one hell of a job." The engineer pumped Wilson's hand again, then his eyes narrowed. "Wait a minute. That was damn near a hundred years ago."

"Not quite." Wilson retrieved his hand and picked up his bag in one motion. "But it's been a spell." He turned to go, but Grissom's voice rang out before he could escort Hugh out of the drugstore.

"I'm filing charges," he yelled. "That was assault. Pure and simple assault. I've got witnesses! You're going to jail, mister."

"You know, Grissom," Pruitt said and took a long pull from his cigar. "You're a royal pain in the ass." He turned and went back to his booth. "I didn't see a thing," he added.

Claude and Hilda stood dumbly shaking their heads over Grissom, who was trying to pull himself up onto his feet. He upset the beach toys display and brought down a shower of plastic buckets and shovels, Frisbees and brightly colored balls on top of him.

"I think you're drunk, mister," the druggist said. "There's a law in this town about being drunk in public." He went back to his telephone, and Hugh took one more look at Grissom's face. Grissom was glowering at him from under an avalanche of yellow, blue, and red plastic.

—≺

"They said 'implode,'" Hugh confided to Wilson once they were back on the street. He wanted to thank the old man for coming to his rescue, but he couldn't find the right words. Pushing his bike ahead of him, he had trouble keeping up with Wilson's pace.

"I've heard tell of it." Wilson stopped for a passing car on Second Street, grimaced, and snapped his fingers, and Goodlett appeared seemingly from nowhere and fell in behind them. "They put a bunch of dynamite at pressure points and set it all off at once. Building just falls in on itself. It's safer'n blowing her up and faster'n tearing her down. When they're done, all's left is to run the bulldozers over her and load up the rubble."

"Well, that's what they're going to do. Grissom said that they had 'stuff' coming in, something called C-1209—a ton, he said."

"Some kind of fancy dynamite, I reckon," Wilson said.

"That's right. He had to go to Chicago last night, and he has to call them today to get permission to use it. It's dangerous, I think."

"Probably," Wilson muttered.

"At least that's what that guy, Mr. Pruitt, said."

"Well, then I guess that's it. They say when?"

"This weekend. Sunday, I guess."

"Well, durn it." Wilson stopped. "That means I can't get out to the place. I'd miss it."

Hugh thought of his own work that awaited him that weekend. "I may not get to see it, either."

They started walking again and turned the corner to the parking lot, where they were faced with a larger crowd than ever. The TV vans were back, and newspaper reporters milled around, pointing out camera angles for photographers who followed them. Carl Fitzpatrick was in place beside his motor home, sitting in a circle of lawn chairs and sharing coffee with three well-dressed men. Lydia was bustling around, handing out pastries to anyone who came by. Linda, Hugh noted, was nowhere in sight.

The Methodist Women were back in business, and the Coca-Cola trailer-concession stand was open and selling soft drinks, coffee, and doughnuts. A number of kids Hugh's age joined the adults, and he decided that the heavy rain must have given some of his working friends the day off as well. Some boys tossed a baseball in the track bed, and older kids wearing sunglasses stood around and tried to look cool as they surveyed the growing party.

"I reckon I'd best go out and see if Ortega'll give me a ride out and back," Wilson said. "He'll want to cut my rate, but they's nothing for her. Spider mites'll have my 'maters, and squash beetles'll be all over the place. Got to spray 'em, and I don't want to be out of pocket when the fireworks start."

Wilson started to move away, then he stopped. "Want to come?"

"I can't," Hugh hung his head. "I, uh . . . there's trouble at home."

Wilson stood still for a moment, then he came back over to Hugh and steered him off to a concrete step that led off of the Main Street sidewalk where they seated themselves. He pulled out his makings and rolled a smoke, then automatically handed them to Hugh.

Hugh reached for the tobacco sack and papers, then pulled back. "It's a little public here," he said.

"If you think so." Wilson put the things away, fired his own smoke, and leaned back. "What kind of trouble?"

Hugh hesitated. He didn't want to repeat it all, not out loud, but something inside him pushed him toward Wilson's waiting stare, so he took a breath and plunged in, starting at the top and working down to the bottom of his troubles. He told Wilson about his neglect of his work, about his father's being fired, about all of it. He even outlined his mother's increasingly heavy drinking, the long silences, and how upset all of it made things. He confessed about his lying to them about going out to Wilson's place the previous weekend and about how his father and he had grown suddenly close since all the business about the building started.

Finally, he broke through completely and told Wilson about Larry's death, the way it stayed around the house like a stray cat, slinking around the corners and inserting itself whenever things seemed to be going all right. The only topic he didn't touch on was his mother and Loretta Thompson, but Wilson knew more about that rumor than he did.

And, because it was somehow connected, he omitted any account of his conflict with his mother about his association with the old man.

Wilson smoked two more cigarettes and listened closely, occasionally nodding.

"I guess," Hugh concluded, feeling wrung out, as if he had been crying, "that I'm afraid. Things just seem . . . well, they seem like they're breaking apart. It's kind of like that building down there." He looked into the crowd that blocked their view of the worksite. "They keep pounding at it and pounding at it, but nothing happens. It crumbles away, a little at a time, but the next morning, it's still there, all beat up and not very pretty. But there.

"But like you said, sooner or later they're going to hit it in the right place, and it's going to fall. Now, they're going to blow it up. I'm afraid Mom and Dad are going to blow up, too. And it's mostly my fault." He sighed heavily, feeling lighter than he had before, but no less confused. "I guess that's it."

Wilson put a hand out and touched Hugh on the shoulder and gave it a quick but gentle squeeze. Then he rose and hefted his sack. "Your daddy's a good man," he said. "I'd do what he tells you and listen to him if I was you. I'll be back tomorrow."

"That's it?" Hugh stood and looked up at Wilson, incredulous. "That's all you're going to say? That's your advice? I thought you were my friend." His fists clenched. "I just spilled my guts to you, and you act like I farted or something. Jesus, you're some friend."

"I don't know if we're friends or not, boy." Wilson snapped his fingers for Goodlett. "But I know I did something today I haven't done in years."

"Yeah, what's that?"

"I went inside a Main Street store," Wilson flexed his right hand to expose the bruised flesh across two knuckles, and Hugh now sensed his anger. "And I hit a man. I ain't done that in longer'n I can remember. I ain't likely to do neither one again for a while, neither."

Hugh started to speak, but Wilson put out the same hand in a flat palm to stop him. "I don't expect no thank yous, so don't give me none. That ain't why I done it, anyway. Like that C. W. feller said: That railroad man needed hitting a long time, and I was just the one to do her. So you don't owe me nothing, and I ain't beholding to you, neither."

"Well, I'm sorry I was the cause of it, anyway," Hugh said, thoroughly embarrassed. "But I do know what they're planning, and I can tell somebody. Mr. Fitz—"

"You keep your mouth shut." Wilson's hand snaked out and landed in a firm grip on Hugh's shoulder. His stubbed fingers bit into the boy's collarbone. "You've said plenty already. You don't need to run your mouth 'bout nothing."

"But if they know, they can stop—"

"Just keep it to yourself," Wilson said. Then he moved close to Hugh and whispered. "This has gone on long 'nough. Carl Fitzpatrick's in the soup, but he don't know it. Let's let him hang hisself with the rope he's got or slip the noose and be a better man for it. There ain't no saving that building. Never was. I was wrong 'bout that. I think that ol' boy back there's the man to do her."

"Pruitt? He said it was a mistake," Hugh recalled.

"It is. Likely. But I seen something in his eyes, something good. The man's going to do it. If Hendershot's has got to be tore down, I say let a man like that do her. He's got a respect for it. Knows what it stands for."

"What does it stand for?" Hugh asked. He wanted to cry again.

Wilson's faded eyes looked up at the crowd. "I ain't seen nothing like this before. These folks is all worked up. They're more together on this thing'n they been 'bout anything for a long time. Maybe some good'll come from it. Maybe not. But in 'nother way, that ol' building stands for other things, things you know better'n me. Things you just said. I ain't sure of that. Only thing I know for sure is that nothin's going to be the same when the Hendershot buildin's gone."

He turned and said over his shoulder, "I got to go. Don't say nothing 'bout nothing. Let's just see what happens next."

Wilson mounted the steps and walked off down Main Street with Goodlett padding along behind, and Hugh turned and moved into the crowd.

—≺

"Did he give you a kiss?" Ray asked Hugh when Hugh sidled up to the concession stand and bought a Coke. Tommy stood behind him and smirked.

The question and its implication shot through Hugh like an electrical charge. Quick sweat beaded on his forehead.

"Why don't you go piss up a rope?" he shot at them, and they giggled.

"Hey, chill out," Tommy said. "We didn't mean nothing. I mean, you used to be an okay guy, Hugh, but ever since you started hanging around with old Looney Tunes, you've gotten weird."

"Yeah," Ray put in, "you're crazier than he is."

"I'm not weird, and he's not crazy." They strolled out by the pylons together and leaned while they sipped their sodas.

"Yeah, well, from what your mom said," Ray shot Tommy a knowing look, "you're in some seriously deep shit."

Hugh stared at his friends for a moment. Two weeks ago, he would have had no hesitation about telling them all that had transpired at home. They were his best friends—shared everything, covered for each other. But now, he found them untrustworthy, just a part of the same stupidity that seemed to surround the whole town. They were people like he used to know a long time ago, a part of a past he had somehow deliberately left behind.

Down at the worksite, the workers slogged around in the mud and drove their bulldozers around the building's perimeter. One man was up in the cockpit of the small crane, and the crowd was speculating as to when they would begin slamming the ball against the building once more.

"Heard your old man got shit-canned," Ray said. Hugh's eyes flared with immediate anger. "Hey, I didn't mean nothing. I just heard it, that's all."

"Yeah, well, 'shit happens,'" Hugh quoted, "even deep shit."

"Listen, man," Tommy said, "we know you're way behind in your mowing business, and . . . well, we were wondering if you needed some partners?"

"Partners?" Hugh thought about his mother's strong admonition that it was his problem and that he would have to deal with it.

"Yeah," Ray said. "I can get my old man's mower. He won't care. He hasn't used it since he started making me cut the grass. Two can work faster than one, and Tommy can rake and bag."

Hugh sipped his Coke. It might get him caught up.

"I'd have to check with my mom," he said. "But—"

"Well, if you don't want to do it, then fuck you," Ray shot. "I—we were just trying to help you out."

"I just—"

"I mean, what the hell?" Ray was almost yelling, and several people nearest them turned their heads to follow the argument. "Ain't we good enough for you? We heard about your sucking up to Linda Fitzpatrick, so I guess you're just too damn good to be seen with us."

"I'm not sucking up to anybody," Hugh started. "Mom just said—"

"Well, you can go home and suck her tit," Tommy said bitterly. He had been standing off to one side and allowing Ray to lead the charge, but now he decided to back Ray and attack Hugh on his own.

"Yeah," Ray put in. "That is, if you've got any suck power left after hanging 'round with ol' Looney Tunes Wilson."

"Well, I guess it'd be okay if you'd—" Hugh started, but Ray and Tommy were already moving away.

"Listen, asshole," Ray whispered loudly enough to be heard by several people, who frowned at his language, "it's open season now. I'm going out today and see how many lawns we can line up. If they're your customers, too darned bad. They'll probably be glad to have someone they can depend on."

"That's not fair," Hugh shouted.

"You should have thought about that before," Ray came back. "We tried to help you out, and you don't want us around, so that's that. It's our business now, and it's our money. There for the taking." Tommy looked uncertain for a moment, but he finally nodded in agreement.

"He's right, Hugh. You've gone queer for that old man or something. Besides, we need the money." Ray grinned a sly grin once more, and they left Hugh standing alone.

"Well, that takes care of that problem," Hugh muttered to himself. "Now, all I've got to do is figure out how to handle the mower payments."

He turned back to his pylon and contemplated the situation. If it dried out by midafternoon, he could get started before Ray and Tommy had a chance to get organized. Maybe he could go ahead and mow the Smiths' and the Blankenships' yards. If he hurried, and it dried out early enough, he might get to one more before dark. The Hatchers' grassy expanse would be needing it badly, but it had a huge incline and often took him more than two hours to complete. That was for in the morning, as soon as the dew dried, provided it didn't rain any more.

Hugh looked at the broken clouds above him. Humidity hung over the town like a blanket, and the air still smelled like rain. He recalled his father's apt description from the night before. It was turning out to be another shitty day—a shitty day, and a shitty summer.

Around him on the parking lot things settled into what had become a morning routine for most of the townspeople. The bleachers were full. Numerous people with regular jobs were there, including Jerry Tallwater, who pretended to ignore Hugh. Hugh wondered if Jerry and the rest of those who usually had to work had taken vacation or just called in sick to come down to watch the show. Linda sat up on a top bleacher by Randy Truman and some older boys, but he didn't want to confront her right then, so he counted out the last of his change, bought another Coke, and then milled through the crowd.

Finally he worked his way over to the Fitzpatrick motor home. Carl was standing outside next to Elton Matthews and the same stranger Hugh saw inside with them the day before. A TV cameraman and a reporter stood inside the semicircle outside the motor home and caught Carl's every word. Hugh leaned against the side of the RV to listen.

"I'm telling you we've got them on the run," Carl announced proudly, putting his arm around the person nearest him. Immediately, he discovered it was Phelps Crane and, with a casual gesture, moved slightly away. Hugh believed he could smell Phelps from where he stood. Phelps blinked at Carl's sudden movement, then scowled into the camera and said nothing. He was filthy, and he had developed a twitch in one eye that made him seem to be winking all the time.

"I called Austin again this morning, and they're finally coming around," Carl went on. "That liberal down there in the attorney general's office has felt the pressure from Washington, I can tell you, and he's changing his tune. It appears there'll be a federal injunction to stop work by the close of business today, Monday morning at the latest. If we get that, then the momentum is definitely on the side of the people of this town, and the building *will be* saved."

The small group gathering near Carl offered a smattering of applause, and Hugh turned to see Carl beaming.

"What if you fail to get the injunction?" the reporter, a youthful blond woman in a short skirt, asked him. "You've tried before and failed, haven't you?"

Carl frowned at the question. "I'm telling you," he repeated his tag line, "we'll either save the building or die trying. This is a total civic effort! It cuts across partisan interests and exposes the true colors of the politically corrupt. It also shows what strong and honest leadership in municipal government can do." He nodded at Elton, who smiled weakly. "We've been taken for a ride by our own—or formerly our own—mayor. But that's behind us, now."

"Does that mean no one will be filing charges against Mayor Thompson?"

"No one will be filing charges," Carl said expansively. "Mr. Thompson has resigned, and the city is now in the capable hands of Mr. Matthews here." Elton nodded and smiled at the camera. "That was not the issue, and it's still not," Carl said. "You've got to be able to put aside personal considerations and take the bull by the horns. Which means, little lady, that we don't need anyone looking over our shoulders and telling us how to run our affairs. Mayor Thompson was duped into believing that nothing we did here would matter to the big liberal muckety-mucks in the Capitol. He thought that once they said 'jump' all we had to ask was 'how high?' Well, things don't work that way. If those folks down in Austin just won't respond to reason and well-prepared legal arguments," he punctuated his speech with a wave of his finger, "then they shouldn't even be down there."

More applause interrupted him, but he waved it aside and went on. "I hope that as your next elected official to state government—" he paused and chuckled, "—if I'm successful, of course—I can do more for everyone in the state, not just for this one town."

"Of course, you'll be elected," Elton piped up.

"I thought you were just running for city attorney," the reporter said. "Are you announcing your candidacy for state office?" The cameraman zoomed in on Carl's sweaty, smiling face.

"Well," Carl said modestly, "that's sort of up to the people. And that's how it should be!"

J. D. Holt, the owner of the cotton compress, one of the largest of the local businesses, stepped forward dramatically and cleared his throat. "I have something to say," he said to the reporter.

The cameraman stepped back, checked his focus, and J. D. judged his distance from the reporter's microphone and cleared his throat again. "I think, Carl," he said in a confidential tone, but one that was spoken loudly enough to be heard even on the bleachers behind them, where several people, including Linda, turned around. "I say, I think that this whole area ought to consider what Carl Fitzpatrick could do for this town, this state, this whole danged country from the Governor's Mansion, not just from here in City Hall." After a beat, there was more sudden, spontaneous applause, and Carl lowered his head in a show of humility.

"I mean," J. D. went on as he was guided by Elton, Harvey Turnbull, and George Ferguson to a nearby pickup's tailgate. He climbed up awkwardly, checking to make sure the reporter and cameraman followed him. "I mean, I think saving the Hendershot building—little as that may seem to anybody who doesn't live right here—is more than just a show of civic responsibility. Indeed, the issue of the building itself is unimportant." J. D. pulled a typed sheet of paper from his pocket and glanced at it. "But I also think," he took confidence and read from the paper in a booming voice, "that such success as we've had already under Carl's leadership shows what can be done when a man of integrity and action goes up against the corruption of one of these big northern corporations. They want to come down here to Texas and run things for us, tell us what to do with our town, our state, our jobs and lives!"

His voice took on more confidence. "That building down there is more than just a piece of local history. It's a monument to what a determined man can do in the face of overwhelming political odds and high-toned moneyed interest."

The workmen down on the site were temporarily forgotten as the crowd on the bleachers stood and faced backward. Those on the ground swelled around the Fitzpatrick motor home. Carl was beaming, and from inside the RV Lydia appeared. She was dressed up, Hugh noticed, stockings and heels.

"And I also think," J. D. went on, unaware that few eyes were on him now. Everyone was watching Carl and Lydia. Other reporters were wandering over, and more minicams were focusing on him. "That once this thing is settled and if the building is saved, that it ought to be renamed 'The Fitzpatrick Building' and remodeled and restored to become a glorious symbol of our city's determination to maintain its history and dignity. And I also think," J. D. checked his notes once more and smiled, "that we ought to consider, seriously, putting Carl here up for governor of this state, and—" his hand shot up to forestall any outburst one way or another, "—I'm prepared to put my money where my mouth is to the tune of a five-thousand-dollar contribution to the campaign, just to get the ball rolling!"

Calls of "Carl for governor" rang out as the crowd roared. Hugh looked around, astonished. It was just as Jonas Wilson had predicted. In the space of a week, Carl Fitzpatrick had raised his ambitions from the city attorney's office to the state Capitol, and he was using the Hendershot building to get there.

Hugh moved off as the pandemonium behind him continued. People were now shouting and clapping, and Carl was now up in the bed of the pickup, waving and trying to speak over reporters' questions and a chorus of cheers from the people around him.

Linda had abandoned her bleacher seat and was now standing by the now-deserted Methodist Women's table. She munched a cookie but scowled as if it were a raw lemon.

"Want one?" she asked when Hugh walked up.

"I'm broke," he confessed.

"It's okay." She handed him an oatmeal-raisin circle. "They said I could have all I wanted. I guess I can give them to anybody I want to."

"Did you hear . . ." Hugh looked over at the crowd. Carl was now shouting a speech to the heavy morning air. The clouds were gathering again, and in the northern distance, Hugh spotted lightning. The storm was returning, it seemed. So much for Ray and Tommy's plans to move in on his territory. So much for his plans as well, he thought.

"I didn't have to." She frowned and bit into another cookie. "He was on the phone with Mr. Holt and Mr. Matthews and half the world all night last night. They had a meeting in Daddy's study before breakfast this morning, if you can believe that! It looks like I'm going to have to do this political family thing for years. It is *so* boring!" Hugh nodded. "I'll tell you something else." She leaned over and spoke quietly. "If there was any way I could tear that old building down myself, I'd do it."

"Don't you want to live in Austin?"

"Do you realize that that's my junior and senior years we're talking about?" she asked him as if he were an idiot. "That means I have to go to a new school, make all new friends, and God knows what else. I do *not* want this to happen! What about my horses? What about being cheerleader? It's going to ruin my life." She looked like she wanted to cry, and Hugh felt sorry for her.

"Maybe it won't," he offered and accepted another cookie. "Maybe they'll tear the building down anyway." He thought of the secret he knew and almost told her about it before Jonas Wilson's voice came to his memory and silenced him.

"Well, that's not going to make much difference, one way or another," she said bitterly.

"What?" Hugh was confused.

"You see that guy in the brown suit?" She gestured toward the stranger, who now was standing well away from the crowd around Carl. Hugh nodded. "Well, his name's Mr. Sapperstein. He's some kind of big-deal lawyer from Austin, and he came up here yesterday to talk this over with Daddy. It was his idea to meet before breakfast, too, I'll bet. I don't like him. I had to get up and get dressed before the sun even came up. If you can believe that!" She leaned over and took Hugh's hand and started leading him away. Shocked by the gesture, he almost resisted. Then he relaxed and let her take him around behind the motor home. Her eyes were narrow with seriousness when she turned to him and spoke.

"Don't you say a word to a soul," she whispered, "but they've got it rigged so it doesn't matter what happens to that old building. Daddy's still going to look good."

"How?" Hugh also whispered and automatically checked around.

She gave him an exasperated expression. "I certainly don't know," she said. "I don't *want* to know. All I know is that this guy and Daddy and that railroad guy—"

"Mr. Grissom?"

"Whatever," she snapped. "All of them were over at the house this morning, and they worked out some kind of deal."

"What kind of deal?"

She put her hands on her hips. "Are you deaf or just dumb?" she demanded. "I told you I don't know. The only reason I know this much is because I had to sit out in the gazebo—because it was raining—and I heard them in Daddy's study talking about it."

Hugh was confused. "How?"

"On an intercom, stupid. Are you going to ask questions or listen to me? They said it was a 'sweetheart' deal, and it couldn't miss." She looked around, then continued, "Mr. Holt came over, too."

"What else did they say?" Hugh's heart was pounding. This was too much like a movie, he thought. It wasn't happening. But then he looked into Linda's indignant eyes, and he knew it was. It was as real as could be, and he had to know more.

"I wasn't *eavesdropping*, Hugh Rudd," Linda insisted. "I was trying to find a radio station. I'm not a spy like you."

"You must have heard something," Hugh said, confused by her explanation but too anxious for details to change the subject. "C'mon. I won't tell. Promise."

"Well, they said they meet to finalize things tomorrow night. The guy from the railroad—"

"Grissom?"

"Yeah, whatever."

"Grissom was at your house?"

"Well, yes. That's what I'm trying to tell you. He's the one who said it was a 'sweetheart' deal. Anyway, he said he had to check once more with his office in Chicago, but that in the meantime, things would have to be a secret."

Hugh thought long and carefully for a moment. "Linda, you have to do something for me."

"No, I don't," she sniffed. "I don't *have* to do one thing. I shouldn't have told you all that stuff to begin with. I'm just p-o'd that I have to move to Austin."

"Do you think they'll meet again at your house tomorrow night?"

"How should I know?"

"Well, you said they were going to meet tomorrow night. Did they say where?" He realized that he had reached out and grabbed her wrist.

"You are hurting me!" she said in a hoarse whisper. "I don't know what you're talking about. All they said was that the whole thing would be over soon, and they were going to meet again tomorrow night—"

"At your house?"

"They didn't say."

"Well, if they do, you have to listen to what they're saying."

"I do not!"

"Yeah, you do," Hugh said. "I have to know what they're going to do. How, and when. I have a pretty good idea already, but I—"

"Hugh, you're asking me to spy on my father. On my family. I won't—"

"Linda," Hugh said. "This is important. Really important. Maybe I can help you. Maybe I can keep you here and out of Austin."

She snorted a laugh. "How could you do that?"

"I don't know," Hugh admitted. "But if I can hear what they're cooking up, then—"

"Well, there's only one way that can happen. You'll have to do your own spying."

"Me? But how—"

"We have a new hot tub," she said. "That's what the gazebo is for." Her tone totally changed. All conspiracy went from it, and once more she was the spoiled little rich girl, teasing him. "I'm having a few friends over for hot dogs tomorrow to break it in, and you can come."

"But I—"

"If you don't want to come, that's fine," she said, turning and starting away. "Six o'clock. Bring a swimsuit. We have towels."

"Wait," Hugh said. "I'll come. But I have to be able to hear—"

"No promises, Hugh Rudd," she said. "Six o'clock."

He nodded, and she flounced away.

Carl was winding up his speech, and the skies began to darken even more. There was no rain falling yet, but thunder rumbled in the distance. A number of people began packing up and preparing to leave. Phelps Crane sulked off to one side by himself and watched Carl shaking hands and accepting congratulations from the mob around him. Suddenly, the old conductor approached Hugh.

"How come your daddy don't come down here?" he demanded. "He's the one got this thing back on the road."

"I don't know," Hugh said. "He . . . he's home." The twitch that had almost closed Phelps's eye disappeared when he looked into Hugh's face. The old man's eyes now seemed tiny in their sockets, mere pinpoints of blackness that shot around suspiciously when he talked. His fingers were black with grime, and the petition he continued to carry was now ragged and torn from handling.

"Well, you tell him we need him down here," Phelps whispered. "Carl's got the wrong idea 'bout this whole thing. Something's fishy here. I can smell it, and I'm not the only one. You tell him I said for him to get down here and take a sniff or two. Tell me what he thinks." Phelps moved off, muttering to himself.

Hugh thought about what Linda told him about the meeting between her father and Grissom. Yes, he thought, there was something fishy, all right.

He saw her again. She was now sitting on a lawn chair under the motor home's awning. She was by herself, her mother and Carl having moved over to stand in the middle of Main Street with the whole downtown area behind them. They were posing for pictures. Five or six reporters now milled around them asking questions.

"Linda," Hugh said when he came up. She looked up at him as if she had no idea who he was and was seeing him for the first time. "I need to know: Did they say anything about when this would all be over? When exactly?"

"I'm sure I have no idea what you're talking about!" she said, her eyes flashing a warning around him. "Keep your voice down," she hissed at him.

"Well, let me put it another way. When do you think they're going to tear down that building?"

"I'm sure I don't know and couldn't care less. That old building is the least of my worries. All I know is that Randy Truman doesn't think they'll finish it anytime soon or maybe not at all. But they are taking bets on it anyway."

"Yeah, I heard."

"Did you bet?" She smiled slyly.

Hugh shook his head. "I'm too broke. How much do they want?"

"Well, they started at five dollars, but nobody would put in that much, so now they're down to two. You guess the hour the building comes down, and if it's not standing higher than one story within that hour, you win."

"So, if you were betting, when would you guess?" Hugh asked, trying to think of a tack that would get around her smile.

"Responsible people do not gamble," she said icily. "Besides, I'm too young. Mother would tan my bottom if she caught me."

Hugh chewed for a moment, then he decided. "Linda, do you have two dollars?"

She stared at him, suspicious. "Maybe."

"Loan it to me."

"Responsible people do not *lend* money for gambling, either," she lectured.

"Just this once. Really!" Hugh looked anxiously at Truman and his buddies. "I'll pay you back. I swear."

She looked appraisingly at him a moment, then swung her small canvas bag off the back of her chair and opened it. "Well, just this once." Her fingers entered the open purse. "But I want nothing to do with gambling," she said. "It is not a loan. It's a gift. What you do with it—"

"Thanks, Linda," Hugh said, snatched the bills from her fingers, then galloped over to the bleachers. Carl finished his interviews. He and Lydia were making their way back toward the motor home. Sapperstein, if that was his name, also started in that direction. From his office window, Grissom watched the whole show without expression. Hugh noticed that all the brooding malice that Grissom had shown all week was suddenly gone. He seemed almost relaxed, relieved. More people were leaving now, as rain seemed to be imminent, and they were unmindful of Hugh's pushing them aside when he climbed up to the top where Truman and Eddy Ferryman sat. A large piece of cardboard with a two-week calendar drawn on it rested between them, weighted down by a small cooler.

Hugh glanced at the tally board. Each day was divided into eight-hour segments, and more than half of the following week and the week after had names scrawled across them.

"Hi, Rudd Junior," Truman, a college dropout in his mid-twenties who had converted his love of high-powered engines and drag racing into a profitable garage and towing service, greeted Hugh with a smile. Truman called every kid in town "Junior"—male or female—because he knew most of their parents but couldn't recall their first names. "Why aren't you off looking at dirty pictures and jerking off or something?"

Then he smacked his forehead. "Damn it! I know what you want." He turned to Eddy and frowned. "I got to go out to the edge of town and pick up his old man's car and haul it in. He called this morning, and I forgot all about it." He started to rise. "Thanks for reminding me, Junior. Maybe I'll save you a foldout next month."

"I want to get in on the pool." Hugh was surprised to find his breath short, a condition not helped at all by Truman's surprised look.

"Yeah, and your old man'll have my butt in traction," Truman said.

"C'mon, Randy," Hugh said and held out the two bills. "I want in."

Truman looked at his companion and shrugged. "Hey, okay. But you tell your old man about it, and I'll whip your ass."

Hugh nodded eagerly, and Truman pulled the board up onto his lap. "Now you understand," he said, "that if they call the deal off and leave it standing, you lose." Hugh nodded again. "And if it happens when nobody has a slot, we keep it all?" Another nod, and Truman pulled a pen from his workshirt. When you want?"

"Sunday noon," Hugh smiled and handed him the bills, but Truman shook his head and refused them.

"Sunday ain't on the chart," he shook his head. "Weekdays only. They don't work on weekends."

"I want Sunday," Hugh insisted. "Sunday noon."

Truman cocked an eyebrow. "You know something we don't?"

Hugh shook his head and grinned through the lie. "I just think with all the rain, they'll probably work through the weekend. I want Sunday noon."

Truman looked deeply into Hugh's eyes, checked his partner, who shrugged, and then sighed. "Okay, what the hell. We'll write it in the margin. If it comes down tomorrow or some other time on Sunday, you lose, and we win big."

"How much is in the pot?" Hugh asked.

"Five-fifty," Truman smiled and took Hugh's money. "Five-fifty-two. They'll be more, since a lot of guys don't get paid until this afternoon. Since they can't get that big wrecker down there, most people are guessing a week from Monday or after. We haven't even got a chart made up for that, yet. Good luck, sucker," he laughed. "Now, I'd better go get your old man's car. You handle the board, Eddy. You try to skim off the top, I'll braid your dick."

Eddy nodded and grinned back.

Hugh looked around. A smattering of rain began to strike the crowd, which immediately broke and fled. Carl was helping Lydia inside the motor home. Linda was nowhere about. Thunder sounded.

"Uh, can I ride along?" Hugh asked. "I'm on my bike. It's downtown. We can pick it up."

"Why not?" Truman frowned as they raced toward his tow truck, which was parked next to the Railway Express Office. "I'm nothing but a glorified taxi service, anyway."

CHAPTER SIX

Contrary to all weather reports and the sporadic showers of the morning, the skies cleared early on Friday afternoon. A strong, warm southwesterly breeze sprang up under a restored Texas summer sky. The ground and the grass that covered it began to dry almost immediately, which meant that by midafternoon, overgrown lawns were ready for cutting.

Randy Truman dropped Hugh and his bicycle off at home, and without even checking inside or eating a bite of lunch, the boy grabbed his Grassmaster, his last box of lawn and leaf bags, and gas can and took off toward the Smiths' house. He completed five customers' yards more quickly than he ever had before. He raced the mower through each yard, hurriedly raked the damp, matted clippings into his bags, and barely had his payment stuffed into his jeans before he was racing off to the next lawn.

He was relieved to find that most of his customers were not downtown, though several asked what he knew about the "goings-on" and wondered if it was "worth the trouble" to go down and watch.

The wet front that had swept through the area left a cool evening in its wake, and even though some of the taller grass was still soaked, Hugh's athletic legs pushed the mower through it without hesitation. His Yankees cap was soused with sweat, his arms and calves ached, but he kept his head down and concentrated on putting one foot in front of the other, anxious to finish as many lawns as he could before dark.

When he completed the Blankenships' lawn, he was nearly exhausted and was growing careless, missing spots and having to go back over them. He tried to convince himself that he should knock off for the day, but the Tallwaters' yard was only a few blocks' distance, so he lowered his head and pushed the Grassmaster in that direction with stoic determination.

Their grass would be higher and wetter than the others, because their front yard with its steep incline was on the south side of the house and had been in shade most of the afternoon.

When he rounded the corner of Pine Street, though, he was shocked to find the Tallwaters' overlarge corner lot neatly trimmed. A dozen stuffed plastic bags awaited pickup at the curb, and he could see Gerald Tallwater, a veterinarian, puttering at his workbench in his garage.

"Ray and Tommy," Hugh whispered, jamming the damaged toe of his sneaker into the side of the Grassmaster. The Tallwaters had been his first customer. He counted on their loyalty. He also had counted on the double charge he made for cutting their expanse. He pushed the mower on and pretended not to see Gerald's wave when he passed the driveway.

The next four houses he visited in the same neighborhood also had newly mown lawns. Finally, he reached the McCartneys' yard, which was still ankle high, and Hugh immediately jerked the pull starter and attacked the grass. With renewed energy derived from this strange sense of competition, he focused completely on making straight lines and raking the yard with special care.

As the sun set, he finished the McCartneys' and the Mineshafts' yards, and with no illumination other than the Trailors' front porch lights to guide him, he completed the last lawn of the day.

It was full dark by the time Hugh, his empty gas can banging against his leg, pushed the overheated Grassmaster up the driveway and parked it in the garage. If he could do twelve yards tomorrow, he calculated, then he would be ready to catch up completely on Sunday—if his mother would let him break the Sabbath.

He went around to the front of the house rather than through the side door from the garage so he could stop and hose down his sneakers, get the wet clippings and mud off before entering. He was startled by the dark form of his father seated on the front porch steps.

"Hey, Sport! Nice night," Harry said as his son approached.

"Yeah," Hugh muttered. He went to the faucet and uncoiled the hose. His father was smoking, and his form was silhouetted against the windows behind him. "How's the car?"

"Lost cause," Harry said. "Dropped a cylinder, Randy says. Ignition system's shot, too."

"What do we do, now?"

"I'll handle it," Harry said cheerfully. "Don't worry, Hugh."

"But, Dad—"

"Don't 'but Dad' me," Harry laughed. "You don't need to be worrying about family finances." He flicked his butt off into the darkness. "You might worry about your batting average, though. You know, one thing this might do is make us think more seriously about a scholarship. I'd like to see you on varsity, next year."

"As a freshman?" Hugh asked, realizing that Harry had just articulated Hugh's most secret ambition. "You wish."

"I *do* wish," Harry said. "In fact, I insist on it. Stranger things have happened. You're a good glove, Sport. Need to work on your hitting, though. Gotten much BP in this summer?"

Self-reproaching guilt swam up from Hugh's stomach. "No time," he muttered and turned on the faucet and sprayed his sneakers. Water immediately invaded the torn soles, soaked his aching feet. "Maybe I won't go to college," he said.

"Maybe the sun won't rise tomorrow," Harry replied.

"Well, you didn't."

"Nope, and look where I am. Stuck in a podunk town, no job, no friends . . ." He let silence fall between them. Hugh finished cleaning his sneakers, and Harry lit another cigarette. "Want one?"

"One what?"

"A cigarette. A smoke."

Hugh said nothing, recoiled the hose, wished he could disappear. "No, I guess not," he whispered at last.

"C'mon, Hugh." Harry thrust the pack out through the darkness. "I know you've been smoking." Hugh said nothing. "Word gets around. I keep telling you, Sport, this is a small town. When you stink, half the town smells it, then they phone the other half to talk about it. And when you smoke, you stink. Even smokers can smell it on you. Here. 'Have a Camel,' as they used to say. They're probably not as strong as that home-rolled crap Jonas Wilson gives you, but that's all right."

Hugh stepped over, his wet shoes squishing slightly, and accepted a smoke from his father's hand. Harry's sweaty body odor hit Hugh's nostrils. Harry still wore the running suit from that morning. Harry lit the cigarette with his Zippo, and for a moment the two of them smoked in silence.

"I don't intend to keep smoking, Dad," Hugh said at last, tossing the cigarette away half finished. "I just—"

"I know, I know," Harry said. "Nasty habit. Don't take it up. Been working hard?"

"Yeah," Hugh sat down beside Harry. "I did a bunch today. Made a dent in it, anyway." He didn't want to admit how many customers Ray and Tommy had stolen from him.

"Did you get to the Tallwaters?"

"Uh . . . they already did it," Hugh said.

"They tell you that?"

"Uh . . . no. I just could tell. I went by, and it was already done. Better job than I usually do, to be honest."

"Anybody else already have theirs done?"

"Yeah," Hugh said reluctantly. "There were a couple. I'm going to hit it early tomorrow. Got that payment to make, and I've to got pay you back."

"Here, Sport," Harry said, reaching into the running suit's pocket. He pulled out a wad of bills and handed them to Hugh. "Maybe this will help."

Hugh shook his head. "No, Dad. This isn't part of the deal. Mom said—"

"I don't think your mother will mind," Harry said in a sudden, strained voice. "At least, not much. Anyway, it's not a gift. Not exactly. That's the Tallwaters' money, and the Bucknells', and the Hatchers'."

Hugh looked at his father's face in the window light. It was filthy with dust and sweat trails. "But how? I mean—"

"C'mon," Harry said, rising and walking suddenly around to the side of the garage. Hugh followed, mystified, but when he rounded the corner of the building and Harry switched on an outside flood, he spotted a large John Deere lawn tractor sitting alongside the building. It reeked of grass and gasoline odors, and when Hugh ran his hand over the engine cowling, it was still warm.

"If I keep it, I've got to build a shed for it," Harry said. "Can't get it in the garage. At least not when we get the car back. Or some car," he added, then brightened. "It's smooth, let me tell you, but it's a bitch to get up those inclines at the Tallwaters'. I turned it over twice. It's dangerous."

Hugh gaped at his father. "You bought this?"

"Well, I've got it on trial. It's a demo," Harry admitted. "I've been thinking about it, and I thought I'd see how I liked the landscaping business." He smiled ruefully. "I don't think I like it very much. It's hard work, even on a machine like this."

"You mowed the Tallwaters' and the others?"

"Well, I had to try it out," Harry grinned. "I think I'll go ahead and buy it—or a new one like it—in any case. It really cuts down on the time it takes to mow those big lots. But it's not worth a damn on the smaller yards."

"I don't get it," Hugh said. He sat down on a stack of bricks.

"You needed help, Hugh. I know you got yourself in this mess, and I know I should have let you stew in your own juices. Sink or swim. But I haven't been much good to anybody lately. I was walking home from Truman's garage and saw you running as hard as you could to get done with the Smiths' yard, and I decided that if I couldn't help you out, I wasn't much good to myself, either. That's almost fifty bucks I gave you. I kept out what you owe me for making the payment, but that plus what you made today and will make tomorrow should catch you up."

"I'm sorry, Dad. I'll work hard," Hugh said.

"Let's go over the list and split up. I'll take the big yards, you handle the small ones. You've got to use a Weed Eater after you go around on this one, though. It won't get close to the trees or curbs. Hell, Sport, we'll be a team!"

They stood looking at the lawn tractor for another moment.

"Well, let's get inside," Harry said. "I'm starving."

"Me, too. What's for supper?" Hugh asked. He remembered that he had eaten no meal that day at all.

"Beats me," Harry said, then under his breath added, "To be honest, I'm sort of dreading it."

—<

Hugh knew that something was wrong the moment they stepped inside. From the kitchen a strange smell wafted down the hall, and he and his father stopped and looked curiously at each other.

"Edith?" Harry called. "The wage-earning element of this family is home! What're you cooking? Boiled socks?"

They entered the kitchen, and both stopped, stunned. Instead of finding Edith Rudd frowning at her tardy family, they were confronted by the sour scowl of Loretta Thompson.

She sat at the kitchen table, a long, brown-wrapped cigarette in her stubby fingers next to a full ashtray. Her brow was knitted, and her small, dark eyes surveyed the two men before her.

"What I'd like to know," she said sternly, "is just where in God's name you two have been."

"Where's Edith?" Harry said, looking around. The odor was intense in the kitchen, and Hugh stepped over to the stove to peer into a large pot.

"Split-pea soup," he muttered, recognizing the bubbling green mess.

"Leave that alone," Loretta ordered. "We'll eat after we talk."

"What's going on?" Harry demanded. "I asked you where Edith was."

"I've called everyone in town," Loretta went on. "I even called the sheriff. I thought maybe you'd been kidnapped by that old man or something. Edith told me that Hugh was—"

"Where *is* Edith?" Harry shouted. "What the hell's going on here?"

Loretta ignored his outburst and only rose and moved to the counter. "You'd better sit down," she said. "I'll make you a drink. Hugh, go wash up. You're in trouble, young man."

"I think I'll decide who's in trouble and who's not, Loretta," Harry said sharply. "I asked you where my wife was. What're you doing here, anyway?"

She turned to face him. She wore stylish jeans that swelled over her abdomen and dropped to low-cut boots. At her waist, a bright turquoise belt held in a yoke shirt, buttoned at the neck, with a silver bolo tie. Her hair was cut shorter than ever, swept back from her plain face. Small hairs traced across her upper lip. Hugh felt a quiver of revulsion.

"And I asked you to sit down, Harry," she said, quickly pouring a strong drink from the bourbon bottle. "I believe I know what's best here. I have something to tell you, and I'm not certain that Hugh should hear it."

Hugh automatically turned and started to leave, but his father's voice stopped him. "I'll sit down when I'm goddamned good and ready. Hugh, stay right where you are. This is *his* house, Loretta. I'll be the judge of what he needs to hear and what he doesn't. So, if you don't mind, I'd like an explanation, and I'd like it now. Where's Edith?"

She put the drink down on the table and then faced them once more. Her features softened slightly, but her mouth stayed tight. "She's in the hospital, Harry."

Harry's face went pale. He looked as if he had been slapped. "What! Why? I'm—"

"Sit down," Loretta ordered.

Harry ignored her. "What happened?" He spun around and started out the door, not waiting for an answer, then he stopped and turned again. "I'm borrowing your car. Where're the keys?"

"She's not in the hospital *here*, Harry," Loretta said with mock patience. "She was, but that was earlier this afternoon. The emergency room, as a matter of fact."

"The emergency—Where the hell is she? What happened? Is she sick? Was there some kind of accident?"

Loretta shot a quick, sympathetic look toward Hugh and sighed. He winced. "She's at Wichita Falls. She had a breakdown, Harry. A total mental and emotional breakdown."

"That's impossible! Where in Wichita Falls?"

"County Memorial. Doctor Richardson said they were better equipped to handle her there."

"This is ridiculous," Harry said. "She was fine when I left. What happened to her? What were you doing here, anyway?"

"*I* was here for her!" Loretta spat her words at him. "*You* weren't! You never are, it seems! She called me about four o'clock." She shot a quick glance at Hugh. "She was hysterical. Babbling. She couldn't find you, couldn't find Hugh. She barely knew her own name. I rushed right over, and when I got here, she was nearly unconscious." She looked at Hugh, then shot directly at Harry. "She drank almost a whole bottle of bourbon."

"When I left, she was fine!" Harry insisted. "A little tense maybe, but who wouldn't be? I mean, the car was in the shop, and—"

Loretta stalked to the telephone. "By noon, people were calling, wanting to know when Hugh was going to mow their lawns." She waved a notepad like a flag in front of them. "She made a nice, hot lunch, and neither of you were around to eat it. So she started drinking and drinking. And then Phelps Crane called."

"Phelps Crane?" Hugh asked.

"That was when she called me. It sent her over the edge. She just exploded."

"Phelps Crane?" Harry was bewildered. "What could that old drunk say to—"

"He said Hugh was still hanging around downtown, gambling and getting into mischief." Loretta shot a mean look at Hugh. "He wanted to know where *you* were, Harry. He wanted to know if you and everybody else planned to let the whole town just go to pot. He cursed her out, called her a . . . a drunk and . . . a lot of other things, mean things, and he hung up."

"I'll kill that son of a bitch," Harry growled, coming to his feet.

"I've already called the sheriff about him," Loretta said, "and he called back a while ago to say that he had him locked up for the night. The man's lost his mind over all this silliness."

"Sounds to me like Edith's the one who's lost her mind," Harry shot at her. "Why'd she call you?"

"Because *I'm* her friend. *You* couldn't be found. Hugh was God only knows where. Where were you, anyway?"

"Well, I hiked down to Truman's. Edith knew that. We had a . . . well, I'm sure she told you we had words before I left." He looked at Hugh. "Nothing serious, though. I called her from Truman's. She was fine." Harry sank down into a kitchen chair and kneaded the bridge of his nose. "Shit," he whispered.

"She might have *sounded* fine," Loretta sniffed. "But she wasn't. She's fragile, you know, but she's stubborn. My God, Harry, you know how high-strung she is. She needed you, and you weren't here." Her tone shifted again, became accusative. "It didn't take you all afternoon to walk back from Truman's."

"I've been helping Hugh catch up," Harry admitted in a confused voice. "I didn't tell her about that. I mean, I came into the house. I used the phone, then I went over to meet Hatcher. Jesus Christ!" He slapped his forehead with his hand. "I thought maybe she was taking a nap or something. Where is she? What happened? I thought we made up on the phone. I mean, a call from Phelps Crane shouldn't have—"

"It wasn't just that call." Loretta joined him at the table. She pushed the drink over to him. "And it wasn't just your having 'words,' as you call them. There have been other calls. Lots of other calls. For days now. Mean and wicked calls. We've had them, too. Pete's beside himself. Ever since that silly meeting the other night, people have gone completely insane in this town."

"She didn't say anything about other calls."

"No, of course not. You've got other things on your mind," Loretta put out her hand to touch Harry's, but he pulled his away. "I told her not to tell you. I told her not to answer the phone. But then, with the way Hugh's been behaving lately, she was afraid not to." She glared at Hugh, but he didn't flinch this time, and she turned back to Harry. "And she had this silly hope that they would call you back to work. She was sure it was some sort of mistake, talked herself into it. I think maybe it was, too."

Harry's shoulders sagged. Hugh was coming to hate this woman.

"Then, on top of everything, there was this foolishness about that old building, what Carl Fitzpatrick and the whole town has done to Pete—"

"What the town has done to *Pete!*" Harry shouted. "What about what Pete did to the town? C'mon, Loretta, why should Pete's problems—"

"Because Edith is a caring, loving person," Loretta said. "And she knows who her friends are, and she's emotional. She suffers right along with everyone else. And you haven't helped. Not one bit. You've just made things worse: losing your job, encouraging this boy to hang around with that old man—"

"Loretta, I don't see how any of this is any of your business," Harry said, rising. "I want to borrow your car. Hugh, get cleaned up. We're going to Wichita Falls tonight."

"It won't do any good," Loretta said, "and I don't have a car. Pete went over to Wichita Falls with it."

"What? Pete? Why—"

"Someone had to go, Harry," she said with a sniff. "Someone had to be responsible, stay with her. I promised Edith I would look after you and Hugh—if I could find you, that is." Harry glanced at the telephone, took a step toward it. "That won't do any good, either," Loretta cut him off. "Pete called a while ago. They have her in isolation, heavily sedated right now. There's no point in your going over there till tomorrow, and there's no point in Hugh going at all. They won't allow anyone under eighteen on the floor, and, besides, he's got a lot of lawns to mow—"

"You let me worry about that." The fire in Harry's voice was gone. In its place was a frigid tone, like skim ice. Hugh had never heard it before. He shuddered. "You had better go home," Harry muttered.

"The best thing for you to do is to drink your drink, eat something, and then get a good night's sleep," she said. "I promised Edith I would take care of things until she came home." She looked around the kitchen. "Pete can drive us over there tomorrow." She folded her hands in front of her. "I think I should be there when you two see each other," she added.

"Butt out and let me handle my family," Harry said, rebounding slightly. He sighed, wiped his eyes once more, then spoke directly to the drink glass. "I appreciate what you've done, Loretta. Your offer to help and all is nice. I'm sorry I yelled at you. But there're limits here. You're not a part of this family—never have been—and I think you'd better go home. Now."

"Harry, you're upset. I know—"

"Go home, Loretta. Get out of my goddamn sight." His voice built in intensity.

"Harry—"

"Go!" he shouted loud enough to rattle glassware in the cupboard. "Now! Get the hell out of my home, and don't come back."

She reared her head back as if he had struck her. Hugh grabbed the side of the counter to steady himself. He had never seen his father so angry. Harry stood in the middle of the room. Sweat ran off his forehead and streaked down his dirty, unshaven face.

"Harry, I've always tried to—"

"Loretta, I've lost my temper," Harry said through clenched teeth. "I'm not going to tell you again to get the hell out of here. I won't be responsible for what happens if I don't see your fat ass going out the door by the time I draw another breath."

She stood for a beat, then two, then whirled past him, grabbing her handbag from the counter. "I'll have Pete come by to talk to you," she said as she left the kitchen. "You're upset and not thinking clearly." Harry remained where he was, his fists clenched, breathing heavily. She moved out of the room with a quick step. "I'll be at home, Hugh," she shouted from the other room. "You call me if you need—"

"Go!" Harry yelled, whirling around and stepping after her. "Go now!" Hugh heard the front door slam a second or two later.

His father came back into the kitchen, picked up the glass, and drained it. For a moment he stood there, his hands visibly shaking. But his voice was steady when he spoke. "I'm going to take a shower," he said. "Then, I'm going to see your mother."

"I want to go with you."

"No," Harry shook his head. "That bitch is right about that much, at least. They probably won't let you in, and you'd be miserable sitting around the waiting room. It's better all 'round if you stay here. Get as caught up as you can on your work. One less thing for your mother to worry about."

"How are you going to get there?"

"If I can't borrow a car, then I'll buy one." He filled the tumbler with whiskey, started to drink, then put it down with a deliberate motion. "Pour that out," he said to Hugh, indicating the whiskey bottle. "Pour it out! And if you see any more in this house—*ever*—pour *it* out, too. That's an order, Hugh."

He turned and swept out of the room. "Throw out whatever witch's brew that is on the stove, too," he called. "Get cleaned up, eat something, and hit the rack. You're on your own tomorrow, Sport. Use the tractor, if you want, for the big jobs—no, belay that. It's way too dangerous for you to handle without some lessons, even then. Wait till I get back. Sunday, if I can." Harry spun and raced from the room.

Hugh nodded and looked around at the empty kitchen. He believed he could almost hear echoes of his father's voice ringing from the wallpaper. He didn't move for a long moment. Finally, he took an oven mitt and picked up the simmering soup from the stove and poured it into the disposal. He rinsed the pot, then stood stock still again, listening. It wasn't until he heard water running in the bathroom that he moved over to the counter, grabbed the whiskey bottle, and dumped its contents down the sink as well.

He was a long time going to sleep that night.

CHAPTER SEVEN

Hugh had planned to rise early on Saturday, but he was so weary and sore from his labors the day before that all he could do was turn over when his alarm went off, shut it down, and try to go back to sleep. He couldn't. And he couldn't find the energy to rise from his bed. He lay there worrying about his mother and everything else that had gone wrong in his life for a long while. He replayed the scene between his father and Loretta Thompson in his mind a thousand times, sometimes kicking himself for not speaking up, for failing to take a part in his father's defense of their home against another invasion by the Thompsons. It was after eight when he rolled out of bed and staggered groggily down the hall toward the bathroom.

After he dressed, he wanted coffee, but he wasn't sure of the proportions, and what he managed to perk was too thick and bitter to drink. So he poured himself a glass of milk, grabbed two Pop-Tarts, and went out to the garage, where he wolfed them down, trying his best to shake the stickiness of fatigue from his body and mind. Grabbing his gas can, he pushed the Grassmaster down the drive. He was tempted to try using the lawn tractor in spite of his father's instructions, but he shrugged off the thought. He had no idea even how to start it.

Hugh was so tired from hiking out to the highway to buy gasoline and more bags from the Allsup's store that he could hardly put one foot in front of the other. Somehow, though, he found a reserve of strength in himself, and he soon was racing along faster than he had the evening before. Each customer greeted him at the end of the job with a compliment on his speed, although more than one reminded him not to allow their yards to go for so long between cuttings next time. He finished six lawns by noon.

The sun was baking him by the time he parked his mower next to the Goosemans' house and trudged home to find some dinner. He also wanted to know if there was any word from his father. The house was empty, though. He tried twice to call County Memorial Hospital in Wichita Falls, but the operator would not put him through to his mother's room. Attempts to have his father paged didn't work, either. He paced back and forth in the living room, listening to that indefinable buzz of emptiness houses often emit, and finally he could stand it no more. He was sore and dirty and hungry, and, he realized, he was painfully lonely. Angry with himself for letting frustration get the better of him, he slammed out of the house, jumped onto his bike, and pedaled hard for downtown.

He stopped by Central Drugs, but it was deserted, odd for the noon hour. Hilda was the only one inside. She actually brightened when he approached the counter and ordered a tuna fish sandwich. She whipped it up in record time. While he ate, he quizzed her as to where people might be, but she only cast her eyes toward the Hendershot building and shrugged.

"Even Claude's gone down yonder. Looky there. You see that coffee?" She pointed toward the Serve Yourself counter. "That's four-hour coffee," she said. "I've never in my life had four-hour coffee on the burner. Nobody's been in here to drink a drop. I'd pour it out, but I don't know if I should make more or not. Four-hour coffee. Can you beat that?"

Hugh finished his sandwich and rode his bike toward the depot parking lot. He didn't get very far before the crush of people forced him to pull up and move on foot. The crowd of onlookers was so large that it spilled out onto Main Street and surrounded the Railway Express Office. People had climbed up onto buildings across the tracks, and Hugh spotted TV crews and people with long-lens cameras on tripods up there as well. Highway Patrol troopers were standing in front of sawhorse barricades to control the occasional car or pickup that wanted by. They were directing them away, detouring them, Hugh suspected, down Spruce Street toward the poorer houses across the tracks.

Eddy Ferryman and Randy Truman perched on the purloined bleachers with their tally board in front of them. Eddy spotted Hugh and said something to Truman, who turned and waved him over.

"Looks like you were right, short stuff," Eddy said with a scowl.

"What do you mean?" Hugh yelled up to them.

"They're going to blast," Truman said. He pointed down to the worksite, where a white truck was parked. The odd triangular symbols for explosives were stenciled all over it, and bright red "DANGER" signs were every-where. "Today or tomorrow for sure," Truman went on. "Going to blow her sky high. The only question is when. We got it busted down into fifteen-minute segments, now. There's more'n a thousand dollars in the pot. You want to stick with noon tomorrow?" Hugh nodded, and Truman shrugged. "You must have inside information, Rudd Junior. That's cheating."

Hugh shrugged. "It's just a guess, Randy."

"If I find out different, I'm going to whip your ass," Eddy said.

Hugh climbed down and moved off.

The crowd was denser than ever as well. Hugh didn't recognize half the people he saw, and by overhearing snatches of conversation, he learned that folks from nearby towns had converged on the small parking lot to see the show. Farmers and ranchers who appeared in town only occasionally stood about talking, chewing tobacco, and smoking under their broad straw hats. T-shirts told Hugh that at least seven different high schools were represented, and a well-dressed man with razor-cut hair and a bright smile moved through the mob handing out fliers inviting "one and all" to an "Old Fashioned Tent Revival" to be held on the banks of Blind Man's Creek Sunday night.

In addition to the Coke trailer, two more concession stands were oper-ating, and the Methodist Women's table was joined by a dozen more enter-prises selling everything from hot dogs to cotton candy. The smell of food mixed with sweat and sweet soft drinks, and more than once, Hugh discov-ered the odor of alcohol in the crowd. It was like being at the state fair, he thought.

"No!" Hugh heard a familiar voice coming from near the Fitzpatrick mo-tor home. "For the last time, Carl, I will not have the Brand Brothers' Car-nival here right now."

The voice belonged to Sheriff Anderson, Hugh realized. He was stand-ing toe to toe with Carl Fitzpatrick, and both men looked overheated. Hugh edged up behind some men near them.

"They have a permit," Carl Fitzpatrick argued. "They're due next week anyway. I don't see what the harm is."

"If they want to set up down on the courthouse square like always, that's fine," Anderson said. "But not down here. It's too congested here now as it is. There's too many people already without all that going on. I have enough trouble every time a bunch of crooks hit town without provid-ing them with a ready-made crowd of suckers."

"But think of the money it'll bring in," Carl argued. "If you stick them down there . . . Hell, Don, that's four blocks away. I don't see why they can't put up the rides right behind the Railway Express. It won't get in the way, and people are already—"

"I said no," Anderson repeated. "I will not add to this, Carl. One of these days, you may have a say-so in what goes on here, but right now, this is still my county, my town, and I will not have a bunch of goddamned bunko booths operating right on top of everything. It's bad enough they're selling goddamned food down here. Nobody's got a permit. You should hear the calls I'm getting from all over town. Half these people are drunk already, and we're just a hair shy of a major riot. No."

Anderson put his finger in the middle of Carl's chest. "The Brand Brothers will not be setting up down here. Not as long as I'm sheriff. You get them on the horn and tell them to stay the hell down in Stamford or Olney or wherever they're stealing people blind till this is over."

He stalked away. Carl started to follow him, but Sapperstein, sharply dressed as always, came out of the motor home and put his hand on Carl's shoulder.

"It's okay," he said to Carl. "Worth a try."

"Son of a bitch is against me," Carl said, pulling out a handkerchief and wiping sweat from his face. "Wouldn't even listen to me. He ought to re-member that he's got to run for office, just like everybody else. I'm going to see to it he won't be elected dogcatcher. Pompous son of a bitch." They went inside.

Hugh moved on through the people, looking for Linda or Tommy or anyone who could tell him what had happened while he had been working. He could see the huge railroad crane still parked on its siding, still covered with its blue tarps, but a grating, whirring sound filled the air, and Hugh was confused. He spotted Tommy and Ray standing near the front of the crowd.

"Well, it's the 'Lawn Doctor,'" Ray said with a sneer. "How's business, asshole?"

"Fine," Hugh said with a thought that he needed to hurry back to work. "Look, guys," he said. "I don't think you understood me yesterday. I'm in trouble with my mom. She said not to ask anybody for help."

The boys looked at each other, then at Hugh. "It's cool," Tommy said. "We couldn't get Ray's dad's mower anyway." Ray looked away, staring at nothing in particular.

Nearly a minute passed before Hugh broke the awkward silence. "So, what's going on?"

"Can't tell," Tommy said. "They brought in some new trucks last night, some new guys. But they've been working inside. They're drilling or something. You can hear them."

Hugh studied the worksite. Several of the men sat or stood around in the shade of a new smaller trailer, smoking and talking. Others, men in white coveralls and yellow hard hats with some sort of symbol on them, moved about near the building. Several large hoses ran from another large white truck to the various doors and windows of the building. The hoses were on huge reels atop the truck's box. Hugh could hear the noise of motors, the source of the grating and whirring. C. W. Pruitt came out of the building and conferred with two of the men in white, then he went back inside.

Tommy and Ray returned into the crowd. Hugh felt a strange, momentary pang of loss when he spotted them hanging around a group of girls from his class, talking and laughing. He longed to go join them, to put things back the way they had been a week before, but somehow he knew that was impossible. He wanted to explain what he was feeling, but he couldn't. He didn't belong to them anymore. They could never understand what he had been through, what his family was going through. The things they shared—school, baseball, dreams of the future—all seemed childish to him now, trivial.

A hollow loneliness crept up on him. Then he remembered his afternoon duties. Some of the largest lawns on his schedule remained to be done. He would be lucky to complete four of them before dark. He shook his head and moved through the mass of people toward his bike.

"Where you been, boy?" Jonas Wilson's voice stopped him when he passed in front of their old spot. "I was counting on you to keep a eye on things. Catch me up."

"I had to work," Hugh said. "I'm way behind." Wilson looked at him through his faded eyes. "I thought you went home."

"Did," he said. "Things was tolerable, so I got Ortega to tote me back this morning. Had to leave Goodlett there. Ortega wouldn't have none of her." Hugh moved over to stand near Wilson. It wasn't easy. People pressed against them, milled about. Few were really watching the work going on down on the site. Most were talking, eating, drinking, and having a great time.

"Mr. Fitzpatrick wanted to bring in the carnival," Hugh said.

"Heard that."

"The sheriff said no," Hugh reported. "Said it was too dangerous."

Wilson reached inside his pocket and pulled out his makings. Hugh waited until he finished, then extended his hand for the bag.

"Ain't it 'too public' here?" Wilson asked, surprised.

"I don't think it matters," Hugh said, working the tobacco and paper.

Wilson nodded and lit their smokes. "You had dinner?"

"Yeah," Hugh said. "You?"

"Yep. Waited on you long's I could."

"Sorry," Hugh said.

"What's wrong, boy?" Wilson eyed him closely. "What's gone on since yesterday? Is it still that little ol' gal, or something else?"

"Nothing," Hugh muttered. "It's nothing, really." He looked down to the site. "What's going on down there?"

Wilson studied him for another moment. "Well, I'm not right sure. But from what all you told me yesterday 'bout them planning to blow her up, I'd say they're drilling blast holes everywhere they can."

"Blast holes?"

"Yep. If it works like it did when I was working on the highway, they'll drill a hole a foot or two deep into the strongest part of her. Then, they'll fill it up with dynamite, wire it all to a battery, then . . ." He made a downward, plunging motion with one gnarled hand. "That'll be all she wrote."

"Think it'll work?"

"Might," Wilson said, scratching his chin. "I been thinking on it. They been pounding on her pretty good near on a week. Got her all shook up. If them fellers in the whites down there know what they're 'bout—and from the looks of things they do—then I s'pect she'll be rock 'n' rubble soon's they throw the switch."

"I hate that," Hugh said.

"Me, too, boy. I hate it worse'n I can say." Wilson's shoulders slumped, then he straightened. "But maybe it won't work," he said. "And maybe if it does work, it'll be for the best. Maybe it's time to think ahead."

Hugh looked up at him. From the shade beneath the battered fedora, Wilson's eyes were moist. "I'm sorry, Jonas," he said. "I know what all this means to you."

Wilson gave him a long look. "You know, I think you just might," he said. "But right now, I want you to quit lying to me."

"What?"

"Tell me what's wrong, boy. What's happened since noon yesterday?"

—≺

"So, are you going tonight?" Wilson asked as soon as Hugh completed outlining the horrors of the past twenty-four hours. As before, Hugh found that unburdening himself to the old man gave him a sense of relief, but throughout Hugh's speech, Wilson only smoked and nodded, sometimes, it seemed, barely listening, hardly paying attention to the agony Hugh was describing in his family.

"I don't know. I forgot all about it until I came down here today. Anyway, a lot depends on my mother . . . how she's doing. I may go to Wichita Falls."

"I doubt your going over there would do much more'n fret her."

"Who asked you?" Hugh said, now angry. "She's my *mother*, for God's sake. Oh, what would you know? You never had a mother." He wanted to wound Wilson, but he wasn't sure why.

"Simmer down, boy," Wilson said. "And watch your mouth. You come real close to calling me a name right then."

"Sorry," Hugh said gruffly. Then he softened his voice. "I'm guess I'm upset. And I'm tired."

"Bet you are," Wilson replied in a matter-of-fact tone.

At that moment a hubbub arose around the Railway Express Office. Voices became shouts, and then came the squawk of a bullhorn. Hugh and Wilson started in that direction, but the mob, pressing in on itself, prevented them from getting close. Everyone was talking at once.

Wilson looked up and pointed. Carl Fitzpatrick emerged onto the roof of the old red-brick structure. At the same time, one of the city's fire trucks had pulled up. A West Texas Utilities cherry picker then rose with Elton Matthews and Sheriff Anderson in the bucket. They stepped out onto the roof to stand by Carl.

Carl was yelling into the bullhorn, but the volume was down, and several people put their hands behind their ears and cried, "Turn it up." Carl fiddled with some knobs on the instrument and tried again. "Let me have your attention!" he shouted. "Let me have your attention!"

"You got it, Carl," a man in the crowd yelled, then laughed. "Seems that's all you want anymore."

"Wait till he's elected," another voice said. "Then you'll feel his hand in your pocket for sure." Laughter was general.

"Let me have your attention," Carl shouted through the bullhorn. "Sheriff Anderson and I have an announcement to make." The crowd quieted, then Carl handed the bullhorn to the sheriff, who took it and spoke in his calm drawl.

"I know it won't do no good to ask you people to disperse and go on about your business," Anderson said.

"You got that right!" a voice shouted back. Hugh recognized Phelps Crane standing in the bed of a pickup at the edge of the crowd. "We got 'em outnumbered," Phelps shouted. "Back off, Anderson. This ain't your business."

The sheriff continued, "But I am informed by officials from the railroad that they intend to complete the razing of the Hendershot building by this evening or tomorrow at the latest."

"Fat chance," Phelps bellowed. "We got the goddamned law on our side, and they ain't going to do nothing."

"Mr. Crane," Anderson said, "if you say another word, you're going back to jail. Do I make myself clear?" There was a chorus of laughter. Phelps folded his arms, sulled up. He was still dressed as he had been for a week, only he had lost his hat somewhere. Gray hair wisped wildly from his balding scalp.

"In any case," Anderson continued, "they are planning to use high explosives. This will be a controlled blast, but it will still be dangerous to anyone within two hundred yards of the worksite. At the point when that happens, whenever that may be, the fire station will blow the siren three times. Three times." He held up three fingers and passed them over his head.

"At that point, you are strongly advised for your own safety to disperse. You will have ten minutes to clear the area. Anyone found beyond the pylons"—he pointed to the far edge of the parking lot—"will be taken into custody for his own protection."

"You ain't the goddamned Nazis," Phelps shouted. "You can't make us 'clear the area.'" The mob muttered an assent. Anderson gestured toward two highway patrolmen, who began moving toward the old man. "And you can't arrest me, neither," Phelps shouted back. "I ain't drunk, and I ain't disorderly. You got no right to arrest me."

The patrolmen pushed their way toward him, but Phelps's voice continued to shout, cracking with emotion. "I was with the Big Red One," he screamed. "We whipped the goddamn Nazis 'fore you was even born, Don Anderson, and I got rights! All I'm doing is exercising my rights of free speech. You tell 'em, Carl. That's all I'm doing! That's what you said the other day, wasn't it? That's what you told 'em. Or have you sold us out, too? Did they buy you off, Carl, just like they did Pete? What do you say, Carl? They going to fuck that building just like they fucked the rest of this town?"

The gray arms of the officers reached Phelps and pulled him down from the pickup's bed. "Take your goddamn hands off me!" he screamed when they wrestled him down to the ground. "I ain't done nothing." But the crowd wasn't watching them. People now turned their eyes toward Carl, who was again speaking through the bullhorn.

"Nothing has changed," Carl said calmly. "We are still working within our rights and actively pursuing a court order to halt this demolition. It looks very promising. I cannot predict with dire certainty, but I do believe that we shall win this fight." The crowd set up a cheer.

"You're lying, Carl," Phelps Crane shouted from beside the DPS cruiser, where he had been taken in handcuffs. "You sold us out, you Nazi son of a bitch!"

Carl smiled again and put up his hand to silence the crowd. "I assure all of you that I am doing all I can to stop this desecration of one of the town's most historic structures. But without any official status, my capabilities are limited. Were I an elected official," he went on, "I am confident that I would have been able to nip this thing in the bud, and we could all be going about our business, confident that the right man is watching the store."

"Bullshit," Hugh heard Jonas Wilson mutter, and he turned and looked up at the old man, shocked to hear a vulgarity from him. Wilson did not so much as glance at Hugh, though. He spat on the ground in front of him and shook his head.

Elton Matthews now accepted the bullhorn. "You folks really ought to go on home," he said in his high, weak voice. "Things have gone too far when people are being arrested around here."

The people milled about but didn't budge, and Elton looked at Anderson and shrugged helplessly and handed the speaker again to Carl.

"I am assured by experts that this parking lot is well outside any danger zone," Carl said. "You people will have to do as you see fit. But please accept the sheriff's warnings, and do not venture beyond the pylons or attempt in any way to interfere with the legal work going on down there."

"You *have* sold us out!" Phelps yelled. "Carl, you're a tin-plated Nazi son—" He stopped in midsentence, but Hugh couldn't see what the officers might have done to silence him.

"I am merely trying to caution you all," Carl continued. "I would be remiss in my civic responsibilities if I encouraged in any way, even by implication, any illegal act or any action on anyone's part which would lead to that individual's arrest or injury."

Applause splattered across the crowd and then dissipated. Anderson took the bullhorn once more. "The All Clear," he said, "will be one long blast on the siren. But even then, the worksite will be dangerous. Do not attempt to approach the building before *or* after the blasting. Is that clear?" He waited a beat. "I will not make this announcement again, but I want to ask you all one more time to disperse." No one moved, and finally the three of them boarded the cherry picker and were lowered from the building's rooftop.

At last, Grissom came to the door of the office and stood there, telephone in hand, and glowered at the crowd. As Carl came around the side of the building, the two men exchanged quick looks, and Carl shrugged before he moved through the milling people back to his motor home.

"Ought to be quite a show," Wilson said softly. "Be a wonder if nobody gets hurt."

"I just hope I get to see it," Hugh said.

"Why wouldn't you, boy?" Wilson asked. "You been here all along."

"I have lawns to mow," he said. "In fact, if I don't get started right now, I'll be so far behind, I'll never catch up. I've got to go."

"You hinting 'round for me to help you, boy?" Wilson's eyes narrowed. "You want my help, all you got to do is ask for it."

Hugh was warmed by an inner heat of resentment. "No," he said. "I don't want any help." To his surprise, he realized that he was telling the truth. This was his responsibility.

"Well, I doubt much'll happen today," Wilson said. "Big doin's'll be tonight, though. You find out what you can. Let me know. This thing's just fixing to get interesting."

"I told you, I'm not sure I can go over there."

Wilson reached out and grabbed Hugh's arm. "You *got* to go over there," he said. "You got to let me know what you can find out. I'm serious 'bout this, boy. Dead serious. This thing's getting out of hand. You go over there tonight and spark that gal if you're a mind to, but you keep your ears open, learn what you can. Then you let me know 'bout it."

Hugh wrenched his arm free of the old man's claw. Wilson's eyes were suddenly hard, fixed on him, and behind them was a panic Hugh had not seen before. There was nothing of the soft nostalgia Wilson had previously shown, nothing of the chuckling irony he so often used to couch his remarks. There was only granite in the milky blue of the old man's eyes now, and all Hugh could do was rub his arm and nod.

In a moment, Wilson moved off, back to his pylon, and Hugh pushed his way through the crowd, boarded his bike, and pedaled away back to work.

—<

It was after three by the time Hugh retrieved his Grassmaster and began mowing again. The afternoon was steamy, preternaturally humid. Sweat stung his eyes and the slight cuts caused by the raking and bagging. His sneaker's sole came off completely, and he had to borrow a strip of duct tape from the Calloways' garage to repair it. The mate, he noticed, wasn't in much better shape.

Just after sundown, he finished the four lawns he had mentally scheduled that day, and he was trudging home in the dusk when he heard a car move up behind him. Too weary to do more than glance around, he moved over near the curb, walked with his head down. He didn't recognize the vehicle, a small red convertible with the top down, and he paid little attention to the fact that the automobile followed him for half a block. Finally, the driver beeped his horn, and he heard his father's voice calling him.

"Hey, Sport, you mad at me or something?"

"Dad?" Hugh spun around. Harry peeked over the windshield. "Is that . . . Did you—?"

"Probably a stupid thing to do," Harry said, cutting the engine and getting out. He ran his hand along the fender. "Always wanted a convertible, though. This isn't really that expensive, and it runs like a bat out of hell. Pretty neat, huh?"

"Dad, are you all right?"

"Never better," he said. "Never paid cash for a car in my life. It felt damn good, I can tell you. I just hope I can get my retirement turned over and into the savings account before your mother starts asking questions. She'll have a blue-collar panic." He chuckled.

"Mom!" Hugh said. "How is she? Have you seen her?"

"Of course, I've seen her," Harry smiled. "Your mother is fine, and she sends her love. She feels terrible about all this. Thinks she's let us both down, but I set her straight on that. It was all a big mistake, and . . . and it wasn't her fault." He looked over Hugh's head in the general direction of their neighborhood. "She'll be home tomorrow."

"But Loretta, uh, Mrs. Thompson said—"

"Loretta Thompson's full of shit," Harry said with a sudden viciousness. "She's the one who caused all this. She didn't come over and 'find your mom nearly unconscious,'" Harry whined in imitation of Loretta's voice. "And your mother didn't call her, either. She came over on her own and fed her alcohol and probably something else until she passed out. They had to pump her stomach. Loretta," Harry said, suddenly bitter, "tried to tell Doctor Richardson that it was a suicide attempt or something, but he saw through that. I talked to him this morning."

"But she said Phelps Crane and—"

"Oh, that crazy old fool did call, I guess. But what other calls there were were to Loretta, not to your mother." Harry looked away. "Loretta wanted your mother to . . . Well, she tried to make your mother say things, do things . . . Well, anyway, after a while, she just went a little crazy. That's all."

Loretta Thompson's face swam up before Hugh. His fists clenched. He couldn't find any words at all.

"It doesn't matter, now, Sport," Harry said. "It wasn't the first time Loretta, uh . . . butted into our affairs. Only before she's been a lot more, uh . . . diplomatic about it. I knew what was going on, but I was too afraid to say anything about it." His voice got small, almost too quiet to hear. "I mean, I never *saw* anything, nothing I could be sure of. And your mother— God bless her—didn't have a clue. But I should have done something any- way." He snapped to, as if he just realized Hugh was still standing there. "Do you have any idea what I'm trying to say, Hugh?"

"I think so," Hugh choked out softly.

"I was afraid, Sport," Harry Rudd said. "Sometimes when you say things, even to someone you love, you can hurt them. Lose them. We lost Larry, and that was hard enough. And—given who the Thompsons were, at the mill and all—I was afraid of losing my job. I guess I was mostly afraid of losing your mother, and you." Hugh stood silent, stiff.

"But all that's behind us now. It took me long enough, but I finally realized that I'm not going to lose one thing. It's time to act, and to hell with the consequences. Your mother's fine. We had a long talk, and everything's fine. She wants to come home, and tomorrow I'll drive over and get her."

"In this?" Hugh found his voice and looked again at the car.

"Sure, in this. We sure as hell can't go in the old boat."

"How did you get to Wichita Falls?" Hugh asked.

Harry grinned. "I went out to Dryden's station, thought maybe he'd lend me one of the junkers he keeps around back out there. But he was downtown with all the other goldbrickers, and the kid he left in charge was afraid to let me have one of them. There was this trucker there, though. Turned out to be an ex-swabbie, like me. He heard me yelling at the kid and offered me a ride all the way there. I saw your mother, talked to the doctors, then talked to her."

He took thought. "You know, Hugh, you can love somebody with all your heart, know them as well as you know yourself. But if you aren't careful, things can get really strange after a while. I mean, one morning you wake up, look at each other, and wonder just who the hell you are, who that is across the room. It's scary. If she hadn't—if Loretta hadn't come over, done what she did, if I hadn't lost my job, if the car hadn't broken down. Hell, if you hadn't been so far behind, none of this might have happened. I might never have said a thing. I might have gotten up one morning and she'd be gone. You, too."

Hugh was suddenly chilled, as if a cold wind was blowing from somewhere. "I don't think that would happen, Dad."

"Oh, it *could* happen. It happens all the time. Oh, not for the same reasons. But it happens, believe you me." He folded his arms across his chest. "But it's water under the bridge now, Sport. Like I said. We talked, and it's all okay. It's okay now, it'll be okay tomorrow. I felt so goddamned good, I went right out and bought the car, and the rest, as they say, is history. Or it soon will be."

"Bought the car," Hugh said.

"Right. I was looking at the ads in the paper there while your mother was getting her bath, and I just made up my mind. I called the Mazda dealer, told him I'd take anything he had in red with no top, and that if he could deliver it today, I'd pay cash. Should have seen the look on his face when I whipped out the checkbook and wrote it out. Didn't even dicker.

Probably never happened to him before. Sure as hell never happened to me."

"And Mom doesn't know?"

"Oh, she knows I bought a car," Harry admitted with a nod and a sheepish smile. "But she doesn't know what kind. Don't worry, Hugh. She'll understand. Believe me, there's going to be a whole hell of a lot more understanding around here, now. Anyway, I stopped off and looked at a new Ford out at Atwell's, too. That one we'll finance, though."

"You've been busy," Hugh commented, still overwhelmed by the car, the news of his mother, and his father's reflective, jovial mood. It was too much to digest all at once. He peered through the dying daylight and tried to see if the happiness in his father's grin was a façade, a put-on for his benefit, but it seemed genuine. Suddenly he wanted to hug him, and he did.

"You have, too," Harry laughed, returning the embrace fiercely, then backing away, holding Hugh's shoulders at arm's length. "You smell like a herd of goats. How's it coming?"

"Getting there," Hugh said. "I think I can catch up tomorrow."

"Sunday? Well, we'll see. Wish you could have used the tractor."

"I'd probably wreck it."

"No more than I did," Harry laughed. "It's just as well. I'm sending it back Monday. Hell with it. I'm not going to spend the rest of my life taking orders from somebody who's dumber than me. I've had enough of that. C'mon, let's get home."

Harry steered the sports car slowly beside his son as Hugh pushed the mower the four blocks to their house. The front windows were brightly lit, and the porch light spilled out onto their own neglected yard. Hugh stored the Grassmaster and pulled his shoes off, realizing that they might not stand up to washing.

"Got to have some new sneaks," he said to his father, who nodded in the affirmative, then opened the garage door. The Thompsons' Cadillac was parked inside.

"What the hell?" Harry exclaimed angrily. He stormed into the house. Hugh was right beside them.

Pete Thompson sat in the living room, a cocktail at his side. He slumped down in the uncomfortable armchair with a newspaper folded on his lap, his shoes kicked off, and his stockinged feet propped up on an ottoman. A ball game was on the television. He looked so installed that Hugh had the impression that he and his father were interlopers in their own home. Harry's body stiffened.

"Don't mind us," Harry said sarcastically. "We're just passing through."

Pete looked up slowly, as if surprised to see them standing in their own living room. He slowly folded his newspaper, shook his head. "You are completely out of hooch," he said. "Had to bring a bottle from home. How's Edith?" he asked, returning to his paper.

"None of your fucking business," Harry shot. "You want to tell me what the hell you're doing here? For that matter, how'd you get in?"

"We have a key," Pete said, startled. "Harry, I know you're upset—"

"You don't know the half of it," Harry growled.

"But you had no call to talk to Loretta the way you did last night."

"I had no call?"

"That's right. You haven't shown a shred of responsibility around here. By the way, there have been a number of phone calls," he said, briefly glancing at Hugh. "That little slut Linda Fitzpatrick has called three times to speak to Hugh."

Hugh almost jumped when he realized what Pete was saying. He was due at Linda's house any time now.

"Loretta faithfully promised Edith that she would watch out for the two of you," Pete continued. "I just don't know what Edith's going to say, now. Her son is hanging around with wild girls, drunken old men, gambling." Pete shook his head, a pitying gesture. "My God, Harry. You've lost complete control here! To say nothing of what you pulled out at the mill. Back when you worked for me, I always thought you were a fairly decent man, and I had no inkling of this side of you at all. The only thing that's clear is that Hugh takes after you completely. If it weren't for Loretta and me, I don't know what sort of state things would be in here."

"Loretta and you," Harry said in a monotone. His jaw was clenched tight, his eyes were narrow, threatening.

"That's right. I mean, yesterday, I chased all over looking for you. Took Edith to Wichita Falls, and today, I've—"

"No one asked you to chase all over anywhere or to do anything." Harry's monotone continued, but his volume came up a notch. "Where we go and who we go with is none of your goddamn business. That's what I told Loretta last night, but she didn't seem to get the message."

"Loretta tried to call Edith all afternoon," Pete said, ignoring the anger building in Harry, "but they wouldn't put her through, and neither one of you has bothered to let her know a thing that's going on."

"I'd say that things are about as they should be, then," Harry said, his voice still low and even. "I'm going to ask you one more time to leave, Pete. Then I'm going to kick your ass out the front door."

Pete put up his hand and came to his feet. "I am going to ignore that, Harry. I came over here tonight for two reasons. One was to let you come home with me and apologize to Loretta for the way you acted—"

"Apologize hell!" Harry shouted.

"That's right. Apologize," Pete went on in a maddeningly patronizing voice. "If not right now, then maybe tomorrow. But you'll come to your senses sooner or later, realize that someone has to take charge around here, turn your life back around."

Harry's mouth opened, but no words came out. Hugh moved against the wall.

"And the second reason is that I've been able to pull a few strings. I'm not sure, but I think if you give Riley a call, apologize to him, maybe they'll take you back on at the mill. I explained what a strain it's been for you—"

Harry walked deliberately across the living room and grabbed Pete Thompson by his shirt collar. "You're so full of shit, your eyes are brown," Harry hissed into the face of the former mayor. His right fist was clenched. Hugh held his breath. He wanted with all his heart for his father to hit the corpulent Pete, to hit him and hit him and keep on hitting him until Pete begged for mercy.

Instead, Harry dropped his fist and his vocal tone at the same time. "I ought to pound you into hamburger."

"Hit him, Dad," Hugh shouted. "Hit him." He meant it with all his heart.

Pete gave a quick, frightened glance toward Hugh. "Don't be ridiculous. Let go of me! Harry, have you lost what little mind you—"

"You and your bull dyke wife came in here and almost destroyed this family," Harry hissed directly into Pete's eyes. Pete struggled to free himself from Harry's grasp, and his shirt front ripped open. White, fat skin spilled out over his belt buckle when Harry let him go and Pete staggered across the room.

"I have no idea what you're talking about, but if it's what it sounds like—"

"*I* don't know what I'm talking about either, Pete."

Harry stepped forward, forcing Pete to retreat toward the front door, once again prompting Hugh to say in a half-whisper, "C'mon, Dad. Hit him."

Instead, Harry's voice remained cold, calm, intense. "I've spent most of my life pretending *not* to know about things like that. But I do know that if she had kept her slimy nose out of our business, we'd be all right tonight. Edith wouldn't be in the hospital, you wouldn't be sitting here in my house acting like the Lord of All You Survey."

Pete shifted his weight nervously and glanced once more at Hugh. "You'd better watch your mouth, Harry," he muttered. "I'm only going to put up with so much for Edith's sake. This is a fifty-dollar shirt."

"You've been a boil on my butt for years," Harry continued. "Back when I worked for you, I thought you were a Class-A Prick and an ass-licker, and all you've done tonight is let me know I was right. You were a lousy mayor, crooked as a dog's hind leg. No matter who comes after you, he couldn't fuck things up as much as you did."

"I'm warning you," Pete said.

"Go ahead," Harry laughed. "Warn me! What're you going to do? Send Loretta over to beat me up?"

"You've lost your mind," Pete said. He pulled his shirt to and turned around. "You surely don't want Hugh to hear any more of this. Why don't we have a drink, sit down, and talk this out like adults? For Edith's sake—and Loretta's. We don't need to—"

"I don't think you understand me," Harry dropped his tone to a level Hugh had heard only one or two times before in his life. Both times, Hugh had been in serious trouble, and he braced himself for what was to come. He was now sure his father's fist would reach out and find Pete's fat jaw. But once more, he was disappointed when Harry said in an even, steady tone, "I want you to get the hell out of my house right now. *Now!*" Harry shouted before Pete could open his mouth. "If you're not out of here by the time I blink, I'm going to kick your crooked ass around the block for drill. The only thing stopping me right now is that I don't want to have to wash off the smell of you when I'm through."

"Harry, I've still got a lot of influence in this town. You'll never find another job here." Pete grabbed the torn shreds of his shirt together over his stomach, scrunched his feet into his loafers, and pushed past Harry, who refused to step aside to give him room and made him walk around him. Hugh sagged with disappointment. Pete would get away clean.

"I've got to move the car so our guest can leave," Harry said, and he followed Pete outside.

Hugh practically raced to the kitchen, found the whiskey bottle, a nearly full one, brought it back and flung it out the door onto the sidewalk, where it shattered. Pete was backing out of the driveway. He pulled away, leaving a streak of rubber behind him.

When Pete's taillights turned the corner, Harry spun on Hugh, a huge grin across his face. "God, that felt good! I haven't felt that good since I belted a Marine sergeant in Naples." He smacked his fist into his palm and raced over to grab Hugh.

Hugh wanted to ask why Harry hadn't hit Pete Thompson the same way. He couldn't understand what had stayed his father's fist. But he didn't have the chance to ask. Harry was laughing and almost babbling.

"*Never* be afraid, Hugh. Never give in to it! God, if you learn nothing else from me, learn that! Fear's a goddamn rock. It'll keep you rooted in place like a statue when you know you should do something." He smacked his fist into his palm. "God, I should have done that years ago when Larry died. Should have done it when I had to work for that son of a bitch! God, how could I have waited so long?" He pulled Hugh to him and bear-hugged him.

"Sport, you stink worse than a roadkill, but God in heaven I love you! What say we go inside, clean up a bit, and head out for a couple of steaks? Goddamn, I feel good!"

Hugh didn't know what to say. He looked down at his dirty socks, tried to feel something clearly.

"C'mon, Sport. Those people have been a weight around this family's neck ever since your brother died. I've cut us free. Free! Really and truly free! Let's get spiffed up and hit the town."

"I can't, Dad."

"What?"

"I said, 'I can't.' I've . . . I've sort of got a date?"

"A what?"

"That's what Linda was calling about. I'm supposed to go out to her house. Swim in their hot tub. Uh . . . you know. It's a party. She's sort of expecting me."

"Well, I'll be damned." Harry put his hands on his hips and stared through the porch light's yellow glow toward his son. "A date! Linda Fitzpatrick? That's high cotton, Sport. Your mother'll have a fit." Then Harry grinned widely and feinted a jab at Hugh, who ducked, bewildered. "But she'll come around. I'll make her understand—I swear it! Go for it, Hugh. Don't be afraid of anything. You're more grown up than I ever was at your age. I sure as hell wasn't dating."

"Uh, no, Dad. It's not really a date," Hugh tried to explain. "It's just . . . Well, I sort of promised. I could call her—"

"Hell, no! A promise is a promise!" Harry exclaimed. "You go inside and clean up. I'll call and tell her—"

"Uh, no, Dad!" Hugh said, panic swimming up inside him. "I'll call her."

"Whatever you say, Sport. This is Independence Day for the Rudds, and nothing you say is wrong."

"I could use a ride over," Hugh said.

"You bet," Harry said, clapping Hugh on the back and pulling him toward the front door. "Whatever you say. Just remember where you came from. The way things are going, I'm going to need your support in my old age. But I'll tell you, Hugh," he stopped and looked deeply into his son's eyes, "for the very first time in my life, I'm not afraid."

CHAPTER EIGHT

Linda met Hugh at the front door of the Fitzpatrick home. "I thought you'd never get here," she hissed, pulling him through the entrance and glancing at the sports car when it sped away. She was wearing a silk cover-up over a swimsuit, but when Hugh looked closer, he saw that there wasn't much suit there at all. His throat involuntarily tightened at the touch of her fingers on his arm. "Who was that?" she asked when she shut the door behind him.

"My dad," Hugh said, staring around the huge entranceway of the Fitzpatrick house. Hardwood vied with gold wallpaper and huge Chinese sculptures. There was no discernible theme or color scheme. It looked more like the fancy department stores at one of the malls in Dallas than someone's home. A staircase spiraled away from a Persian rug in a half-circle to the second story.

"We got a new car," he muttered as his eyes traced a bright mural along the wall. It depicted a seascape, complete with whales and other creatures cavorting in choppy swells. Seabirds floated overhead in blue skies, but high on the second landing, Hugh could see that purple storm clouds were descending on the happy scene.

"A convertible," Linda said. "That is so cool! C'mon, you're late. They've been here for hours."

"Oh," Hugh said and blushed. "I'm sorry. I thought you said everyone would be here at—"

"Not *them*, silly," Linda threw her eyes toward a set of double doors off the entranceway. "*Them*. We're the only kids here."

She took him by the hand and led him down the hall by the staircase and through a swinging door to the largest kitchen Hugh had ever seen. It was bigger than the kitchen in the old hotel. An enormous double-door refrigerator and a freezer stood in a line on one wall, and a huge chopping block table with built-in grill and a double sink sat in the middle of the floor. Everything, including the floor tiles, was either lime green or pink.

Lydia Fitzpatrick, dressed in electric blue tights and a halter top, sat on a bar stool by one counter watching a small portable color TV and dabbing at a bowl of ice cream with a silver spoon. She turned when the pair came through and put on a pair of red-rimmed glasses.

"So, *someone* showed up, after all," she said. Hugh nodded, and Linda continued to pull his hand through the room toward a back door.

Lydia studied Hugh. "Aren't you the Rudd boy?" she asked.

Hugh stopped and nodded again. Lydia's hair was now almost white. Shorter than Hugh's own curly mop, the platinum wisps parted here and there to reveal a pink scalp beneath. Her nails were painted with dark maroon polish. Hugh tried not to stare at her pointed, braless breasts that strained against the halter and threatened to push it aside.

"I hear your mother's in the hospital," she said matter-of-factly.

"Uh, yes, ma'am. She's coming home tomorrow."

"I'm glad to hear that," Lydia said. "But you tell your father that if there's anything I can do—give you a ride someplace, or fix something to eat and bring it over—he's to call me," she said.

You? Hugh's inner voice shouted at her. You of *all* people? Lydia's tone was purely sympathetic. There was no note of enmity or sarcasm in it. She seemed genuinely concerned. Then he realized that everything he knew about Lydia Fitzpatrick—everything his father knew, as well—had been filtered through the vileness that was Loretta Thompson. He studied this silly, frowzy woman sitting in her expensive kitchen and expressing what was apparently genuine sympathy for him, for his family. How many other people in this town had been judged strictly because of rumors, lies, misunderstandings, he wondered.

"I'll tell him," Hugh said. "But we'll be fine."

"Well, you tell him," she said. "I've always liked your mother. I'm sorry we never got to know one another better. Everyone's always so busy these days. Time just gets away. Anyway, you can tell your father we heard what happened at the mill, also," she went on, her eyes returning to the TV. "and we think it's wrong. As soon as this silly business downtown is over, I'm sure something will be worked out." Her eyes found him again. "I guess you know that Linda's father has decided to run for governor."

"Uh . . . yes, ma'am."

"Well, he may well be in a position to make some changes in the way things are done around here," she said.

Hugh nodded once more and gave in to Linda's tugging, which, he realized, hadn't stopped since her mother started talking.

Linda led him outdoors, across a covered patio and then a well-trimmed lawn to a redwood gazebo structure that housed the hot tub. The roof was open to the sky, but Hugh could see that it was made to be covered for winter use. The walls were thick and had removable windows. She directed him to a small room on one side, where he shed his jeans and abused sneakers and put on his swimsuit. When he came out, Linda was already in the water.

It was hot, much hotter than he expected when he lowered his body into it. He almost leaped out.

"You have to get in slow," Linda explained. "There're minerals in it. It's good for you."

Hugh gently lowered himself into the foaming water, trying not to stare at Linda's body beneath the white bubbles. His mind told him she was wearing a suit, but for all he could see, there was nothing blocking his view of her entire body in the occasional clear spots that rumbled to the top.

"Mother is *so* boring," she said, drawing his eyes up to meet hers. "She has decided that we're moving to Austin next year no matter what."

"Well . . ."

"Is that all you can say? I am *not* moving to Austin. I am not leaving here until I leave for college, and I am going to college in California. That much I know."

"I wish I could be that sure of things."

"I am sure," she insisted. "And I am sure that if I am the daughter of the governor of Texas, I'll have to go to some Texas college. And in the meantime, I'll have to go to some private high school where they don't even have football and probably don't have any boys. I am depending on you to help me get out of this, Hugh."

"What? Me?"

"Yes, you. My mother's gone completely crazy, and so has my father. You're the only person I ever talk to who's sane."

She continued to talk, but much as he wanted to, he found that he couldn't listen anymore. He studied the water's surface and the bare sky above them for a moment and realized that his entire body was relaxing, that he was almost drifting away to sleep. Aching, tired muscles unknotted as his limbs floated in the bubbling water.

"So, are you ready?" Linda asked, and Hugh opened his eyes, aware suddenly that he had almost been dreaming.

"For what?"

"To be a spy. That's what you're here for, isn't it?"

Hugh, now wide awake, stared at her, and she laughed, splashed him playfully, then climbed out of the tub. "Come here," she said.

Hugh followed her, but he was instantly distracted when he started to climb over the edge. Her suit consisted of what appeared to be slightly less than a square foot of flesh-colored material. One small patch covered her crotch, and two more even smaller pieces hid the nipples of her small breasts. The trio of tiny coverings was linked by a spaghetti-thin series of strings, one of which rose from between her buttocks. Hugh's breath quickened, and he lowered himself back into the tub, embarrassed instantly by his body's reaction.

"C'mon," she said, turning and framing her bare stomach with her fingertips. Her golden hair, the ends wet, fell down across her chest and naked shoulders. "What are you waiting for? This is what you're here for, isn't it?"

"Uh, that's some suit," Hugh muttered. He had to fight to keep his eyes off her body, to concentrate on looking at her face.

"Of course, it's 'some suit,'" Linda said. "My sister got it for me in Hollywood. On Rodeo Drive. It's from France. Now, c'mon."

"Right," Hugh said. He grabbed a towel from the rack on the side of the tub, pulled it quickly around his waist, and dripped over behind her. "Chilly out here," he said.

"I swear, Hugh Rudd, you are such a wuss." She pointed to a series of electronic components built into the wall of the hot tub's redwood housing. Hugh recognized a tuner-equalizer combination and a CD player. "Look here. You do know what this is, don't you?"

"Stereo," he said. "CD."

"And," she announced with a flick of her long finger, which lit up the tuner's LED dial, "an intercom."

Instantly, the gazebo was filled with male voices coming from four speakers ingeniously placed around the tub. "Daddy had it installed all over the house and out here as well," she said. "That way, we can all call each other from any room at all, even the bathrooms."

Hugh strained to hear what the voices were saying.

"I want you to know that *officially* I do not approve of this," Linda explained carefully. "Eavesdropping is *not* respectable, and spying on my own father would get me in deep you-know-what. But I'm desperate. If you think you can hear something that will stop all this nonsense and get things back to normal, then—"

"Can you turn it up?"

"Sure," she said, fiddling with a button. "I sneaked in and turned it on in the den while they were eating dinner in the dining room. Daddy always takes men into the den for drinks after. But they've been in there for a while, like I said, so I don't know what they've said. I was waiting for you—"

"Shh," Hugh said. Carl was speaking, he realized, and Hugh tuned his ears to pick out any other voices that might answer him.

"I want it understood," Carl said, "that this arrangement is completely above board and on the level. I will not be surprised by any 'revelations in the press,' as they say. And I will *not* do anything illegal."

"It's all on the up-and-up," another voice—Hugh believed it was Sapperstein's—said. "That's the way I work, the only way I work. Everything goes through me. If anybody's got a problem with that, now's the time to say so."

"It's no big deal," Carl said. "Small potatoes, really. But I don't want to have to deny anything in the press. And I want it clear that I am not enriching myself at all with any of this."

"I wouldn't call a quarter of a million dollars a small deal," another voice, which Hugh recognized as Grissom's, spoke up.

"It's chicken feed compared to what it'll cost you to call this whole deal off, pull the crews out, and then try to explain to your bosses what happened," Sapperstein said.

"Well, I still don't like it," yet another voice came through.

"Shut the hell up, Elton," Carl said. "The only reason I brought you in on this is to keep you honest."

"Honest, my ass," Elton replied. "If *you* get caught, *I* get caught. The only reason I'm here is because you couldn't grab the mayor's office when you dropped the hammer on Pete."

"I'll tell you what, Elton," Carl said. "Why don't you just pick up your goddamn scruples and get the hell out of here right now?" There was a pause, and Hugh listened to the hiss-buzz of the intercom broadcasting dead air. "I thought so," Carl said. "You'll be set up for the next election, and everybody's happy. Right?"

"Right," Elton said, then coughed. "But I wouldn't mind a few thousand to ease my conscience."

"Nobody's making any personal money on this," Carl insisted. "Not me, not you."

"Okay, okay," Elton said. "I'm in. I told you I was in."

"So sit down and shut up."

"Can we get back to business?" Grissom asked. "What I want to know is how you're going to keep that mob down there from going ape-shit when that building goes up? Half of them think you've sold them out already. I don't see how you're going to come out of this as clean as you think you will."

"I got that figured," Carl said. "We just couldn't get the judge to move fast enough on that court order."

"What court order?" Elton said in a sarcastic tone. "You never filed for any court order."

"I'm telling you to shut up for the last time, Elton," Carl said. "Of course, I filed a court order. Or a temporary restraining order anyway. But don't worry about it. Judges don't just hand those out like campaign fliers. I had my secretary slapping together affidavits all afternoon. It's all so general, there's no way in the world a judge is going to rule in our favor. In fact, when I took the papers down to the courthouse, I had to point out—candor in the court, you know, just doing my duty and all—that there's a recent case right on point that goes against us. He'd have to rule that the Hendershot situation was worth overturning precedent."

"How likely is that?" Elton asked.

"There's no way in hell that any judge is going to add to his reversal on appeal rate by ruling against a verdict handed down just three years ago. That would be political suicide, especially when a national corporation is involved. Anyway, we filed the papers, so the reporters can go and look at them, and they'll tell the waiting world that we did what we could, but it wasn't enough. That's all. We fought the good fight, and we lost."

"So it's over," Elton said.

"Not quite," Carl continued. "To show that the railroad has the town's best interest at heart, they're going to put up a park right there on the lot behind the Railway Express Office, which we'll convert to a museum, and—"

"What?" Grissom shouted. "What park? What museum? That's not part of the deal."

"Yeah, it is," Sapperstein said. "That was part of the deal."

"Not a park. Not on top of everything else. That'll cost another half mil."

"Naw," Sapperstein laughed. "Maybe fifty grand. Couple of picnic tables, a tree or two, and a plaque saying this was some kind of big-deal rail terminal once upon a time. Tourists'll go nuts for it. That'll satisfy all the downtown merchants who've jumped on this bandwagon, and the local civic leaders all look good. The railroad buys itself a shitload of publicity and goodwill, and you get your goddamn wye. Hell, I'll donate a couple of thou myself out of my end."

"Your end?" Elton's voice asked. "I didn't think anybody had an end. Carl, you—"

"I don't work for free, small time," Sapperstein responded.

"A park. A museum," Grissom moaned. "They'll crucify me in Chicago."

"They'll give you a medal," Carl said. "Which is more than they'll do if you don't finish this job. And you can believe me that I can hold this up for another week, maybe a month. Court order or no court order."

"But—"

"Look," Sapperstein interrupted again. "The deal on the money and the park and museum has been cut already. What's your problem, Grissom? You come out of this smelling like a rose. You get your wye, the town gets its monument to history, and the railroad gets a new governor who's remarkably sympathetic to corporate needs."

"And Fitzpatrick here gets rich," Grissom said.

"No," Carl put in. "Fitzpatrick is *already* rich. I get to be governor. Then maybe senator. Who knows? Sky's the limit. The money goes to Sapperstein, and he runs the campaign. It's a sweetheart deal, and nobody gets hurt."

"So the building comes down as scheduled?" Elton asked.

"Noon tomorrow," Grissom said. "That's the—"

"Just what in the world do you think you're doing?" Lydia Fitzpatrick's voice shot through the gazebo and froze both teenagers in place. Hugh and Linda instantly swung around to face her mother, who stood in the doorway, a tray of iced drinks and snacks in her hands. Linda instantly snaked out her finger and casually flipped a switch on the stereo system, instantly filling the small room with loud heavy metal music. Hugh's heart thundered in his ears. He almost turned to run away, but there was no other door.

"Turn that down!" Lydia shouted.

Linda obliged. Hugh still couldn't move. His skin tingled with shame and fear.

"I asked what in the world you think you're doing?" Lydia demanded as she stalked into the room and set the refreshment tray down on a small table.

"We are trying to find a decent radio station!" Linda said. "I told Daddy he needed to hook the FM up to cable."

"It sounds like you've found the demons of hell," Lydia said, frowning at the music surrounding her. "But that's *not* what I was talking about. I want to know just what you think you're doing, young lady?" Lydia marched to the rack and pulled a towel free. "I told you that you were not to wear that suit in public."

"This isn't public," Linda said, shocked and, Hugh could see, relieved. "This is our backyard."

"*He* is public," Lydia said, jerking a thumb toward Hugh. He wanted to crawl under the boards beneath his feet, but Lydia wasn't looking at him. She wrapped the towel around her daughter and pulled it tight. "You are naked, and I will not tolerate that, do you understand me?"

"I am not naked! Megan says—"

"Your sister is a grown woman, and she can do as she pleases, with or without my consent. You, however, are still a child in this house, and you will not prance around naked in front of anyone, especially some boy you hardly know." She turned to Hugh. "I'm sorry, what's your first name?"

"Uh . . . Hugh?"

"Hugh. I'm sure you are a very nice boy, and I am going to apologize for Linda's behavior. I'm very sorry, but I'm afraid you are going to have to leave. Linda has directly disobeyed me. It has nothing to do with you, and you are certainly welcome to come back another time. But this party is over. I hope you understand. Please get dressed and leave as quick as you can."

"Uh . . . yes, ma'am."

"I'm sorry. I hope there are no hard feelings. Linda, you are to go upstairs at once. You are grounded for a week."

"A week!"

"All right, a month! Goodnight, young lady." She pointed toward the house, and Linda, with a small secret smile for Hugh and a bit of mischief in her eyes, passed through the door and across the lawn. "Can you find your way out? Do you need a ride home or anything?" Lydia asked when Hugh went into the dressing room for his clothes.

"Yes, ma'am. Uh, no, ma'am. I can walk."

"Fine. Be sure to let your parents know that I asked about them." Then she was gone.

—≺

Hugh let himself out of the house, then started the long walk home from the Fitzpatricks. He thought of stopping at Dryden's gas station on the highway and phoning his father to come get him, but he also wanted to let Jonas Wilson know what was going on, and he needed to do it that night.

It was late when he reached the downtown area and found it almost deserted. Only a few cars and pickups with camper shells were parked here and there. Hugh suspected that some of the out-of-town folks had bedded down in them, but he steered clear and walked along the sidewalks, peering into darkened storefronts.

He walked over to the abandoned corner gasoline station across from the hotel and looked up to the third floor. Sure enough, a small light was visible from the window of the room in back, but when Hugh set his foot on the street to cross, Coach Kruickshank emerged from the building's front door, a flashlight in one hand and a large plastic bag in the other. He weaved uncertainly as he moved around the corner of the building and toward the trash cans in the back.

Hugh looked up again, but now the light was out. He wished Jonas would come out for a walk or something. Kruickshank returned and went back inside. Wilson did not appear. Hugh discovered that he did not have the courage to sneak into the building. The ghost stories he had always heard now seemed silly and far away, but the thought of mounting the old, creaky steps in the back of the building was too daunting. A lump rose in his throat when he contemplated it, and he remembered the fear he felt when Coach Kruickshank was looking for him. "Never be afraid," his father had told him, but Harry Rudd had never faced the dark interior of the rear staircase of the hotel.

After waiting another several minutes and finding no new reservoir of courage inside him, Hugh turned away, feeling ashamed but no more able to enter the old building. He strolled down toward the parking lot.

He was shocked to see how it looked, as if a huge army had camped there, then moved on, leaving anything it didn't want behind. Fifty-five-gallon drums hastily set up as garbage cans were overflowing. Trash and bottles were strewn about everywhere, blown by the soft night breeze. The quiet of the downtown area seemed to fill the open expanse as fully as the noise of the crowd had done earlier. He wondered what time it was, but he had no watch on. He knew it was late. It even felt late, later than he had ever been up, alone at night.

He heard some noises coming from the worksite, and when he reached the pylons and looked down, he was surprised to see that large spotlights had been rigged to illuminate several of the entrances to the old building. A few men in white coveralls moved busily from their trucks to inside the building and back again. For a moment, Hugh feared they were about to blow the building up at night, when no one was around.

A dark shape moved up from the shadows of the site: Phelps Crane. He was bent over, trudging up the incline. He emerged onto the parking lot and stood for a moment, his body heaving with the effort of the uphill climb. Hugh could see something—maybe a long toolbox—in his hands. Phelps looked around, then reached into his overalls pocket and pulled a pint bottle from it. He opened it, tilted back his head, and drank deeply. Then he smashed it against one of the pylons, then slumped off toward the far side of the Railway Express Office.

Hugh shuddered. Phelps looked like a monster, he thought, a hunch-back or a Frankenstein, sloughing off into the darkness, away from the light.

The small trailer Hugh had seen down at the worksite earlier was now pulled up near the opposite side of the REO from where Phelps disappeared. There were lights on inside. Hugh moved over for a look through the open door. Inside sat a man in white coveralls, his heavy workboots propped up on a table. He was reading a magazine and drinking coffee. Suddenly, he sensed that he was being watched, and he dropped the magazine and stared directly at Hugh.

"What'cha want, kid?" he asked. "Ain't it a little late for you to be hanging around here?" His accent reminded Hugh of gangsters he had seen on TV.

"I'm waiting for my dad," Hugh said, shocked with the ease of lying once again. "I've been at a friend's house, and Dad was supposed to meet me, but he didn't make it."

The man studied Hugh's face in the light spilling from the doorway. "Tough break, kid," he said. "Want some java? I'd offer you a Coke or something, but coffee's all that's on the menu tonight."

Hugh nodded and entered the trailer. The table was crowded with equipment. There were coils of wire and tape and in the center a small black box with red and green knobs on either side and a small triangular hole in the center.

"Curious about that, ain't you?" the man said when he set a cracked mug full of black coffee in front of Hugh. "Well, that's the little dinger that's gonna do the job," he said. He sat down, reached out, and patted the box. "Hook one wire in there," he pointed to the red knob, "one in there," he pointed to the green. "Hook the whole gizmo up to a six cell. Take this here key." He pulled out a large brass T from his pocket. "Stick it here in the middle. Give her a turn. And boom!"

"Implosion," Hugh said.

The man's bushy eyebrows rose. "That's right, kid. You got it. Ought to be using a remote control, but they won't do it. This old box'll have to do."

"What's it look like when it happens?" Hugh asked, staring through the doorway into the darkness.

"Never seen one?" Hugh shook his head. "Well, let me tell you, I done forty, forty-one of these. Me and C. W. has, anyhow. And no two is alike. Sometimes, there's lots of noise. Sometimes, the roof goes off. Just flies off, like it was jerked off or something. Sometimes the walls fall out and away like somebody just pushed them all over at once. Sometimes they fall inside. Hard to say. Always lots of noise in them kind. Sometimes there ain't no noise at all. Sometimes, there's these little puffs of smoke coming out the drill holes and windows and doors, and then she just falls in on herself, just like somebody let all the air out of her.

"Sometimes, she just stands there a minute or two, then just falls apart all at once, like she was a mirage or something that you got too close to. Only two things is ever the same. One is that there's a hell of a mess of dust and dirt blowing all over the place, and two is that when it's all over, she ain't there no more. That's the same every time."

"How do you think it'll go on the Hendershot building?"

"The what? Oh, that old lady down there? Well, it's hard to say. C. W. says she's solid as a brick shithouse—pardon my French—but I don't know. I never seen one that wouldn't go sooner or later. That's one tough old lady, though. She's going to put up a fight."

"Seems like she already has," Hugh said. The coffee was black and bitter.

The man winked, then pointed at a small carton marked "High Explosive." "See that?" he asked. Hugh nodded. "That's C-1209 Explosive Gelatin. Unstable as hell. Developed top secret by the CIA back in the seventies, but so far as I know, they never used it. Army put the kibosh on it, too. Claim it's dangerous, and they're right. That tiny little box there has enough to blow this whole town to Kingdom Come. The army got careless with it over in Cambodia and blew a hole the size of Brooklyn right there in the jungle. Wasn't more than a couple of pounds there, but I can tell you, it made a bang. Hushed it up, but nobody cared one way or another, anyhow. It's potent stuff, though. We only use it on tough old ladies like that one down there."

He rose and picked up the carton and tossed it to Hugh. Hugh jumped up from his chair, spilled the coffee, and barely secured the greasy carton in his hands before it hit the trailer's floor. When he looked up, sweat beading on his face, he found the man doubled over, laughing.

"Whoo," the man gushed out. "I never seen a boy move that fast. You'd make one hell of a tight end," he said. "Fast hands. You play ball?"

"I didn't think that was funny. You could have—"

"Hell, boy," the man reached and took the carton from Hugh's shaking fingers. "When it ain't charged, this stuff's harmless. That's the beauty of it. When it's raw like this, unfused, it's stable as a table in a uptown restaurant." He banged the carton on the table hard enough to upset his own coffee cup. "If it'd bounce, you could shoot hoops with it. You can shoot a bullet into it, drop it out of an airplane, set fire to it, it won't go up. You can do what you want to with it. Except . . ." He winked and looked around. "Set a electrical charge through a blasting cap. Then, my boy, you got yourself one hell of a lot of bang for the buck. Sometimes, more bang than you paid for. That's what's wrong with it."

Hugh set his chair upright. "Seems dangerous."

"Not in the right hands," the man said. "We—C. W. and me—we're the right hands. You might call us the 'good hands people' when it comes to using Homer Easy."

"What?"

"HE. High explosive. We got enough stuffed in that old lady that if it don't kill her, it'll sure as hell put her in orbit. C. W. says we ain't taking no chances with multiple goes." He grinned. "More coffee, kid? You ain't touched that you spilt."

"No, thanks," Hugh said. "I guess I'd better be going. My dad'll be here in a while. I need to get out and watch for him."

"Right," the man said. "You're a good sport. You got a name?"

"Hugh. Hugh Rudd."

"Gerald Tortelli," the man said. He shoved out a beefy hand. Hugh accepted the shake, felt the heavy calluses. "You remind me of my own kid. Ain't seen him in six months. Lives with his mom. He's a ballplayer, like you. Heavier, though. Got a neck on him like a bull. You're too tall and thin for football. Bet you play a little cage, though."

"Uh, yeah. Well, baseball mostly."

"No shit!—Pardon my French. God, I didn't think kids played baseball anymore. When I was a kid, my dad used to take me to the Ebbets Field, watch 'Da Bums' in action, go over to the Bronx to see the Yankees. Hell, I seen Ted Williams homer. Mantle, too. Maris. All the big sticks. That was something, I can tell you. You a hitter?"

"Uh, yeah. I can a little," Hugh muttered.

"Secret's in the head. Keep it down." Tortelli stood and took a batting stance, made an imaginary half-swing and formed a triangle with his arms. "In the hole. That's the stuff. Keep the head down, and it's a frozen rope. You can't hit what you can't see."

"Yeah, that's what Coach—"

"Always wanted to play. Had me a shot, too." Tortelli sat down and lit a cigarette. "Tried out with the Yankees, and got me a Rookie League contract right out of high school. Hell, I was hitting .400 that year. Well, .389, anyway."

"You played?" Hugh asked, suddenly interested.

"Naw," Tortelli's smile turned down.

"Got drafted. Did two hitches in 'Nam, fuc—uh, screwed up my leg." He took a drag off his smoke. "That was a long time ago." Then he brightened. "But you keep after it, kid. You got good hands, and you're tall. You pitch?"

"Outfield," Hugh said.

"Damn good. Too many kids want to be pitchers. Game's won and lost in the outfield. That's a hard lesson to teach kids. Too damn many big-shot pitchers owe their ERA's to some no-name in the outfield who scoops 'em up, throws 'em out. Whole problem with the majors today. Bunch of over-paid puss—uh, sissies. All wanna be pitchers. You ever hear of a pitcher who could hit?"

"Babe Ruth pitched," Hugh said with a small smile.

Tortelli gave Hugh a long look. "I can't tell if you're a wiseass or straight up, kid. What was your name again?"

"Hugh Rudd." Hugh's smile involuntarily widened into a grin. He liked this big northerner.

"Tell you what, Hugh Rudd, you come by here tomorrow 'round noon, and I'll let you watch me throw the switch. Get you a box seat. Big thrill, I can tell you. Home run. Grand slam, all the way. I never get tired of it." He winked. "It's better'n sex. Better than jerking off, anyhow, pardon my French."

"No, thanks," Hugh muttered, looking away, then trying to explain. "I don't . . . I'm just not sure I want the building to be torn down. It's kind of a . . . a monument, you know?"

"Yeah, I know. I know all about it," Tortelli said, a crooked smile on his face. "I remember Ebbets Field, see? And the Polo Grounds. And I under-stand, believe it or not. Hell, I seen grown men cry when the old Stork Club went. But there's monuments, and there's monuments, and like it or not, that old lady's going to be dust come this time tomorrow."

"Yeah," Hugh said. "But I don't think I can make it."

"Change your mind, you come by anyway. Give you something to tell your own kids. You don't want to miss the show."

"No," Hugh said, "I guess not. Uh, thanks for the coffee." Tortelli gave him a wide grin, then picked up his magazine as Hugh walked away.

Hugh left the trailer and walked through downtown. A single car paused at the flashing yellow light at Main and Third, then proceeded slowly down the street. Hugh stepped inside a doorway when he recognized the vehicle. Behind the wheel, Grissom's face was masked by a dull expression. Both of his hands gripped the wheel, his eyes stared straight ahead with glassy blindness. Hugh waited until Grissom pulled up beside the little trailer next to the Railway Express Office, then he ducked around the corner.

Hugh walked to the next street and stood looking up at the hotel's third floor. All was dark there, but a lamp burned in the downstairs shop. He now was confident that Coach Kruickshank was asleep or drunk. He thought once more of the dark, dirty rear staircase, and the lump of fear returned to his throat. But he had to do it, he knew, fear or no fear. Now more than ever, he had to tell Wilson what he knew. With a heavy swallow, he forced his steps to take him around to the back of the building and the open window.

—≺—

"So, how's that little gal feel 'bout you spying on her daddy?" Jonas Wilson whispered to Hugh in the darkness of his room on the third floor of the hotel.

"I don't know," Hugh admitted. He hadn't given much thought to Linda's motives. To her, he decided, this was all some kind of game, a sort of trick being played on her father and his cronies. "We didn't get much chance to talk about it."

He had told Wilson almost all of what had happened that night. He even told him about his father's blowup with Pete Thompson. The story made Wilson chuckle and retort that, to his mind, Hugh's father had turned out to be "hotter'n a two-dollar pistol."

"Told you Pete Thompson was too much like his daddy to be any damn good," Wilson said. "I'm glad your daddy done it."

"I wanted him to hit him," Hugh confessed. "I wanted him to hit him the way you hit Grissom in the drugstore."

Wilson was silent for a beat, then he said, "That ain't no way to settle things, boy. Shows a weakness."

"Weakness? But you—"

"What I done needed doing," Wilson said, waving Hugh's question off. "That don't make it right. Don't make me more of a man, neither. That railroad man made me mad, and I hit him. Shouldn't of done it. Don't make more of it than it was."

"Mr. Thompson—Pete needed it, too." Hugh protested. "But my dad—"

"Your daddy done the right thing. Kept his fist in his pocket where it belongs. You can hurt a man a whole lot more with your tongue'n you'll ever hurt him with bare knuckles. Take a lesson, boy."

"But—"

"Ain't no buts 'bout it," Wilson said. "When a man hits another man and knows he's not as good as the other man is, that man's made hisself smaller'n the other man. Your daddy shown hisself to be a better man. Better man'n me, actually. Sooner you learn that, boy, sooner you'll come to see the right of things. Go on, boy," Wilson spoke through a light cough. "What else happened?"

Hugh continued. When he got to the part about the overheard conversation at the Fitzpatricks', though, Wilson turned serious.

"Well, I don't know what to do," Wilson said. He scratched his grizzled chin. He had been sound asleep when Hugh knocked at the door. The climb up the stairs had taken, it seemed, forever. Every footfall seemed to echo through the old building. Hugh forgot that the last time he made the ascent, there had been a loud thunderstorm outdoors to mask the noise. That night there was only the quiet of the street to compete with.

"Seems to me, ol' Carl's got it all figgered out. You put the dog on his yard, all right. But he's done his business and come home. I didn't figger on there being a rag on the bush."

"What?" Hugh said.

"Didn't figger Grissom and the railroad would deal," Wilson explained. "Didn't figger Carl'd call hisself in a hired gun like that Sapperstein feller. Just goes to show you, you can't trust nobody."

"Right," Hugh yawned.

"Trouble is," Wilson said, "when you lie down with dogs like that, you're bound to come up with fleas. Carl's never been worth a durn. This time, he's in way over his head, but I doubt serious he has any notion of what ol' boys like Sapperstein can do to him. Once they get their hooks in you, well, you're theirs for life."

"Right." Hugh yawned again.

"Way I see it, now," Wilson said, "this thing's got a whole lot bigger'n it was. We got to figger a way of putting a stop to her 'fore Carl and the whole shooting match goes down along with the building."

"I don't see how," Hugh said. "They're down there putting the final charges in place, from what I can tell. If that stuff's half as powerful as that guy said it was, the building's gone."

"Oh, Hendershot's a goner, all right," Wilson rose and walked back and forth across the room. "And that's too bad. But I ain't talking 'bout no building no more. But I'm trying to figger how we can take Carl out of the game 'fore he does more hurt to hisself. What was that feller's name, again?"

"Tortelli."

"Eye-talian, you say?"

"I guess so, but—"

"Never had much use for Eye-talians. Bunch of slick-livered cowards, if you ask me. When I was a young'un, not much older'n you, I was working for a feller name of Petralli—"

"Look, Jonas," Hugh interrupted in an annoyed tone.

"I don't recollect giving you notice to use my first name," Wilson snapped. "You're making a habit of it. That's twice today, already. You're getting a notion of yourself, boy."

"Jonas," Hugh insisted and ignored the flinch in Wilson's face, "I'm tired of this whole mess. It's wrecked my family, made my friends mad at me, and turned me into some kind of secret agent. It's stupid. All this for some silly building nobody really cares about anyway, not even you."

Wilson was silent for a moment. "I do care 'bout it."

"Well, I can't help that, Jonas." Hugh stood up. What had been sleepiness now returned as a kind of internal weariness that pulled him down, made him irritable. "But I'm through with all of this. I've told you what I know. If you can do something about it, use it to save the building, great. If not, I'm sorry. I really am. I don't care what happens to the Fitzpatricks. I don't care what happens to the town. My mom's in the hospital. Can you at least try to understand that? You haven't even asked about her."

Wilson looked hurt in the dim glow of the lantern, and Hugh sighed. "I know you care about the building, and you should know by now that I care about you, about what you care about. I've tried to be your friend, but I can't do anything anymore. I've got my dad and mom to worry about." He stood up and looked down at Wilson, who studied him with a curious expression on his face.

"And I have to work tomorrow," Hugh sighed. "I've got to go. You'll have to save the building on your own." Hugh moved toward the door.

"I told you this ain't 'bout saving that building no more," Wilson said in a soft voice. "It's 'bout saving something maybe a whole lot more important. It's 'bout stopping this thing 'fore it goes too far. Now, you've started this, and you're bound to see it through."

"You don't understand, Jonas," Hugh almost shouted before he remembered himself, lowered his voice. "I don't care anymore. I just don't! I feel sneaky and dirty all the time. I've broken my word to people. I've learned to tell a lie like it was my own name, and I don't care. I just don't care."

"I care," Wilson said. "I truly do, Hugh. You got to help me see this thing through. It means something to me. I can't tell you why, but it does, it means something to me."

"What are you going to tell me?" Hugh asked. "What tale are you going to tell me now? I'm not a kid, Jonas. I'm not! I may be young, but I know when you're lying to me. If you want me to help you, you've got to tell me why."

"I can't," Jonas said, looking away. "I can't say why. I . . ." He trailed off, for the first time in Hugh's experience with him at a loss for words. "I need your help, Hugh." The old man's voice was high, cracked with emotion.

But Hugh was unmoved. "My parents need my help," he said, walking toward the door. "My dad—" He stopped, his hand on the old knob. His shoulders slumped, but he spoke without turning. "I can't help you, Jonas. Not anymore," he said. "I quit."

"I don't think so, boy," Wilson growled at him. "I think you're just taking a breather."

Hugh didn't respond. He opened the door and ran down the hall, bounded down the stairs, uncaring if Coach Kruickshank heard him or not, and, ignoring the fatigue that pulled at every muscle and threatened to smother him with exhaustion, he jogged all the way home.

PART III: THE MONUMENT

CHAPTER ONE

It was after nine o'clock Sunday morning when Hugh Rudd forced open eyes sticky with sleep and stumbled out of bed. He scrambled into his clothes, hoping against hope to complete mowing four lawns before noon. It had been late when he fell into bed, sweaty and exhausted from his run home from the hotel. Fatigued as he was, though, his mind would not relax and let him sleep until it was already growing light outside. He worried about so many different things that he could only toss and turn and bite his lip until it was bloody and raw. Images of his mother lying in a hospital in a distant city vied with a vision of her drunk and incoherent, being fawned over by Loretta Thompson. Her evil smile was matched in his imagination by a narrowing of her eyes into a virtual dragon's face as she mixed drink after drink and forced them down his suffering mother's throat.

Only after making himself a firm promise that he would set out the next day to stay straight with himself, to make everything in his life all right again, could he fall completely asleep. It seemed he had barely closed his eyes when his alarm went off.

All plans were changed, though, when he limped on his flapping, torn sneaker into the kitchen and found a neatly typed note from his father.

Hugh,

I took off early to get your Mom. Should be back before noon. One thing I didn't warn you about, Sport, was that your Mom is still going to be a little under the weather for a while. Now don't worry! She's fine. She'll be better than ever. But we're going to have to watch our p's and q's for a while, 'cause I think it's not going to take much to upset her. So, don't do any mowing today. Sunday and all. Don't sweat it, Sport. I've still got that tractor for a day or two, and I'll pitch in and help you get caught up on Monday. We're partners, remember? Anyway, I know you want to be downtown today, so go ahead. But be careful.

Hugh, I love you, and your mother loves you, and we know you love us. Be careful as hell, Sport, but have a good time.

Love,

Dad

A half-full pot of coffee sat cold on the burner. Hugh poured a cup and reheated it in the microwave, then opened the refrigerator and found a nearly empty milk carton. He drank what remained to wash down a peanut butter and jelly sandwich, then started toward the garage.

He stoically resisted a nagging urge to go downtown. He had sworn to himself that he would have nothing more to do with all that business, with Jonas Wilson or Linda Fitzpatrick and her father, or with any of it. But something was drawing him there, kept pulling his thoughts toward the whole mess.

No, he said firmly to himself, all he would do was sit on the front porch, sip the old coffee, and feel numb, tired all over. His eyes tingled with a need for more rest, and his body ached, but he didn't really feel sleepy, just stupid, helpless.

"You know something, boy," the echo of Jonas Wilson's voice spoke to him through the hazy morning sunlight. "You're bound to use what you know. It's a obligation." The voice was so clear that Hugh looked around, expecting to find Wilson right behind him. But he was alone.

"*You* use it," Hugh said to the invisible Wilson. "I'm just a kid."

Hugh shook his head to dispel the daylight ghost. He looked at their overgrown front lawn and wondered if his mother would extend the ban on Sunday mowing to their own place, then decided she would, and turned away from that. He wandered out to the end of the driveway and looked up and down the empty street. The sky was clear, blue, and as yet it was cool, but the morning was warming rapidly. Cicadas sang in the trees, and he heard the Methodist church bells tolling ten o'clock. It had been weeks since they had been to church. If cleaning up and dressing hadn't posed such a daunting prospect, he thought he might go.

Before he realized what he was doing, he returned to the garage, mounted his bike, and pedaled off aimlessly down the street. It was just something to do, something to keep his body active and his mind away from deeper thoughts that inevitably led to a sense that he was, once more, being irresponsible. Block after block passed beneath his wheels while Hugh's inner voice argued back and forth, planned what he would say to each person he encountered. His eyes were glazed, not even watching for traffic at intersections. He just rode on in what seemed to be a haphazard meander.

He hardly knew where he was until he turned the corner on Main Street and was confronted by the largest crowd of people he had ever seen in his life.

Yesterday's gathering of curious onlookers had spilled onto and blocked Main Street down by the old U-turn and depot parking lot, but today's mob was twice that size. People jammed the street for a full city block away from the parking lot, and Hugh could see that television crews were filming the hubbub from atop the hardware building and the auto parts store across the tracks from the worksite. Cheery voices rose in a wave of babble that was rivaled by people moving through the crowd selling everything from balloons to soft drinks.

Hugh chained his bike to a pole in front of Central Drugs and hiked toward the crowd. When he reached the perimeter, he was amazed by how hard it was to push through the human thicket. There was a good deal of shoving and other small movement in the crowd's center, and along the edges, small groups gathered to stand and talk. Everyone, it seemed, wanted to be up by the pylons so they could have a clear view of the old building. If Hugh had been an adult, he probably wouldn't have made it through the crowd's center. Angry exchanges broke out when someone tried to shoulder his way closer to the parking lot's far edge. Because he was just a kid, though, people only glowered at him when he weaved through and dodged elbows.

He spied a knot of his friends gathered by the concession trailer.

"What's going on?" Hugh asked Tommy, who held a hot dog in one hand and a cup of Coke in the other. The edges of his mouth were covered with mustard.

"Man, it's great," Tommy said. "Ray and I carry Cokes and stuff to people on the bleachers, and they tip us. I've made over forty dollars this morning. And we eat for free! I'm so full of hot dogs, I won't eat another bean for a week."

Ray pushed through then with a fist full of bills. "I'm heading home," he said. "Mom's got this deep plastic serving tray. I can carry six or seven hot dogs and Cokes on it at one time. Oh, hi, Hugh." He scowled at his former friend. "Listen," he said with a quick glance at Tommy. "We've got this locked up with the concession stand. Don't try to cut anyone else in. I mean it."

Hugh put up his hands. "Don't sweat it," he said. "I'm just watching."

"That's right," Tommy grinned. "You've got high noon on Randy's board, right?"

"Uh, that's right." Hugh nodded. He had forgotten all about the wager. He looked at the spectators high on the bleachers. Randy and Eddy were in position. Eddy had a stopwatch around his neck. The bleachers were filled completely, and several kids were trying to climb up the back and squeeze next to those on the top row.

"Look, man," Ray said to Tommy, "I'm going for that tray. You do what you can till I get back. Don't let anybody cut in on us." He pushed off through the crowd.

"Back to work," Tommy said to Hugh. Then he winked. "Listen, man, don't listen to Ray. We can get you in on this. There's plenty of work for everybody."

"No, thanks," Hugh said. "I just came down for a quick look."

Tommy shrugged, stuffed the remainder of the hot dog into his mouth, and waded through the crowd toward the concession trailer's back door.

Hugh weaved through the mob. He dimly realized he was looking for Jonas Wilson but would settle for almost anyone else. He spied Sheriff Anderson flanked by two DPS troopers and another man who wore a star on his shirt shouting through a bullhorn from atop the Railway Express Office, but no one was listening, and only a word or two were discernible over the hubbub of the crowd. Large speakers mounted on the building's corners weren't being used.

He made his way as close to the pylons as he could, but the worksite was visible only in glimpses when the crowd parted briefly here and there. For the most part, the crowd's mood was apprehensive and happy. Noise from the mass hovered overhead like an invisible cloud. Hugh stood between a large man in a suit and his well-dressed wife, who insisted on holding hands and blocking the way. He waited for them to notice him, let him pass, but they pretended not to see him, so he tacked off and ran right into Loretta Thompson. Pete stood behind his wife. A pair of binoculars hung from his neck. Loretta carried a Polaroid camera.

"Hello, Hugh," she said. "I see you're not in church this morning. Again."

"You're not either."

Loretta sighed. "You know, Hugh, I never thought I'd ever hear such smart aleck remarks from such a sweet boy."

"I've got to go," Hugh said, backing away and crushing the instep of a man behind him. The man cursed and shoved Hugh forward, causing him to stumble slightly into Loretta.

"Sorry," he muttered, jerking away from her hands as if they were on fire. Her cloying perfume filled his nostrils, and he crabbed away in another direction.

"You tell your mother I'll come by this evening," Loretta called after him. "I'm certain your father has come to his senses by now."

"I don't think I'd do that, if I were you," Hugh shouted over the crowd's noise. He didn't wait for her reaction.

Hugh worked his way over toward the REO. The crowd was thicker there, but he pushed and threaded his way to the front, trying to hear what the sheriff was saying from atop the building. It was still unintelligible, only a series of loose words. None of it made sense except "warning," "get back," and "signal." From his vantage point, Hugh took his first unobstructed view of the worksite.

The trailer and all the vehicles except a white Suburban were gone from around the Hendershot building. The yellowed concrete exterior baked in the late morning sun, and beyond it, the cemetery and sparse houses of the northern outskirts of town swam in dusty silence. Except for the absence of windows and doors and open, rough places where the small wrecking ball had knocked off some facing, the old structure looked as it always had. The first crew of workers was nowhere to be seen, but men in white coveralls moved here and there through the openings in the building. Several more were gathered around Gerald Tortelli's trailer up by the REO. All of them had walkie-talkies on their belts, and from time to time, one would take off a handset and speak into it.

The Fitzpatrick motor home had returned and was parked near the REO, parallel to Tortelli's trailer, their open doors facing each other. The area between them was guarded by more DPS troopers. Hugh scooted closer. George Ferguson and Harvey Turnbull gathered with several other men. They were talking and gesturing with Grady Cartwright. The old deputy had a jaw full of tobacco and carried a shotgun. He stood with his feet spread over a bunch of wires that had been bound together with duct tape and ran from the trailer to the REO. He also had a walkie-talkie mounted next to his flabby belly.

"I don't care what you say, I ain't moving," Grady shouted at George and Harvey over the noise of the crowd.

"But I'm telling you, he's gone plum crazy. There's no telling what he might do. You need to tell Don to keep an eye out," George insisted.

"I'm keeping a eye out," Grady shouted and spat. "What you think this thing is for?" He waved the shotgun dangerously. "I ain't worried about no crazy drunk right now. Half this crowd's drinking. There ain't never been this much booze in town."

Hugh moved closer. Harvey pushed George aside and tried once more to reason with Grady himself.

"Look, Grady," he said. "Nobody's seen him since the Highway Patrol let him go last night. He called me this morning before daylight and told me to call 'the boys' and to be sure to be here to see him 'fix the railroad's wagon.' I called him back, but he wasn't home. His daughter told me he must have come home, though, 'cause he tore up the garage—"

"I'm telling you, I've been ordered to stand guard right here!" Grady shouted. "Phelps Crane is the last of my worries, but you're getting to be a pain in the ass." He spat and brought the shotgun to port arms.

Hugh stepped forward.

"I saw him," he said, and the men turned to look at the boy. Hugh stepped out of the crowd and approached them. "He was right over there."

"When?" Harvey asked, peering through the mass of people uncertainly.

"After midnight. Maybe later," Hugh said. "He was—"

"You people have *got* to move back," Sheriff Anderson's voice, at last amplified by the huge speakers atop the REO, suddenly spread out over the parking lot and stunned the crowd into silence. Hugh peered up into the sunlight. The sheriff was speaking into a microphone. "Anyone found outside the line established by the Highway Patrol will be arrested," Anderson went on. "You have five minutes to clear that area. I mean it."

Harvey, George, and the men around them fell back automatically with the crowd, but after a few half-hearted steps, most of the people stopped and held their ground. The Highway Patrol began moving barricades into place between the REO and the pylons.

Hugh stepped aside and stood next to Grady, who glared menacingly at the vanguard of the crowd.

"You're late." Hugh heard Linda Fitzpatrick's voice to his left, and he spun around to face her. She wore her sunglasses again, a dressy pink sundress that showed off her tanned shoulders. Her hair was pulled back in a golden ponytail. He stared at her and allowed his eyes to drop to his sneaker tops. Memories of last night's adventure swam over him, but it was her suit, her face, her body that came back, not the other part of their private party. She gave him a big smile. Something inside him fell when her teeth flashed in the sunlight. He detected a sweet, pleasant scent from her. Suddenly the crowd surged forward again, pressing around them, and they were almost thrown into each other's arms.

"Get back!" Anderson ordered from the roof of the building. "Damn it, I said get back!"

The crowd's collective voice was plaintive in reply. Several people called out that they were trying, and more cursed those who stood around them and jockeyed for position. Everyone was trying to move one way or another, but none wanted to give up a view of the old building down the way. Every other person seemed to have a camera or video camera in his hands.

"I thought you were grounded," Hugh said, reaching out to hold her upright while the crowd moved and jostled. It was the first time he had put his hands on her in such a way, and he was shocked at how soft and yet, at the same time, how strong she felt beneath his fingers.

"I am," she said. "I can*not* have another party or go to another party for two weeks." She frowned. "We worked out a compromise. I have to throw away the suit, though. It cost me two months' allowance."

"But you're here."

"Yeah," she sighed. "Daddy said we had to be. So here we are. He's going to be on TV. They're going to take a bunch of pictures, too. He says Mother and I have to be right beside him, but I'm not going to do it. I'm going to sneak out at the last minute." She scowled. "Looks like we're going to Austin, no matter what. I'd better just get used to it."

She squirmed out of his grip. "You know, Hugh, I can stand up all by myself. You don't have to hang on to me."

Hugh let his hands fall away to his sides and stood blushing. "Sorry," he said.

"Can you dance?" she asked.

"What?"

"I mean, *really* dance. I know you can do all the fast dances, but can you do things like waltz and two-step?"

"Uh . . . I dunno." Hugh began looking around in the crowd. Grissom stood in the REO's doorway. He was speaking furiously into his telephone. Behind him in the dusty shadows of the interior, Carl Fitzpatrick sat at an old desk. Standing next to him was Elton Matthews, and in front of him was Tortelli's detonator box.

"Well, I think I'd like to teach you," Linda said. "Mother didn't say a word about not being able to have some dance lessons. I think I could talk her—"

"Look, Linda, did anything else happen after I left last night?"

"What? Oh, that. No, I don't think so. They stayed down in Daddy's den forever, I guess. I was already asleep when they left."

She looked at her father, then turned back to Hugh. "Listen, I've been thinking about what we heard last night. I know it sounded bad, but I don't believe Daddy would do anything wrong. I'll bet it's some kind of trick. I think we ought to just forget everything and—"

"It's too late, Linda," Hugh said, his head down. "I don't know much about it, but I know it's wrong."

"I don't believe you! Daddy would never do anything wrong! He's leading them into some kind of trap."

"No, I don't think so," Hugh said. "I think he's about to blow up that building down there, and I think he's going to make a lot of money—"

"And you're going to stop him?" She put her hands on her hips and stared at him.

"Me?" he asked with a quick memory of Jonas Wilson's admonition the night before. His vow to himself to remain uninvolved from here out also came back to him. "Not me. But somebody—"

"I think you've got an overactive imagination, Hugh Rudd," Linda cut him off. "I think you're going to get us both in trouble. I'm sorry I ever invited you over and helped you spy on him. I only did it to show you I can be a real person who cares about others. I care about you, Hugh. I like you. Can't you tell that? Oh!" She stamped her foot. "You had your fun, got me in a lot of trouble already. Can't you just forget it?"

"No, I can't," Hugh heard himself saying. "I know things, Linda. *We* know things. We need to tell somebody. Somebody needs to stop this. I thought—"

"Oh, you silly boy," she said. "You're so immature! You don't know anything. I don't know why I thought—" She stopped in midsentence, turned, and pushed her way through the crowd and crossed the empty space toward the old Railroad Express office. Grissom lowered his phone and stepped forward to stop her, but when he saw who it was, he smiled grimly and stood aside to allow her to enter.

Hugh didn't hesitate. He broke through the people nearest Grissom and walked deliberately toward the office door right behind her.

Grissom recognized him. "Stop! Where do you think you're going?"

"I'm with her," Hugh said and continued.

"Like hell you are!" Grissom shouted and stepped in front of him. "You're spying on me again, you little shit. I don't know what you're up to this time, but it won't work. Now, get the hell out of here, or this time I *will* call the sheriff. Go on. Get!"

"Hey, kid! Mr. Hugh Rudd?" Gerald Tortelli shouted. He stood in the opening between the trailer and the Fitzpatrick motor home with a grin on his unshaven face. "Change your mind, kid? Thought you might. I told you, this is better than"—he winked—"than anything you ever done." He mockingly went through a batter's swing. "Grand slam! Remember?"

"This kid, this *spy*, is dangerous," Grissom shouted at Tortelli. "He's caused more trouble than anyone else in this whole damn business."

"Gee, Mr. Grissom." Tortelli scowled, walked over, and pretended to study Hugh up and down. "I don't think he's carrying no weapons or nothing." He turned to Grissom. "You're a little skinny in the butt, but I think you could take him if he jumps you. I dunno, though. He might know kung fu or something."

"Oh, for Christ's sake," Grissom swore.

Tortelli gave Hugh his crooked grin. "You come to watch me throw the switch?" he asked. "Do that old lady in down there once and for all?"

"I, uh . . ." Hugh started. His eyes left Tortelli's bright face and scanned the noisy crowd near him. He was not at all surprised to see Jonas Wilson's battered fedora floating in the human sea. The old man pushed to the front of the crowd, stared at him intently.

"Well, what about it, kid?" Tortelli asked. "Get you a box seat. First base dugout. You'll see it all. Back there," he pointed to the crowd, "all you'll see is dust and smoke. That's bleacher seats."

Wilson gave Hugh one quick nod, although there was no way he could have heard the conversation between Hugh and Tortelli, not with the noise the crowd was putting up. "Uh, yeah," Hugh nodded vigorously. He swallowed the lump that formed in his throat. "If it's still okay."

"It is *not* okay," Grissom insisted. "Look, Tortelli, you're not even the second banana on this project. You work for Pruitt, and Pruitt works for me. I'm the one who gives him his orders, so I'm the one who says whether or not this kid can hang around here. He's caused me enough trouble, and I want him out of here. Now." He spun around and pointed into the crowd. "Get back over there, you little shit," he ordered.

Grissom's regular uniform—white shirt, tie, and dark slacks—was soaked in sweat. His hair was plastered to his forehead. There was pure fatigue in his face.

"If he don't go in, then I don't go in," Tortelli said, grinning.

"What's going on here?" C. W. Pruitt emerged from the trailer and walked over. "You fighting with this kid again, Grissom? He going to have to call his granddaddy to whip you one more time?"

"I told the kid he could come in and watch me throw the switch," Tortelli explained. "Promised him. One outfielder to another." He gave Hugh a quick wink. "Now, Mr. God Almighty here says the kid causes him some kind of trouble. I don't see the harm."

"That's your end, Ger," Pruitt said, glancing at Hugh, then giving Tortelli a shrug. "You're in charge in there."

"This is stupid!" Grissom exploded and flapped his arms as if he were trying to take flight. "Pruitt, get your people ready." He looked at his watch. "It's eleven forty-two. I want this to go off on time. And I want this kid out of here."

"Look, C. W., do we have to put up with this crap?" Tortelli asked seriously. "Seems to me like we got control of this project or we don't."

"What's going on?" Carl Fitzpatrick came out. He looked fresh in a full dress suit and a large straw hat. "Grissom, we have a deadline. I've called a press conference in five minutes. Oh, hi, uh . . . Hugh, isn't it? Hugh Rudd?" He frowned. Hugh nodded. "What's going on here, Grissom, Pruitt? Is there a problem?"

"No problem, Mr. Fitzpatrick," Pruitt said. "Mr. Grissom here seems to think this boy's some sort of troublemaker."

"Hugh?"

"That's right, Carl," Grissom said. "If it wasn't for him—and his father—this whole job'd be over by now, and I'd be gone."

"Seems to me," Pruitt said, "if it wasn't for him, you'd still have some pretty expensive bridge work." Carl looked a question at C. W. "Old man over yonder had to whip his ass to keep him from kicking the kid around the block," the engineer said.

"No shit," Tortelli said, whistling through his teeth. "Wish I'd seen that."

"What'd you do, Hugh?" Carl asked.

"I—"

"He didn't do a thing," Pruitt said. "Not a thing. Grissom's got a bug up his ass, that's all."

"What I have," Grissom insisted, "is a crew drawing triple time to do a job that should have been completed a week ago. If it wasn't for this little shit spying on me and blabbing my every move around to everybody in town, I'd be back in Fort Worth right now."

"I don't know nothing about any of that," Tortelli put in. "All I know is the kid come by last night and kept me company for a while, and I appreciated it. Reminds me of my own boy. Good kid. Ballplayer. You ever play any ball, Grissom?"

"I—" Grissom gaped at Tortelli.

"Didn't think so." Tortelli now ignored him and spoke directly to Carl. "So, I asked him if he wanted to come by and watch me turn the key when we take that old lady down, and he said okay. Promised him he could see the whole show. That's all. Give him my word, C. W." He grinned at Hugh. "As an outfielder."

"He needs to go now," Grissom whined. "I'm sure he's up to something. He turns up every time there's trouble, the little son of a bitch."

"I didn't do anything," Hugh said. "I just—"

"Your girl's inside. She says she doesn't want to stay, though." Sapperstein stuck his head out the door and interrupted. "We need to get this show on the road."

"You tell her to stay put," Carl said, glancing at Hugh. "She's going to be on television." A gleam came suddenly into Carl's eye while a thought took shape. "You know, it's not a bad idea. Not a bad idea at all."

"What?" Grissom yelled.

"It'll be a symbol," Carl mused, half to himself. "The two of them standing together, side by side, watching the whole damn thing. Is that possible?" He looked at Pruitt, who, in turn, looked at Tortelli. The big man nodded. Carl went on, "Young people watching progress in the making. Make every paper in the state. Hell, I might make network news."

"I—" Grissom started again.

"Shut up, Grissom," Carl said. "It'll just be for a few minutes, for the cameras, then we'll send them out. C'mon, Hugh. Let's get those reporters in there and get this show on the road."

At that moment, from atop City Hall five blocks away, the fire station's siren began the first of three long, mournful notes.

CHAPTER TWO

The outer office of the Railway Express Office was cramped. Most of the building was given over to warehouse space. In the past, tractor parts, household appliances, furniture, and even disassembled combines, cultivators, motorcycles, and automobiles had passed through the old building. Once, the materials for an entire three-bedroom Custom Cottage—complete with picket fence and rosebush trellises—were received from Sears, Roebuck and Company in Chicago.

The business office itself was about twenty-five feet square. When operational, it had been bisected by a chest-high, marble-topped counter that had long since been transported out to the country club and refinished, where it served as a bar in the ballroom. Now, all that remained of the commerce the business had once enjoyed was a large dusty desk with no drawers, a lopsided swivel chair, and two or three straight-back office chairs. A double door led to the warehouse space behind the office, and three transoms, open to the outside air, were pushed wide open up by the tall ceilings. The walls were covered with peeling and cracked plaster, and the wooden floors were carpeted in oily dust that now showed the tracks of recent traffic between a messy array of extension cords and electrical lines. A large fly-specked picture window faced the worksite and offered an excellent view of the Hendershot Grocery Warehouse.

The office was filling with more people when Carl Fitzpatrick ushered Hugh inside past Grissom's continuing but futile protests. Reporters came through the back door and were led by Sapperstein to a position near the front window. Each reporter had a notebook. Photographers and minicam crews jammed into the small room. Bright lights were snapped on, and the reporters called occasional questions to Grissom, who ignored them.

Grissom's face was bright red. He glared at Hugh several times and mouthed something Hugh couldn't lip-read. Then Grissom went outside and began conferring with DPS troopers, instructing them to begin moving the crowd back as best as they could. Anderson's voice continued to boom through the speakers, and Hugh could see that the troopers were stringing a bright yellow tape that read "POLICE LINE DO NOT CROSS" from the front door of the office on a direct line toward the pylons. The crowd, which had grown louder since the siren blew, now fell back in a noisy mass. Protests from those in the rear of the mob could be heard roaring as toes were crushed, food and drinks were spilled. Those at the top of the bleachers could be seen struggling with latecomers trying to climb up, and scuffles broke out. TV cameras from atop the buildings caught it all.

Hugh looked around and blinked into the cameras' lights. He was confused and wanted to leave. His original purpose in trying to come in here, he reminded himself, had been to talk to Linda, but now, that wasn't going to happen. She sat in the swivel chair. Her long calves raced upward from her skirt's hem, crossed at the ankles next to the detonator box atop the desk. She refused to meet Hugh's eyes. He was miserable and wanted to go home.

Elton Matthews sulked in one corner, his hat in his hands. Lydia Fitzpatrick sat on one of the office chairs in the opposite corner from Elton. In a bright print frock and wide blue straw hat, she appeared to be dressed to go to a wedding or other festive event. She snapped gum and pretended to read a paperback while activity swirled around her.

When the second siren blew at the fire station, once more stunning the crowd outside into momentary silence, Carl led Hugh over beside his daughter and explained what he wanted them to do.

"On *TV*? With *him*?" she exclaimed, giving Hugh a chilly look. "Together? I don't want to. He—"

"Do it," Carl hissed at her through clenched teeth. "Stand here together and smile. If they ask you any questions, keep your answers bright and short. Hear me?" He looked at Tortelli, who fussed with some wires and looked up and threw an occasional grin at Hugh.

"Daddy, you promised—" Linda started.

"Do it, damn it," Carl whispered through a tight smile for the reporters. "Soon as we finish, you can leave."

"I want to go home, now!" she demanded.

"Don't give me any shit, Linda," he growled through the forced smile. A photographer snapped the family argument, and Linda turned toward the camera and stuck out her tongue. "Stop it, Linda," Carl ordered aloud, and he took her by the arm and tugged at her. "Stand up."

Linda gave Hugh a mean, condemning look and sighed deeply. She pulled her legs down and sat with her hands folded in her lap. "This is all your fault, Hugh Rudd," she whispered. "All I was supposed to do was stand by them while Daddy answered a bunch of questions. If I have to say anything that makes me look dumb, you're going to be very, very sorry."

Pruitt and Tortelli now took up positions beside the desk near the box and talked incessantly into their walkie-talkies. Tortelli fussed some more with the duct-taped wires that led through the open door, checked his connections, then removed the key from his pocket and winked at Hugh.

"Linda, you and Hugh hold hands," Carl ordered. "You people might want to get some shots of this," he suggested to the photographers.

Linda stood up beside Hugh, her fingers grasped his. Her touch sent an electrical sensation through him, but then he noticed that her palms were moist, and he glanced at her. She was visibly quaking.

"I don't like this," she said in a shaky whisper. "I want to go home."

Tortelli glanced at them, then raised his fingers up to block one eye, winked at Hugh, and slanted his eyes toward Linda. "I know what I told you, kid," he whispered, "but I sure didn't think you'd have it this good. Try to keep a hold on yourself."

"I want those kids out of here before anything happens," Grissom said. "This is no place—"

"I think we're about ready," Carl boomed, cutting the railroad man off.

Sapperstein stepped to the center of the room and handed Carl a microphone attached to a wire that ran up the wall, through the transom, and, Hugh guessed, to the speakers on the roof.

"Testing, testing, 1-2-3," Carl said tentatively into the device. His voice echoed off the downtown buildings.

"He can count, everybody, he can count!" someone in the crowd yelled, bringing a chorus of laughter. Sapperstein nodded and stepped back.

"Ladies and gentlemen, members of the press," Carl announced suddenly. "This is Carl Fitzpatrick. You all know me, and I have a statement to make. I don't think there will be time for questions right now, but I'll be happy to give you all the answers I can later." He removed a folded paper from his suit coat pocket and opened it.

Several more catcalls came from outside, and Grissom came back in and stood in the corner near the door, scowled at his wristwatch. The third siren blew. Carl waited patiently until it died out.

"That was the final whistle," Carl announced sadly, reading from the paper. "That means that in spite of all the efforts this city and its elected officials could mount . . ." Carl's face lifted to peer into first one camera lens, then another, ". . . we, the good citizens of this community, have not been able to stop the total destruction of one of our city's most sacred and cherished historical monuments.

"The Hendershot Grocery Warehouse is and has been for many years a concrete symbol of the pioneer spirit and courageous entrepreneurship that built this state, even this entire nation. I—that is, *we*—have worked diligently to save this structure since we learned of the intentions of the Burlington Northern Railroad Corporation to raze it in order to construct a much-needed wye. I have personally spoken to the governor, the attorney general, members of the State Railroad Commission, and leading members of the Texas Legislature in an attempt to prevent the loss of this important piece of this city's history. I have even gone as far as Washington, D.C., in my personal efforts to save this historical testament to this city's development. And I have tried my best to negotiate with executives of Burlington Northern. All to no avail.

"I—*we*—have filed motions in every court in the state, approached judges and politicians and influential people of every stripe. But once again, we have not been successful. The sad truth is that politicians today have no interest in preserving monuments, in saving a piece of this fair city's skyline from the wrecking ball."

The crowd murmured, and Hugh could see several of them shaking their heads.

"In approximately five minutes," Carl continued, "I regret to say, the Hendershot Grocery Warehouse will exist only in our memories. Our city's horizon will be changed forever. Possibly, some people might have thought to stop this desecration of our community by extraordinary means. But theatrical gestures would not alter the outcome. The course of progress established by history itself will not be denied."

Carl took a long breath and consulted his script once more. The crowd was absolutely quiet. Hugh realized that he was holding his breath and let it out in a soft whistle. Linda looked at him and frowned.

"Rather than continue to stand in the way of what, in the final analysis, will be a positive and progressive step toward this community's future associations with the Burlington Northern Corporation and its many enterprises, I, as a civic leader and candidate for governor of this state, have decided that it is better to have fought the good fight and lost rather than to continue to stand in the way of the inevitable. Futile and imprudent gestures belong to the chaos of the past. There is no glory in struggling for lost causes. It is time to put away history and to focus on the future."

Another wave of muttering began outside, but Carl continued reading.

"I, therefore, on behalf of this city, this community, and its citizens, am pleased to accept the generous offer of Burlington Northern's representative, Mr. James Grissom, to construct a brand new downtown historic park for the amusement and recreation of the good people of this city, and also to convert the old Railway Express Office—the very building in which we're standing—into a museum of local history for the edification and education of all our citizens, not only of this community but of this state and nation. Whenever people pass through our county and wonder what elements of progress have brought us so far, they will have a concrete testimony to this community's courage and pioneer roots."

There were a few cries of dismay outside, but a light shout soon arose, took shape, and grew, spreading through the parking lot and into the overcrowded intersections, drowning out anyone who raised his voice in protest. It then burst into a demonstration of whistling and whooping. The Hendershot Grocery Warehouse was finally doomed.

Carl took advantage of the camera crews' hasty swinging of their lenses toward Grissom to hand Sapperstein the paper, then to mop his brow with a handkerchief.

"Stand up straight," he hissed at Linda. She squared her shoulders and gripped Hugh's hand more tightly than ever. "Are we ready?" he asked Tortelli, who glanced at his watch and nodded. "Then, let's do it."

"Not with those kids in here," Grissom said, moving forward. "It's too dangerous."

Carl put his hand over the mike. "It's just for the cameras, you idiot," he whispered, then smiled once more for the reporters.

Hugh and Linda looked at each other. Sweat broke out on her forehead. He could feel her pulse in her fingers. His own heart was beating furiously, and he again looked into her eyes and again saw fear. He put his other hand across and touched her forearm.

"I'll get you for this," she whispered.

Tortelli spoke once more into his walkie-talkie, nodded at Pruitt. Carl observed the exchange and began speaking. Tortelli stepped forward and put the key into the box. He kept his hand on it, his eyes glued to the building.

"Ladies and gentlemen," Carl said, and again the mob outside went quiet. "Although most of you cannot see them, and although many of you know them, I would like to introduce my daughter Linda, my wife Lydia." Lydia shut her book, stood, and nodded toward the cameras, then took her place on the other side of Linda. "And Mr. Hugh Rudd, a friend of our family's, and the son of one of our most prominent citizens."

Hugh peered into the bright lights when the cameras swung back.

Carl continued, "Most of you know these young people. As a symbol of that future, I have asked Mr. Grissom if these two children could join hands and bear witness to this historical act of bringing down the past and making way for progress. He has consented."

Grissom turned away, and Hugh couldn't see his face.

"It is much more than a mere gesture," Carl went on, "for this is a monumental event, one that will bring prosperity and progress to this whole community for generations to come, one that will enrich everyone who lives here."

"And what's in it for you, Carl?" a soft voice asked suddenly.

Hugh didn't have to look to know who spoke. In the doorway, just to the side of the reporters and in front of Grissom, stood Jonas Wilson. He looked taller than ever. His gnarled hands were at his side, but his fists were half clenched. "Just what do you get out of it?"

Carl's eyes flicked between Wilson and the reporters. "Turn the key!" he ordered.

"Don't do nothing," Wilson said. "Just hold her steady."

"Who's this guy?" Tortelli asked. His hand was still on the key.

"Turn it, goddamnit!" Carl shouted. His voice shot from the loudspeakers and bounced back from the downtown buildings. He stared horrified out the window, where the crowd looked on curiously. Some were laughing.

"He ain't going to turn it, Carl," Wilson said. "Not if he knows what's right. And what you're doing is just plain wrong."

Hugh looked at Carl, who, in turn, looked at Sapperstein. The reporters were now all giving their attention to the shabby old man in the doorway.

"I'll stop you if I have to—if you don't stop yourself. You know I can do her, and you know how. Don't make me, Carl. *You* stop it. Here and now."

"Who *is* this guy?" Tortelli repeated.

"I knew it, goddamnit," Grissom swore with a glance at Hugh. "I told you this would happen."

If Wilson noticed the cameras pointed at him, he didn't react. Then, to Hugh's surprise, Carl Fitzpatrick's voice lost all of its anger, all of its booming confidence. "He's a nobody. A drunk," Carl spoke rapidly to the reporters, who turned around again to stare at him. "A derelict, and a convicted criminal, a troublemaker. Pay no attention to him. Where is the sheriff, anyway? Someone ought to arrest him right now."

"Oh, you give me too much credit, Carl," Wilson chuckled. "Oh, I take a drink now and then, and I been in the joint. You know that better'n most." He fixed his eyes on Carl and stepped toward him. "But I'm stone sober now, and you know that, too. I may not can stop you going on with this. That ol' building down there don't mean nothing to you, and there ain't no reason why it should. It don't mean much to nobody, truth to tell, not even me."

He turned and spoke to the reporter nearest to him. She was scribbling furiously on her notepad. All the cameras now focused the best they could in the small space of the office on Wilson's battered face.

"But you made too much out of it," he continued. "Yessir, you did. So you go ahead on and bring her down, if you can. But don't lie 'bout why you're doing her. Time for lying has stopped. Tell 'em what you're getting out of it. 'Cause if you don't, I sure as blue deuces will."

"I don't know what he's talking about," Carl insisted. "He's crazy!"

"What's going on here, Carl?" Hugh heard Sapperstein ask in a loud whisper. "Do you know this guy?"

"Show 'em all the legal papers you been talking 'bout," Wilson said. "Show 'em all them fancy court orders and such." He smiled grimly, holding his eyes on Carl. "He can't show you," he said. "'Cause there ain't none. Never was none. Not from the start." Wilson jerked a crooked thumb toward Grissom, who bowed his head and brought his fingers up to knead his forehead. "Him and this feller here cooked all that up. Ain't that right, Carl? He used this whole deal, ain't that right, Carl? You just used it."

"Who *is* this old man?" Sapperstein demanded furiously, his hand on Carl's shoulder. "Who let him in here?"

"I'm telling you. He's crazy!" Carl finally found the volume he had lost and raised his voice. "He's a drunk, and he's crazy! Grissom, tell them to throw that switch or the deal's off!"

"Do it," Grissom said evenly. "Do it now."

No one moved. Tortelli's hand remained protectively over the key, his face searched Pruitt's. Pruitt, in turn, was looking first at Carl and then at Grissom. "What *deal?*" Pruitt asked. "What the hell's going on here?"

Hugh looked down and saw his knuckles turning white under the pressure of Linda's fingers. Her eyes also fell to their locked hands. She stared at them as if they belonged to someone else.

"Don't do a thing, Ger," Pruitt said. "Just what is he talking about, Grissom? I thought you said this was all cleared through Chicago. Do we have the legal right to proceed with this or not? I'm not putting myself at risk here."

"What?" Grissom said, smacking his fist in his hand. "You don't know one goddamn thing, Pruitt. You're a hired contractor! Now, this has gone far enough! I'm ordering you to throw that switch. Now!"

"Let's hear what he has to say, first." Pruitt nodded toward Wilson. "I'm not going along with anything crooked. I don't need to spend the next five years in court trying to explain how you fucked things up and hung me out to dry." He addressed Carl. "I think I'd like to see some of those papers everyone's talking about."

"Get away from that key!" Grissom ordered Tortelli, stepping toward the desk. "I'll do it myself. Take your hand away!"

Tortelli kept his right hand on the key but put out his left hand and pushed the railroad man back easily. "Stand away from here," he said gruffly. "I don't take orders from you."

"Pruitt," Grissom screamed, "for the last time, I'm telling you—"

"Go on, Carl," Wilson said. "You do it. You turn it. Don't ask nobody else to do your dirty work. It's time for you to find your own hind legs."

"Me?" Carl asked.

"Yeah, you," Wilson gestured. "Go on, Carl. You take her down, if it means that durn much to you. But don't try to make more of it'n it is."

Carl stood still, stared at Wilson. Sweat ran down his face.

"Go on," Wilson repeated. "Go on. Do it your own self. Don't lay it off on these folks. They're just trying to do their jobs, same as me when I helped build that building. You ain't never built nothing, and you never will. Let's see if you got the guts to tear something down. Go on."

Carl didn't move. Wilson reached into his pocket and removed the tobacco and papers and calmly rolled a cigarette. "You ain't never going to be governor, Carl," he said. "I might of been proud of you for it one time or 'nother, but not this way. Go on! You blow the building. If you got the guts. But I doubt you do. 'Cause it ain't right, and you know it."

Carl's shoulders sagged, and his suit coat, sopping with sweat, hung off him like a sack. "Don't say anything else," he said to Wilson.

"Don't have to, Carl. Reckon you've said enough for both of us."

Linda's grip on Hugh's hand relaxed. He freed his tingling fingers, allowed his arm to fall by his side. She stared at her father. Lydia also stared at Carl, a look of confusion on her face.

Carl stood for another long moment, sweat dripping from his nose. Then he dropped his face and looked at the floor. "All right," he said. "All right. I can't. I won't." He looked hard at Grissom. "The deal's off. If you blow that building, I'll sue you blind."

"You gave me your word," Grissom spluttered. "You said you wouldn't do a thing—"

"Some things is more important'n a man's word," Wilson said, lighting his cigarette. "Some things is just bigger'n any of us. You could of been a good man, Carl. Could of been proud of that. Maybe it ain't too late, though. Maybe all you ever needed was a little push. I hate that it's me has to give it to you, but I couldn't just stand around and let you play this whole town for fools just to make yourself bigger and worser'n you have any right to be. It ain't worth it."

Carl stared at Wilson for a long moment. His hands were shaking as they opened and closed. Then he turned to his wife and daughter. "Let's go home."

"Shit," Hugh heard Sapperstein whisper, "might have known. Small town hicks." He pushed past Hugh and Linda and crossed to the office door and left.

The reporters, once again animated, began shouting questions at everyone. Carl ignored them and continued to stand and stare at his wife and daughter. Linda's hand once again found Hugh's, but this time there was no panic in the pressure, only something that he sensed to be a need to hold on to something solid. Outside, Hugh noticed, the crowd was still quiet, waiting for the explosion. All eyes were focused on the Hendershot building. Elton, with a contemptuous glance at Carl, who remained where he was, went out behind Sapperstein.

Lydia looked down at the floor, and in a moment she also left, brushing past Carl's outstretched hand. Carl dropped his arm and watched her go. Linda didn't move. Finally, Carl reached out and took her hand from Hugh's and led her around the desk and past Wilson. "Let's go, honey," he said, leading her away.

Hugh started to follow them, but he stopped when he reached Wilson, trying to put it all together. He stared into the old man's milky eyes, but Wilson said nothing. He just shook his head and lowered the brim of his hat toward the floor. Carl pushed aside a minicam and started out the door.

"You're just leaving?" Grissom suddenly yelled at Carl's back. He stopped and waited in the doorway. "Just like that?"

"Just like that," Carl said without turning around. "I told you: The deal is off."

"The hell it is!" Grissom shouted. He leaped across the desk, struck Tortelli in the middle of the chest, and reached for the detonator box. Tortelli bounced against the wall and rebounded, and Pruitt jumped forward, but before they could secure Grissom's arms, he grabbed the key and gave it a hard twist to the right, then back to the left.

Immediately, everyone spun around and stared out the picture window toward the Hendershot building. Several puffs of smoke discharged from the door and window openings of the top three floors. More rocketed up from the high corners of the building. Jets of puffy gray smoke shot out and upward into the hazy atmosphere. There was almost no sound at all. The huge mob outside was as silent as if the people were praying. No one in the office said a word. More smoke and dust escaped from the fourth and fifth floors of the building, but it didn't collapse, didn't implode. It just stood in the noon Sunday sun, covered by the shadows of small clouds of dust and smoke, and defied the puny assault on its solidity.

Hugh was afraid to breathe.

"It's done," Grissom gasped, standing erect and shrugging off the engineers' hands. His chest heaved, sweat dripped off his nose. "With or without you, Fitzpatrick, it's goddamn done. You can sue me forever, but the goddamn building's gone."

"Something screwed up," Tortelli said, almost in a whisper. "All the charges didn't blow." He spoke furiously into his walkie-talkie. Pruitt raced out the door, pushing Carl and Linda into the reporters and cameramen, who were furiously snapping and filming through the window.

"What?" Grissom turned to the big man and shouted. "What are you talking about?" He reached again for the key and jerked it right, then left, then completed the circuit again. There was nothing. He did it once more, and the key snapped off in the box. Grissom held the broken cross-piece up to his eyes as if it was a precious gem he had discovered only to have it shatter in his hand.

"What the hell is going on?" Grissom demanded. "Why didn't it blow?"

"Charges didn't blow," Tortelli explained while he tried to listen to the scratchy voices on the handset. "The secondary detonators didn't go off. Some of the charges on the opposite side and the upper floors went. But those are primaries. That's what you saw. But the secondaries, the C-1209, didn't go, not by a long shot. Something's wrong."

Reporters all began shouting questions at the men, but Grissom slammed his hand down on the desk, upsetting the box. Carl stood transfixed in the doorway, Linda's wrist still in his hand. Hugh stepped back against the wall next to Wilson. He thought he could feel the railroad man's fury.

"Well, fix it! Fix it! Goddamn it, what am I paying you for?" Grissom yelled, pounding on the desk in front of Tortelli. He turned back to the box and tried to refit the broken key into its hole, but then a burly, smelly figure emerged from the double doors that led from the office to the storage area.

"You can't fix it," Phelps Crane said. He stood alone in the doorway, hair wildly spraying over his head, his tiny eyes narrow and ugly, but with a black, crooked grin on his face. "*I* fixed it. Fixed it good." He stepped into the room. "With or without you, Carl, I'm going to stop this. It just ain't right. Goddamn railroad's screwed this town for the last time."

"Is this whole town crazy?" Grissom shouted.

"Phelps, you're insane," Carl said, stepping toward the old conductor. He still held Linda's hand and unconsciously pulled her right along with him. "Get out of here."

"Just hold it," Phelps said. From the greasy pocket of his overalls he pulled out an ugly black automatic pistol. Every person in the room moved back a step. "This here's a German Luger," he said. "Took it off a Kraut major. Killed him with it, and I guess I can kill you, too, Carl, if you don't do just what I say."

"Phelps," Carl said. "Just—"

"Shut up, Carl, and come over here," Phelps said. Carl didn't move. "I said come over here," Phelps repeated, and Carl released Linda's arm and once more approached him. As soon as Carl was at arm's length, Phelps drew the pistol high over his head and hit Carl across the bridge of his nose. Carl collapsed, Linda screamed, everyone in the room surged forward.

"Get back! Get back!" Phelps ordered, swiveling his arm about and threatening everyone with the gun's narrow black barrel. "Now," Phelps said when everyone stopped. He held the pistol directly on Carl, who struggled to his knees. Blood gushed from his nose, poured down his face.

"Damn it, Phelps!" Carl yelled. "You crazy son of a bitch. You *hit* me!"

"Too damn bad," Phelps said. "Get up." Carl staggered to his feet. He pulled a handkerchief from his pocket and held it against his face. "Let's just see what we can do, now," Phelps said, turning to Grissom. "Fixed your wagon, didn't I? Railroad son of a bitch. Should of been you I hit."

He looked again at Carl. "Fixed your wagon, too. Sorry about all your big plans," he said. "Looks like things just didn't turn out so good. Fixed all of you," Phelps went on, turning on the room and waving the pistol a bit. "I tried to do it right. I got me the petition, just like you said." With his other hand, he reached behind the bib of his overalls and pulled forth the filthy, wadded sheets he had carried around for more than a week and waved them around. "I got folks to sign it, just like you said. But then you wouldn't even *look* at it! Wouldn't give me the goddamn time of day. Ain't that right?" He yelled, flinging the papers at Carl. The ream hit him and flew apart, settling like fallen leaves around his feet. "Ain't that right, Carl?" he screamed.

The reporters and camera crews fell back, but they didn't stop filming. "I told you, Carl," Phelps went on, "you can't sell us out. I knew you was going to do it. So I had to stop you. I don't much care if you run for goddamn president of the United States or God Almighty. But you ain't going to blow up this town or any part of it to do it. Not when you're in cahoots with the goddamn railroad."

"Look," Tortelli spoke up. "It's too late. The detonators have already blown. We've got a dangerous situation down—"

"You don't got shit!" Phelps shouted back. "And don't lie to me, Mr. Fancy Engineer Yankee Railroad Son of a Bitch. You don't got shit!" Spittle sprayed from his mouth. His eyes were red and darting around the room. His free hand opened and closed constantly. His clothes were filthy, and a ten-day growth of whiskers sprung away from his face, giving him a mad, grotesque mask.

"While y'all was up here drinking coffee and looking at dirty pictures last night, I went down there and moved a few things around. Took a few things away, too. She didn't blow, did she? Well, I'm in charge now, and ain't nobody going to blow that building up. Not without taking one of our most important civic leaders with it. You're going with me," he said to Carl. "We're going down there, and we're going to wait her out. See how handy they are with that fancy dynamite then."

"I'm not going anywhere with you," Carl said. His voice was muffled beneath the handkerchief that was now completely scarlet. "You've lost your mind, Phelps. You need help."

"Oh, you'll go, all right," Phelps opened his mouth and exposed his black teeth. He raised the pistol again, and Hugh felt himself being pulled back by Jonas Wilson's hand on his shoulder. They pressed against the wall, as far away as they could. Hugh believed he could still smell the old man from across the room, but then his heart jumped when Phelps calmed down once more and trained his red-rimmed eyes on Linda.

"And she's going, too. Half the folks out there'd buy a two-dollar ticket to see you get blowed to hell, Carl. Me, too. But they'll think twice 'fore they hurt her. C'mon, girl," he said. He stepped over to Linda, and before she could twist out of the way, he grabbed her ponytail. He jerked her hair hard. Hugh stepped forward, but Wilson's hand on his shoulder held him back.

"Let her go," Carl yelled, dropping the blood-soaked cloth and lunging for Phelps.

The pistol came up and down again, this time catching Carl on top of his head and bringing forth gouts of blood from his scalp. Carl collapsed again.

"Daddy!" Linda screamed. Phelps jerked her head back once more. "That hurt!" she barked at Phelps. "Let me go!"

Once more Hugh started forward, and once more Wilson's hand gripped him from behind. The gnarled fingers bit deeply into his skin and jerked him back hard.

"Not now, boy," the old man hissed in his ear. "Bide your time." Linda struggled to free her hair from Phelps's fingers, and he jerked her hard up against him.

"Get back!" Phelps waved the pistol at the room's occupants. "Get up! And tell her to simmer down, Carl," Phelps threatened. "Or I'll blow her head off and shoot you next."

"You're insane," Carl gasped from the floor.

"Maybe," Phelps said, holding the gun up. "But I got the gun, and you don't got shit."

Wilson's grip on Hugh's shoulder relaxed. At that moment, Sheriff Anderson's form appeared passing by the picture window. Two DPS troopers followed him. None had a gun drawn. They had no idea what was going on.

"Stop right where you are, you goddamn Nazi," Phelps shouted when Anderson stepped inside the doorway. "Drop them pistol belts, and do it now."

The officers almost stumbled over each other when Anderson halted abruptly in the doorway.

Anderson looked down toward Carl's bleeding form rising to his knees and set his jaw. "Phelps, put that pistol down right now. You are under arrest—"

"Go to hell, Don Anderson," Phelps growled. He jerked Linda's head back once more and made her cry out. "You drop them guns, or by God, I'll make a mess in here you and all the storm troopers in the world can't clean up."

Silence filled the office, and outside, when the crowd nearest the door began to understand what was going on, voices rose in panic. People began to push toward the office.

"You're under arrest, Phelps," Anderson repeated without moving. "Drop the gun."

"Go to hell," Phelps responded, now pointing the ugly pistol at the sheriff's face and pulling Linda more tightly to him.

"Daddy!" Linda shrieked.

Carl climbed shakily to his feet, one hand now clasped over the crown of his head. "Back off, Anderson," he gasped. "He's crazy. He might do anything."

One of the troopers put his hand on the sheriff's shoulder, and the trio slowly backed away. "I'm backing out," Anderson said softly. "Don't do anything stupid, Phelps. You're in enough trouble as it is."

"Go on, then. Get out of here. Get them people back!" Phelps yelled at him, then cackled again. Anderson backed completely out of the doorway, and in moments the troopers were screaming at the crowd to clear the area.

"All right," Phelps breathed deeply, panting as if he had been running hard. "We're going down there. Me and Carl and," he pulled Linda's ponytail once more, "her."

"I told you, we're not going anywhere," Carl said calmly. He drew himself up to his full height and looked Phelps in the eyes. Carl now seemed cool, completely unexcited, almost bored with what was happening around him. "It's all over, and we're not going anywhere," he said in a tired voice.

"Oh, you're going, all right," Phelps yelled. He swung the gun around to cover everyone in the room while he backed toward the door, spoke to Tortelli. "I fixed it so that you couldn't do it. Not on the first try. You try it again, and we all go up together."

"Let her go, Phelps," Carl cried. "I'll go with you. All right. But not her. Let her go."

"I'll let her go. You, too, when you do the right thing, Carl. When you do what you was supposed to do in the first place and put a stop to them ruining this town. You let me down, Carl. You let all of us down. So I fixed it down there so you'd have another chance to make it right."

"What did you do?" Tortelli asked, his voice rising. "What've you done, exactly?"

"Just fixed your wagon is all," Phelps snarled. "Now, you got one hour to clear out of here. Take your fancy crew with you. I mean it! I'm not fooling." He dragged Linda over to the front door of the office and motioned for Carl to follow them.

"Just take me," Carl said. "Let her go, Phelps. Please."

"Shut up," Phelps said. Then he yelled out the door. "Don Anderson, you listen to me!" he yelled. "I got me a gun, and I'm going down there, and it won't do to try and stop me." He pushed the pistol out the door and waved it around. He yelled, "I got me a gun!"

The hubbub from the crowd, which had pulled back considerably, immediately increased from a loud curious series of shouts to panic and screams. People fell back all at once, stampeding into the street and away from the small office. Hugh could see through the window that the DPS troopers immediately went into a crouch and began backing away, their pistols drawn. Grady Cartwright lumbered over to a barricade and leveled his shotgun. Phelps spied him.

"I mean it, Grady!" Phelps yelled. "And if you or that Nazi sheriff tries anything, somebody's going to get hurt bad."

Phelps looked back at Grissom and smiled. "Get the railroad to back off," he said. "Leave that building and this whole damn town alone." With that, he gave Carl a push with the pistol's barrel and dragged Linda outside behind his staggering form. Hugh saw the terror in her eyes. He had never felt so useless.

Phelps jerked Linda out behind him and gave Carl another blow, this time on the shoulder, with the heavy pistol. Carl stumbled, regained his balance, and then grabbed Linda's hand. Phelps swiveled unsteadily, waved his pistol briefly in the direction of the crowd while it surged away from him, then pushed Carl and Linda on ahead of him. The sheriff and the troopers watched helplessly while he pulled them past the pylons down toward the Hendershot Grocery Warehouse.

—≺—

For a moment, no one in the office moved. Hugh finally could hear people in the room beginning to breathe again, as if they had been dead and were coming back to life. He wanted to collapse. A sick, sour taste filled his mouth. The DPS troopers rushed in and began shouting questions at everyone, and the reporters milled about, shouting into cellular phones. Grissom began pacing. Hugh swallowed deeply.

"I'm holding you fully responsible for this," Grissom shouted at Pruitt when the engineer came inside again and began conferring with Tortelli. "Those people down there are your responsibility, not mine. If you had done your job, none of this would be happening."

"Now, hold on," Tortelli said hotly. "I told you to use radio-remote control, didn't I? All them wires were just an invitation to trouble. But, oh, no! You had to have your goddamn way. You said you wanted complete control. Too many things could go wrong, you said. So that's what we set up."

"Well, something went wrong anyway!" Grissom shouted. "And who the hell's fault is that? Look at this mess! My God, he's got *hostages* down there. People are going to get hurt. Jesus!" He paced away waving his arms over his head. "He should have taken me! This is the end of it," he argued with the thin air. "This is the end of my life."

"What did he do?" Pruitt was muttering over and over. "Just how crazy is he? Would he actually hurt them?" No one in the room had a ready answer. Pruitt's walkie-talkie squawked, and he held it to his ear to hear. Tortelli was inspecting the wires connecting to the box. "He's apparently done something to the boosters and the wiring," Pruitt said to Tortelli.

"How?" Tortelli asked. "When could he have gotten down there?"

"I saw him last night," Hugh said. Both men turned to him. "He had something in his arms that he was carrying up. Tools or something, I guess. I didn't know what he was doing." Pruitt spun on his heel and raced out the door. Grissom went right behind him.

"And you didn't tell me?" Tortelli said. "Thanks, kid. You could have saved us—and your girlfriend—a lot of fucking trouble. Pardon my French."

"I didn't know," Hugh repeated. He slumped against the wall, out of breath and numb.

Everyone in the office seemed to be screaming, angry, confused. Hugh looked around for Jonas Wilson, but he was nowhere about. A cigarette butt lay on the floor where he had been standing, but he had disappeared, as if he had been a ghost. To Hugh, the whole episode seemed like a dream, a blur of reality that had no focus. Tortelli spoke quickly into his handset, then he went out the door, and, after a beat, Hugh followed.

"Way I see it," Pruitt said as he and another man came out of the trailer to meet Tortelli with a large roll of paper, "he must have shifted some charges around or taken them away, maybe moved the secondaries away from the ground floor. He's done something to the boosters, too. But he couldn't have gotten to all of them. That would have taken two days, even if he knew where they all were. It took a whole crew working around the clock to put those things in."

"That's why only the top floors blew," Tortelli said. "The primaries would have taken care of that by themselves. Hell, they should have collapsed. What's holding them up?"

"Who knows?" Pruitt peered down to the old warehouse. "We were only guessing about how much it would take. Hell, it might not have gone if every charge went at once."

"Which they didn't," Tortelli said.

"No way," Pruitt agreed. "But they might any time. They're still live, and there's no question that the boosters are still hot. Grissom broke the key, and God only knows what that old idiot did to them. Maybe he crosswired them some way. There's no way to tell."

"So the building could still go up?" Hugh asked.

They seemed surprised to see him standing there.

"No 'could' about it, kid," Tortelli said. "Even if he dismantled half the charges, that old lady's a goner. The boosters down the line are still pouring the juice to her. Can't say what might happen. Only, she won't 'go up.'"

She's already done all the 'up' she's gonna do. I don't know what's holding her together right now. When the secondaries blow, it'll all be over."

Tortelli looked at the building. "Them folks are in serious trouble," he added. He took off his hard hat and scratched his head. "You see, it's a chain reaction, bottom to top. One charge, then another, all the way up. Any time now the secondaries could get hot. But it probably won't be all of them, and it sure as hell won't be in the right order. Shit, C. W.," he said. "We got us a time bomb down there."

"I want those people out, and I want them out right now!" Grissom burst from the trailer. He held his phone in his hand and was practically screaming at the two men. "And I want that building down as soon as they're clear!" Grissom came between the men and pointed at the telephone as if it were a tunnel to his office. "I've been on the phone with Chicago, and they're saying this is my fault. I'm the one who's going to be liable." The engineers said nothing. "Do you *understand* me? I want them out of there, and I want that building down, now!"

"Look, Mr. Grissom," Pruitt said. "We need to defuse the boosters, first. Then, we'll have to send a team in to make an inspection—"

"Don't give me this horseshit!" Grissom screamed. "You get off your butts and get down there and find out what's wrong! Hook it up, wire it up. Do something! Get those people out, and as soon as it's safe—the goddamn *second* it's possible—bring that building down, now!"

"I think you better calm down, Mr. Grissom." Sheriff Anderson approached from the other direction. "We got us a situation down there, and nobody's going to do anything—"

"Down now!" Grissom erupted once more. The railroad man's face was bright red, and he was breathing heavily, almost panting. "You don't understand. None of you understand. I've personally authorized enough shit to demolish this whole damned town. And now that crazy old man's got people down there." He pounded his fists up and down in front of him like pistons.

"This isn't happening!" he shouted. "That building's going down today!"

"Don't do one thing," Anderson cut Grissom off and addressed the two engineers. "Anybody touches anything that causes that building to fall in on those people, and they'll be under arrest for murder. Is that clear?"

Grissom stared open-mouthed at the sheriff, then at Pruitt and Tortelli, then at Hugh. He started to shout again, but then he lowered the phone to his side. Tears filled his eyes. He stumbled off to the trailer, muttering to himself.

Tortelli turned to Anderson and began explaining exactly how dangerous the situation surrounding the Hendershot building was.

Hugh had heard enough. He was sick to his stomach. He stumbled off to the side of the Fitzpatrick motor home. Nearby, Lydia was surrounded by reporters and two DPS officers as well as the man in plain clothes with the badge on his shirt. Her hat was off. She was crying, waving her arms and speaking in a demanding voice. Behind her, the crowd, its courage recovered, returned to the old lines in spite of everything the officers could do to restrain people.

Tommy and Ray pushed their way through the crowd and came running up to Hugh.

"What's going on in there?" Tommy demanded. "God, old man Crane had a gun! I saw it. What's he doing with Linda and her old man? This is like TV." Ray nodded soberly, then put a hand out on Hugh's shoulder. "You all right, man? I mean, he didn't shoot you or nothing, did he?"

Hugh looked into the faces of his friends, but they appeared to him suddenly to be strangers. He just shook his head.

"C'mon man, give!" Tommy said, his eyes excited and dancing. "Did anybody get shot?"

"Go away," Hugh gasped. His stomach cramped painfully. "Just leave me alone."

Loretta and Pete Thompson appeared behind Tommy and Ray.

"Hugh?" Pete said, "Are you all right? You boys get away from him and leave him alone." Tommy and Ray backed up a step or two, then stood their ground.

"Come along, Hugh. We'll take you home." Loretta reached for his hand. "We'll wait for your parents, there. I'm sure they will want to know that you're all right."

"Go away," Hugh swallowed back bile in his throat. "All of you just get the hell away from me!"

"Hugh Rudd!" Loretta looked as if she had been hit across the face. She snapped, "I will not hear such language from you or anyone else. Your mother is very ill, and your father is in no condition himself to—"

Hugh spun away from her outstretched hand and raced around to the back of the old Railway Express Office, where he bent double and emptied his stomach's contents onto the gravel. Rising, he limped over to a pile of old bricks on the far side of the building and sat down, putting out a hand to brace himself.

It was funny, he thought, and raised his eyes and looked down the vacant gravel street that led over to the hotel. Around here, if one didn't listen too closely to the noise from the parking lot, one might think it was a typical Sunday noonday. There was no traffic, no people moving about. In the distance, Coach Kruickshank was walking around outside the hotel. A dog barked somewhere, and Hugh could hear the buzz of insects in the weeds nearby. In the distance, he heard a church tower striking the quarter-hour.

"Lost the pool," he said. He put his head down on his knees. He was weak. He told himself that this wasn't his fault, but he didn't believe it. He was somehow guiltier than he had ever been from the beginning, and now, he was more helpless than ever.

"You going to just sit 'round here all day and sull up?" He heard Jonas Wilson's voice. The old man positioned himself between Hugh and the sun. When the boy looked up, all he could see was a silhouette. Wilson had a crowbar in one hand and a coil of rope in the other. "Way I see it, we had a hand in getting Carl into this mess. Guess we ought to go get him out."

"Down there?" Hugh asked, standing and looking in the direction of the Hendershot building.

"Can't do much up here," Wilson said. "C'mon, boy. This thing might get ugly if we don't hurry."

CHAPTER THREE

By the time Hugh and Jonas Wilson reached the rear of the Hendershot building, they were breathing hard. Hugh's shortness of wind, though, was caused as much by fear as by the half-running gait they had taken down the tracks to Stuart Street, then around the crumbling buildings and wasted yards of the Projects, across North Main Street where it bent away to join the highway to Oklahoma, and finally through the newest addition to the County Memorial Cemetery. After they drew within a hundred yards of the old warehouse, they both knew that at any moment the world around them could explode and drown them in a cloud of dust and collapsing concrete.

Whereas the south and west sides of the Hendershot Grocery Warehouse were situated to face directly toward the depot parking lot and downtown area above, the north and east sides pointed toward the cemetery and a cotton oil plant just beyond. The way they had come was the most roundabout way they could have chosen to reach the building, but the only other routes were guarded by police barriers and roadblocks. By taking the circuitous approach, they were able to come up on the building from the northeast, the only side left unguarded. Weedy lots jammed with mesquite and discarded junk, barbed wire, and surplus railroad ties bordered the cemetery's near side, but there was no fence or barricade between the graveyard and the building. Most important, there were no people anywhere about on that side.

Twice during their circuit away from the crowd's eyes, the man and boy had heard muffled explosions coming from the building. Each time, they stopped, listened for an indication that the secondary charges had finally blown and that the building, Phelps Crane, and his two hostages had collapsed into a mountain of rubble and rock. The second time, Hugh scrambled up a dead hackberry tree to try to see if anything had happened, but the building still stood. A cloud of smoke and dust swirled around the top, but the outer walls showed nothing but strength as they shimmered in the noonday sun.

Twenty minutes after they left the Railway Express Office, Wilson and Hugh, with his torn sneaker sole slapping with every step, scrambled across the uneven ground, broken and rutted as it was by the workmen's machinery, and flung themselves against the cool concrete on the shady side of the building. As far as Hugh knew, no one knew they were there. He tried not to ask himself why he *was* there or what he thought he might do now.

"Whew-boy," Wilson panted. "I'm wore out. Too old for this kind of nonsense." Like Hugh, he was sweating freely, and he pulled out a bandana and wiped his face and eyes.

Hugh jerked his baseball cap from his head and drew his wrist across his dirty forehead. "Now what?" He both knew and feared what Wilson might say. He had no intention of going inside the building.

Wilson tipped back his hat and peered up the side of the structure. "Up yonder, see?" He pointed to a place where there was a slight recession in the wall. Over it were two large, petrified posts sticking out of the building's wall. "Them's joists," Wilson said. "That's a old doorway. Used to be a fire escape. Hendershot actually had it put in so he could come and go in private, 'thout nobody seeing him. Didn't use it much, far's I could tell. Finally had it boarded up."

"We're not going in there," Hugh said rather than asked. "I mean—"

"Don't know no other way. Them folks up there'll fiddle-foot 'round and flap their jaws all afternoon, till it's too late." He looked up again. "We'll go in right up yonder."

"Why not go in the front?" Hugh argued. "Or the side? All the doors and windows are open."

"'Cause if that durned fool Phelps sees us coming, no telling what he might do," Wilson said. "He ain't looking for nobody to come calling at the back door." He stepped back and uncoiled the rope. He fussed with one end for a moment, then stepped back another step or two, twirling a lariat. Hugh looked up at the joists.

"You're going to try to rope them?"

"Lasso 'em, yep," Wilson set his jaw and flung the rope, but it fell loose and harmlessly back onto the ground. "Been a spell since I done this. You don't lose the knack, though," he said, gathering the rope again for another throw.

"This is stupid," Hugh said. "Let's just go on in the front—"

The entire building shuddered with a rumbling explosion from deep inside it. The ground beneath their feet trembled. Hugh put his hand out against the wall to steady himself, but Wilson dropped the rope, grabbed Hugh, and pulled him ten or twelve yards away. For a moment they stood there and stared at the blank concrete wall, listening.

"That's good 'nough reason," Wilson said, taking up the rope once more.

"Jonas, we can't go in there. We'll get killed."

Wilson stared hard at him. "You never struck me as a coward, boy."

The look hurt worse than the words. Hugh winced. "I'm not," he said weakly. "But, Jesus—"

"Watch your mouth, boy."

"Damn it, Jonas," Hugh yelled. "Didn't you feel that? It's blowing up inside."

"That's why we're going in up yonder," Wilson said, moving back to the side of the building. "That'un was down here, right on this ground floor. You go running inside there, you're like as not to get blowed up, if you don't get squashed by flying concrete."

"Why won't that happen just as easily up there?"

"'Cause 'hind that door is a separate stairs. Goes up and down the whole building. Got its own casement. Every staircase in the building is built that way. Like a building inside a building, don't you see? 'Less they opened her up and set charges right inside every one of 'em, it's pretty safe."

"But they might be on the ground floor," Hugh continued to argue.

"Doubt it," Wilson said. "That's the third time something's gone. If I was Phelps, I'd be going up. High as I could get." He tried again to rope the joist, failed again. "Ever go coon hunting? Or possum?"

"Uh . . ."

"Well, I have. Lots. You chase them critters into a thicket, and they'll shinny up a tree if they can find one to get away from the dogs down on the ground." He turned to look at Hugh. "Old Goodlett's a good possum dog." He flung the rope once more, and again it dropped uselessly at his feet. "Not as good as some, but better'n most. Anyhow, when the dogs get to yapping 'round the bottom of that tree, old possum or coon'll get up as high as he can. There ain't no getaway, don't you see, but it don't stop him from going up to the tiniest little old branch he can find and hanging on for all he's worth."

"This isn't a coon hunt, Jonas. And a tree's not a building."

"And you ain't no coon dog," Wilson said in a sudden, sharp tone. "Look, boy, if you're scared of going in there, then get on out of here. I'll do it best I can on my own."

"But why? It's—"

"'Cause I stuck my nose in and caused this ruckus. Way I see it, you did, too. I didn't figger old Phelps'd go off his rocker. But he did. I should of seen it. You should of, too. It don't matter, now, who did what, who said what. What matters is that Carl and his little gal is in trouble. Way I see it, we helped get 'em into it, and so we got to take a hand in getting 'em out. Now, I'm fixing to do my part. What 'bout you?"

Hugh shrugged, but Wilson didn't wait to see it. Instead, he turned, spun the rope again, and let it fly. This time it neatly looped the left joist and held. Wilson pulled the noose tight and hung on it a few seconds to make sure it would hold.

"What I was trying to say was the way I figger it, old Phelps is a lot like a possum. He's scared, and he's crazy. He's going to go high as he can. Roof likely. But he still might be watching his backside, so this is the best way to go. We'll come in his blind side. Here." He thrust the crowbar into Hugh's belt. "I'll set a anchor on her. You shinny up that rope and get you a footing. Then try to pry that door open. Get you good leverage, now."

"Me?"

"Yeah, I'm a old man. I can't climb no rope."

"I'm not sure I can, either," Hugh said.

"Thought you was some kind of athlete."

"I play baseball," Hugh whined. "I'm not . . . I mean, I can't . . ." he trailed off.

Wilson shook his head and took a position to steady the end trailing on the ground. "Go on, boy. Get up there."

Hugh touched the line. The rough hemp already burned his palms. He hesitated again, then looked at Wilson, who nodded once. Finally, the boy opened his hands, spat in them, then reached up and started pulling himself up, bracing himself with his torn sneakers against the wall of the building. He slipped and almost fell. "I can't do it."

looked around, and located Phelps Crane. Crane was seated next to a rusty ventilation duct, and next to him, slumped down and clinging together, their heads buried in each other's shoulders, were Carl and Linda.

Carl's suit coat was washed in blood, and more streamed from his face and head. Phelps sat fully on his hips, his legs splayed out in front of him, a dead cigar butt in his teeth and a nearly empty pint bottle of whiskey in his left hand. The pistol was still in his right, but he held it in his lap in a desultory fashion. His head was down, his hair still wild, and his overalls and heavy workshoes were covered with white dust. Linda's dress was torn in places, and she had dusty marks and dark smudges on her legs and arms, but she appeared to be unharmed. As Wilson had predicted, Hugh thought, Phelps had gone as high as he could. Each of the explosions drove him up and up, but now there was no place to run.

From where they were, Hugh realized, none of the trio could see him. He slipped from the opening, and, holding the crowbar close to his side, he crept away at a right angle to Phelps's form. He hid behind another ventilation duct and looked forlornly back at the opening to the roof. What should he do now? Where was Jonas? What if he emerged all at once and Phelps started shooting? Panic crept up his back. He had to do something, and he had to do it now.

He studied the crowbar, judged the distance from where he crouched to where Phelps Crane sat, and waited. He couldn't throw the heavy bar with any guarantee of accuracy, and if he charged the old man, he doubted that he could make it there before Phelps would hear him and simply pick up the pistol and shoot him. Hugh was terrified of what might happen when Phelps realized he was there. Crazy as he was, Phelps was an adult. How could he actually strike him with something as heavy as a crowbar? Hugh looked behind him. Where the hell was Jonas?

The afternoon sun baked Hugh's head. None of the three had moved much, except that Linda occasionally tightened her grip on her father, and Carl shifted his legs and arms a bit to try to hold her more closely. With each movement, Phelps raised his eyes to them, then relaxed. No one talked.

Hugh looked around one more time. It was time to act, with or without Wilson. He stood, revealing himself but not seeing any alternative. He prayed that Phelps was frightened enough to give up, or maybe to let them go. If Hugh got close enough, Hugh thought, he would just hit him where he could and hope that would be enough.

Suddenly, the entire building trembled, then violently heaved and rolled. Hugh fell, and the others tried to come to their feet but were thrown down and tumbled over onto one another as the cracking boom of several shuddering explosions came from below. Linda screamed. Carl grabbed her and dragged her to the rusty old duct. She wrapped her arms about his neck, and his hands grasped the base of the crusted metal. Phelps scrambled over to join them. The noise rumbled again, then erupted once more into a splintering roar that forced all their hands to their ears.

The building swayed and bowed. It seemed to Hugh that it was about to turn completely over. He rolled around to his right, hanging onto the crowbar, afraid it would stab him as he fought for control.

Dust and smoke suddenly belched up from the roof stairway's opening, and dark clouds of dirt and debris blew high overhead while the building heaved again, then settled and was quiet. Hugh grabbed the duct and struggled to his feet. His legs were still shaking, and his breath came in quick, narrow gasps. But he gathered himself together and was about to step forward, launch himself toward Phelps, when, off to his right, a few feet from the duct where Phelps, Linda, and Carl still clung, a section of the roof collapsed and fell into the building in a ripping, tearing avalanche.

The first deafening crash gave way to a second and then a third as large sections of floor after floor gave way when the falling weight of the crumbling concrete struck. Another enormous cloud of dust and noise gushed up through the hole with the collapse of each of the floors below. As if propelled upward by an unnatural power, chunks of concrete and brick erupted skyward, borne up by the force crashing down beneath the building's rooftop, blotting out the sun with swirling dirt.

Hugh fought to maintain his balance and crouched down behind the duct. The roof, or what was left of it, felt solid enough beneath his feet, but his legs were shaking. Boards and bricks, hunks of concrete and steel reinforcement blasted up from below now littered the remainder of the roof.

"Will you let us go, now, you crazy old fool?" Carl shouted at Phelps. "Let *her* go, anyway. While there's still time." Phelps shook his head. "For the love of God, Phelps! Give it up."

"I told you to shut up." Phelps turned on them. He struck Carl again and again with the pistol's barrel. Linda screamed and flailed her arms uselessly at him. He brushed her attack away and continued to pound Carl with the gun. Carl fell and dragged Linda down with him, and Phelps stood up and shouted at him. "I told you, they're just trying to scare us."

Linda grabbed her father, hung on tight. "I'm scared, Daddy! Take me home!" she shouted into her father's shoulder. Carl didn't move.

The old conductor studied them a minute, then shrugged and stepped gingerly over to the edge of the raw hole where only moments before solid roof had been. He peered down into the swirling dirt and smoke below him.

"Got it good that time," he said.

Hugh took three running steps and sprang at Phelps.

In spite of what he had let Tortelli think, Hugh was never much of a hitter. Choppers in the hole past the shortstop were sort of a specialty with him. It was caused, Coach Kruickshank always told him, because he was late in dropping his shoulder, and he never would learn to choke up when he had two strikes and a man on base. Basically, he tended to top the ball, hit into 6-4-3 double plays a lot.

When Hugh bounded toward the foul old man standing on the brink of the huge smoking maw in the roof of the Hendershot Grocery Warehouse, Hugh made up his mind that this time he was going for the fences. He gripped the heavy crowbar in both hands and pulled it back, took an imaginary stride toward an imaginary pitcher, leaped across the last five feet between them, and swung.

Linda screamed when she saw him in midstride.

"Huh?" Phelps said, and he turned around faster than Hugh imagined possible. Phelps's small, red-rimmed eyes flicked toward the back-swung crowbar, and he ducked neatly. Hugh tried to adjust to the lower target, but it was too late. The bar whiffed directly over Phelps Crane's balding head, came all the way around, and struck Hugh in the back of his left leg, sending him sprawling toward the ragged hole in the roof. He rolled to one side and tried to hang on to the crowbar. He had but one thought: You're out!

Phelps staggered away from the boy, lost his balance, almost fell into the opening behind him. Hugh lay at his feet, pain rifling from his thigh, but he began scrambling away. Phelps waved the pistol around and shouted at him, started toward him. Hugh pulled himself erect, and with his teeth clenched against the tearing pain in his leg, he shuffled toward the far edge of the roof. Phelps staggered after him.

"You little punk!" Phelps screamed, saliva roping from his open mouth. "I'll fix you."

Hugh collapsed on the two-foot-high lip of concrete that formed a slight ledge around the building's roof. The swirling dust overhead had blown away, and he looked south, up toward the depot parking lot, where he could see the crowd of people and, he thought, could hear them shouting. Phelps came on, yelling something at him and pointing the pistol at his head. Hugh pulled himself as upright as he could. He still had the crowbar in his hand, and he brought it back to defend himself. But he focused only on the ugly black pistol in Phelps's hand.

"Fix you, you young punk!" Phelps snarled. "Who you think you are?"

Hugh looked down and grew dizzy. Black spots danced before his eyes, he waved his hand uselessly to clear them away. He spun away, looked down once more.

On the ground between him and old Market Street, trailing through the dusty weeds and gravel, he saw the wires. They ran haphazardly, it seemed, from the building to small gray and black boxes, where they were brought together for a more organized route up toward the Railway Express Office. Hugh imagined he could hear the sizzling pop of electricity from the boosters, could see the movement of the wires as they strained to deliver their load.

He turned back. Phelps was almost on top of him, waving the gun like a club.

Then, over Phelps's right shoulder, Hugh spotted Jonas Wilson standing beside the hole in the roof. The coil of rope was over his shoulder, and his clothes were white with concrete dust. His left arm stuck out oddly at a right angle to his body. Hugh's stomach tightened when he realized he could see the ragged end of Jonas's arm bone sticking though his shirt sleeve. The old fedora was gone. Wilson's silvery hair blew in an unnatural breeze that emerged from the hole.

"Get them out of here!" Hugh yelled, pointing the crowbar at Phelps to ward him off. "Get them—"

"C'mon, boy," Wilson shouted back. He moved in a shambling gait toward Carl and Linda. She rose and pulled at her father's coat. "She's a goner, now, boy," Wilson yelled. "Let's go! Don't dillydally."

Phelps paid no mind to Jonas. He lunged out with his left hand for the crowbar, but the boy jerked it away and on the backswing struck the old conductor hard on the left shoulder. In spite of the sickening crunch and the yielding sensation of Phelps's bone and muscle collapsing under the blow, Hugh grinned grimly. Base hit, he thought.

Behind Phelps, Wilson used his good arm to haul Carl to his feet. The lawyer leaned on his daughter and let Wilson jerk him toward the opening to the roof stairs.

"C'mon, boy," Wilson yelled. "Stay in the back stairs all the way down, and jump from the second floor."

Hugh had no time to respond. Phelps danced in close once more, and Hugh swung again.

Phelps dodged the blow this time, stumbled and fell, and Hugh also lost his balance, collapsing on top of the old man. Panicked, he crab-crawled away, gritting his teeth against the pain in his leg, and propped himself up on the roof's ledge. He glanced over to see Wilson pushing Carl and Linda down through the casement opening. Wilson waited, looked at him.

"Go on!" Hugh yelled. "Hurry!"

They disappeared down into the narrow opening, and Hugh rolled to one side and took another wild swing at Phelps, who was up and on the attack again. Phelps dodged once more and shoved out his hand. The crowbar caught him squarely in the palm and swung him around. He collapsed on his face. Hugh brought the bar back again, but Phelps recovered, and with his injured hand holding his wounded shoulder, he swung the pistol at the boy in a ferocious lunge. Hugh fell away, stood up, and swung again, missed again, but it was Phelps who lost his footing this time. He plunged forward at Hugh's feet.

Hugh didn't hesitate. He stepped over Phelps, dropped the crowbar on top of him, and scrambled around the smoking hole that blocked his way to the stairway opening. Dust and dirt poured from the ventilation shafts suddenly, but Hugh didn't notice. His breath filled his ears. He was intent on trying to get to the opening, down the stairs, out of the building. All at once, he seemed to be running uphill, but he barely noticed. He limped, tripped over boards and debris, and then, just when he reached the torn-away edge of the casement, he stopped. He couldn't move his uninjured leg. His foot seemed nailed to the roof.

Hugh looked down to see that the torn sole of his sneaker had jammed itself under a board, a piece of heavy wooden flashing that had once surrounded the staircase's opening. He looked down the stairs, hoping that Wilson would appear to help him get free, but the concrete steps were empty and now covered with shards of broken concrete and splinters of wood. He jerked at his foot, but the sole was stuck hard under the board, and the movement sent slivers of sharp pain throughout his body. A nail had embedded itself in the loose sole, fastening it to the heavy lumber. Hugh pulled and tugged with all his strength, but pain swam wildly through his body until he lost his balance and fell over.

Phelps, again on his feet, lumbered toward him, the pistol still in his hand, his eyes glazed. His mouth was open, and spittle roped away from his grizzled chin. Hugh ripped at his shoe's laces, knotted them, then amazed himself by finding the strength in his fingers to break them in two. He jerked and pulled, but the shoe was still bound too tightly to his foot.

Phelps's shadow now covered him, and Hugh fought the pain, stood up. Tears clouded his eyes, and his leg was on fire. But he brought himself erect and faced the old conductor. Phelps stood before him for a moment, panting hard. He quickly checked Hugh's hands for a weapon, then brought the old pistol high over his head. Hugh put up his arms to ward off the blow, but before it could come, Phelps began to rise in front of him, moving up as if gravity itself had loosed its hold and the crazy old man was being called to heaven.

But they were both rising, Hugh realized. A grotesque roar filled his ears, shutting out his own scream. The entire building seemed to launch itself upward all at once beneath Hugh's trapped foot. He could see the horizon disappearing behind the ledge around the roof, and the few white fluffy clouds that had drifted over the small town grew nearer. The sun seemed incredibly bright above the dust and clouds, and when he looked down, Hugh saw that the roof was gone. Phelps was gone. Surrounding Hugh now, black, blinding clouds of smoke and dirt swirled so that he could see nothing at all. The last thing he heard was a deafening, crashing, crackling roar that seemed to come from somewhere inside himself with such violent ferocity that it shut his lungs and forced his arms to fold themselves over the top of his head. The last thing he remembered was a sensation of falling, as if the world itself had lost its foundations and he was descending into nothing.

—≺

When Hugh opened his eyes, all he could see was white. It took a while, maybe as long as several minutes, before he realized that he wasn't dead, that what he was looking at was not a cloud but only a strip of gauze bandage that had slipped down across his eyes. When he tried to reach up to remove it, however, he discovered his right arm was fixed somehow, heavy and numb. His left was too sore to move at all, and when he flexed his fingers, terrible pain shot up his arm. Dazed and dopey, he decided not to worry about it and went back to sleep.

"You're in pretty good shape, Sport," Harry Rudd's voice said when Hugh next awoke, "for a complete idiot."

Hugh realized that his father must have been speaking for a while, but the words hadn't registered. He gestured for water, and Edith stepped forward out of a hazy gray fog and offered him a straw.

"Mom?" he said thickly, then swallowed again. "Are you okay?"

"Oh, Hugh!" she said, then she turned away, back into the fog.

"What, what happened?"

"Well, you got yourself blown up, Sport," Harry Rudd grinned at his son. "Ought to go into the *Guinness Book of World Records*, or at least get you on one of those talk shows. Don't know of anybody who ever did that before."

"Shut up, Harry. It's not funny," Edith Rudd insisted, coming once more into Hugh's view. She was crying. "It's not funny at all."

Hugh learned that he had broken both legs—one as the result of his misguided swing with the crowbar, he thought—and fractured his right arm, as well. He had a serious concussion—two separate concussions, really.

"From what I understand," Harry explained, "you fell into some sort of stairwell that ran up to the roof. The casement sides were strong enough to hold together, though you wound up in the basement. Mr. Pruitt said it was sort of like being inside a mobile bomb shelter. You got banged up pretty good, but you stayed alive." Harry fiddled with an unlit cigarette and looked seriously into Hugh's eyes. "And you're damned lucky," he concluded.

The fog around the room was lifting now. Hugh understood that he was in the hospital.

"It took all night to dig you out," Edith said, dabbing at her eyes with an abused tissue. "They said you were dead." She broke down completely and began crying. "You can't imagine what you put us through, Hugh," she said. "I mean—"

"I know what you mean," Hugh said. Pain was now coming on strong. His legs hurt badly, and his arm was itching beneath the plaster cast. He also had a thick, heavy headache.

"'Nobody could live through that,'" Harry quoted. "That's what everyone said. And now, they're saying you'll never play the violin again. But what the hell, you never did before." He laughed.

"Harry, you are a complete fool. Did you know that?" Edith said, bitter.

"Really, Hugh," Harry said. "You're going to be fine. The doc says you'll be back in centerfield before you know it."

"Shut up, Harry," Edith barked through new tears. "You can say whatever you want, but don't think I don't know whose fault all this is. I know," she said with a firm nod that reminded Hugh of the way a small child underscores a statement with internal surety. "I know."

Harry shrugged, then looked into Hugh's eyes. "Told you to be careful, Sport."

"Oh, Harry!" Edith exploded.

"Did Phelps . . . uh, Mr. Crane . . ." Hugh asked, trying to grab a fix on what had really happened.

Harry shook his head. "No, Hugh. He's gone. You want to know the hell of it? That old pistol wasn't even loaded. Didn't even work. No firing pin."

Hugh tried to laugh, but his head ached. He closed his eyes.

"You sleep now," Edith's voice said. "They'll come give you a shot in a minute."

Hugh shook his head, but he saw a nurse coming into the room and felt the prick of a needle in his hip. "What about . . ." he said, hearing his voice slur as he tried to pronounce his words correctly.

"They're fine," Harry said. "Both Linda and Carl got out just before the whole thing blew. They got some scrapes and cuts, and Linda turned her ankle badly. Carl's got a fractured skull, too. But they're both going to be okay."

Hugh shook his head, fought for consciousness, for one word. "Jonas."

"That's what they're saying," Harry said from somewhere in the gray fog. "He got them out. He's a goddamn hero."

"That old man," Hugh heard his mother say in disgust. "It's all his fault, too."

Hugh forced his mouth to ask. "What happened to . . ."

"Jonas is gone, Hugh," Harry said. "He got them out, but he died in the explosion. He was coming back to get you, but he didn't make it."

"I told you not to tell him that." Edith's voice was sharp. "The doctor said not to tell him that. Besides, we don't know that it's true."

"He loved that old man," Harry said gently. "And he deserves to know what happened to him." Harry leaned down and ran his hand across Hugh's cheek. "And I think he knows more about the truth than you or I will ever learn."

"Harry," Edith started in a warning tone, "for the last time, I'm telling you . . ." But the fog closed in completely, and Hugh didn't hear the end of the argument.

CHAPTER FOUR

FOUR YEARS LATER

Hugh Rudd skidded his Yosemite mountain bike to a halt on Main Street in front of Central Drugs, then walked it up and chained it to a parking meter behind which sat a new, red Ford F-150 4×4 pickup. It belonged to Randy Truman, Hugh recalled with a pang of envy, and it was precisely the kind of truck he wanted. He had a poster of one thumbtacked to his wall at home.

The vehicle was outfitted with ground effects, racing wheels and tires and had two thick white racing stripes traced sharply down its length. Hugh stood for a moment admiring the vehicle, trying to decide if red was the color he would have selected, then shrugged and turned away.

He was distracted, though, by a small, navy blue BMW Z-3 Roadster parked, top down, next to the pickup. It had California plates and looked brand new. He studied it for a moment, shrugged again, and walked into the drugstore.

George Ferguson and Harvey Turnbull sat around the Serve Yourself counter. They frowned against the morning sunlight when Hugh came through the door, but their downturned mouths quickly parted in friendly recognition.

"Great game, Hugh," George said.

"Four for four, six RBIs," Harvey seconded. " How'd that homer feel?"

Hugh grinned back and shook his head in modesty.

"No kidding," George said. "Regular clothesline!"

"Frozen rope!" Harvey laughed. "Right over the four-hundred-foot sign. That some kind of record?"

"Maybe for me," Hugh said.

"Guess you showed 'em a thing or two, huh?" Harvey said.

Hugh bobbed his head and grinned, then moved along the counter toward the prescription window.

"Dad's medicine ready?" he asked Claude Cutter.

"In a minute," the druggist replied irritably, then he looked up and recognized Hugh. "Get a cup of coffee, slugger! On the house." He smiled broadly and pantomimed hitting a ball with a bat. "Great game, Hugh. Like to give me a heart attack, though. I thought McMichaels was going to give it up in the bottom of the sixth. But you come through. Yessir, you did."

Hugh grinned modestly and turned to the counter. At eighteen, he was handsome, tall, and lean. His face and forearms were deeply suntanned, and he moved with an easy, confident athlete's gait. His hair was closely cropped under a Cubs cap, which he wore with confidence, as if it was a natural part of his body.

Sunday night he had played in the Connie Mack National Finals, effectively the World Series for high school–age summer league teams. Somehow, through a combined miracle of luck and unique teamwork, the Eagles had struggled from their dusty old WPA-vintage ballpark to Farmington, New Mexico, where they actually got to play in the final round of the tournament. They held their own through the brackets, finally giving up two games to West Coast teams and dropping out of the competition. They wound up in fourth place, but that was better than not winding up at all. No team from the town and only a few from the whole state had ever gone so far, and, the old-timers around town loudly proclaimed, none ever would again.

Sunday's game had been televised on a special closed-circuit cable hookup, and everyone in the whole county must have watched. Hugh had heard nothing but enthusiastic praise for his game-winning homer for the past two days. No one commented on his lackluster performance in the two losing contests that ended their chances.

Hugh walked over and took a counter stool. "Coffee," he said to Hilda's back, and she turned with a big smile on her face.

"Coming up," she said. "Great game, Hugh. You're something, you know that? Made this whole town proud."

"Made them pay attention to baseball for a while, anyway," Hugh said.

"Oh, that's for sure," Hilda replied. "Where's Tommy and Ray?"

Hugh grimaced, shook his head. "Guess they'll be by," he said. And they would, he knew. Right now, they were probably picking out their new sports cars or something. All three boys had played on the same team, and although Hugh's performance in Sunday's game was heroic, the consistent play of his two best friends not only in this season but throughout their high school careers had attracted the notice of pro scouts and also landed them scholarship bids from major universities. Tommy would leave next week for California, where he would pitch for USC's squad, and Ray, the only kid in the high school ever to win three gold gloves in a row, was off to Florida State and a full ride as an infielder.

Hugh had also been fortunate, but not that fortunate. No pro scouts talked to him at all, but one or two junior colleges had come forward with partial scholarship bids.

"It's just as well, Sport," Harry Rudd had told his son when the news of his friends' scholarships was announced. "It'd kill your mother if you went too far away to college."

Hugh was amazed, truly, that Harry could still give much of a damn about what would hurt Edith and what wouldn't. Since the divorce, she rarely spoke his name, and when she did, her voice filled with bitterness. But that was the way Harry was, Hugh knew: loyal to the death. Nothing could ever change that. In a deep way, it made Hugh glad.

Hugh unconsciously reached down and massaged his legs. There was no pain, no discomfort at all, never was. But the old injuries still came to mind when he thought about his future. Not being able to play until his junior year had hurt, set him back, but he never let himself think of just how much.

"Here you go, slugger," Claude came up behind him and handed him a small sack. "How's Harry doing?"

"Oh, he's fine," Hugh smiled. "Long as he stays on his medicine."

"Business booming?"

"Well, it's summertime," Hugh said. "People fish."

"Yeah," the druggist smiled. "I got a slot picked out the end of August. We're heading up to Texoma for a week."

Hugh smiled again, finished his coffee, and swung around on the stool. His eye was caught by a flash of golden hair coming his way. He froze. Memory hit him like a line drive, his breath grew short when the beautiful girl—woman, really—approached the counter. She wore a delicate yellow blouse over white slacks, and a delicate scent filled the space between them. She carried a plate with a tuna fish sandwich on it. One bite was missing from a corner.

"This tuna is *old*," she said primly to Hilda, "and stale. It's dry as can be, and you put mayonnaise in it. I specifically said 'no mayonnaise.'"

"I always put mayonnaise in my tuna fish," Hilda quarreled. "It's already made up. I can't go opening up a new can for everybody who walks in here. Anyway, it ain't old. It was fresh this morning." Hilda looked at Hugh for support, but he wasn't paying attention. His eyes were solidly on the beauty standing next to him.

A swarm of old feelings buzzed around his head. He was too warm but, at the same time, experienced an icy sensation somewhere in his chest. He cleared his throat, surprised to find his mouth dry, his tongue thick.

"Linda?" he asked, reaching out before he thought and putting a finger on her shoulder.

She turned to face him, a sneer forming on her lips. Then, when their eyes met, her severity fell away, and she stared incredulously at him.

"Hugh? Hugh Rudd?"

"That's me all over," he grinned.

"Hugh Rudd," she said, spreading her long fingers on her sides and standing back to look at him. "I don't believe it."

"God, Linda. I never expected to see you again." His breath would not fill in his lungs, and he almost became dizzy. His eyes ran uncontrolled up and down her form. Her hair fell naturally to her shoulders, and her eyes were still striking blue, her teeth white, perfect beneath full lips. Her skin was deeply tanned, and each of her fingers ended in a carefully manicured nail.

"Why not?" she asked. "I mean, Jesus Christ, Hugh, this is *still* my hometown."

"You want to watch your language, young lady?" Hilda asked.

"You want to make me another sandwich?" Linda replied without looking at Hilda. "And this time, no mayo, and whole wheat, if you please." Hilda turned away in a huff.

Hugh couldn't take his eyes off her. He was sincere. He had thought he never would see her again. By the time he had been aware enough to ask, Harry told him that they were gone. Carl left the hospital early, against doctor's orders, and packed up the whole family and left a week after the building was destroyed. The news that they had already moved to California before Hugh was up and walking without crutches was both a relief and a disappointment to Hugh—who was unsure what he might say to her, or her to him— but he often wondered if he'd ever hear from Linda again.

"But what are you doing here? I mean . . . visiting or what?"

"Oh, we sold that old house," she said. "You know, it's been rented all these years. The lake house went pretty quick—right after we left—but the house here in town was too expensive for the market. Anyhow, it finally sold, and Daddy came back to sign some papers or something." She looked away. "I decided to come with him. I'm off to Europe in a week. You know: France and Italy." Hugh nodded wisely. "And I start Stanford in the fall, of course."

"That's your Beemer, right?" Hugh's eyes slanted out the window.

"Graduation present." She smiled. "I wanted a Mercedes, but Daddy says they're too expensive. We drove all the way here, too. Daddy says German cars have to be broken in at highway speed."

"How is . . . uh, how are your folks?"

"Oh, the same," Linda said with a frown. "Mom's in San Francisco, living with an artist." She drew out the last word and rolled her eyes. "Daddy's running for mayor of Santa Monica, you know." She read the slight surprise on Hugh's face. "Some things never change, Hugh." She rolled her eyes again and laughed.

There was silence for a moment. "You still ride?" Hugh asked.

She nodded. "Not competitively. And you're playing ball."

He nodded. "Not competitively."

She narrowed her blue eyes. "Don't lie to me, Hugh Rudd. Dad insists we subscribe to the local paper. I'm glad you're doing well."

"Not as well as some," Hugh said with a renewal of the earlier pang. "Tommy and Ray got scholarships."

"Yeah. I read about that. *The Eagle* gives *great* coverage to local news. 'Hammerin' Hugh Rudd,'" she quoted and forced him to blush. She smiled. "And you? What did you get?"

"All I got was couple of small offers. JC down in Corpus Christi was one. I had hoped for a Division 1 school, at least. But I didn't have the grades, even if I got the offer," he added.

"Corpus Christi," she repeated as if it was the capital of a third world country.

"Yeah." Hugh flushed a bit. "I'll live with my grandparents. Get to see my mother more often."

"How *is* your mother?" Linda looked suspiciously down at a new sandwich that Hilda set in front of her.

"No mayo," Hilda grumbled. "But I'm out of whole wheat. You'll have to take it on white." Linda glanced at her, then looked at Hugh again. Hilda shrugged and moved away.

"She's okay. Really doing fine. I see her three, four times a year. It's hard during school, during the season. But now, I'll be living right there, and I'll have to come up here to visit Dad."

"Is she . . ." Linda's eyes trailed down to the sandwich.

"She's fine," Hugh insisted. "She's on medication, still. Will be, I guess, for a long time. You know. Depression. But she's fine. Grandma and Grandpa take good care of her. Said they'd buy me a car when I come down. 'No public transport in Corpus,' is what Grandpa told Dad."

"What're you going to get?"

"Pickup," Hugh grinned. "Ford, I hope."

Linda frowned. She lifted a corner of the sandwich. "Corpus Christi," she said again. "Well, at least it's near the ocean."

"Or the Gulf," Hugh said. "What's with the 'no mayo'?" he asked to change the subject.

"No-fat diet," she said, patting her flat stomach. "I'm going to be eating French cooking and Italian pasta for a month in Europe, I'm sure, so I don't need to carry any extra pounds over there with me."

Hugh examined her figure. Her breasts flowered into nicely rounded mounds beneath the blouse, and even with the slacks on, he could tell her legs were still long, muscular, well developed.

"Don't look like you're in any danger of getting fat."

"Well, it pays to watch it. I hear girls routinely put on ten pounds their first semester, and if I'm just back from all that great food, I'll have a head start. I doubt I'll be able to work out over there, either."

"Well," Hugh said, grinning. "You look pretty good to me. I think you could stand a cheeseburger and a malt for old time's sake. What'd'ya say? My treat."

She hesitated for a second, then smiled and pulled three bills out of her purse and smacked them down next to the untouched sandwich. "Why not?"

─⟨

They took Linda's BMW and spent two hours at the Dairy Mart after they finished two greasy cheeseburgers and chocolate malts, followed by a shared banana split. Linda proclaimed she hadn't had such a good burger since she left, and Hugh told her about the odd way the restaurants in New Mexico served such fare.

"They put ketchup right on the meat," he said, "and if you want, you can get green chilies on it."

"They do that in California, too," she laughed. "The ketchup, not the chilies. They might put pineapple on it, though."

He told her about his mother's final breakdown, one that sent her to a hospital in Houston and, finally, to Corpus, where she was finally taking regular treatment for chronic depression and living in a kind of halfway house near her parents' home.

"The divorce was hard on Dad," Hugh said softly. "He almost didn't get over it. Couldn't believe that he was part of the problem."

"Was he?"

"I don't know." Hugh shook his head. "Her doctor told us that ever since Larry died, she's been blaming herself for anything bad that happened to us. Said Loretta Thompson wasn't really the problem after all, although she probably made things worse. She was just trying to help, I guess. But she didn't know how. Neither did Dad. Mom 'needed to learn to love herself' is what they said."

He shrugged. "He—the doctor—was the one who said they ought to get a divorce. I stayed here, live with Dad." Hugh took thought. "Things are better now," he said. "Dad's running a kind of combination sporting goods store and fishing guide service. I help out, too. We're sort of partners. He bought this custom bass boat, and he takes guys from here to some of the big lakes, shows them where to fish. He does pretty well."

"Is he seeing anyone?" Linda asked.

"Huh?" Hugh looked up suddenly, then caught her meaning. "Uh, no. I don't think so. He still loves Mom, I guess. He keeps talking about her coming home when she gets well."

Hugh looked out the window at traffic passing on the highway. "He had a heart attack last year," he said softly. "It was a small one. Happened down on Possum Kingdom. He was out by himself. He brought the boat in, put it on the trailer, got in the truck, and drove himself to the hospital. He's all right," Hugh said. "But he has to watch his blood pressure. Take pills."

"Are *you* seeing anyone?" she asked with a slight smile.

Hugh flushed in spite of himself. "I was going with Trish Gordon for a while."

"Trish Gordon!" Linda exclaimed. Then, suspiciously, she sneered. "*Little* Trish Gordon? My God, did she ever get those horrible braces off? And those gross pimples!"

Hugh was angry. He thought of Trish, how she fit so neatly under his arm when they walked away from the fieldhouse after a game, how his letter jacket practically smothered her, and how she had to use nearly a whole roll of dental floss to make his senior ring small enough to fit her tiny finger. She was pretty, he thought, not stunningly beautiful, but still pretty. And smart. He liked her, even though a month ago she told him that he wasn't a "good enough Christian" for her and that she thought that since she was planning to go to Baylor and then to become a missionary and marry a minister, they ought to break up. He still had hopes that she might change her mind.

"She's turned out pretty good," he said. "You ought to go by and see her."

"No, thanks." Linda picked up a cold French fry and drew a pattern in the melted ice cream. "I might get jealous. After all, you're always going to be my hero. I'm sure you're a big deal to a lot of folks around here." She beamed insincerely at him, and he looked away. He didn't know what to say. He hadn't seen Linda in four years. They hadn't written even once to each other. It was like she died in that building.

"What's happening with everyone else?" she asked after a moment of silence. "Who's pregnant? Who's in prison? C'mon, give me the dirt on everybody."

Hugh relaxed and outlined the histories of several of their old classmates, then shifted to an account of the recent spring commencement exercises. He mentioned several other people slightly, then the conversation began to peter out once more. They were silent for a while, and then Linda brightened and talked about her life in California. She admitted freely that she lost interest in cheerleading and other "silly high school stuff" pretty quickly and that she was engaged for a while to a senior at UCLA.

"Tony or whatever his name was?"

"Who?"

"Never mind," Hugh said. "How did it work out?" Hugh asked, not at all surprised to hear her take this tack, this tone with him.

"Not too well," Linda said lightly. "I was too young. He was too old. He married a law student from USC." She fingered the empty banana split dish. "What do you do, Hugh? I mean how can you stand living here? It's *so* boring."

Hugh thought for a moment. "Oh, I get around," he said. "I was in New Mexico last week, you know. We stopped off for the night in Santa Fe. It was pretty cool." She frowned and shook her head, as if in sympathy for him. He looked at her, then decided. "You really want to know what I do?" he asked. She nodded again, this time more sincerely. "C'mon, I'll show you."

They drove through town and took the U-turn in the old depot parking lot. A refurbished Railway Express Office greeted them on the near side of the turn. A large yellow sign proclaimed that it was a museum. Behind it was a large park, mostly gone to weeds. As they finished the turn, Hugh noticed that Linda did not so much as glance down to where the Hendershot Grocery Warehouse once stood. She focused on the opposite direction through the whole maneuver, as if she wanted to avoid seeing the site. There wasn't much to see, Hugh thought, when she swung back onto Main. Now, as if it had always been there, a railroad wye sat steaming in the summer heat. On a siding nearby a Burlington Northern engine hummed in wait for a switching procedure to begin.

Coming back down Main, Linda obeyed Hugh's directions and took a right and drove out the old highway, some five miles beyond the city limits. When they reached Jonas Wilson's place, Hugh instructed her to pull up to the barbed wire gate and wait while he opened it. Then he got back inside, and she pulled up to the old boxcar house and parked.

He stepped out and was immediately assaulted by a large dog the color of concrete. She came bounding up and leaping on Hugh's leg. He went over to a shelf nailed under the makeshift porch, found a bag of dogfood, and poured some out into a metal dish.

"It's Goodlett," he reminded Linda while she got out of the car and looked around. "Blind in one eye—some varmint got her, I think—but she won't leave the place."

Linda was looking around, sunglasses on against the sun's glare. The garden area, though not so large as it had once been, flourished in a bounty of summer growth. Peas and beans staked out the north end of the rectangular tract, and along the rows, corn, squash, tomatoes, and a variety of other vegetables grew up from well-cultivated and heavily fertilized soil. A series of soaker hoses ran the length of the garden from an electric pump near the well in back, and peck and bushel baskets were stacked neatly against the wall of the boxcar.

"You do *this?*" Linda asked incredulously. "*You?*"

"Well, me and Dad," Hugh said. "And Ortega, the guy who runs the vegetable stand. We're sort of partners." Linda walked around. "Watch out for snakes," Hugh called. "They come up and get water when it's dry like this. Goodlett can't keep them down anymore."

Linda jumped a little at the warning, then smiled shyly and stepped up and down the rows with care. "This is incredible," she said. She sounded sincere.

"Yeah, well, it's a lot of work, too," Hugh admitted. "We give a lot of it away, whatever Ortega doesn't want to sell. He and his boys come out and do the heavy work, the fertilizing and cultivating. All Dad and I really do is water it after we get the sets and seeds in and come out to try to keep the bugs and weeds down. It's kind of a hobby, I guess, but it pays pretty well. Better than mowing lawns." He grinned at her, but she didn't grin back, so he stooped down and picked some leaves off a tomato plant and examined them. "Bugs are bad," he said. "Feel like helping out?"

She didn't, he could see from her casual shrug. But she also didn't refuse.

For an hour, she helped him spray a mixture of detergent and water up and down the rows. Then, inspired by the labor, he began pulling a few weeds at the base of the vegetables. She worked half-heartedly, and they didn't speak. It was a hot, dirty chore, and in spite of her unenthusiastic participation, her white slacks were soon ruined. She pulled her golden hair back into a ponytail, sparking an uncomfortable recollection in Hugh, when he glanced at her and noted the dirty streaks on her hands and forearms. After another hour, both of them were sweating and straining in the sun, but when they finished, they sat on the broken chairs of the makeshift porch and sipped cool well water. She rose after a bit and went to the car, coming back with a small beaded bag.

"Want some weed?" she asked.

Hugh, trying to hide his shock, shook his head. "Can't break training," he said weakly. Several of his teammates, including Tommy and Ray, became thoroughly stoned while they were in New Mexico. He had not tried it, even so. He had never seen it handled as casually as Linda did when she pulled a perfectly rolled joint from the small bag. She put it on her lip, and then lit it with a gold-plated butane lighter.

"Wonder what Jonas would say?" Hugh thought aloud.

"He'd probably take a hit," Linda smiled, extending the slender cigarette. "I'm surprised he didn't include home-grown in all this." Hugh accepted the carefully rolled smoke, examined it, felt a prick of guilt, then sucked in the smoke. It burned his throat, and he forced himself to stop, to hold the bulk of it in his mouth for a moment while he handed the joint back to her, then blew it out.

It was suddenly comfortable sitting there with Linda. Although she was dirty and her face was covered with dry sweat trails, she was still lovely, still alluring. He wanted to do nothing more than reach out and touch her, and he was about to do just that, when she leaned forward, her hands on her knees, and spoke to him.

"You saved my life, you know," she said. "Mine and Daddy's."

"I really didn't," he said, embarrassed. "I was just there."

"You're too modest, Hugh. You made the national news. CNN gave you two whole minutes. I know. We have it on tape."

"I never saw it."

"I don't believe you, but I'll send you a copy, anyway."

Hugh looked off into the heat waves rising from the garden. "I wasn't really—"

"Oh, sure you were." Linda gave him a narrow, thin smile. "'Local Junior High Kid Saves Local Politician.' And his daughter," she added. "Made you famous. Probably had girls hanging all over you for the last four years."

"Linda—"

"Oh, that's right!" She exclaimed sarcastically. "You've got little Trish. No need for other girls."

Hugh blushed. "I—"

She interrupted him. "I spent a lot of time wondering what was in it for you. Why you did it. I mean, if you had just gone on and minded your own business, everything would probably have worked out the same, anyway. What did you have to gain? That's what I kept asking myself. And my therapist." She gave him a hard, straight look. It was cold. "You know I've been in therapy for the whole four years?"

"No, uh . . ." Hugh had no idea what she was talking about.

"Well, I have. That's why I came back with Daddy. 'Doctor's orders,' you know. 'Confront the past.' That's what I'm told. Get rid of the guilt."

Her stare warmed. "I helped you, you know. Helped you ruin my father's career. Helped you ruin my family. I'm as responsible for all this as you are." Her anger was now hot, palpable. Hugh sat back, slightly afraid. Her blue eyes flashed raw fire, but just as suddenly they cooled. She folded her arms, leaned back, and stared at him, as if she was sizing him up, assessing him.

"I'm not really the one who did it." He looked away, again. "I was just . . . there."

She waved her hand as if to dispel his words. "Oh, you *did* it, all right. I just never could figure out *why* you did it. Not until today. Now, I think I know. I mean, here you are, keeping this stupid garden going, feeding that stupid dog. And why? It's because of *him*, isn't it? Because of that silly, stupid old man. It's like you brought me out here to show me what a great job you're doing keeping it all alive. That's it, isn't it?"

Hugh waited, but she didn't say more. Instead, she sucked smoke out of the joint and studied him with a mean, narrow look. "So tell me, Hugh," she asked him, her eyes now turning soft and serious, "is little Trish one of your big admirers? Is she any good in bed?"

It was as if she had slapped him. A hollow feeling opened in his stomach. He abruptly stood up.

"That's why you did it, isn't it?" she went on, her voice rising. "You thought if you saved me, I'd fuck you, right? Give you what you wanted but didn't have the guts to take even when I was trying to hand it to you? Was that it, Mr. Baseball Stud?"

He spun away from her, his head reeling, and stalked out into the sunshine and toward the back of the boxcar house. Weeds and junk still obscured the ground, but right along the fence toward the end of the property, there was a broad, clear space, covered with green grass. Hugh stopped, took a breath to calm himself, then turned on a faucet and extended a hose and began spraying the grass that covered a grave with a small, marble stone.

"Jonas Wilson," it read. "A Good Man. Forever is a Long, Long Time."

"I didn't know what else to put on it," Hugh said when she walked up beside him. She stood there in silence, finishing her smoke, holding the joint like an ordinary cigarette and blowing the smoke out of her nose.

"You know," he said softly, "it wasn't me. *He* saved your life. I was just there." He smiled. "He had to talk me into it. Tell you the truth," he said, "I don't think he could have, if I had thought about it."

"Why not? Wasn't I worth it?" Her voice dripped sarcasm.

"I'm not sure," he said seriously. "I'm really not."

She took a deep, shuddering breath, as if she had been crying. "I guess I deserved that," she said, looking up at him. "I'm sorry, I shouldn't have said those things. I've been waiting a long time to say them, and I should have just forgotten it. Dr. Pascal told me to forget it, but I didn't listen. I'm sorry."

"I guess in a way you're right," Hugh said. "I should have minded my own business."

"No," Linda said. "It was mean of me. And tacky. It wasn't your fault any more than it was mine. And Daddy's. And I'm sorry. I shouldn't have laid all that shit on you. Like Dr. Pascal says, they're my demons. I have to deal with them. This," she said, sweeping a hand in the direction of the garden, "this is your demon. And I guess you're dealing with it the best way you know how."

"I don't see it as a 'demon.'"

"You call it what you want to," she said. "It amounts to the same thing."

Hugh didn't know what to say. A light breeze had come up, bathing their sweaty bodies with hot, summer air. In the distance Hugh heard a dog barking. Goodlett, who slept next to the boxcar house, raised her ears, but then returned to her doze.

"Linda," Hugh asked, almost fearfully, "why'd your father give this place to me?"

"My father? Daddy?"

"Yeah. He gave it to me. Or practically. He sold it to me for twenty-two hundred. There's a well on it. He could have gotten ten times that."

"I don't know what you're talking about."

"When I got out of the hospital, I found out that I had won the pool on when the building would come down. Actually, it was Dad who won it. Randy Truman got him to place a bet on it, and when he found out that I had twelve noon, he took the next four slots. Bought them in my name. So, anyway, Randy brought the money by the house, and six weeks later, I get a call from the bank telling me that your dad wanted to sell this property and wondered if I was interested. Y'all had already gone to California by then. Anyway, he wanted to sell it."

"For twenty-two hundred."

"Right on the money."

"And you bought it."

"Didn't think twice. But what I've always wondered is how he came to own it in the first place. I thought Jonas owned it."

"In a way, he did," Linda said, shaking her head and thinking. "I don't know how, exactly, but there was some kind of trust. I don't know. I mean, I could guess, but so could you. You were the only one who knew him, you know. You were the only one who was nice to him or cared about him. I didn't know about that, though. About Daddy selling it to you."

"Well, he did," Hugh said. "I thought maybe you might know why."

She sighed deeply, then shrugged as if shaking off a loose coat. "You know he was my real grandfather," she said rather than asked.

Hugh went cold inside. He should have guessed.

She nodded and went on. "That came out in therapy, too. Daddy always knew. But he was the only one."

Except Jonas, Hugh thought.

"He and my grandmother had what I guess they called 'an affair.' He worked on their ranch—you know the one out south of town? Anyway, that's all I know. That's all Daddy knows, too, I guess."

Hugh said nothing. He was trying to absorb all this information at once, but it would not dissolve. It explained a lot, he thought, but not enough. "That's all Daddy would say in front of me. It's been a problem for him all his life, knowing that the town loony was his real daddy, always being afraid that somebody would find out."

"He wasn't a loony," Hugh said quietly.

"No," Linda admitted, "but nobody liked him. He was always in trouble. Even before Daddy was born, he was in and out of jail all the time."

"He was a union organizer," Hugh said. "In the twenties and thirties, he went all over and tried to organize workers into unions. He was a member of the I.W.W. before that."

"The what?"

"International Workers of the World," Hugh explained. "'Wobblies,' they called themselves. 'I Won't Works' is what the companies called them. They were always going out on strikes, getting beat up and killed, getting thrown in jail."

"I didn't know they did that sort of thing around here," she said.

"Well, they didn't. Not much. But Jonas believed in them. He went to their meetings. He once took a train all the way to Atlanta just to try to see Eugene V. Debs in prison. They wouldn't let him in. Beat him up and sent him home. But he didn't quit. He went down to Mexico and tried to join the revolution there. When that didn't work, he came back and worked to unionize the farmers around here. During the Depression, he went all over. Tried to get the dockworkers down in Galveston to join up. Even tried to organize the roughnecks in the oil patch. He'd take any kind of job, then he'd try to get people to join up with the union. He went all over. But he always came back here. He'd set up a soapbox downtown and make speeches about the evils of capitalism on Saturday afternoons. He was a pacifist, too. Did you know that?"

"No."

"Well, he was. He was always making speeches against war. Everybody thought he was crazy anyhow, and nobody listened to him. Then, when World War II started, everybody thought maybe he was some kind of spy or something."

"That's ridiculous."

"Well, there was an airbase nearby, over near Childress, and everybody was jumpy. The sheriff arrested him, kept him locked up for a month one time. Then, when he got out, he went right back to talking about how we didn't need to be fighting the war, about how it was all a crooked scheme."

"I'll bet that got him in trouble."

"Yeah," Hugh said. "Lots of people from here were being killed over there. You've seen the 'honor roll' on the courthouse square." She nodded. "That's why Phelps Crane hated him so much, too, you know. Anyway, about that time he was working as a janitor in the old hotel. A bunch of soldiers were home on leave, and they threw a party. A girl got killed. She jumped out of a window—or was pushed. You've heard that."

"Yeah, but not much more. I don't even know who she was. I always thought it was a ghost story."

"Well, it wasn't. Her name was Bessie Tillman. She was from Oklahoma. Anyway," Hugh went on, "when they went upstairs, everybody was gone, except Jonas, who said he was passing by and he just went up there to see what happened when he heard the girl screaming. When he came in, there was no one there. Anyway, they arrested him, and he went to prison. Then they found out that she was engaged to two of the soldiers at one time, and they were fighting over her when she went out the window, or, like I said, they pushed her out. It never was clear what happened. But Jonas got a pardon, came back here. Right back to his own place. Everyone still hated him, and nobody would give him a job, so he started this garden, and he traded what he grew for whatever he needed."

"How do you know all this?"

"My dad told me most of it," Hugh said. "And Sheriff Anderson told me some more. He said everyone really knew he was harmless, but he was always getting complaints about him, people making up stuff and blaming him for all sorts of things. And," he nodded toward the boxcar house, "there's a lot of old letters and things in there. Clippings and junk. Mostly about the I.W.W. and stuff," Hugh said with a slight grin, then he turned serious.

"Back in the sixties, he got into some real trouble. A bunch of hippies— eight or ten of them—came through, and their van broke down right out there. Jonas took them in. Turned out that several of them were draft dodgers, deserters from the army."

"Did he know that?"

"I doubt he would have cared very much." Hugh smiled. "It was his kind of thing. Pacifism and all. That was during the Vietnam War. He made a lot of speeches about that, too, till the sheriff told him to quit or he'd lock him up again. Anyway, he let them stay here until they got enough money to get their van fixed. He fed them and took care of them for a month or so. Finally, one of them got busted for drugs, and they came out here and arrested everybody in sight."

"Oh, shit," Linda said.

"That wasn't all. Some of the girls were underage. Runaways. And that plus the deserters and stuff brought in the FBI, and he was in deep shit. They put him in jail again," Hugh said bitterly. "Six years in the federal prison. Called it 'aiding and abetting,' or something. Tried to get him on kidnapping, too, but the girls' families wouldn't press charges. Hell," Hugh spat into the weeds, "I'll bet he was past seventy. But he got paroled and came back again, if you can believe that."

"He was tough," Linda admitted.

"Tough as nails," Hugh said. "Everyone called him a 'kid stealer,' and all sorts of things. But he didn't care. He just kept on farming this place, trading his vegetables, and getting by. Everybody hated him, but you know something?" Hugh looked at her, and she shrugged. "No one really knew why. I guess a town just needs somebody to hate, and Jonas was the one here. I always wondered why he stayed, though. Now, I guess I know."

"Daddy," Linda said.

"Yeah," Hugh said with a nod. "That explains a lot. You see, the one thing nobody could figure out was how he hung onto this place all those years. I mean, he didn't have any money. How did he pay taxes and stuff?"

"Daddy," Linda almost whispered.

"I guess so," Hugh said. "Your daddy was his lawyer on the last thing. Did you know that?" Linda shook her head. And Hugh fell silent.

Linda shrugged again. "Well," she said. "You have it now."

"Yeah," Hugh said. "But why would your dad give it to me? I mean, like you said, I'm sort of responsible for what happened to you."

"You're also responsible for saving our lives."

"That was Jonas," Hugh said, shaking his head. "Not me. I didn't do anything but what he told me to do."

"Maybe . . ." Linda started, took a breath, and continued, "Maybe when all of that happened, Daddy just wanted you to have it. He knew you would keep it like it was."

"Maybe," Hugh said.

"Maybe that's the way Daddy dealt with his demons." She reached behind her head and loosened her ponytail, then brushed hair away from her face. "God knows he's got enough of them."

"Maybe we all do."

"Maybe we do," she agreed and reached up and kissed him lightly on the cheek. Hugh was so stunned, he stepped away. But she didn't seem to notice. "Look, I've got to get back," she said. "I look like a Mexican, I'm so dirty. I told Daddy I'd meet him at Mr. Givens's house hours ago. He'll be furious." She stalked back toward her car.

Hugh shut off the water, coiled the hose around the faucet, gave Goodlett a quick pat, then did a brief check of the area around the garden, and they drove out to the highway.

"Do you keep the house up, too?" Linda asked when he returned from securing the gate.

"Nope," Hugh said. "I can't. You have to live in a place to keep it up. I don't know enough about it, anyway. I ride my bike out here, mostly." He looked back at the boxcar house receding in the distance behind the Johnson grass and mesquite. "To be honest, I don't go inside much."

"I'm sorry for what I said, Hugh," she almost whispered. "But one thing's true. I did have the biggest crush on you." She looked down at her lap. "I think I still do."

He didn't reply.

Linda sped toward town. The wind ruffled her hair, and she put her sunglasses on again.

"Corpus Christi," she said when she slid into the parking slot near where his bike was chained.

"Yeah," he said. "If I can get the grades, I might get a transfer to Texas or A&M or someplace."

"Maybe some school in California," she said with a bright smile.

He grinned.

"Well, listen," she said, shifting into reverse. "We're leaving tomorrow, early, so you write and give me your address. I'll be back from Europe when school starts."

"Yeah," Hugh said. "I'll do that."

"You write now," she said and pulled out into traffic. "Write me at Calvin Hall. 1010 Old Bay Road, Palo Alto. That's my dorm. It's private and exclusive, so they'll make sure I get it."

"Right," Hugh waved from the sidewalk, and she moved out with a quick twiddle of her fingers over her head. Too late he remembered that Harry's pills were still on the BMW's floorboard. He would have to call her at the motel, he thought, if that was where they were staying, or he could go in and get Claude to make up another batch. That was the best plan, he decided. But he didn't want to do it right then. It could wait until tomorrow.

He was empty, hollowed out, alone. The afternoon had become a burden of memories that stood like ancient statues in his mind. He got on his bike and pedaled down to the old depot parking lot. Dismounting, he walked over and stood against the pylons and stared down into the work area where the trains now switched a turnaround on the wye. Boxcars and flatcars jammed against each other in that curious chain reaction of crashes that was unique to railroad work. He felt dirty, sweaty, yet somehow cleansed by the late afternoon heat.

He remembered Linda's deliberate refusal to so much as glance at the site when they drove by earlier. He wondered if the demon she really needed to face was down there somewhere in the late afternoon heat, and he wondered if she was still too afraid to confront it.

What was the name of that dormitory? he wondered. He tried to think. Cline Hall? No, something else. He shook his head. "It don't matter," he heard a familiar voice in his mind speak while he took another long look at the wye and the Burlington Northern engines at work. "Some things are just best forgotten." Some demons, he added, are better left at rest.

Suddenly, he remembered that Harry was grilling steaks that night. They would eat them and watch the Rangers take on Detroit. Maybe drink a beer or two. He grinned, set his cap back on his head, got on his bike, and pedaled off as fast as he could for home. Harry hated it when he was late for supper.